"Smart and funny and all sorts of raunchy in the best way.... Dazzles, entertains, and squeezes in more than a few laughs.... *Razzmatazz* is another success for Christopher Moore."

—*San Francisco Chronicle*

"Moore and his merry band of miscreants are firmly on the right side of history—and they will make you laugh until it hurts."

—*BookPage* (starred review)

"There is literally a laugh on every page of this book (several, on some pages), and with its fast-paced, deliberately helter-skelter storyline, it sinks its hooks deeply and never lets go."

—*Booklist*

"A humorous romp.... Moore's fans and those who like their noir with a side of slapstick and the supernatural will enjoy."

—*Publishers Weekly*

"*Razzmatazz* is marked with the same sort of coarse charm that permeates all of Moore's books.... There's chaos at play throughout—there's a LOT going on—yet Moore handles it deftly, resulting in a book whose myriad fractured storylines ultimately come together in a delightfully droll denouement."

—*The Maine Edge*

"*Razzmatazz* is Christopher Moore once again at his unique best. Bravo!"

—*Fredericksburg Free Lance-Star*

RAZZMATAZZ

A Novel

CHRISTOPHER MOORE

WILLIAM MORROW

An Imprint of HarperCollinsPublishers

RAZZMATAZZ. Copyright © 2022 by Christopher Moore. All rights reserved. Printed in the United States of America. No part of this book may be used or reproduced in any manner whatsoever without written permission except in the case of brief quotations embodied in critical articles and reviews. For information, address HarperCollins Publishers, 195 Broadway, New York, NY 10007.

HarperCollins books may be purchased for educational, business, or sales promotional use. For information, please email the Special Markets Department at SPsales@harpercollins.com.

A hardcover edition of this book was published in 2022 by William Morrow, an imprint of HarperCollins Publishers.

FIRST WILLIAM MORROW PAPERBACK EDITION PUBLISHED 2023.

Library of Congress Cataloging-in-Publication Data has been applied for.

ISBN 978-0-06-243413-5

23 24 25 26 27 LBC 5 4 3 2 1

TRIGGER WARNING

This story is set in America in the first half of the twentieth century. While this story and its characters and events are entirely fictional, the language and attitudes portrayed herein regarding race, culture, and gender are contemporary to that time and may be disturbing to some.

A DRAGON IN BIG TOWN

So, about three hundred years ago, when the Qing dynasty isn't even old enough to buy a beer, there comes a wave of barbarians out of the north with such fury and numbers that it kicks nine shades of shit out of the Emperor's army, causing much embarrassment and fear among the aristocracy, and a large number of corpses among the peasants and military. You can't walk a block without tripping over a widow or an orphan, the sky is black with the smoke of burning villages, and it is widely agreed throughout China that the soup of the day is Cream of Sadness.

So the Emperor calls his ministers together and says: "Who are these mugs? Why do they vex me thus? And will no one rid me of them?"

And one of his ministers, a toady whose name is lost to history, but let's say he's called Jeff, says: "These are the same mugs from the north that have invaded us regularly lo these many years." But he does not say, "They vex you thus because you have opened up the aristocracy to anyone who can afford the ducats, including merchants and lawyers, so you have a kingdom very top-heavy with bums, but you have not spent any of that sweet cabbage on walls, weapons, or the training of soldiers." Jeff does not say this because he is one of those selfsame bums of which he speaks. But he does say, "I hear of a Buddhist monastery in Fukien Province where the monks train day and night in the art of fighting and are said to be so fierce that one of them punches out a yak's lights when he goes outside to take a leak in the morning—rings the bell of a wild yak with one hand on his willy and does not get even a drop on his robe."

And the Emperor says unto Jeff, "Yeah, go get those guys. Offer them substantial cheddar and powerless positions at court to save our bacon."

So Jeff journeys to the mountaintop where the monks keep their clubhouse, and asks them will they rid the kingdom of the vicious barbarians from the north, and the abbot answers thus: "Nope. We have some chanting and meditation to do, and after lunch, fighting practice."

"But," says Jeff, "we will give you titles, stacks of cabbage, fine outfits, a feed bag of the finest fare, and gorgeous dames with feet so tiny they can tap-dance on a bottle cap."

And the abbot says, "We're good. Now, if you will excuse me, I'm going to have some tea and punch a yak."

So Jeff spake thusly: "But many peasants have been killed, there are widows and orphans coming out the wazoo, villages are burning, and there is much suffering in the land. Besides, what's the point of training at fighting all day if all you are going to do is knock out random mountain beefs?"

And with that the abbot says, "That is an excellent point, toady. We'll do it."

And so it comes to pass that one hundred and thirty-eight monks, outfitted for fighting, march north (leaving home one guy for ringing the gong and another to milk the yak). And before three days have passed, those barbarians who were not killed or wounded are more than somewhat discombobulated, and they retreat to their own land, while not a single monk is lost (although a couple have blisters on their thumbs from their fighting sticks and the abbot quotes the Buddha to them, saying, "Life is suffering," and "You should put some ointment on those," and they are comforted). Then they return to their monastery, shut the doors, and resume their routine.

Meanwhile, there is much rejoicing in the land, and in the Celestial City, the Emperor is praised for his strength and wisdom and says thus: "So these daffy mugs don't want *anything*?"

"Nope," says Jeff. "They say they are content to have lessened the suffering and oppression of the people and would I please go piss up a rope."

"Buddhist parable," explains one of the other ministers. "Probably."

"Something's fishy," says another toady. "How do we know these guys aren't up to something?"

"And what if they start to think that *we* are the ones oppressing the people?" says another.

"Which, you have to admit, *has* come up at meetings."

"Yeah," says the Emperor. "I don't trust a guy who doesn't want anything."

"Maybe," says a younger toady, "we—" And here he makes the gesture of cutting someone's throat and makes a croaking sound.

"How?" asks Jeff. "They are the best fighters in the land and I think we can admit that in comparison, our guys are shit."

"Maybe we give them a little *flaming medicine,*" says one of the more clever ministers, referring to what they call gunpowder at the time. "I hear recently from one of the Dutch white devils that it can be used for croaking guys as well as entertainment."

And around the great hall goes a collective "hmmmm" of thoughtfulness.

See, gunpowder has been around for hundreds of years, but up until then it has only been used for firecrackers on New Year's and to blast that one guy to the moon several centuries ago, which, it is agreed, would have worked if they hadn't made his rocket ship out of bamboo. But recently, traders from the West have introduced the flaming medicine for making bombs and loading cannons, thus giving it the new name.

"Make a plan," says the Emperor.

So it comes to pass that a small force of the Emperor's soldiers sneaks into the mountains in the night and sets fire to the monks' clubhouse, stacking barrels of gunpowder at the gates and tossing bombs over the walls until the entire joint is in flames. When the monks run to one gate to meet their attackers, it is blown up, and when they run to another, it too is blown up, until most of the monks are dead or in flames and it is not looking good for those few who are not.

But then the Immortals look down from the heavens, and despite the fact that the Buddhist monks don't believe in them, they are moved by their discipline and good deeds, and they send a thunderbolt down to blow a hole in the back wall of the monastery, through which the surviving eighteen monks escape, leaving the Emperor's soldiers thinking the monks are toast to the last man.

Hidden and nursed by the peasants whom they saved from the barbarians, all but five of the monks perish from their wounds. Those five, who are called the Five Ancestors, vow to oppose the reign of the Qing Emperor and all those of his descent, as he is now regarded throughout the land to be a first-rate douche bag, and they also vow to restore the previous Ming dynasty, which everyone agrees was swell, and much better for the people. To each of the Five, the Immortals bestow a talisman of the Five Great Dragons: dragons of wood, earth, metal, fire, and rain, whose power they will represent on Earth.

So the Five Ancestors adopt a banner of three red dots, which is the symbol of the Ming dynasty, and for that they are called the Triads. They spread out through the cities and villages, recruiting members to the secret resistance, and eventually, to make ends meet, they evolve into great criminal organizations, always with the goal of overthrowing the Qing emperors, as well as making a few doubloons on the side. A couple of hundred years go by, gold is discovered across the salt in the Land of Golden Hills, the Triads establish benevolent societies called tongs, and many sons of the working class are recruited and helped to immigrate to America to find their fortunes. The tongs become very powerful among the Chinese in America, and become very proficient in running gambling, smuggling, prostitution, and extortion operations. In the New World, the tongs are competitive to the point of war, and adopt all kinds of spooky rituals, calling on their noble Triad history to recruit and earn the loyalty of their soldiers. There are even rumors that some of the talismans of the Five Great Dragons made their way to Big Town (San Francisco) and that the tongs promised the power of the immortal dragons could be summoned against their enemies at any time.

But you know, rumors. Dragons? In San Francisco? C'mon. What are the odds?

MOTHER SUPERIOR AND THE BIG BLACK DONG

Sammy

When we pulled up to Jimmy's Joynt on Pier 29 the doorman was beating a skinny guy in a tux with a black rubber dildo the length of a Louisville Slugger and the diameter of a soup can, hitting him only in the soft parts—the thigh, the shoulder, the caboose—so each blow sounded like a butcher smacking a fat ham.

We had the windows of the cab down, as it was a warm night for November, with only a light wind, and the fog hadn't even crept through the Golden Gate yet, despite it being the small hours of a Sunday morning.

"Boy, you don't see that every day," said Milo, whose cab I was driving. Milo often assumes passenger duties in his own taxi, as he was soundly blown up while driving a tank at the Battle of the Bulge and so sometimes gets jumpy behind the wheel.

"Well, Butch likes to keep a tight ship."

Butch, who was also wearing a tux, as she always does when working, performed a two-handed golf swing that sent the dark dangler into the thin guy's nut sack with a sickening thud, to which the guy, Milo, and I all responded with explosive *oofs*, although the *oofs* were only sympathetic from Milo and me.

The thin guy sank to his knees, then rolled over on the pier, trying to catch his breath, while Butch menaced him with the point of the dong. "And don't come back," Butch said, "or it won't go as well for you."

"It does not seem to be going that well for that guy *this time*," said Milo.

The guy, still gasping for air, scuttled away from Butch, passing on my side of the cab.

"That guy looks like he could be good for a return fare," I said to Milo. "Pac Heights or Nob Hill. You want I should flag him down?"

"Nah," said Milo, pulling down the brim of his checkered cabbie cap like he couldn't even see the guy. "That guy has a pencil-thin mustache, and it is well known that no one grows a pencil-thin mustache except douche bags and Errol Flynn."

"Are you saying that Robin Hood is a douche bag?"

"I am saying no such thing. I said douche bags *and* Errol Flynn. I'll wait. You want I should keep the meter running?"

"First, I do not know how long I will be, and second, since I drove here, the flag has not been dropped on the meter to date, so third, and in conclusion, no."

"Fine. Off the meter. You sure you don't want to drive back?"

"I have to see to the Cheese," I said.

"Well, she can drive back. I don't mind a dame driving."

"We will not be returning to Cookie's," I said, referring to the diner in the Tenderloin where I often rendezvous with Milo and various other citizens for late-night coffee and philosophical discourse. "I am accompanying the Cheese to her place, where I intend to attend to her various wants and needs and vice versa."

"I'll be back!" shouted the pencil-thin-mustache guy. "I know people! Important people. You'll be sorry! You, you, abomination!" Then he scuttled off down the pier past a line of parked cars where two dames were smooching furiously against the side of a Studebaker.

"You wanna come in?" I asked Milo. "I'll buy you a drink."

"Nah," said the diminutive Greek, "I gotta get back to Cookie's. I might just sit here a minute and watch those two dolls swap spit, you know, pick up some pointers I can use on Doris."

"You are a thoughtful fellow," I said as I climbed out of the cab and screwed my hat down tight against the breeze. "Always thinking of Doris's happiness, Milo."

"She is a stand-up dame," said Milo.

"That she is," I agreed. Doris is the graveyard biscuit-slinger at Cookie's Coffee, and despite her being ten years older and several stones heavier than Milo, and being in possession of a very large Swedish longshoreman husband called Lars, Milo is deeply smitten with her, and vice versa, it would appear. "Well, hold down the fort," I said, tapping the hood of the cab. "I will see you tomorrow at Cookie's."

"*Adieu,* ya mug," said Milo, sliding over behind the wheel as I strolled away.

"How's it hanging, Sammy?" called Butch, holding the dildo in a menacing manner (and it occurred to me then that menacing is about the only way one can hold a yard-long rubber dong).

"You an abomination now, Butch?" I asked.

"Taking night classes," said Butch with a shrug. "Something to fall back on." She stood five feet ten, weighed maybe a buck-ninety, so my size plus about twenty pounds of shoulders, giving her a linebacker V-shape that unruly patrons had come to fear or at least respect. Her hair was short, black, and slicked back in the manner of a lot of the dames who frequented Jimmy's Joynt.

"Well, that is quite a respectable pasting you gave that guy. This a regular thing?" Being a barman myself, at Sal's in North Beach, I am acquainted with various methods of managing unruly patrons. I appreciate the art.

"Regular enough. Some guys get sored up when they find their missus joining us here on the sunny, sunny side of the street. Such guys are often of the opinion that they can push a dame around by virtue of their sex, and I am obligated to correct their way of thinking, sometimes rendering them unconscious before my point is made."

"Point taken. I, too, have resorted to such tactics, although I use a sawed-off pool cue to help make my point, rather than—" I bounced my eyebrows at Butch's weapon.

"Oh, this," she said, holding up the dong like a marine saluting with a dress sword (her weapon wiggling disturbingly with the gesture). "You'd be surprised how few guys want to report to the cops that a dyke down at the wharf just beat the stuffing outta them with a big black rubber dick."

"That is a very savvy angle, Butch. Very savvy indeed. They ever come back with some pals to get revenge?"

"Nah, although one guy comes back the next night and offers me a C-note to do it again, only slower."

"You take him up on it?"

"Nah, the boss does not like us to pursue personal business while at work. Jimmy has asked that we attract as little attention from the gendarmes as possible. I keep the corporal punishment very much on the QT, what with the Mother Superior vowing to rid the city of all forms of fun."

The *Mother Superior,* or *Dunne the Nun,* is Captain James Dunne, the San Francisco Police Department's new head of vice, a starched-shirt, churchgoing flatfoot who is trying to claw his way into the mayor's office on the backs of many respectable citizens such as hookers, gamblers, hustlers, strippers, lady-lovers, pansies, pimps, pornographers, panderers, and people who like jazz—in other words, the guys and dolls I call my friends.

"Still, you got that as a fallback, if working the door gets you down."

"I don't think so," Butch said, tucking her dark dingus behind the podium where she stood guard, as she functioned as both the doorman and the host on slow nights. "Taking money for it would be weird."

"Yeah, you wouldn't want it to get weird. Well, you got style, pal, I'll give you that."

Butch raised an eyebrow of skepticism. "Don't go sweet on me, Sammy. I know you got a talent for falling for the wrong dame, and dames don't get any wronger than yours truly."

"She inside?"

"Holding court at the bar. Not a dry stool in the house."

"What's the damage tonight?" I reached into my pocket for the toll for the cover, which changes from night to night, depending on the time and how much the joint is jumping.

Butch tossed her head and a well-oiled forelock broke loose from her coif. "Get out of here with that, ya mope."

I tipped my hat as I went by. "You're a gentleman and a scholar, Butch," I said, which made her laugh until she snorted.

The main room at Jimmy's Joynt was once a warehouse, now painted black to cover the hooks and hoists in the rafters. A low ghost of cigarette smoke hung in the air over about forty tables where dames, only dames, in dresses or men's suits, were paired up, looking sad and urgent as, up on the stage, a skinny dame in white tux and tails with a painted-on mustache squeezed out a slow song about lost love in a sultry alto. The joint looked like some daffy Sapphic goddess had sprinkled an abandoned coal mine with melancholy lesbians, then taken a powder in a puff of smoke. On the dance floor three couples rocked in rhythm to a stand-up bass coming out of a dark corner where a tall blonde in a long green evening gown was giving it an expert fingering for their pleasure. It was three in the morning and whatever high time there was to be had had been had, whoever had somewhere to go had gone, and now everyone was just marking time until last call, when they had to go somewhere they didn't want to be or home to someone they didn't want to see.

A few faces turned toward me as I walked in and for all the

welcome in their expressions I felt like a leper wearing a dead skunk for a tie. I don't take it personally. A lot of these dames have grounds for giving a general stink-eye to citizens of the guy persuasion and no use for us whatsoever.

Just like Butch says, Stilton, a shapely blond biscuit of whom I am more than somewhat fond, was perched on a stool up at the bar, looking bright as a summer day in her white dress with the big red polka dots (despite it being November, and dark as Dracula's dirty drawers) and red Mary Janes, tall heels hooked into the rail of the bar. The Cheese, as I and my pals refer to Stilton when she's not around, was surrounded by a bevy of broads of various sizes and shapes, attired in men's suits, smoking and laughing and hanging on the Cheese's every word like she was the Blessed Virgin passing out tips on a hot horse at Bay Meadows.

But before I could catch the eye of my *one true*, I heard, "What's the scam, Sam?" Which came from Jimmy Vasco, who was flanking Stilton on the starboard side, smoking a coffin nail in a long black holder that she chomped between her pearly whites so it bounced a little when she talked. Jimmy was slicked-back, sharp as a tack, in a satin black tux and tails tailored to flatten her curves; maybe five-two and a C-note soaking wet, and though she is little, she is fierce, as the Bard says, and a stand-up dame—she lends me her car and a sweet little Kraut pistol on occasion. Jimmy Vasco owns the joint.

Jimmy gave me a respectable punch on the shoulder by way of a hello.

"This jamoke bothering you, Toots?" said the Cheese. In this scenario, Jimmy is the jamoke, and I am, well—

"Don't call me Toots," I replied.

One of the dames on the other side of the Cheese sneered at me—actually sneered—I suppose sensing that Stilton and I have enough chemistry to put Union Carbide and Dow Chemical in the soup line.

"Hi, Sammy," chirped Myrtle, a tall Olive Oyl–shaped redhead who works the lunch counter at the Five & Dime with the Cheese and who had been decorating Jimmy Vasco's arm nigh unto half a year.

"Hey, Myrt," I replied with a wink. "Looking very fetching this evening. Very fetching indeed."

"Aw, pshaw," Myrtle said, and hid her smile like she was embarrassed instead of basking in it. And she did look good. Jimmy had wrapped her in various sheaths of satin and sequins since they started dating, at least when Myrtle was in the club, and rather than looking gawky like when I'd first met her, she was threating elegant. In fact, that long green number on the blond bass player in the corner had made its maiden voyage on Myrtle a month or so back. (Jimmy Vasco is nothing if not efficient.) I like Myrtle. She's a good pal to the Cheese and she says things like "pshaw."

"You ain't so bad yourself," said Myrtle, batting her eyelashes, flirting for Jimmy's benefit.

"Me? I'm a sack of old sweat socks compared to you, hot stuff." And I sort of was, still in my bartender togs, smelling of stale liquor and cigarettes, my tie tucked into my shirt, my tweed overcoat thrown over the whole mess.

"*My* sack of socks," said Stilton, who pulled me over to her and bit me on the ear, a little harder than was strictly necessary. And with that, all the dames who had been trying to make time with the Cheese moved away, dispersing into the room like mosquitoes who just tried to take a bite out of the Tin Man. The one who'd sneered at me before harrumphed as she walked away.

"Hey, I'm trying to run a business here," said Jimmy. "It's hard enough these days without you dancing in and crushing everyone's hopes and dreams."

"That your business, Jimmy? Hopes and dreams?"

Jimmy stepped to me and let a stream of smoke trickle out of her nose as she tried to look sinister. "Very dark, very damp dreams,

Sammy." Then she grinned around her cigarette holder. "Also dancing and moderately priced liquor. Whaddaya drinking?"

"Vodka gimlet," I said. Jimmy nodded to Mel, the bartender, a lean, androgynous dame in the same outfit as me, sans the overcoat and fedora, plus a cameo on a velvet choker at her throat. She started building the gimlet without a word.

To Stilton and Myrtle I said, "Don't you two have to be at work in about"—I checked my Timex—"three hours?" The girls are generally pushing pancakes at the Five & Dime by six. In fact, the Cheese and I had decided we would take a night off, as I did not get off work at Sal's until two, and she had to be at the Five & Dime by six, so I was more than somewhat surprised when she'd called me at Cookie's Coffee, where I was enjoying coffee and narrative with my pals, and invited me to join her at Jimmy's Joynt, as Jimmy had something she wished to discuss with me, after which, the Cheese implied, we would retire to her place for much nudity and merriment.

Gimlet in hand, I tipped a toast to Mel the bartender, then turned to Jimmy and said, "So, what's on your mind?"

But before Jimmy could answer, there came the sound of a whistle, such as a coach might use, tootling through the club, although I was sure it was not the tootling of a coach.

"Fucking cops," said Jimmy by way of explanation, and with that she grabbed Myrtle's paw, who in turn grabbed the Cheese, who grabbed me, and we were led willy-nilly behind the bar, through a door, and into a long, badly lit hallway with walls painted black. I had been there before, and I headed for Jimmy's office down the hall, but I was whipsawed in the grasp of the Cheese as Jimmy stopped and bumped a shoulder into the wall, from which snapped open a hidden door, revealing a narrow staircase.

"Pull that shut behind you," said Jimmy, and I did.

Jimmy led us up the stairs to another hall, barely shoulder width, where she pulled a chain, snapping off the single lightbulb, leaving us standing in the dark listening to each other's breath as well as no little shouting by cops and patrons coming from the club on the other side of the wall.

"They can't see—" I started to say when I heard a scraping sound, which was Jimmy opening a little port that revealed a peephole the size of a quarter, which Jimmy filled with her eyeball.

"The fuck happened to Butch?" she asked.

"Butch has a button on the podium that warns everyone," explained Myrtle.

"Maybe they sneaked up on her," the Cheese offered.

"There's a dozen cops down there," said Jimmy. "No one sneaks up on Butch."

"Why the commotion?" I asked. "You ain't doing nothing illegal. I mean, serving after hours, but that's maybe a ticket or a bribe, not a raid."

"Three articles," said Jimmy, and she pulled away from the peephole to give me a gander.

I looked down to see the cops lining all the dames dressed in men's suits against the wall, while herding all the dames in dresses over to the stage.

"Masquerade law," said Myrtle, casting no more light on the subject than the peephole did on the dark passage.

Below there was much protest from all involved and a little sobbing and sniffling from a few. The uniform cops did indeed number a dozen, which surprised me no little, because if you had asked me, I did not think there were a dozen cops working all of Fog City at this time of the morning. As I observed, two plainclothes mugs made their way in, one a dumpy mope with a boiler trying to escape his pants and jacket, and a very tall, hard-looking cop with a jaw like a hatchet and creases in his pants that would cut butter.

While I watched, the tall cop went from one dame to another, pulling up her jacket and pulling out her waistband, inspecting each in the most invasive way. "I don't know what he's looking for," I said, "but it ain't weapons."

Jimmy Vasco pushed me aside and fitted her eye to the peephole. "That cracker-crunching mackerel snapper is checking their underwear."

"Cracker cruncher?" I asked Myrtle with a raised eyebrow. My peepers had adjusted to the dark, and between the light from the peephole and what was coming over the top of the fake wall, I could see just fine.

"Body of Christ," said Myrtle, crossing herself.

"Sorry, doll," said Jimmy. "I forgot. It ain't he's a Catholic, it's he's a holier-than-thou cocksucker of a Catholic."

"That's Dunne?" I'd never seen the new head of vice.

Jimmy shushed me, finger to her lips. We could hear cops rummaging around in the hall below us, slamming doors, tipping stuff over.

"Looking for you?" I whispered.

Jimmy nodded. "'Swhat I wanted to talk to you about."

"Well, I'm not going to hide you. My apartment's small and you're bossy."

"Nah, I was gonna ask you to take care of him like you did Pookie O'Hara."

"I did not scrag Pookie," I said. And I didn't. Pookie O'Hara, SFPD's previous head of vice and a certified creep, mysteriously disappeared a few months ago while the Cheese and I were having an adventure up in Sonoma County. Many citizens attribute his disappearance to me.

"Right," Jimmy said with an exaggerated wink that not only was visible in the crepuscular light of the passage, but looked like she had wiped a cut lemon across her eye and was trying to squint away the burn.

Stilton pushed through and put her eye to the peephole. "Now they're looking at their socks. What kind of loopy shit is going on down there?"

"Masquerade laws," said Jimmy. "Started back in the 1800s. If a dame is dressed like a guy she's got to be wearing at least three articles of women's clothing or she's in violation of the law."

"Three-articles law," said Myrtle.

I heard a click and a flick and Jimmy's Zippo lit up and she held it down by her feet while pulling up her pants leg, showing a lacy sock with pink embroidered roses. "Embarrassing," she said.

"Most girls wear a pretty pair of panties, too," said Myrtle. "I know I do."

"Aw, Myrtle," said Stilton, "you got feminine for miles."

"Well, those socks make two," I said to Jimmy, then, with an elbow to her ribs, "What else you got hidden to keep you out of jail?"

"Things get rough, I figure I can jump into Stilton's panties."

"Well, you're shit out of luck tonight, buster," said Stilton, still looking down on the club. "Unless you want to hike up the hill and get 'em out of the hamper."

And I was thinking, *What kind of bum lets his girlfriend go through life with only one pair of skivvies?*

"Hey!" Stilton yelled. "Let go of her!"

"Shhhhh, doll," I said, and Myrtle and Jimmy were shushing her for all they were worth, too.

"Well, he's roughing up Betty Anne. She's a swell gal."

I looked through the peephole and sure enough, Dunne was going down the line, whipping each of the dames up against the wall while the uniforms were cuffing them. Not exactly punching their lights out, but being much rougher than the situation called for. Dunne is a big guy, maybe six-six, and well over two hundred, a church tower of a guy, one of those sturdy English church towers with the slots on top for your church archers to shoot through. He was whipping these dames around like they were rag dolls, calling them perverts and dykes and various other unflattering sobriquets, and let me tell you, dykes can call themselves dykes all night long and laugh it away, but a guy tries that one on and he will have some severely sored-up lesbians on his hands. But these poor dames were growling or crying and I did not care for the scene at all. I do not care for guys roughing up dames, even if they are wearing suits that are nicer than mine, and just as I was about to comment thus, Dunne whipped this tall, thin dame around by the shoulder, and she had nothing but fire for him. She couldn't have been more than twenty-two, twenty-three, wearing a black pinstripe suit over a silk blouse unbuttoned to her navel, and not a stitch under that I could see. Her hair was black, short, in a bob like that silent film star Louise Brooks had, long, pointed sideburns sweeping down near to the corners of her mouth. She was a looker, in a pissed-off, vampire-who-wouldn't-drink-your-blood-if-she-was-dying-of-thirst sort of way.

Dunne dropped his tone and said something I couldn't hear. The thin dame gave him a sneer. Whatever she said, it made Mother Superior Captain James Dunne look like he'd run into a solid wall of nope.

"The fuck?" I sort of let drool out as I watched Dunne order all his uniforms to uncuff the dames against the wall. While they were still sniffling and rubbing their wrists, the cops cleared out, Dunne called the uniforms back out from Jimmy's office, then made a tucked-tail exit with the tall, thin dame stepping right behind.

"Jimmy," I said. "Look, look, look. Who's the tall dame trailing Dunne?"

I stepped to the side and Jimmy fitted her eye to the peephole.

"The fuck?" Jimmy said.

"What? What? What?" said Myrtle, pulling Jimmy away from the peephole.

Jimmy looked up at me. "The fuck?"

I shrugged so hard my hat tipped. "She said something to him and he nearly pissed himself."

"Oh yeah, I saw her come in after you," said Myrtle. "Wait. Look, look, look." Myrtle pulled aside to give me a look.

So I looked. "The fuck?" On her way out, the thin dame threw an arm around Mel, the bartender, who had been lined up against the wall with the others, and laid an Argentine backbreaking tongue-tango on her while catching the back of Dunne's jacket so he was whipped around and had to watch.

I stepped aside quickly so Jimmy could see. "The fuck?" she said.

"Who is she?" I asked.

"No idea, first time I've seen her," said Jimmy. "But I'm glad she's on our team."

Two minutes later we were downstairs on the dance floor, the lights all the way up like you never want to see in a bar at three in the morning, and Jimmy had gently but sternly told everyone they had to get the fuck out, so they shuffled off, some of them still sniffling from their run-in with the Mother, the bass player carrying her axe like an oversized baby.

Jimmy herded us out last, turning off lights and locking doors as we went. I helped her bring the host podium in and noticed that Butch's dingus of death was still tucked behind it.

"Can't figure what happened to Butch," Jimmy said. "That's not like her to take a powder on a work night."

"You want us to help look for her?"

"Nah, I'm beat," said Jimmy. "I'm staying at Myrtle's place. You two need a ride?"

Jimmy keeps a small apartment behind her office and has a pearl-black '36 Ford coupe with a rumble seat that would be a snug but welcome fit about now. I did not relish climbing the 387 steps to Stilton's place on Telegraph Hill or finding a cab to my place at that hour.

"Sure," I said. "Thanks."

"We can find out Butch's story in the P.M.," said Jimmy, the P.M.

being the hours in which we in the hospitality trade actually begin to stir, as opposed to the morning for normal citizens.

But what we found out in the P.M. was that at that very moment, Butch was bobbing facedown in the bay about fifteen feet below where we stood.

2

THE DRAGON'S BEARD

Sammy

An arrow thunked into the door by my head and before I could see where it came from, the kid came howling out of the stairwell and tomahawked me in the danglers. I snatched him up by the back of his overalls and chucked him back over the railing into the stairwell, where he hit a wall and slid down onto the steps, leaving a bright red stain on the wallpaper. I took a knee and tried to catch my breath, and while down there picked up the rubber tomahawk (which was somewhat lighter in hand than it had felt impacting my man pouch). I flung it into the stairwell after the kid.

"Die, paleface!" said the kid.

"What's the matter with you, kid?" I am kind of a mentor to the kid, and as his pops was scragged in the war and his mother was out most of the time, or entertaining various uncles in their apartment, which was downstairs from mine, I often took a moment to teach him life lessons. "You can't just go hittin' a guy in the sack like that, kid; it's bad manners."

"Apaches don't have manners."

Despite my best efforts, he was a horrible little kid. "You're not an Apache, you little monster."

"*You're* a monster, ya dirty turpentine."

I could hear him coming up the steps and I dug in my pocket

for my keys, thinking I could get through the door before he made the landing, but then there he was, in his overalls, no shirt, streaked with red war paint, which looked suspiciously like lipstick, and a band around his head with a bent red feather sticking out. He was fitting the nock of an arrow onto the string of his little bow.

"Turpentine is paint thinner, kid."

"No it ain't, you're a stinkin' liar."

I looked at the arrow pointing at me, then at the one sticking in my door, then at the kid drawing his bow. The kid let fly and the arrow thawanged into the door next to the first one.

"Goddammit, kid, you keep that up, they're going to put you in a home for fucked-up little kids."

"Let 'em try. I'll scalp the sons a' bitches."

"The fuck did you get arrows with metal tips?"

The kid dropped the bow to his side. "My uncle Clappy give 'em to me."

"Uncle Clappy? Your uncle a clown, kid?"

"Nah, Clappy ain't his real name, it's Goneril or something."

"Gonorrhea?"

"Yeah, that's it. He gets sored up if you say it on account of him being Italian."

"Gonorrhea ain't an Italian name, kid."

"You don't know. Uncle Clappy says if I stay away till four he'll get me a tomahawk with a real blade; then you're in trouble, buster."

I pulled the arrows out of the door and inspected the holes they'd made. It's an old redwood door, original to the building, which goes back forty-some years ago to the earthquake, but redwood is soft and the door is showing some wear. If the landlord saw the holes, he might ding me a sawbuck for a repair he'd never do.

"Gimme my arrows back. I only got three," said the kid.

"Two." I showed the kid the arrows to make my point.

"I got three. One is in the holy cow window at Saint Pee-Pee's."

Saints Peter and Paul's is the Catholic church a couple of blocks away on Washington Square Park. It has a stained-glass window with a winged cow with a halo on it. It's a daffy thing to put on a window, if you ask me, but I'm sure it hadn't been improved by the kid's arrow.

"Well, these two are mine," I said, trying to work my key in the door.

"It ain't locked," said the kid. "I left it open for ya."

The kid has a key to my place he claims I gave to him one time that I don't remember, but I have been known to have lapses of memory after long evenings of merriment and consumption of spirits, so he might not be lying. I used to leave the apartment un-locked for the kid to have a place to go if his mom was entertaining an uncle when I was at work of an evening. I keep some bread, butter, milk, and cornflakes around for him to eat in case Ma also forgets to feed him. I need to have a chat with her one of these days about her parenting skills, but when I think about it, I can't get past the part where I am busting the chops of a war widow who has to go on the hustle because she forgets to marry the kid's dad before he croaked, and so I just buy more cornflakes.

Sure enough, the door wasn't locked, and I slid into my place and threw the bolt. I needed a shower and a shave, although I had caught thirty-seven winks at the Cheese's place because she deigned to grab some shut-eye before work, rather than giving me the razzmatazz, as is her habit, and which saddened me no little. I sent her off to the Five & Dime to work a little before six, then slept until ten thirty before making my way down the hill home.

I had not even turned on the water to heat up for my shower before the kid was pounding on the door.

"Give me my arrows, ya mug!"

"Go away, kid. Why aren't you in school?"

"It's Sunday. No school."

"You shot an arrow through the church window on a Sunday?"

"*Into* the window. The arrow's still stuck up there. I gotta wait until dark to climb up and get it."

The holy cow window was about three stories up on the face of the church, next to the holy eagle, holy lion, and holy random halo guy windows, all equally daffy. I was going to ask him why he was shooting at a church window in the first place, but the answer would boil down to what it always did: he was a horrible little kid.

"Take a hike, kid."

"Gimme my arrows or I ain't giving you the message I took."

I paused, then sniffed my towel to see if I could get another shower out of it. It smelled like someone had used it to beat out a fire built of mildewed mice. Good for another round.

"What message?"

"My arrows or you can just pound sand, ya stinkin' penicillin."

"Penicillin is medicine, kid."

"No it ain't. My ma got stuck in the butt by a penicillin and she said it hurt like crazy."

I unlatched the door and opened it just wide enough to hold the kid's arrows outside, above his head.

"Gimme!"

"Message."

"That Nip cocksucker called."

"Eddie Shu?" The kid always referred to my Chinese pal Eddie as a Nip spy.

"He didn't say."

"Then how did you know it was him?"

"By his Nip accent."

Eddie is second-generation Chinatown and has no more accent than I do, except for some hepcat jazz jive he picked up at the club where he works. But the kid grew up during the war, and even two years after it ends he is still on the lookout for Japanese spies and aircraft.

"Fine, what'd he say?"

"He said you need to meet him at the Dragon's Dong at noon. He's got a job to do for Gao Mao Yow. What's that, some kind of Jap code?"

"Yeah, some kind of code." I dropped the arrows in the hall, pretty sure I was going to regret it later. Gao Mao Yow wasn't code, it was Eddie's Cantonese nickname for his uncle Ho: *the Catfucker*.

◇◇◇◇◇◇

I knocked out a hard ten minutes on the heavy bag hung in the alcove of my apartment, as is my habit; executed a shit, shower, and shave; and was crossing Broadway into Chinatown on Grant Avenue in fresh street togs before the bells at Saint Pee-Pee's were ringing out lunch. Broadway is the border between North Beach, the Italian neighborhood where I work and live, and Chinatown—the distinction is so sharp a mug could find himself reaching for his passport before stepping off the curb on either side of the street. Red, white, and green flags and the smell of garlic and baking pizza on the air gave way to red pagoda roofs, five-spice chicken, and joss sticks.

What the kid called the Dragon's Dong was, in fact, an ice cream joint called Dong's Dragon, Dong being the name of the proprietor and Dragon the name of his specialty, the *dragon's beard*, a sweet treat Dong claims was invented for the Emperor by his ancestor going back two thousand years and handed down to him so he could serve it to guys and dolls of the American persuasion who stopped by on a night on the town to enjoy an exotic Oriental novelty while giggling up their sleeves over the proprietor's name.

Eddie "Moo Shoes" Shu was waiting on the sidewalk outside Dong's, a slim Chinese guy with a carefully oiled Sinatra forelock curling down his forehead, dressed in a light gray flannel suit and white linen shirt with no tie. He was holding his Panama hat, which seemed excessively tropical for a November day, but it was warm and sunny and Eddie only owned two hats.

It being Sunday, a cohort of kids gamboled around Eddie, waiting to get into Dong's or strafing the sidewalk with dripping ice cream cones, making Moo Shoes look not a little nervous about any getting on his sharply pressed flannel or his black-and-white wingtips with the Holstein pattern, from which he gets his moniker.

"What's shakin', bacon?" Moo inquired.

"A job for Uncle Ho?" I replied.

"I wasn't sure you got my message. The kid is—"

"He's a horrible little kid," I said.

"You should get a phone for the Cheese."

"Such is my ambition, but alas, I am somewhat short on doubloons, which is why I am here. A job?"

Moo flipped his forelock toward Dong's door and led me inside, where Uncle Ho, looking like a statue of Confucius constructed from dried apples and worn leather, was sitting at one of the eight stools at the counter, worrying a cone of green ice cream, a little of it frosting his wispy white mustache.

"Ho," I said, with a slight bow.

"*Gwai lo,*" said Ho, with a nod, not looking up from his ice cream.

"I am not a white devil," I said to Moo Shoes.

"He means it affectionately," Moo explained, giving me a slight shake of the head as if to say, *Please, do not fuck this up as I am desperate and my shoes are ridiculous.*

"You want some ice cream? I'm buying," said Moo.

I looked at the menu above where old Dong was furiously scooping ice cream, backed up by his two adult sons, all in white jackets and soda-jerk paper hats. *Chocolate, Vanilla, Strawberry, Praline,* and *Coconut,* and below that, five flavors written in Chinese characters.

"What are those?" I asked Moo.

"Lychee, passion fruit, pangolin, pork, and toad," said Moo Shoes.

"Toad? Toad? Goddammit, Moo Shoes, if this job is about giving stiffies to the nut-sack guys again I will bop you in the beezer."*

"Nah, nothing like that. Uncle Ho needs us for—I'll tell you outside."

Hearing his name, Ho glanced at me over his ice cream long enough to let me know that whatever he needed from me, I would probably disappoint him.

"You're eating toad ice cream, aren't you, Ho?"

Uncle Ho grinned briefly, showing his seven or so teeth, then quickly looked back to his ice cream. I looked to Moo Shoes and continued as if Uncle Ho weren't there at all, which is how we usually talked around him. Ho spoke convenience English, which was none at all unless it was convenient for him. If he had something to say, he'd speak up.

"Chocolate in a cone," I said, "and don't use the toad scoop on my chocolate."

Moo said something to old Dong in Cantonese and one of the young Dongs started scooping my cone. The other son was heating a cake of molasses about the size of a bar of soap over a flame, then stretching it in a metal tray of cornstarch, then doubling it, and stretching it, then doubling and stretching it again, until the brown molasses was a sheet of hair-thin white threads. Then he took crushed peanuts and toasted coconut and wrapped them in the fine white fiber and handed Moo Shoes a bite-sized pellet. It reminded me of the owl pellets my brothers and I used to find in the barns outside Boise—compact fur-turds wrapped around bones and cartilage from some digested gopher.

---

* Moo Shoes, Uncle Ho, and I had a short-lived business selling poisonous snake whiz mixed into noodles at Tall House of Happy Snake and Noodle over on Pacific Street to a bunch of guys who were so old and wrinkly that they looked like they were made entirely out of scrotum skin, so I named them the "nut-sack guys," out of respect. The snake whiz was supposed to help them get boners, and I don't know if it ever did, but we made some respectable folding cabbage until the snake died.

Moo Shoes raised a toast to me with the pellet. "Beard of the dragon," he said, then he bit into it and white sugar-hair trailed down his chin—the beard of the dragon that gave the joint its name.

The other Dong son handed me my cone and, with it, a fortune cookie. Eddie paid him, took a fortune cookie for himself, and handed one to Uncle Ho.

"To the dragon's dong," I toasted Moo with my cone before giving it a lick.

One of the Anglo kids waiting for ice cream laughed. Old Dong silenced the kid with a glare. I got the feeling that if you made fun of old Dong's name you were getting either no ice cream or, worse, an extra scoop of toad.

"The name Dong comes from a Cantonese word for *boss,* very respected," Moo Shoes said, giving old Dong a wink, like, *I'll set this* gwai lo *straight.* "Not like *dong* in English."

I gave my ice cream a lick and tossed my head toward the door. "Step into my office."

Eddie headed out the door. Ho sat on the stool. "You, too, ventilated elder," I said.

"Venerated," Eddie corrected.

"We'll see," I said.

I led them up the street a few doors until we were clear of all the kids and stopped in front of a shop with red Peking ducks hanging in the window.

"What's the skinny, Minnie?" I asked Moo.

Uncle Ho crunched down the last of his cone, then held a skeletal finger up for me to wait while he swallowed it. Moo Shoes started to talk but Ho shushed him with the same finger in his face.

"You find black dragon," Ho said to me.

I looked at Eddie, who shrugged. "It's a statue," he said.

"I'm gonna need a little more to go on. Also, why me?"

"Us," said Eddie. "He asked me to call you."

Ho nodded. "Need *gwai lo.*"

"He knows that now that I don't need him I will punch out his lights, right?" I asked Moo. "Even if he's old and crispy. I don't mind."

"Two grand," Eddie said.

"What?" I inquired.

"Two Gs. We split it. C'mon, Sammy, I need this."

"Well then, why don't *you* find the black dragon and keep the whole two grand?" Don't get me wrong, I could have used the money. Maybe get the Cheese a phone, maybe get a bigger place where we both could live together.

"Uncle Ho says I need a *gwai*—an Anglo to find the dragon, because where it's at is Anglo country now. And you're the only round-eye he trusts."

Well, now I felt bad about threatening to punch the old guy's lights out. Sure, I'm a white devil, but I'm his *favorite* white devil. "Now? Where is it? And furthermore, before you answer, if we know where it is, why do we not just go get it?"

"Locke," said Moo Shoes.

"The fuck is a Locke?"

"In the Sacramento River valley. It's a town. Used to be an all-Chinese town. Like Chinatown, only agricultural. That's where Uncle Ho last saw the black dragon."

"When was that?"

Moo asked Uncle Ho something in Cantonese. The cat fucker replied in the same.

"Forty-one years ago."

"He lost his statue forty-one years ago and all of a sudden it's worth two grand to get it back?"

"No. Getting his business back is worth two grand. The dragon is for another guy, the Squid Kid."

"Moo Shoes, do not try to run that *phonus bolognus* inscrutable Eastern mystic game on me. You are highly scrutable. I can scrute both you mugs five out of six days a week."

"No game. Tommy—the Squid Kid—Fang, local gang boss.

Moved in on Uncle Ho's business and won't give it back until Uncle Ho coughs up the dragon."

I looked over at Uncle Ho, who nodded. Far as I remembered, Uncle Ho had several very large fellows of the ornamental persuasion working at his opium den, so if he was being muscled out of his business, this Squid Kid must have had some serious juice indeed.

"What's the deal with this statue? Made of gold or something?"

Uncle Ho spoke to Eddie, who translated a windy story for me, which reduced to this:

Squid Kid is the grandson of an old boss of the Ghee Sin Tong from the days of the fighting tongs. He grew up listening to stories of the fighting tongs' power and wealth back in the late 1800s. In those days the tongs ran everything in Chinatown: drugs, women, gambling. They even sponsored peasants from the old country to come here to find their fortune. All the local businesses paid the tongs for protection, and the tongs fought among themselves for territory, sending out squads of hatchet men to battle in the streets and alleys, sometimes starting a minor war over the theft of a single whore. They existed with much secrecy and ritual, and in those days to be Chinese was to either be in a tong or live in fear of them. Unwedded sons from the provinces would leverage their loyalty for a chance in the Land of Golden Hills. Gentle farm boys became brutal criminals in the service of their tong, which claimed a higher purpose of revolt against the Emperor and the Qing dynasty. Their legitimacy came from their claim of succession back to great rebel warriors, warriors of the people, back three hundred years to before the dynasty. The symbol of that connection for the Ghee Sin Tong was the black dragon, which they smuggled to the New World to show their young initiates. But around the turn of the century, one of the initiates stole the black dragon and hid it away somewhere, and soon, whether through curse or history, the tongs fell. Squid Kid thinks the black dragon will restore his gang to the glory of the tongs.

Uncle Ho stopped talking and grinned as he waited for Moo Shoes to finish translating.

"You?" I said, and the old guy grinned wider. The sneaky bastard actually had eight teeth. (He'd been hiding a tooth on the sly.) "You took the black dragon?"

"You find dragon, *gwai lo*."

"I might, *Catfucker*."

Moo Shoes cringed like a salted slug, grabbed me by the sleeve, and dragged me three doors down the street for a private consult.

"I told you, you can't call him that," Moo said.

"He keeps calling me white devil, I'm gonna call him Catfucker."

"You agreed."

"I agreed when he was doing us a favor. Now he's asking a favor, so he can piss up a rope."

"It ain't a favor, it's a job. Play nice. I need the cheddar, Sam."

"It's two days after payday; you always need the cheddar by now."

"No, I need a chunk of change. I can't be on the hustle forever."

"And you want to start a driving school with Lois Fong? Then what, settle down, have a bunch of kids, buy a house in the Sunset?"

"Something like that. Uncle Ho says he'll stake me, on top of the two Gs, if I help him get his business back."

"Moo Shoes, while Lois Fong is a certainly a dish of the most delicious aspect, if I may, she does not seem the type to want to settle down." (More the type to slip a guy a mickey and steal his wallet, I was thinking, but I did not mention that because Moo was in love and seldom had more than twenty bucks in his wallet, which he would have gladly surrendered to Lois sans mickey.)

"Nah, she's on board with the driving school. You should see how she brings them in."

"How?"

"Well, I had her pass out flyers at Tall House of Snake and Noodle."

"She is hustling the nut-sack guys?" I was trying to imagine

Lois in her satin cheongsam, the slit up the side, a pair of getaway sticks to make a priest weep for his lost life, and all the creepy nut-sack guys paying a fortune to drink poisonous snake urine to tent their trousers at her, and I said, "Sure, I can see how that might work, but do they show up for the driving lessons?"

"Dunno. We can't schedule them. We don't have a car."

"I thought Milo was going to let you use his cab during the day."

"He was, but then Doris's husband went on the graveyard shift at the docks, so he's home during the day, so Milo and Doris got no place to go to do the razzmatazz. Doris told Lars she's working days and Milo found an empty warehouse in the Mission where he parks the cab and him and Doris have at it and afterward harvest some Zs."

Due to his discomfort with driving, Milo seldom has enough cabbage for rent, although sometimes he rents a room at a single-room occupancy hotel in the Tenderloin so he can grab a shower, but those joints, set up for defense workers during the war, do not allow overnight or even daytime guests, to keep them from becoming bone palaces for streetwalkers.

"You could lend them your place and stay with the Cheese," Moo Shoes added, bouncing his eyebrows like I might think that nonsense was a good idea.

Lately the Cheese had been sending me home more than I liked to admit, and I did not relish the idea of having to vacate my digs in the early A.M. so Milo and Doris could bump uglies on my sheets just to give Moo Shoes a car in which to teach ancient ornamentals to drive.

"What do you need for a decent used jalopy?" I asked, feeling hopeful. I had about fifty bucks stashed at home. "One—two hundred bucks tops, right?"

"Yeah, that, and we need to rent a storefront, get some signs painted. Lois wants a uniform."

"A driving instructor's uniform? Does she even know how to drive?"

"Not the point. The nut-sack guys will expect her to be in the car and she wants an outfit. Something official looking, but sexy."

Lois is a dancer at Club Shanghai, where Eddie works as a host. She has access to a bushel of sexy outfits, most of them composed of less fabric than an eye patch, but probably not official looking.

"But I don't know how to find stuff," I said. "I've never even heard of this Locke place. Look, I got fifty bucks, I can—"

"I need this, Sammy. And we find the black dragon, you can take your share and take the Cheese on a trip, maybe get a place big enough for the two of you to share. You don't mind me saying, Sammy, dame like that, she ain't going to be short of offers. You got to lock her down."

I didn't want to tell Moo Shoes that a dame like that would bloody a guy's nose who talked about locking her down, but I also didn't want to admit he was getting to me. Fucking Moo Shoes is a hustler, and he was plying his skill on a pal.

"Fine," I said. "But he's got to stop calling me white devil."

I made my way back to Uncle Ho, who had just snapped open his fortune cookie. The old guy looked at his fortune and grinned like an eight-toothed opossum. He held it out for Moo Shoes to read.

"*Destiny and prosperity are one and the same for you,*" read Moo.

"Ha!" said Ho, like he'd hit the daily numbers.

"He knows that fortune cookies aren't even Chinese, right?" I said. "I read they were invented by the Japanese guy who designed the tea garden in Golden Gate Park."

Uncle Ho rattled off some nonsense in Cantonese.

"He says he is open to the new ways as well as the old," Eddie translated.

"If he understood me, why didn't he answer in English?" I said.

Eddie shrugged, cracked open his own fortune cookie, and read,

"*Friends and family are forever blessings for you.*" Eddie grinned, a full set of gleaming choppers, unlike his uncle. "Smart cookie. Go on, Sammy."

I cracked open my cookie and pulled out the little paper message. There were Chinese characters over the English translation. I read, "*He who steps on the dragon's tail will have his dick bit off.*"

I heard a wheezing, like someone cranking the starter on a tiny asthmatic Oldsmobile: Ho the Cat-Fucking Uncle was doubled over laughing.

I chucked the bits of cookie in the gutter, turned on my heel, and headed back to the ice cream shop, waving the thousand little kids lined up for ice cream out of my way with my fortune as I went. "Goddammit, Dong, you gave me a defective cookie!"

"Come by Cookie's after work," Moo called after me. "We'll make a plan to find the dragon."

3

LONE JONES AND TOO MANY COPS

Sammy

The only customers in Sal's when I showed up for my shift were a raggedy, drunken couple, leaning forehead to forehead at a high-top table at the back, and a rotting cop at the bar pass-through by the front door. Daytime Bennie had rolled a fresh keg of lager out of the back of the ramshackle shotgun saloon and was wrestling it to the hookups under the bar, handling the buck-and-a-half-pound barrel like it was as empty as his big blond noggin. Bennie was a good kid, if a little slow. (Kid? He was only a couple of years younger than me, maybe twenty-five.) He'd seen some shit during the war that had scrambled his eggs more than somewhat, but he'd been better since Sal croaked and I started paying him more than tips so he could get a place to live besides a doorway down on Third and Howard with the rest of the poor shell-shocked mugs who came back broken. He hadn't gone on a bender for months, and he showed up for work every morning at six to set up shots for the day drunks who migrated across North Beach with the sunrise, and ran things all day until I showed up at four. He even restocked the bar and switched out the keg if it was needed, something our late padrone and douche bag, Sal Gabelli, had never done.

"Hey, Sammy," Bennie said. "The Cheese just called. Said she's takin' a night off tonight."

"You didn't call her the Cheese, did you?"

"Nah, you kidding? I called her ma'am."

"Attaboy," I said. I slipped out of my coat and made my way down and around the bar, headed for the phone on the back bar wall. "*Just called* like five minutes ago or *just called* like an hour ago?"

"Right as I was bringing the keg out of the back."

"Two minutes, tops," said Fitz, the old cop, who looked like he'd crawled out of his grave that morning and had come to the saloon to embalm himself right through the afternoon.

"Hey, Fitz," I said. His name was Fitzsimmons, or Fitzhugh, or Fitzgerald—I don't know—all anyone ever called him was Fitz. He'd worked homicide at SFPD back in the days of the dinosaurs and retired to drink and bitch about everything. Most days he'd crawled back in his grave before my shift started.

I held a finger in the air to pause conversation while I dialed the Five & Dime, where the Cheese worked the lunch counter. It rang for long enough that I had to give the handset the stink-eye like it'd been talking bad about my mother before I hung it up. "No one's answering at the Five and Dime," I said with a shrug.

"Wouldn't be," said Bennie. "They ain't open on Sunday."

Wait. That was true. But then, where had she called from? More important, where had she gone when she crawled out of bed at the crack of dawn to head off to work?

"Ah, dames," said Fitz, his voice like a pepper grinder full of dried mice. "Whaddaya gonna do? Can't live with 'em, can't bury 'em in the basement under the furnace."

"You married, Fitz?" asked Bennie, trying to draw fire away from me.

"You wanna bury them out in the woods somewhere," Fitz ground on, ignoring the question. "Or better, drop 'em in the drink a couple of miles offshore with a couple of cinder blocks tied to them. Am I right, Sammy?"

I shook off my confusion for a second. "What the hell are you talking about, Fitz?"

"You want to get rid of a body, you do it somewhere far away from your stomping grounds. Somewhere no one will ever look. Like up in the redwoods in Sonoma County, know what I mean?"

"No idea what you mean, Fitz." I pushed the garters up on my sleeves, made sure my tie was tucked inside my shirt—made a show of getting ready for my shift. I knew exactly what he meant.

"I mean like Pookie O'Hara."

I affected a look that I hoped approximated the surprise of a babe in the woods what has just fallen off a turnip truck and landed gently in a puddle of oblivion.

"Pookie just disappeared, didn't he? Heard he left town."

"Not a chance. Someone scragged him. Put him in a sack. Dropped him in the bay."

"Allegedly," said Bennie. "I think you're supposed to say *allegedly*."

"You'd need a pretty big sack," I said, speculating. Pookie was a big guy.

"Or several sacks," said Fitz.

"Several sacks, *allegedly*," Bennie corrected.

I looked at Bennie. Fitz looked at Bennie. Bennie looked quickly to each of us like he was watching us play ping-pong.

"What?" Bennie said. "I spent a lot of nights in jail. You pick stuff up."

Fitz lit a cigarette and coughed until I grabbed a bottle of Old Tennis Shoes out of the well and poured him a shot to settle his cough. The old cop downed it and blinked smoke and tears out of his eyes. I hovered the bottle over the shot glass in case he started coughing again.

Fitz said, "Last anyone saw Pookie was in the wee hours six months ago outside of Cookie's Coffee in the Tenderloin. He was beefing with some skinny guy with a cane."

I poured him another quick shot. He knocked it back and emerged gasping for breath like he'd surfaced from a dive.

"Witness was snockered, though. Couldn't remember what happened after that."

What happened after that was Pookie O'Hara reached for the forty-five in his jacket and the skinny guy landed a home-run swing of his cane right upside Pookie's enormous coconut, rendering the cane broken and Pookie conscious and more than somewhat steamed. Allegedly.

"You used to walk with a cane, didn't you, Sammy?" asked Bennie. I gave him a look that could weld steel.

The old cop put his hands up like he was surrendering. There was trembling there. "Look, Sammy, whoever did Pookie O'Hara did this world a favor. That miserable son of a bitch thought he was cock of the walk. Head of vice? Vice! He never did an honest day of real police work from the time he came off the beat. This fucking Goody Two-shoes, Dunne, is even worse. At least Pookie didn't pretend he was some straight shooter."

I was about to repeat my complete ignorance, unconcern, and profound innocence in the disappearance of Inspector Pookie O'Hara when the door swung open behind Fitz and a very large Black fellow in a tuxedo, carrying a top hat under his arm, rushed in the door: Thelonius Jones.

"Oh Sammy, I'm glad you here. It's just awful. Just terrible. He dead. Oh, what my gonna do now, he dead!" The big man leaned on the bar, cradled his head in his hands, and began to wail softly, his dump-truck shoulders quaking with a sob.

"Who's dead, Lone?"

"The president. What my gonna do, Sammy? The president dead."

◇◇◇◇◇◇

Thelonius "Lone" Jones was one of the charter members of the Cookie's Coffee Irregulars, a loosely organized group of mugs that included yours truly, Eddie "Moo Shoes" Shu, Milo Andreas the cabbie, and lately Jimmy Vasco, who was the only cross-dressing lesbian member of the group, although Milo insisted that she, like him, was of Greek heritage, being as the island of Lesbos abided in the Greek archipelago. Lone had migrated west from Alabama with his mother during the war to find work in the shipyards of Fog City. I met Lone at the Hunters Point Naval Shipyard when I was assigned to a welding crew of all Black guys due to my inability to shut my yap when confronting the boss. Lone had saved my bacon more than once when my crew and a number of the residents of the "all colored" barracks where I was assigned also expressed their dissatisfaction with my unshut yap by attempting to pound me into frothy pink pulp. Lone had taken me under his wing and taught me how to fight, something he'd done as a bare-knuckle amateur back in Alabama in the *fucking enormous* weight class. After seeing a newsreel during the war of President Roosevelt with his Secret Service detail, Lone had resolved to become one of the elite bodyguards, not letting his race or lack of education get in the way of serving the president who signed Executive Order 8802, which banned discrimination in hiring at defense plants, allowing Lone to get the first job in his life where he didn't have to beat people up for his supper. None of us'd had the heart to tell Lone when President Roosevelt died two years ago, but evidently, today, some jamoke had spilled the beans.

◇◇◇◇◇◇

"Oh gosh, the president!" said Bennie. He beelined to the far end of the bar, where we had a radio, clicked it on, and did a little-kid-having-to-pee dance in front of it while waiting for the tubes to warm up. The couple at that end of the bar were engaged in a smooch so sloppy that they looked like they were breathing through each other.

"It's okay, Lone," I said. "It'll be okay."

"But I was gonna be a Secret Service for the president, and he dead. What my gonna do?"

Fitz shook off his haze and sat up. "What the fuck is with this loopy eggplant?"

"Shut up, Fitz," I said. I poured him a shot. He shut up long enough to knock it back, but nearly went over backward off his bar stool in the process.

"Uh, Sammy—" Bennie had given up on the radio and returned to my end of the bar. The goof was holding out a bottle of unlabeled brown liquor like I was about to run out, which I wasn't. I waved him off.

"I was talkin' to this new songbird singing up to the club," Lone said, wiping away a tear with the sleeve of his doorman's jacket. "She colored, but they let her sing 'cause she light skinned. Just a pretty little thing. So I tell her I understand her vibe, because I also ain't colored, 'cause I'm gonna be a Secret Service for President Roosevelt, so I'm only in disguise as colored, and she laugh at me and say the President Roosevelt done died two years ago. Two years, Sammy! Why don't no one tell us?"

Fitz said, "Sammy, you let this stupid fucking tar baby come in and—"

"Another word, Fitz," I said, my index finger a hair away from a spot between the old cop's eyes, "and I will knock you off that fucking stool."

"You ain't tough, kid. You ain't going to hit a cop over this—"

"Yeah, even money says I will and I have, pops. And I liked Pookie O'Hara a helluva lot more than I like you." I snatched the shot glass from in front of the old cop and chucked it over my shoulder, but looked back to make sure it didn't hit Bennie in the noggin, and when I turned back, much to my surprise, Fitz had drawn a .38 snub-nose and was tracing wobbles in the air to get a bead on me. He was pretty quick for an ancient wet-brain.

I slapped the pistol out of his hand and it clattered across the wooden floor. On the backhand I slapped knuckles across the old man's kisser, knocking him over backward. I'm pretty quick for a smart-ass bartender with a limp.

I checked to make sure Fitz wasn't going to scramble for his gun, but he just lay there, his overcoat having slipped over his head, looking like a pile of dirty laundry. I checked my palm for blood—my blood—the revolver's sight had left a gouge along my lifeline, which would have been an omen if I believed in that kind of spooky shit, but to me it was just a harbinger of some iodine and a Band-Aid.

The pile of laundry began to shake, and before I could lift the pass-through on the bar to get the gun, Fitz had rolled over to a sitting position and begun to wail like a mashed cat. Tears, snot, and a little blood streamed down his face.

Lone Jones slipped off his bar stool, knelt by the old man, and braced his shoulders. "Sammy!" scolded Lone. "I didn't teach you to fight so you could beat up an old man and make him cry."

"I wanted to go home," Fitz moaned. "But I stayed late to talk to you."

"He pulled a gun on me," I explained.

"It ain't polite, Sammy. He a sad, stinky old man. Say you sorry."

I threw Lone a clean bar towel and the big man wiped Fitz's face.

"I know your girlfriend is hanging out at Jimmy's Joynt and one of the dykes got murdered there last night," said Fitz. "I thought you should oughta know." He sobbed a couple of times and Lone rubbed his shoulders.

"Wait, how do you know all that?" I asked.

"I'm a goddamn detective inspector. I know things."

"Say you sorry, Sammy," said Lone. "I done raised you better than this."

"Raised you?" said Fitz.

"He's my mom." I bounced my eyebrows at the cop. "Didn't see that one coming, did you, Detective Inspector?"

"I'm sorry, sir," said Lone. "I try to teach him, but he is my first white boy, and like Mama always say, 'The first pancake is why you have a dog, so you have someone to give it to who appreciate it.'"

I said, "All due respect to your mom, Lone, who is as lovely as the day is long: she's crazy as a goddamn bedbug."

Lone shot me a very stern squint of *I will kick your snowy white ass* disapproval.

"I—" Fitz started to say something, then slumped back into Lone's arms.

"Now you done it, Sammy," Lone said. "He dead."

"He's not dead," I said. "He's snoring."

Bennie tapped me on the shoulder and I turned to see him standing behind me, still holding up the unlabeled fifth of hooch. "You can't pour full-strength booze for these old day drunks like that, Sammy. Especially the cops, drinking for free. They'll stay all day and pass out. I keep this bottle, four parts iced tea, one part Old Tennis Shoes, in the well for them. After the first two, they never notice the difference. Fitz usually staggers home by lunchtime."

Lone said, "He dead, just like the president." The big man shook his head mournfully.

"He's not dead," I said.

"Well, he gonna be mad when he wake up. You don't need no police mad at you, Sammy. Even if he old and damp."

"Damp?" I leaned over the bar to see a wet stain expanding around the front of Fitz's pants.

"You want me to take him home?" asked Bennie.

"Would you? You know where he lives?"

"Yeah. Just a couple of blocks. I've done it before. Can I use the hand truck?"

"Sure thing, Bennie. You're the tits, kid. Thanks."

As Bennie and Lone got Fitz into position and strapped onto the hand truck, I headed to the phone and dialed Jimmy's Joynt. Jimmy Vasco answered on the second ring.

"It's Butch," Jimmy said, after we made quick niceties and I inquired about the murder. "Fisherman spotted her floating under the pier about ten this morning."

"Drown?"

"Nah, some kind of wound to the back of the head. They don't even know yet what it was. I'm gutted, Sammy. Butch has worked for me from the jump. I shoulda known something was up when she wasn't at the door last night when we left."

I didn't know what to say, so I said, "Butch could handle herself. No way you could know."

"Look, Sammy, you need to lay low. That cop, Dunne, he's asking about you. Someone said you were the last one to see Butch last night."

"Me? I wasn't even close to the last. Why me?"

"Someone remembered you. Maybe because you were the only man in the joint. You kind of stand out. Look, whoever saw you only had your first name and a description of you, but they know you're with the Cheese, and North Beach is a small town, so it won't be long before Dunne figures out who you are."

"They didn't call her *the Cheese,* did they?"

"Not that I heard. But everyone in the place knows her and they know she works with Myrtle at the Five and Dime. Cops are heading over to Myrtle's to interview her now. Just a matter of time."

"I don't want Stilton in this. I'll be over to talk to the cops as soon as Bennie gets back to cover the bar."

"You don't want to do that, Sammy. What if Dunne brings up that jazz about Pookie?"

"Then he can write me a thank-you note. The only reason he has his job is because Pookie disappeared." Then a light went off like a bolt to the bean. "Hey, what's a vice cop doing investigating a murder, anyway?"

"Dunno. Fuckin' cops," Jimmy said. I could feel her shrugging through the phone. "Look, Myrtle won't say squat to this mook. I'll get the skinny and call you. You stay put."

"I will," I said, and I hung up. "Fucking cops," I said to no one in particular.

"Sammy," said Lone Jones, who had helped Bennie to the door and come back to a spot across the bar from me. "You shoulda told me 'bout the president."

I was about to explain, but I heard a rattle behind me and looked to see the couple in the back giving each other the razzmatazz against the jukebox.

And as much as I am a romantic at heart, a poet really, I yelled, "Knock it off, you two, that jukebox cost the joint a fortune."

◇◇◇◇◇◇

Two hours later I had talked Lone Jones off his ledge and convinced him that he could still be a Secret Service for President Truman, who was a swell guy and would probably love to have a giant colored fellow catching bullets in his stead, but he had better get to work or it would look bad on his permanent record. (My ma was a high school English teacher and had impressed us kids with how bad something would look on our permanent records, especially if one of us dawdled while fetching her gin or cigarettes from the store.)

There were a few early drunks at the bar: three fishermen who were catching one last one before they hit their bunks for a way-too-early 3 A.M. wake-up, and Father Anthony from Saints Peter and Paul's, who slipped in after saying vespers to wet his whistle and study a racing form in quiet contemplation.

I was warming up the radio to listen to the new Groucho Marx quiz show, *You Bet Your Life,* when the Mother Superior came through the door, flanked by two fresh-faced young flatfoots in uniform. I made my way over to Father Tony.

"Let us pray," I said under my breath.

"Huh?" said the priest.

"Rattle off some of that Latin nonsense you guys do."

"It's not nonsense," said Father Tony.

"Well, not if you speak fucking Latin, but how 'bout you do me a favor and do a couple of your greatest hits." And with that I refreshed his shot with some top-shelf Irish whisky and bowed my head. "Let us pray."

And Father Tony rattled off a long, quiet string of Latin of which I understood not a word, while the cops at the end of the bar fidgeted and looked uncomfortable, first the baby cops, but soon even Dunne, who, after about five minutes of low-level Latin, all of which Father Tony executed without taking his eyes from his racing form, cleared his throat loudly.

I looked up from my prayerful pose to give the tall cop the side-eye.

"Do you still have your hat on?" I asked.

"Wha—" said Dunne, reaching for the crown of his fedora like he wasn't sure it was there.

"Take it off. I got a man of the cloth here, ya mook. What are you, some kind of fucking Philistine?" I turned quickly to Father Tony. "Forgive me my language, Father. I know not what I do."

Father Tony traced the sign of the cross in front of me, picking up his shot on the downstroke, downing it, then returning to his racing form. "*Ego te absolvo a peccatis tuis,*" he said, which I am pretty sure was Latin for "You are not going to pull this off."

"Sammy Tiffin?" Dunne asked, with no regard at all for my communion with the Holy Spirit and whatnot.

"Aloysius Fisher?" I replied.

"Are you Samuel Tiffin?" he asked.

"Who's askin'?" I replied. The two young cops were looking more and more like they felt they should be let off the leash to beat the tar out of me.

"Inspector James Dunne, SFPD vice."

"So not Aloysius Fisher?"

"No." He held up a leather badge wallet and let it drop open.

"Of the Anal Fishers?" I further inquired. "The family resemblance—"

Dunne moved to the spot across from me and puffed up his six-foot-six frame like he was going to drag me over the bar.

"Hello, my son," said Father Tony, which stopped Dunne like he'd hit an invisible wall.

"Father," said Dunne.

"The power of Christ compels you!" I said. "The power of Christ compels you! *Am-scray!*"

"It doesn't work on cops, Sammy," said Father Tony.

"I almost went to seminary," I explained, not really that surprised that I was not able to exorcise the cops from my bar.

"So you *are* Sammy Tiffin?" said Dunne.

"My name is Legion, for we are many," I said, quoting gospel, much to the annoyance of the inspector.

"Tits," said Father Tony with a thumbs-up, by way of complimenting my biblical chops.

"Tiffin," said Dunne, acting like I was not busting his chops, "I need you to come downtown and answer some questions in connection with a murder."

I was very close to cracking wise again, but if Dunne got me downtown, and out of the protective gaze of Father Tony, I was going to get busted up more than somewhat, as that had been the reaction by gendarmes to my razor wit in the past.

"Well, I'd like to help in any way I can," I said, folding like a paper crane.

Dunne pulled a notebook out of his jacket, flipped it open, and threatened it with a pencil. "What can you tell me about Natalie Melanoff?"

"As God is my witness, she said she was eighteen."

"She was thirty-five," Dunne said.

"See? Anyone could make that mistake. Wait. What? Who the fuck is Natalie Melanoff?"

"Worked the door at Jimmy's Joynt," Dunne said.

"Butch? Butch's name is Natalie?"

"Was," said Dunne. "She was found floating in the bay late this morning. Someone bashed in her skull."

"Oh man, who would do that? Butch was a stand-up broad."

"And you were the last one to see her alive."

"How do you know that?"

"Because you were seen talking to her just before closing."

"Well, whoever saw me talking to her was the last one to see her alive, so ask them what happened to her. She was fine when I walked away."

"You were the last one in the club last night."

"Not strictly true. There was that slim dame in the black pin-stripe that twisted your sack up until you curtsied, remember? But I'm sure you already questioned her, right?"

Dunne swallowed hard. The two young cops looked around like they were trying to spot spiders in the corners. I wondered if they'd been at the raid when Dunne pulled everyone out. I decided to throw the Nun a bone, see if he might forgo dragging me in and beating the various humors out of me.

"Butch was fine when I saw her. But she was having a beef with a guy when I walked up. Sent him away more than somewhat purpled up for his trouble. Slim guy, five-nine or -ten, maybe a buck fifty. Mid-thirties, wearing a tux, slicked-back hair, pencil-thin mustache."

"Did she say what the beef was about?"

"She'd eighty-sixed him, I don't know why. But he was hot as a griddle. She said guys like that get sored up all the time, but she had it under control. The guy limped off while I was standing there."

"You think he mighta come back, Inspector?" said one of the young cops. Dunne gave him a look usually reserved for puppies that piss on the rug. The kid looked for spiders.

Dunne said, "I didn't see you in the club. Where were you?"

"Hiding behind the stage. You mugs were checking everyone's skivvies and I'm shy."

"When did you leave the club?"

"Right after you did."

"Did you see Miss Melanoff on your way out?"

"Nah, Jimmy figured she scrammed when you guys showed up."

"And where did you go after that?"

"Jimmy dropped me off at my girlfriend's place on Telegraph Hill, where I stayed until about ten this morning."

"And your girlfriend, a Miss Cheese?"

"What?" Jimmy was right, one of the dames in the club who was trying to put the moves on Stilton had ratted me out. I smiled at the thought of how mad Stilton would be at a cop calling her Miss Cheese. "Oh, yeah, sure. Margaret Cheese. She goes by Maggie, though."

"And what is Maggie's address?"

"I dunno, somewhere on the Greenwich Steps. Not like there are numbers for all those little hovels up there."

"What's her phone number?"

"No phone."

"Well, where does she work?"

"No idea."

"But she's your girlfriend?"

"She's a very private dame."

Dunne flipped his notebook closed and slipped it into his inside jacket pocket; the pencil went in there after it.

"Did Miss Melanoff seem depressed when you saw her? Was she drinking? Taking pills? Talk about hurting herself, maybe?"

"What, you think she bashed in her own brains and jumped into the bay, but made sure to finish her shift first?"

"Just answer the question."

"She was jolly as a jester. You can write that down."

"Let's go," Dunne said, tossing his head to the baby cops, who skedaddled out the door. Dunne started to follow them, then paused, one hand on the open door, and turned back. "Tiffin, I got your number, see. I've heard the rumors about you and Pookie O'Hara, but there's a new sheriff in town, and I'm cleaning things up. You and your lowlife friends are not welcome in my San Francisco. And that goes for Jimmy Vasco and the rest of her bunch of freaks, too."

"Well, Fog City's got a good hundred-year tradition of smugglers, hustlers, Gold Rush profiteers, whores, tong warriors, Barbary Coast outlaws, shanghaiers, and plain old pirates, so good luck with that."

"They haven't met me yet. Put the word out, Easy Street is closed. And don't leave town. We might not have enough on you for this one, but we'll get you on the next one, and if not that one, the one after that, maybe the one after that, but we're going to get you."

"You're going to let me get away with three murders before bringing me in? No wonder you're still working vice."

Dunne growled, audibly growled, which is very unprofessional, and started after me. Right then Father Tony stood up, made the sign of the cross, and said, "Go with God, Inspector."

Dunne harrumphed and headed out to the street.

Father Tony looked at me. "You think he thinks you got something to do with Butch's murder?"

"I think he wants me to think he knows something he can't know, because I don't know. He's vice. He's probably been talking to a lot of hookers who think I rescued them from Pookie. You know how stories get out of hand, Father. I don't think he knows his ass from a hot rock. '*Was she depressed?*' What kind of daffy shit is that? That broad could swing a dick like DiMaggio."

Father Tony raised an eyebrow of curiosity at me.

"She loved her work," I explained.

"I gotta scram," said the priest, reaching into his pocket for his wallet to settle up. I waved him off. "Thanks, Sammy. You want to go to the track with me in the morning?"

"Nah, thanks. I gotta find the Cheese and warn her about Dunne. Besides, I don't have a car."

"Me either. I was going to take the bus down to Bay Meadows."

"You're taking a bus to the track?"

"Vow of poverty," said Father Tony.

"Me, too. Playing the ponies probably helps with that, huh?"

"I bless guys' betting tickets for a buck apiece, too. I do okay if I don't bet more than I get for the blessings."

"I gotta find a racket like that," I said. *Like Uncle Ho's dragon*, I thought.

4

PAPER SONS AND STEEL DAUGHTERS

The Rain Dragon

I must tell the story of Ho, because this, and many other stories, Sammy does not know. I know everything, but you do not know me. You do not want to know me. To know me is to find a place among your ancestors, and you know those bums always want to borrow money.

Shu "Gao Mao Yow" Ho was born in Guangdong Province in the year of the Dragon, the month of the Ox, day of the Dog, half past the hour of the Tiger, an hour well known for birthing scoundrels and big-footed women. The second son of a landlord farmer, Ho would never inherit, but because his father owned the land they worked, if fortune smiled, he might have one day gained wealth, had a family, perhaps even bought land of his own. He didn't do any of that, but instead became Ho the Cat-Fucking Hatchet Man.

Ho was a gentle, sensitive child with a great affinity for animals, all, his father thought, completely useless qualities in a farmer. While the other children were working in the fields or attending to their lessons, Ho would often be found wandering among the chickens and ducks, making friends with creatures the family would later eat for supper. When Father Shu noticed that his second son was a little bit loopy, he tasked his number one son, Shu Chang (who would become Eddie Shu's grandfather), with teaching his younger brother proper behavior, adherence to duty, and self-discipline. So, upon their father's instruction Shu Ho shadowed his older brother in all his movements. Number one son planted rice, so did number two, even if Shu Chang had to drag Ho away from a conversation he had taken up with a group of frogs to get him to do so. If number one son was tasked to feed pigs, so too was number two, after naming each of the pigs and asking after their well-being—until before long, Shu Chang referred to Shu Ho as the *annoying shadow*. But being a dutiful and disciplined son, Shu Chang never complained to his father about his task, for did Confucius not teach, "Let the will be contained to the path of duty, and don't be a fucking whiner, kid"?

But trouble arose one day in the year of the Tiger, when Ho turned ten. They were feeding the pigs together, as duty dictated, and as Chang chucked buckets of rotting cabbage and rice straw into the sty, Ho struck up a lively conversation with the pigs, at which his elder brother snapped.

"Why do you do that? Why do you talk to them? They are pigs! They don't understand you."

"They like me," said Ho. "See how they gather when I come to the pen?"

"They gather because you feed them."

"No, they like me. They told me."

"They did not tell you. They are pigs. They do not talk."

"They do," said Ho, as calm as a pond on a windless day. "They said if I pushed you into the pen they would be happy to eat you."

"They did not."

"They asked me to. They think you would be delicious."

"They did not. And tell them that I am not delicious."

"I told them that you would probably be bitter, but they don't believe me."

"I am not bitter."

"I will tell them."

With that Chang tossed the last bucket of rubbish on Ho's head and stormed off to sulk and await his punishment. But evening and morning came without a word from Ho to Father, and Chang was grateful that his annoying brother had not ratted him out, so as they made their way over to the market that day to sell some yams, he said, "Thank you for not telling Father about yesterday."

Ho waved off the offense as if brushing a cobweb from his path and said, "Can we stop to look at the cranes wading in the rice paddies?"

To which his brother replied, "Do you have to be so fucking spooky all the time?"

"Yes," said Ho, shifting the great basket of tubers on his back.

On the way home that day, Chang led the way, carrying the coin they had received, and Ho followed, the basket on his back a third full of fresh prawns for the family's supper, but when they reached home, the prawns were gone.

"What did you do with them?" cried Chang.

"They asked to be let go in the rice paddy, so I released them."

This time Chang struck his smaller brother, knocking him to the ground, then squatted over him, pummeling Ho with his fists, shouting, "You idiot! You simpleton!" until Father Shu pulled him off.

Chang was beaten to stripes with a willow switch and forbidden from eating with the family for a week, which only caused his resentment for his younger brother to grow until it bloomed one early morning, when he went outside to relieve himself and found Ho, wearing his shirt but no pants, crouched over one of the farm cats, petting it as it arched its back and purred. Why his brother had gone outside pantsless at dawn, Chang did not know. Although later Ho would say that in his morning urgency to reach the privy, he had peed down the front of his trousers and had hung them on a post to dry, no one would believe him.

Chang heard the snapping of a cattle crop and looked up to see a neighbor farmer and his son leading an ox over the road by their farm, and he shouted, "Cat fucker!" pointing to Ho. "Cat fucker!" he shouted, frightening both Ho and the cat. "Cat fucker!" he yelled as Ho snatched up the cat to comfort it and stood, holding it squirming in his arms, as the farmer and his son looked over.

"Cat fucker!"

Ho began to run, pantsless, the poor cat squirming in his arms before him.

"Cat fucker!"

The farmer and his son pointed and laughed. Others working their plots nearby, or just out in the morning, watched as the half-naked boy with the cat ran by, a number one son shouting behind him as he went.

"Cat fucker!"

They were all farm people. Even the youngest child knew how animals mated. And with a quick glance at the odd second son running pantsless with a cat in arms, they concluded that indeed, some cat fucking had been going on.

So on that day, Shu Ho, second son, became known in the village, on the farms, in the market, and in school as Shu "Gao Mao Yow" Ho, or Ho the Catfucker, and nowhere did he go that he was not teased by other boys, chased, chided, and humiliated. When he came of age, and Chang and his younger brothers began to take wives and have families, Ho, the village joke, wanted only to be shed of this cruel place with its cruel people.

"We see now which brother is the bitter one," the pigs told him.

And then there arrived in the market a traveler, a stranger, and in a place where people often passed their entire lives within a mile of where they were born, a stranger was a mysterious marvel. He approached Ho on the raised road between the rice paddies as he was making his return to his father's farm.

"You seemed burdened, little brother," the stranger said.

"No," said Ho, "I have sold all of my yams."

"Burdened by oppression," said the stranger.

"Well, yes, that seems true," said Ho. "But I am the second son and it is my proper place and duty."

"How would you like to go somewhere that it doesn't matter what order you were born in? Where a man's fortune is based on his own work, and you could become rich, have land and a wife, and many sons of your own? How would you like that?"

"I would like that," said Ho.

"Come with me, then," said the stranger. "Become one with the Guild for the Protection of Virtue."

"I don't understand," said Ho.

"We will take you to the Land of Golden Hills, America, where there are mountains of gold for the picking, and you can find your fortune without the foot of an unjust emperor on your neck."

Ho had heard of the Land of Golden Hills. Men of Guangdong Province had been going there for years, and some had even returned with their fortunes, but he had heard that the white devils had made it illegal for Chinese to come to America, and he said so to the stranger.

"Not if your father or your uncle is born in America. We shall make you a paper son. When you get off the boat you will have a paper that makes you the son of a Chinese born across the water, and you will be able to live and work in the Land of Golden Hills."

"I will lose my name?" asked Ho.

"Only while you are in America. When you return, you can take back your old name."

"What if I want to stay a paper son?"

"You can have anything you want if you serve the guild loyally."

"How much is passage?" Ho had only the money he had earned for the sale of his yams that day, but he felt sure his father would gladly give it to be rid of his disgraced second son. Ho poured the few coppers from a pouch into his hand. "This is all I have."

"It is not enough," said the stranger. "But you may keep it. You need only pledge to work for the brotherhood for your first three years. We will pay your passage."

Shu Ho felt tears of joy begin to rise in his eyes at the thought of leaving behind the name of Catfucker, for even after all the shame, Ho was a gentle, sensitive boy. "When can I leave?" asked Ho.

"Soon," said the stranger. "Go home, pack a bundle, and meet me here two days from today. Just bring clothes, a blanket for sleeping, and, if you have one, a hatchet."

"A hatchet?"

"If you have one, paper son," said the stranger.

Myrtle

Sundown painted the city pink as Myrtle stood outside her apartment building on Fourth Street, wearing a set of grease-stained canvas coveralls, with a wide webbed belt and rolled-over work boots that looked like they'd escaped a *Li'l Abner* comic. Her hair was tied up with a blue bandana, but a long thin strand of red had escaped at her collar and trailed down onto her shoulder, which would have gotten her a scolding from the foreman at the shipyard during the war.

"Did I tell you about the dame that had her whole scalp ripped off her head by a lathe? Ears and all. I got a picture. You wanna see pictures? Secure that hair, missy!"

She hadn't had on this outfit since the war and she'd forgotten how naughty letting a strand of hair fly free could feel. She was twirling it around her finger and projecting a coquettish smile at a pee-pants hobo across the street when a big black Chrysler pulled up and Stilton yelled, "Get in!"

Myrtle got in. Stilton pulled away.

"Where'd you get this thing?" Myrtle asked. Stilton was wearing work clothes similar to Myrtle's, except her hair was tied up with a red bandana and a fountain of blond curls was shooting out the top.

"Borrowed it," Stilton said. The Chrysler's gas and brake pedals had been extended to just under the seat, so Stilton was sitting with her legs splayed out on either side of the wheel like she was playing bongos.

"Why am I dressed like this? Why are you dressed like this? Why are we dressed like this? And why haven't you said anything about Butch?" She'd told Stilton over the phone about Butch's murder and the cops.

"Butch was a tough cookie," Stilton said. "I liked her, but she rubbed a lot of guys the wrong way. That broad could fill out a tux, though."

Myrtle sighed. "I feel like a sack of potatoes in this outfit. What are we doing?"

"Have you ever been inspired, Myrt?" Stilton grinned and took her eyes off the road for way too long while she waited for an answer.

"Look where you're going!" Myrtle said, pointing to where they were going, which was into the back of a streetcar if Stilton didn't slow down.

"I mean," Stilton went on, "have you ever just wanted to do something because you feel like it needs to be done? I don't mean like helping the war effort. I mean like you feel it bubbling up from inside?" She shimmied in her seat and the Chrysler lurched like they were riding on rough seas.

"Is this about becoming a lesbian? Because, I gotta tell you, Tilly, I love you like a sister, and you are a dish, but you ain't my type. Besides, I'm new and I ain't that good at it yet."

"Nah, nothing like that. This is about art."

"Well, I ain't that good at art, either. And if it's about art, why are we wearing our Wendy the Welder duds?"

"Because I got inspired, and I need you to help me with something." They had swung down to the waterfront and were headed through an industrial area, mostly warehouses, factories, and machine shops—the smell of coffee coming from the old Hills Bros. coffee plant was tall in the air.

Myrtle said, "This is the way they usually take you when they're going to hide your body in the mud flats. I saw it in a movie."

"Relax," Stilton said. "You're so skinny, I want to get rid of your stiff I'll just drop you off right at Portsmouth Square, throw some bread crusts on you, and let the pigeons finish you off."

"Would that work?"

"Well, not if you're moving around and talking and stuff. You gotta sit still."

"Yeah, makes sense," said Myrtle.

"So, a couple of months ago," Stilton said, now turning the Chrysler along a row of tall metal warehouse buildings, "I wake up in the middle of the night with this picture in my head. Just fully detailed, like I was looking at a blueprint like we used to work from at the shipyard."

"Well, strictly speaking," Myrtle said, "over in the Sausalito yard, I just welded what the crew boss told me to, but he was always working from blueprints."

"But you saw them, right?"

"Oh yeah. I learned to read them a little."

"Well, just like that. All the measurements and angles and whatnot popped into my head. For stuff I've never seen before. Inspiration! I just sort of knew all of a sudden that I have to make something. Make this thing I got a picture of in my head. And I can't shake it."

"Like what, a painting, a statue?"

"I'm not sure. I gotta show you. I think I got it as far as I can get it on my own. I need help."

"Well, I'm supposed to meet Jimmy at the club at ten, and we got work in the morning."

"We might not finish tonight," said Stilton. She pulled the Chrysler into a deserted gravel parking lot by a corroded steel warehouse and killed the engine. "We're here."

Myrtle looked around, looked at Stilton, looked around again at the rust, the chains, the barbed wire, the puddles of water, maybe sewage. "Swell," she said.

"You go on in, I'll be right there." Stilton waved toward a rolling door the size of a house, then got out of the car and ran around to the trunk and opened it. "Go on," she said. "I gotta get some stuff."

"You need some help?" Myrtle asked.

"No!" Stilton barked, then giggled like it was a joke and said, "I mean, nah, I got it, thanks. Go. Go. Go."

Myrtle shuffled across the gravel about as slowly as she thought she could go without actually standing still. It was almost dark and there were no lights coming from inside the warehouse and there were certainly none in the parking lot and she did not want to be here, but she especially did not want to be here on her own. She heard Stilton's voice and turned. "What?"

Stilton looked around the trunk lid. "What? What?"

"You said something?"

"No, I didn't. Oh, here they are." Stilton came up with a handful of eighth-inch welding rods, holding them like a bundle of arrows. "Got 'em." She trotted across the lot and joined Myrtle.

"What did you say back there?" Myrtle asked.

"Nothing. Just talking to myself." Stilton strode over to a normal door cut in the corrugated warehouse wall that Myrtle hadn't even seen before.

"How'd you find this place?" Myrtle asked.

"I know a guy," Stilton said.

Jimmy was always saying that: "I know a guy." Everyone in North Beach was always saying that. "I know a guy." Why did everyone know a guy but her?

Stilton unlocked a heavy padlock that was holding a chain that ran through the door and the wall, then let the chain fall, threw the door open, reached inside, and hit a light switch.

"Voilà!" Stilton said, presenting the open, now brightly lit warehouse like a magician presenting the newly reunited halves of his assistant.

"Holy moly," Myrtle said.

"It's just in the early stages," Stilton said.

"That's not going to be enough welding rods."

"Not by a long shot."

"We're not going to be finished by ten."

"Nope."

"It's a lot bigger than I was thinking."

"That's why I need your help. This place has some rails, a crane, and heavy block and tackle, but if I'm going to assemble the big pieces, I'll need some help. I wish I could show you the whole picture in my head. Wait until it's all put together."

"Will it be a boat?"

"Could be, I guess."

"Looks kinda like a rhinoceros."

"Too big to be a rhinoceros, I think."

"Well then, what the hell is it?"

"No idea," said Stilton. "But it's inspired."

"It looks like it's moving. Why is it moving, Tilly?"

"I dunno. Breathing?"

"Oh, that's just swell," said Myrtle.

5

COOKIE'S COFFEE IRREGULARS

Sammy

By the time I stepped out of Sal's at the end of my shift, the fog had swallowed the city like a damp woolen crocodile. I locked up, pulled up the collar of my peacoat (courtesy of the lost and found), and limped up Grant toward Chinatown. I caught a cab on Broadway, where the clubs were still emptying out, and jumped out in front of Cookie's Coffee in the Tenderloin. The big neon coffee cup was floating in the fog like a steaming pink ghost.

"Happy New Year!" shouted the gang milling around on the sidewalk as my cab pulled away. Since the theater and club crowd was always working on New Year's Eve, Cookie's celebrated New Year's 365 nights of the year. There was a crowd outside because years ago Cookie had lost his liquor license (and it would have been after hours anyway), so the only source of hooch was my pal Milo, who was leaning against his hack, pouring shots into citizens' coffee out of a pint of Old Tennis Shoes from the inside pocket of his car coat for two bits a shot. It was a living. The cops mostly looked away.

Inside, the joint was jumping, mostly show people, actors, dancers, singers, and musicians in their street clothes (the Tenderloin had been the theater district since the twenties); stagehands and ushers still in their tuxes; drunk couples dressed to the nines, looking for something to soak up the booze before taking each other home to Pound Town; working stiffs off the late shift; cabbies, stevedores, janitors, truck drivers, a couple of cable car conductors still in uniform, and a trio of streetwalkers sitting in the booth, painted up but looking very much not open for business, at least until they finished their burgers. Maybe the fog had chased them indoors during prime hours. Doris was inside chugging around the joint like a bosomy tugboat, pouring coffee, pulling plates, and barking orders to the cook, a sad-sack mug with forearms that looked like hairy hams.

I tipped my hat to one and all and joined Milo and Moo Shoes, who was helping to hold up the cab and sipping from a cup of joe with a cruller balanced on the saucer.

"What's the haps, paps?" said Moo, toasting me with his cruller. "New coat?"

"Lost and found," I said.

"Ain't we all?" said Moo Shoes.

Milo said, "You hear about that broad works the door at Jimmy's Joynt got scragged last night?"

"Yeah. Butch. She was a stand-up dame."

"You think it was that guy she was beating with that big black dick?"

"What?" Eddie asked Milo. "What?" he asked me. "What? What?"

"Butch kept a big rubber dildo under the host stand," I said. "Used it to convince difficult patrons to take their business elsewhere."

"How big?" Moo asked around a bite of cruller.

I gestured the length like I had caught a fish, then the girth like I was holding a baby bottle.

Moo Shoes whistled at the dimensions.

Milo added, "She was pasting a skinny guy with a pencil-thin mustache last night when I dropped Sammy off." He held a finger in the air to mark his place while he splashed some hooch into the cups of two guys in canvas coveralls who had come out of Cookie's holding their cups like they were collecting alms for the poor. "Go with God," Milo said.

"Happy New Year," said the guys.

"We keep a leather sap at the host desk for that," said Moo. "Also a couple of gorillas on standby for backup."

"Half a pool cue under the bar," I volunteered.

"Sawed-off shotgun under the front seat," Milo said.

Moo Shoes and I turned to Milo for an explanation.

"What? Guy left it in the back of the cab a couple of weeks ago."

"Where'd you pick him up, a bank robbery?"

"Nah, front of a church in the Fillmore. Although he did seem like he was in a hurry. Nah, I'd have heard an alarm."

"You know," said I, "the gendarmes will be most perturbed if they find a sawed-off in your cab."

"That is why I try to stay off the streets during business hours."

"Which are all hours," said Moo.

"Solid strategy," I said. "You see anything outside of Jimmy's after I went in?"

"Nah, I watched those two dames smooch for a while, then took off. I lost track of the guy with the pencil-thin mustache."

Just then Doris rolled out the door and across the sidewalk, carrying a cup of joe, which she handed to me.

"Cream, two sugars, handsome?" she said. The other patrons loitering on the sidewalk looked on in wide-eyed wonder at my special treatment.

"Doris," I said, tipping my hat, "you are as swell as you are lovely."

"Yeah, I had to fight off two little girls to keep them from taking it on my way out," she said, thus busting my chops for my java preferences. "You want I should put in an order for you?"

"Nah, I'll come in later. Thanks."

Doris turned and rolled away.

"Wow," said Moo Shoes, "Doris is in the weeds and she brings your coffee out here, just the way you like it. Wow."

"Well, she thinks you're the tits," said Milo.

I took a sip, and indeed, the coffee was just the way I liked it. "First," I said to Moo, "Doris has never been in the weeds; her ability to frighten a citizen into submission by telling them to sit the fuck down and shut the fuck up until she gets to them renders her weedless. And second, no, Milo, you may not borrow my apartment to use as your bonk closet."

"I'll let you use my shotgun," said Milo.

"We're going to need a car to go to Locke for that thing we're doing for Uncle Ho," said Moo Shoes.

I was about to tell Milo that I had no use for a shotgun, and Moo Shoes that I had a line on a car if we needed it, when I heard a clicking coming from down the street in the direction of Union Square. The fog was so thick you could barely see a block; all our coats and hats were glistening damp.

Click de click de clickity-click, click de click de clickity-click.

"Lone," said Milo, squinting into the fog.

"Yep," I said.

Click de click de clickity-click, click de click de clickity-click.

I asked Lone Jones once why he had taps installed on his size-sixteen wingtips.

"'Cause I'm light on my feet. I can come up on someone and surprise 'em on accident. People don't like to be surprised by someone look like me. It give 'em heart attacks and the willies and whatnot."

The big man appeared first as a soft silhouette in the wash of a streetlight, then clickity-clicked into the light coming from Cookie's, in full view, top hat and all, beside him a slim Black girl in a red satin sheath and a fur wrap, her hair tied up under a gold silk scarf, in stocking feet, holding a pair of tall Mary Jane heels by the straps.

"Happy New Year, Lone," Milo called out.

The big man smiled, caught himself, then frowned at Milo. "Y'all shoulda told me about the president."

"Oh yeah," I whispered to Moo and Milo, "I forgot to tell you, Lone found out that President Roosevelt is no longer with us."

Moo Shoes cringed so hard he spilled his coffee.

Lone stepped up to us and presented the girl beside him. "This here is Della," said Lone, taking his hat off out of respect. "She the new singer up to the club."

"Hello," Della said, like she would have rather been filing her nails.

"And these three lyin'-ass motherfuckers are my friends," continued Lone.

"Charmed, miss," I said, tipping my hat. Moo and Milo performed similar greetings under Lone's gaze, which had enough disappointment to wilt flowers, turn milk sour, and damage a delicate child.

"Aw, Lone, you can't be mad," said Moo Shoes. "We were just trying to keep you chipper."

"I ain't mad," said Lone. "I'm sad, and I need y'all to buy me a meatloaf."

I caught Doris's eye with a salute as she was pulling plates from the booth by the door. She spun, hands full of plates, and butt-bumped the glass door open.

"What? You can come in and get your refills, buster. I'm busy."

"Nah, doll, we're gonna need a meatloaf for Lone."

"One blue plate." Doris looked the songbird up and down like she was measuring her for a casket, the way dames do each other. "Big booth in the corner is about to leave, but anybody bleats, you mugs keep it fluffy; there's two plainclothes dicks at the counter. Vice, I think."

Which explained the forlorn hookers inside eating burgers instead of peddling their wares.

Lone said, "Ma'am, I'ma need a whole meatloaf, please."

"A whole meatloaf?"

"Yes'm. And mashed potatoes, please." Lone held his hat over his heart.

"We'll be right in," I said.

Doris harrumphed and looked to the cook at the window. "Butcher's revenge, murder the whole cow, bomb it with Boise!" she shouted. She gave us all a last once-over, a look usually reserved for dog shit on your shoe sole, then she was off to deliver joy to all she met.

"I'm from Boise," I said to Della, because in my experience, nothing impresses a dame like a guy with Idaho sophistication.

"She seem nice," said Della.

"She's Milo's sweetie," said Moo Shoes.

"Vice?" said Milo. "I should probably stop selling hooch for now."

The sidewalk had already cleared of revelers drinking Milo's spirits in their coffee.

"For a while," said Moo Shoes.

"Well, I'ma go eat my meatloaf," said Lone. He headed to the door. "Y'all better come along because I'm sad and I ain't got no money. C'mon, Della, they buy you a coffee."

Milo and Moo Shoes followed Lone into the diner, I started after them, but Della didn't move. She was looking up the street. "Let's go," I said. "Doris won't bite. And your dogs gotta be barking." I nodded to her stocking feet, her nylons already running ruined up her ankles.

"I got to meet a fella at a club on Fillmore Street—sing a late set," she said. "Lone was just walking with me."

"Well, you still got a ways to go. Why didn't he put you in a cab?"

She braced her fist on her hip, holding her shoe straps, and looked at me as if to say, *Why do you* think *he didn't put a Black woman in a cab at two in the morning, you goddamn anvil?* But she didn't say that, she just waited for the very dim bulb to go on in my brain.

"Oh yeah," I said.

"Yeah," she said.

"Well, come on in, warm up, and Milo can drive you to your club."

"They gonna serve me in there?"

"Oh yeah. Lone came in with us a couple of years ago and Cookie was too flustered to kick him out."

"Lone told him he wasn't colored, he was in disguise, didn't he?"

"That may have come up."

"Big dummy told me the same thing." She scoffed. "Secret Service."

"You didn't have to tell him about President Roosevelt. We wanted to let him down easy."

"How easy you gonna make it, the man been dead nearly three years. What, Lone your trained monkey, you was just going to lie to him and laugh at him behind his back?"

"No, we didn't tell him because we didn't want to break his heart."

"You sayin' I broke that big dummy's heart?"

"No, doll, you wouldn't do that, would you?" I opened the door and held it. "Shall we?"

The entire joint gave me and Della the hairy eyeball as we went to the booth. I might have traced that same path two hundred times and no one would have noticed me if I'd dropped my pants and fired a flare, but in the company of this stunner of African descent in red satin, I might have been licking lepers at the county fair for all the loathing they were laying down. Even the two plainclothes cops at the counter, who would have normally looked bored at everything, were giving us the side-eye.

"It always like this?" I whispered to Della.

"You know it is, Snowflake."

"Lone told you about that, huh?" Lone's nickname for me from back on the welding crew at Hunters Point Naval Shipyard during the war.

"He said you're his first white boy and he gotta look out for you."

"I wish he wouldn't tell people that."

She grinned at me over her shoulder and slid into the booth next to Milo, across from Moo Shoes and Lone Jones, who was menacing a whole meatloaf in the middle of a mountain range of mashed potatoes. Doris had served it on a platter.

"Eighty-six meatloaf," the cook called from the kitchen.

"Eighty-six meatloaf," Doris called back.

"See that, Lone," I said. "They're making you eighty-six more meatloafs." Which cheered the big man up not at all.

We all drank our coffee and watched Lone eat. It wasn't whole-sale carnage, as Lone's mother had brought him up to have exquisite table manners, so rather than shovel down the beefy slab like coal into a blast furnace, Lone carved out each bite precisely, then speared and dragged it through spuds to its fate. He chewed quickly and thoroughly, then down the hatch to return to the next steaming cube waiting to go in. In all, it was like watching a building being deconstructed, block by block, and fed into a crusher. None of us could stop watching. Other patrons craned their necks to see, then looked away quickly when one of us at the table caught their eye. In a field somewhere, cows wept ketchup tears for their fallen brethren.

As Lone approached the final third of the meatloaf, the crowd called, "Happy New Year!" and Moo Shoes looked past Della to the front door and said, "Uh-oh."

I turned around to see a tall, wide-shouldered guy of about forty-five, blond going gray, giving Doris hell at the register. He was kind of yelling, but also kind of whispering to keep his voice down, so mostly what we got at our end of the diner were a lot of hisses and gestures, but it was clear he was somewhat sored up at Doris.

"Lars," said Milo.

"Uh-oh," said Moo Shoes.

"He didn't even say happy New Year back," said Lone.

"Huh?" said Della.

"Doris's husband," I explained. I'd never seen Lars before, but he fit the image I had in my head. Stevedores tend to be pretty beefy mugs or they don't last. You can't sling cargo around a dock eight hours a day for very long unless you're packing some muscle.

"Doris, your sweetie's husband?" Della asked Milo.

"Yeah, this is it. I'm going to kick his ass."

"No you're not," I said. "He doesn't know who you are, he doesn't know anything is going on. He's just steamed to find Doris at work." To Della I said, "See, Lars was working the day shift when Doris was working graveyard, so when he was sleeping, Doris was working, and when he was working, Milo and Doris were giving each other the razzmatazz."

"As is written in scripture," said Moo Shoes, who was much more amused than a pal really should be at such a situation.

"But a couple of weeks ago," I continued, "Lars gets his shift at the docks changed, and he's also working graveyard, so Doris tells him she is working days, so she and Milo can continue their various shenanigans while Lars is sleeping."

The intensity at the register stepped up somewhat, with Lars actually yelling now and Doris coming around the counter and facing him down, her chin nearly poking him in the sternum.

"That dame's got spunk," said Moo Shoes.

"I'm gonna get my shotgun," said Milo, squirming against Della to get out of the booth.

"No you ain't," said Della. "Those cops are looking, everybody in here looking. The cook looking out the window. Big blondie ain't gonna do shit. Just let him yell himself out."

"He hits her, I'm going to get my shotgun," said Milo.

Doris was pointing to the door and backing Lars out of it, yelling something about not bugging her at work and how she'd deal with him at home and why the fuck wasn't he at work?

Lone Jones paused with a cube of meatloaf hovering on his fork. "I would whip his ass for you, Milo, but I'm grieving."

Della rolled her eyes so hard at Lone I thought she was going to pull a muscle. "You just eat your meatloaf, dummy."

"Hey!" I said.

"I gotta do something," said Milo.

"Well, we can't kill him," said Moo Shoes, jumping a little more ahead in the story than we were all ready for.

"No, Milo and Doris got motive out the wazoo," I said.

"And he's huge," said Milo. "His body is probably floaty. Swedes, you know."

"Y'all do know there are two cops sitting right there?" said Della. "In voice range?"

"Are Swedes floaty?" asked Moo Shoes. "How do you know this?"

"Yeah, murder is definitely out," said Milo.

"You two could run off together," I said. "Just two desperate kids running from danger, nothing but love and the road ahead." I bounced my eyebrows. "I see Doris in her waitress outfit, except for the little paper hat, because you have the windows down. You have a pack of smokes rolled up in your T-shirt sleeve."

"Sounds like a lot of driving," said Milo. "Also, I would like to wear my hat."

"Yeah, you, Doris, driving into the sunset, naked—"

"Naked?" Milo said.

"You'll have your hat."

"Oh, okay then."

I continued: "Driving to the edge of adventure, just two plucky kids, your hat, and a dream."

"Well, he going away now," said Lone.

We all turned and watched as Lars made his way down the side-walk and past the window at our booth.

"That mug is extra gorilla size," said Moo Shoes. "Watch yourself, Milo. Maybe you should hide out at Sammy's place for a few days. Lois and I will keep an eye on the cab for you."

"Moo Shoes, can it with the hustle. Lars doesn't even know about Milo."

"I'm done with my meatloaf," said Lone, placing his fork and knife at ten and two on his plate. "You want, I can go whip his ass now, Milo."

"Nah. That's okay. I gotta get outside and sell some shots."

Doris had grabbed a coffeepot and was making her way down the booths, topping off everyone's java. When she got to us I shook off the refill.

She said to Milo, "Don't worry, pumpkin, he's just a big sack of chowder. They had some kind of chemical spill at the dock and sent everyone home early. He was sored up when I wasn't home when he got there. I told him Debbie was sick and I got called in."

"You'll be fine, *pumpkin*," I said to Milo.

"Yeah, *punkin,* don't worry yo' little head," said Lone Jones.

Della giggled. Milo cringed and slid down in his seat.

"You mugs," said Milo.

"What if he asks Debbie?" asked Moo.

"There ain't no Debbie," said Doris. "But we're going to have to figure something out now, Milo. He's on high alert."

"Don't y'all shanghai people anymore?" asked Della.

"Huh?" said everyone.

"Place where I'm staying has this book about the Barbary Coast, and they talked about men all the time getting shanghaied. Barbary Coast, that here, right?"

"Yes," I said. "It was. Is, I guess."

"Well, can't y'all just shanghai this Lars dude?"

"We could do that," said Moo Shoes. "Easier than murder."

"Cops still right over there," said Della, tossing her head toward the cops.

"Do we know how to do that?" I asked.

"Lars ain't naturalized," said Doris. "You get him out of the country, it's gonna be hard for him to get back in."

"He's not a citizen by marriage?" I asked.

"We ain't officially married, exactly."

"Well then, why don't you just leave him?" Moo Shoes asked.

"Lars ain't the kind of guy you just leave. I tried. He brought me back and I had to get my jaw wired back together." Doris turned and refilled the cops' coffee at the counter.

"Well, I will definitely whip his ass, then," said Lone.

"Shotgun," said Milo, fired up now. I could tell this was the first he'd heard of the jaw.

"Still cops," said Della, toss of the head.

I said, "Look, Milo, give Della a ride over to the Fillmore; we'll swing by her place and grab that book. You're staying in the Fillmore, too, right?"

"Just down from the club."

"I don't know, Sammy," said Milo. "That's a lot of driving, and this is my busy time."

"Then give me the keys and I'll drive her. You can just lean against the light pole to sell your hooch for no longer than I'll be gone."

"What will I say I'm doing if the cops come by?"

"You think the cops didn't know what you were doing when you were leaning on your cab?"

"Motherfuckers are right *there*," said Della.

"Can I ride along, Sammy?" asked Lone. "You know where I live."

"Sure. Keys, Milo. Hand 'em over."

I stood up. Lone stood, top hat in hand. Della gathered her wrap, slid out of the booth, and stood. She started down the aisle toward the door.

"Someone need to pay for my meatloaf," said Lone.

I paid. Because we really should have told Lone about Roosevelt.

We caught up to Della next to Milo's cab. She waited for Lone to open the door for her. He did, and waited for her to get in and gather her wrap, then he closed it with a firm push, not a slam, the perfect doorman passenger load.

He looked at me. I looked at him. Della rolled down the window.

"Get in, dummies. Let's go get the book so you can learn how to shanghai your friend's girlfriend's husband. I'm late for my set."

Lone went around the back of the taxi and got in with Della. I went around the front and jumped in behind the wheel.

"In my defense," I said, "in Boise there is very little shanghaiing."

6

DAMES, DAMES, DAMES

Sammy

I dropped Della at a rooming house on Laguna Street. She ran in, got the book, and was back before I could get a smoke lit—tippy-toeing in her tall Mary Janes like a cartoon down the walk and around the big Checker. She got in and threw the book on the seat, *Tales of the Barbary Coast.*

"There, now you can fix the world for your friend the cabdriver who afraid to drive."

"Milo's tank got blowed up in the war," said Lone. "He don't mean to be difficult."

"Fillmore and Clay," said Della.

"Yes, ma'am," I said, pulling the Checker into gear.

We were there in less than two minutes and I docked the taxi at the curb in front of a darkened waffle house. I expected one of the after-hours clubs that had sprung up in the Fillmore since the war. By the wee hours there was often a crowd spilling out into the street, sometimes even a piano and some horn players laying down the bop.

"It's a waffle house," I said.

"Look at you, reading signs like a grown-ass man," said Della.

"Street-savvy, doll. Nothin' gets by me."

"But it's dark," said Lone Jones.

"It ain't dark in the back and downstairs," said Della. She popped the door and slid out. I could see a light through the window, like someone might be burning the midnight oil in an office in the back.

"You gone be okay by yourself?" said Lone.

"I'll be fine. They expecting me."

"That joint is not jumpin'," I said.

"It's after hours. The party moved downstairs at two."

"Nobody cares about after hours in the Fillmore," I said. "I've seen traffic stopped outside that club on Washington from people dancing in the street after hours."

"You ain't been to Dark Town in a while, have you, Snowflake? They's a new sheriff in town, they call *the Mother,* and he ain't having no after hours in the Fillmore. We gone underground."

The Mother—Dunne again.

"I still think I should go with you," said Lone.

"You ain't going nowhere but home. I don't need your big goofy ass following me into a club." And with that she scampered away, leaving Lone Jones looking like someone had shot his dog in front of him.

"I may need to eat me another meatloaf, Sammy."

◇◇◇◇◇◇

I pulled up outside of the earthquake shack that Lone Jones shared with his mama. It was a little clapboard place with two bedrooms. Thousands like it had been thrown up as temporary housing after the earthquake and fire of 1906, but they were still in use. Mrs. Jones had planted red geraniums in window boxes under the two front windows and there were lace curtains inside.

"Light still on. Mama up. You need to come in, Sammy."

"I'd love to, Lone, but I need to get Milo's cab back to him. Besides, what's your mama doing up at"—I checked my Timex—"three fifteen in the morning, anyway?"

"That how old people are. They keep gettin' up earlier and earlier and fallin' asleep all day in a chair until they don't really even know the difference of day and night unless they got church that day."

Lone climbed out of the cab on the curb side and looked back in. "Get your ass out that cab and come in with me. Mama know you out here, and I don't bring you in she twist my ear off."

"You know if you don't bend over she can't reach your ear."

"Get out the damn car, Sammy."

I did, and followed the big man up the walk.

Lone unlocked the front door and opened it a crack. "Mama, I got Sammy with me, put your robe on."

"I got my robe on, bring him on in."

Lone ducked to get through the door, stepped in, and stepped aside into the small parlor—just one chair and a broken-down sofa with an afghan thrown across the seat to calm the escaping springs. Mrs. Jones stood in the doorway to the kitchen, a tiny woman in a housecoat, fuzzy slippers, and a pink satin hat decorated with an array of feathers and silk flowers that looked like someone had bludgeoned a parakeet to death with a wedding bouquet.

"Hey, Sammy," she said.

"Mama, why you wearing your church hat? It the middle of the night."

"Had me one of my spells earlier, and I figure if the Lord take me I want him to recognize me. He sees me every Sunday in this hat."

Lone moved to his mother and bent down until he was looking her in the eye. "You okay, Mama? You know you can call me at work and they let me off to come home."

"I know, baby." She wrapped her arms around his neck and kissed him on the forehead. "But what you gonna do, anyway? It my time, I'm going." She grabbed him by the ears and held him at arm's length. "That meatloaf I smell on you?"

"No, ma'am."

"Don't you lie to me, Negro." She let go of his one ear and

wound up to twist the other. "Did you have a meatloaf down to the diner?"

"No, Mama, I didn't have no meatloaf."

"Sammy, did Thelonius have a meatloaf down to the diner?"

"Yes, he did, Mrs. Jones." I knew I was a dirty stinkin' rat fink, but she would have known, then it would have been me with his ear all wound up like a rubber-band airplane, and nobody wanted that. Well, I didn't want that.

She cranked Lone's ear like she was turning over the ignition on a Ford, and he bellowed like he was gonna backfire any second. "No, Mama, I was sad because President Roosevelt dead."

She let go of his ear. "Who told you that? I will whip his ass." She reached down and pulled off one of her slippers and held it like it was a blackjack and she would sap the choppers out of the next mug who said the wrong thing. "Sammy? You? You know Thelonius tenderhearted, you can't just go telling him things make him sad."

"No, ma'am. I gotta be going. Nice to see you again."

"Boy had his heart set on being a Secret Service."

"No, Mama, it wasn't Sammy," Lone said. "Was the new songbird down to the club."

"The pretty one?"

"Yes, ma'am. She called me a dummy, Mama."

"You can't trust them pretty ones, son. They heartless. Ain't that right, Sammy?"

"Yes, ma'am."

"How that pretty little girlfriend of yours? What her name? Cheddar?"

"Stilton."

"Yeah, how you two doing?"

"I don't know, Mrs. Jones. Not so good, I guess." I'd never really said it out loud, but the Cheese had a been a little distant lately.

"You givin' her that *special* razzmatazz, right?"

"Um—"

"Sammy, you a fine-lookin' young man, and I know you work hard, but you ain't got no money or future, so you want to keep that girl interest, you gotta give her the *special* razzmatazz. Don't look at me like that. I know how you—"

"Mama, please," Lone moaned.

"Hush, Thelonius. Thelonius don't need that mess, he naturally gifted like his daddy—that man had a dick like a ball bat—but you white boys with your little white bunny dicks, you got to give a girl the *special* razzmatazz. You gots to touch her in that special spot."

I once had my foot crushed by a forklift and was less uncomfortable than I was right then. I said, "Yes, ma'am."

"You know what I talkin' about, don't you? Woman got a special spot, right on her business, that make everything better. Don't be embarrassed you don't know nothin'. According to the ladies I know—we talk amongst ourselves—*most* men don't give that special spot proper attention. Look here, I can show you." She started to lift up her housecoat and nightgown. "It right here."

"No, Mama!" Lone lurched forward and yanked down the hem of her nightgown so fast it caused her hat to fall down over her eyes.

"I know, ma'am. I know," I said. "Thank you, Mrs. Jones. I really need to go, ma'am," I said, backing out the door.

She pushed her hat back out of her eyes. "You want me to fix you some breakfast before you go? Thelonius, you want some breakfast, baby? Or are you too full of diner meatloaf?"

"I'm good, Mama."

"Well, take care. I'll see you soon," I said. And I almost made it out the door, almost had the door pulled shut behind me—

"Sammy!" she called.

"Yes, Mrs. Jones."

"What you gonna do?"

"Give her the *special* razzmatazz."

"And how you gonna do that?"

"Gonna pay attention to her *special* spot, ma'am."

"You a good boy, Sammy."

"Goodbye, Mrs. Jones. See ya, Lone."

◇◇◇◇◇◇

I was back at Cookie's by four and was lucky enough to score Milo's normal parking spot in the front. I must have looked shaken up or something, because when I handed Milo his car keys he didn't ask me for any gas money.

"Everything copacetic?" Milo asked. "You get the book?"

"Yeah, front seat. Did you know that Dunne was cracking down on after hours in the Fillmore?"

"I hate that guy," said Milo. "I've never even seen him and I hate that guy."

"Playing jazz after hours isn't even vice, it's a sacrament."

"You don't say?" Milo pushed his cabbie hat back by the brim.

"I almost went to seminary."

"Well, you would know. You look rough, Sam. You okay?"

"I might be in shock. Lone's mama tried to show me her cooter."

"Tried?"

"Yeah, Lone stopped her at the last second, but I braced myself so hard for the impact I think I pulled a neck muscle."

Milo handed me the pint of Old Tennis Shoes from his jacket and waited while I took a hard, burning pull, then clutched my arm like I was an old lady he was helping across the street. "C'mon inside, slugger, I'll buy you a burger. Drunk Nob Hill rich guy tipped me a fin."

Cookie's had emptied out more than somewhat and nobody even yelled happy New Year when we walked in. Moo Shoes was sitting by himself at our booth, studying some booklet between bites of a patty melt. The two vice cops, a tall one and a round one, rumpled suits, shoes with too many miles, were still sitting at the counter, two hours after I'd first seen them. I was beginning to think they were not at the top of their protect-and-serve game.

"What's the tune, June?" Moo Shoes said.

I slid in beside him. "The songbird gave Lone the brush-off. He's heartbroken."

Moo whistled at the enormity of the tragedy. "That and Roosevelt in the same day? We may have to buy him another meatloaf."

"That's what he said," I said.

"Also," said Milo, "Lone's mom tried to flash Sammy her cooter."

Moo Shoes looked up from his booklet of traffic laws, which was what he'd been studying.

"Near miss," I assured him. "I'm fine."

"I'm going to buy him a burger for his drama," Milo explained.

"You can't use my apartment, Milo."

Milo raised his hands like he was being robbed. "Ah, Sammy, it ain't like that. I'm just being a pal because you were dramatized. Besides, I think me and Doris might be on a break after the Lars visit." He waved Doris over and ordered me a burger and fries.

"You get that book?" Moo Shoes asked.

"Seat of the cab," I said. "What's the story on these mugs?" I tossed a thumb at the cops.

"Waiting for something," said Moo. "They check the door every time someone comes in."

Then there it was, what they were waiting for, or so it appeared. Jimmy Vasco came through the door in a sharp, shiny black suit, white cravat with a black pearl stickpin, hair slicked back, eye makeup heavy enough for a raccoon, carrying a cane with a cut crystal knob on the end—looking two parts Dracula, three parts Jiminy Cricket.

The two cops swiveled on their stools as she passed and gave her the hairy eyeball—even sitting down they towered over her.

Jimmy wasn't having it. "The fuck you cocksuckers looking at, you never seen a lady before?"

One of the cops started to say something and Jimmy rolled right up to him.

"You want to check my skivvies for masquerade?" She tossed her cane and caught it in the middle, a dance move she'd obviously practiced, then pulled out the waistband of her trousers. "Give it a look, flatfoot. That enough proof for you? I know you've never seen one, and you'll probably never see one again, so take a good look."

The two cops fidgeted. Normally they would have sapped a mug and cuffed him, he talked like that, but they were unprepared for a tiny dame dressed like a guy stirring their shit and flicking it in their faces. They looked away, embarrassed-like.

"Inspection passed?" asked Jimmy, still holding out her waistband. "You wanna give 'er a sniff for memory, huh? Nothing. That's what I thought. Don't you mugs have a murder to solve?"

"We're vice," the round cop offered.

"Yeah you are. And your captain took the case and dropped it like a hot rock, fucking coward."

"We don't like him, either," said the tall cop.

"Well, tell him he knows where to find me." She dropped her cane behind her, let it bounce on the tip, then spun and caught it, another dance move she made look threatening. She headed to our booth and slid in across from me. The two cops gathered what was left of their dignity and oozed out the door.

"You are impressively unarrested," I said.

"I've had it," said Jimmy. "One of them was waiting at the club when I left. Tailed me here. I can't figure their game. I thought I'd make 'em show their cards."

"That what you were doing?" I said. "Showing your cards?"

Jimmy ignored my wiseass retort. "You seen Myrtle? She's not at her place. She said she was doing something with the Cheese."

"The Cheese said she was going to have an early one. We took a night off. We could run up to her place."

"Been there already. Dark. No answer. I need to find her."

"You need to get that broad a phone," Milo offered.

I felt a tinge of worry that the Cheese wasn't in residence in these wee hours.

"They're probably just gassed, out dancing," said Moo Shoes.

"They're not dancing this late," said Jimmy. "I don't even know where to look."

I checked my Timex. "Well, they have to be at work in less than two hours. They could've gone early to the Five and Dime, caught a few Zs in the back room before their shift," I said, but I wasn't believing it. And I'd never seen Jimmy, normally as chilly as a winter morn, this wound up before. Her hands were shaking.

"You okay, Jimmy?" Moo Shoes asked.

Jimmy reached into the pocket of her jacket and slammed a piece of paper on the table. "This was on my windshield when I left the club."

It read YOU'RE NEXT in big block letters. The ink had run a little from the damp.

"Shit," I said. That explained the cane. She was probably packing her Walther, too.

"Yeah," Jimmy said.

"Do you recognize the handwriting?" Moo Shoes asked.

"Yeah, I compared it to the *Big Book of Dykes* I have everyone sign at the door when they come in the club, ya mook."

"Sorry," said Moo.

"You think it was the cops?" I asked.

"Dunno," said Jimmy. "Whoever it is is trying to mess with me, and that means they know enough to put Myrtle in danger, too."

"You know," said Moo, "when you find her, you two wanna lay low, me and Sammy can take your car out of town, lead anyone who's tailing you on a wild-goose chase."

"Not now, Moo," I said.

"What? It works out, Lois and I could give a lesbian discount at the driving school."

Jimmy looked at Moo Shoes with black-eyed fury. "You know, come to think of it, I don't mind the idea of using you as bait."

"Let's check the Five and Dime, Jimmy," I said. "We'll find her."

The Rain Dragon

She doesn't know it, but Jimmy Vasco is not next. I know, because I, your narrator, know everything. I know, for instance, that in the small hours of that very morning, while Jimmy was still driving around looking for Myrtle, a wave of fog was rolling up out of the bay like a damp ghost, straight up Broadway into North Beach, right when Francine "Frankie" Fortuna was making her way from Mona's 440 to her car, which she had parked in an alley off Kearny Street, a couple of blocks away. "Where Girls Will Be Boys" was the motto on the cocktail napkins at Mona's 440, and *that* was Frankie's stock-in-trade. She'd just knocked out a set of Sinatra, Perry Como, Hoagy Carmichael, and Frankie Laine songs to an all-dame audience, who didn't even notice that she sang everything an octave higher than the guys she was imitating. She had the look, and she crooned romance that would make an ingénue swoon, with enough flirty camp to bring everyone in on the fun. To the untrained eye, in the fog, she looked like a featherweight guy in a nice suit, a blue number, with a red silk tie. She preferred wearing a tux during her set, it looked classier, but Rose O'Neil, "the female Fred Astaire," who opened the show that night, said a tux and tails were as essential to her act as tap shoes, so Frankie graciously ceded the penguin suit. She didn't have to strap her boobs down quite as tight in the suit, anyway, so it was better to move in.

She heard the door back at Mona's open and laughter spill out into the street. She thought for a second, just for a second, about turning back. It was late, and she was bushed, but there was still fun to be had and she kept thinking about that thin dame sitting stage-side—a Veronica Lake platinum blonde complete with the bangs over one eye, in a sapphire satin halter jumpsuit with long hostess pajama bell-bottoms—delicate bare shoulders, big ruby lips, and pure flirt in every look. Frankie should have known better. She made a living on the flirt, and that dame had come to play the game—but every time Frankie looked down, *there she was.*

Go back? Nah, there was a warm Ovaltine and forty winks calling her name at home, and a dame like that was nothing but trouble. Hell, you couldn't even wear her clothes—Frankie had put on a getup like that once for a dance bit with Rose O'Neil and felt like a drag queen escaped from Finocchio's down the street. Ovaltine and forty winks, that was the way to go.

But when Frankie turned the corner, *there she was.* Frankie had been about to light a cigarette but just sort of let the coffin nail dribble out of her mouth.

There she was, leaning against Frankie's Studebaker like a sparkling sapphire dream.

"Hey, sugar," the blonde said. "Got a light?" She put a cigarette between her perfect lips.

"Sure, sure," said Frankie, digging in her jacket pocket for her Zippo, realizing it was already in her hand. "You're gonna catch your death out here, doll," she said bringing up the lighter. The blonde had some kind of cream-colored wrap around her shoulders, cashmere maybe, but it wasn't enough for a November night in the fog.

The lighter lit the blonde's face from below, and up close Frankie could see her real hair peeking out from under the wig. *Good,* Frankie thought. *Blondes are nothing but trouble.*

Frankie snapped the Zippo shut, dropped it in her pocket, dazzled a big grin, and said, "So, what's a nice girl like you doing out on—"

But she never finished that sentence because an ice pick had entered her skull just above the first neck vertebra and switched her off like a light.

Frankie was next.

7

STILTON SLEEPS WITH THE HAMSTERS

San Francisco, 1904

The white devils in Big Town were like grains in a bowl of rice—so many that it was hard to see one and not see the mass of them. They were everywhere and looking at them hurt Ho's eyes after so long below deck.

"Don't look at them," said the boss who picked them up at the dock. "Don't be afraid of the *gwai lo,* they are not your concern." Ho was pleased to hear that he should not fear the *gwai lo.* He had spent the whole month on the ocean seasick and afraid, and now that he was in the Land of Golden Hills, he did not want to be either any longer.

The boss led them to a *gwai lo* customs man with a big mustache and brass buttons on his coat who looked at a piece of paper the boss gave him. "Are you Bai Da Wong?" The white devil said the surname last, rather than first, as was the custom in China.

"Yes," said Ho. It was the only English word he knew, and he had been coached to say it when spoken to by the mustache man at the dock. Ho, like the nineteen men behind him, was now a paper son, a nephew of Jing Fan Wong, who had been born in Sacramento forty years ago. The boss slipped the customs man an envelope, then led Ho and the other paper sons through the crowds at the docks, across the Embarcadero, down Washington Street, across Battery and Kearny Streets, the financial district with its banks and brokerage houses (where the paper sons paused to marvel not only at all the horses, but at the cable cars, gleaming red and gold, with brass bells sounding, which seemed to move by magic), and into Chinatown.

One block of Chinatown had as many people as Ho had ever seen in one place. All of them seemed to be running from one place to another, or bartering, barking, and doing business in one spot. A miasma of smells washed over him: lye from the laundries; garlic; fish; cabbage, both cooked and rotting; human sweat; horse shit; and the odd sweet whiff of incense, sandalwood, coming from the joss houses, tiny temples wedged between gambling houses, vegetable stands, brothels, factories, and storefronts of every kind. Ho marveled at the commerce and all the moving money it represented. And the people. So many of them, all of them men.

The boss herded the paper sons into the guild hall, a four-story building on Dupont Street, and with four other lieutenants of the Ghee Sin Tong (Guild for the Protection of Virtue) saw that they were washed, fed bowls of hot rice porridge (jook), as much as they wanted, and installed with their meager possessions into closet-sized rooms, each with six narrow bunks stacked on either side to the ceiling in a rough wooden building on an alley behind the guild hall. They were given clean clothes, simple spun-cotton shirts, black trousers, and jackets, and one by one sent next door to the barber, who shaved the fronts of their heads, braided their long queues, and cleaned their ears. They were required to wear their queues to show loyalty to the Qing dynasty, the very principle of which the Triads and the tongs had vowed to overthrow, and indeed, some of the lieutenants wore their hair in the Western style, which Ho thought quite strange, but the tong did not need its new recruits to stand out among the residents of Chinatown, not at first, anyway. It needed, it demanded, only loyalty.

"You are welcomed into the Ghee Sin, the Guild for the Protection of Virtue," said one of the lieutenants, a fierce-looking fellow of perhaps thirty-five, with half an ear missing on the right side and a rude white scar in his Western haircut from whatever had taken the ear. They were gathered in the big room of the guild hall. The bosses, dressed in robes of silk, sat on a dais on either side of an altar at the head of the room, where joss sticks trailed their fragrant smoke over a charcoal brazier. On the altar sat the statue of a dragon, carved in polished black stone, about the size of a house cat, its eyes inlaid with bright green jade: the Rain Dragon.

"Everything you do is a matter of loyalty, every act of loyalty is a matter of honor, and preserving the honor of the tong is a matter of life and death," said the boss.

Then, with the lights turned out (the first electric lights that Ho had ever seen) and candles lit around the room, they told the recruits of the legacy they had inherited by becoming part of the Ghee Sin Tong. They told the story of the five ancestors, of the great battle and great escape, of the gift of the great dragons and the establishment of the Triads and the tongs after them.

The boss telling the story threw pinches of gunpowder into the brazier when he made a point, and the flash and smoke mesmerized the recruits.

"Tonight you will give your life to the Ghee Sin. You will be brothers with everyone here and everyone who has come before you. It is your sacred duty to preserve the honor and virtue of the tong. Better you die a thousand times than bring dishonor to this guild or a loss of face to any of our leaders. You can pick up your hatchets on the way out."

Then, one by one, they brought the recruits forward, made them swear an oath to the guild and the ancestors, and to seal the oath, a red-hot brand was pulled from the brazier and the symbol of the Rain Dragon burned into their right forearm. They were told that should they cry out, they would dishonor the guild, and their life would be forfeit on the spot.

Ho watched, and afraid as he was, he tried to steel himself against the pain. It would be hellish, but when it was over, he would have left his old life in China. He would not be a second son, scorned by the village for a cruel joke. He would be a new man. He would find his fortune, have a wife and family; a future would open.

When Ho's turn came, he repeated his oath and swore fealty to the tong, but despite his resolve to begin anew, he was very afraid he would cry out. He was a gentle boy, never a fighter, and he had not learned to endure pain. But when the boss took his arm and the iron was pressed into it, he heard the sizzle, saw the smoke rise, but he felt nothing. It was as if someone had pressed a piece of ice against his flesh. He unclenched his jaw, peeked through eyes squinted in anticipation of the pain, and saw the Rain Dragon's eyes pulsing with green light. Then he heard the dragon's voice in his head for the first time. "*Already I have saved you. Ha! Welcome to Big Town, Catfucker,*" it said.

Sammy

When I finally caught up to the Cheese, she was dealing breakfasts off her arm at the Five & Dime, running coffee to a half-dozen mugs reading the *Chronicle* at the counter, and generally looking no worse for wear, even though I had imagined she had been kidnapped and murdered a dozen times in the preceding three hours or so.

"Flapjacks and willies, slam 'em in the screen door!" she called to Phil, the fry cook, a rangy mug who hated all things morning and looked like he'd just been chucked out of hobo camp for looking too rough. He groaned in response.

"Waffles and sausages," the Cheese explained to me with a wink as she flipped the cup set up on the counter in front of me and splashed some coffee in. "What's shakin', Toots?"

I wasn't going to fall for it. She calls me Toots. I tell her not to call me Toots, because she is just busting my chops for me calling her Toots the first time we met, then I forget that I have been distressed, distraught, and generally worried about where she's been out all night, and how she's got a lot of goddamn nerve looking so fine and fresh in her pink waitress togs when I feel like a bag of mashed assholes. Nope, not falling for it.

"Where you been?" I asked as I added cream and sugar to my java.

"Busy. Me and Myrt got a project we're working on."

"All night? Jimmy went by your place looking for Myrtle. You weren't there."

"Ah, we worked late, decided to bunk here for a couple of hours. It's nice, everything kind of smells like comic books, hamsters, and cedar chips, and in the morning you got your pick of toothpastes you can use."

"I like the spearmint," shouted Myrtle, who was taking an order at one of the booths maybe twenty feet away. That broad could hear an ant fart in a hurricane. "Tar and feathers on a raft," she called to Phil.

"Black coffee and scrambled eggs on toast," Stilton translated.

"You don't gotta call the coffee," Phil said.

"I know, but I got a system," Myrtle said. "Do I tell you how to cook the eggs?"

"Every order."

"Oh yeah," Myrtle said. "I'll get the coffee." She swooshed by us to grab a coffeepot. "Hey, Sammy."

"Hey, Myrt," I said. "You need to call Jimmy. She's worried sick about you. Was out all night looking for you."

"I will when I get a minute. Thanks, Sammy."

Stilton did some laps around the counter and booths, pouring coffee and breaking hearts, then made her way back to me. "Get you some breakfast, Mopey?"

"Who you calling Mopey? I got every right to be worried."

"Don't be so touchy," she said, looking surprised, which was a special talent she had. "Mopey is my favorite of the seven dwarfs."

"Mopey is not one of the seven dwarfs."

"He is, too," she said, starting to count on her fingers: "Mopey, Squeaky, Daffy, Scruffy, uh—" She was stalling out.

Myrtle came up behind her and continued counting on her own fingers: "Lonesome, Dopey, and Doc. Dopey is my favorite. Those ears. I'd give that little mug the razzmatazz all night long."

"Nah," said Stilton. "But I'd give Mopey the grand tour of Tuna Town."

The guy next to me sprayed his coffee all over the counter.

She snort-laughed and punched me in the shoulder. "Huh, Mopey?"

"Myrt, order up!" Phil yelled. He also dinged the little bell that signaled the same thing.

I said to the Cheese, "I'm not mopey, I'm worried. Do you know there's a big black Chrysler parked out front of here? Just like the one those G-men had. I nearly had a heart attack when I saw it." (We were pursued and almost somewhat murdered by some G-men in black Chryslers some months back, and even now when I spy a black late-model New Yorker it makes my man marbles shrivel.)

"Ah, there are Chryslers all over the city, Sammy. Those guys are long gone and they aren't coming back—how 'bout tonight we—" Then she stopped and was staring over my shoulder at the door. The little bell had rung, but I hadn't really noticed. "Whoa," Stilton said.

I turned to see Milo staggering into the diner, catching himself on the door, then sort of smiling through bloody teeth when he spotted me. His eyes were purple and nearly swollen shut; there was a deep cut on his right cheek.

I jumped up and took him by the shoulders, steered him to the empty stool at the counter next to mine, and helped him onto it. "Pal, what happened?" I asked.

"I met Lars," Milo said.

The Cheese came up and handed me a rolled-up dish towel, steaming hot. "Thanks, doll," I said.

"Look here, Milo," I said. He was trying to stare at his hands, which he held folded on the counter, but he was also trying to keep them from shaking. He looked up and I dabbed away some of the dried blood on his cheek.

"I gave Doris a ride home after work. Even dropped her off a block away. Got out, gave her a good-bye smooch. He hit me when I was headed back to the cab. He was hiding in a doorway. I knew I shouldn't be driving."

"Yeah, pal, driving was where things went wrong. What about—" I looked around. I didn't want to say the thing I was about to say if anyone was listening, just in case Milo had made use of the thing I was about to refer to. The guy who had sprayed coffee on the counter was stacking some coins in front of him to pay his bill, but he was paying attention. "What about that thing under your front seat?"

"Never even made it to the cab. He blindsided me with the first punch and rang my bell, then I guess he hit me a bunch of times after that, but I don't remember anything but waking up to bright light and a headache."

The Cheese had taken another clean dish towel over to the pot of hot water they keep on the burner for tea, wetted it down, and brought it to me on a saucer. I switched it out for the bloody one I'd been dabbing with.

"Is Doris okay?" asked the Cheese.

"Dunno," Milo said. "When I came to I sneaked by their place and looked in. It's a basement apartment down by South Park. I could see in and Lars was sitting at the table, drinking, but Doris wasn't there. That was maybe twenty minutes ago."

Just then Myrtle came out of the back looking distraught and made a beeline for us at the counter. When she got to where she could see Milo, she pulled up. "Holy moly, what happened to you?"

"He was driving," the Cheese said.

"Can I help?" Myrtle said.

"Maybe put some of that hot water in a cup with some salt," I said. "He can rinse his mouth out."

To Milo I said, "You break any teeth?" He shook his head.

"I'll get the salt water," said Stilton, "if you could refill my customers."

"Sure," said Myrtle. She snagged a coffeepot off the burner and started away, then turned. "Oh yeah, I was gonna tell you guys. I just talked to Jimmy and she's a mess."

"You guys were missing all night," I said.

"Nah, not that. Well, yeah, that, but she was better after I told her I was okay. She just got the news that one of the singers down at Mona's 440, gal called Frankie Fortuna, got murdered last night."

"I don't know her," said Stilton. "Do you know her?"

"Nah, I'm new. I don't get invited to the meetings yet," said Myrtle.

◇◇◇◇◇◇

I had just helped Milo to the second-floor landing when we heard the scream.

"Kid," I explained.

"What?" Milo said.

The kid came swinging down from above on a rope, screeching like a flaming owl, arcing in the air in front of us and smacking face-first into the ceiling of the landing, then losing his grip on the rope to drop about five feet and land flat on his back with a great explosion of air and spit.

"Huh," I said. "Would you look at that. He got a rope."

"You didn't tell me you had a kid."

"Not my kid. Just *a* kid."

The kid seemed to be having some trouble catching his breath, a little gaspy.

"He gonna be all right?" Milo asked.

"Kid, you gonna be all right?"

"Cocksucker," the kid coughed.

"He's fine," I said.

I led Milo around the kid and looped his arm around my neck to help him assault the second flight of stairs. We figured Lars must have kicked Milo while he was down because his knee was swollen up to about a hundred and fifty percent, and he was having some trouble with stairs. Even with me doing a lot of the work, he winced on every step.

"I'm worried sick about Doris," Milo said.

"I know, pal." I sat Milo down on one of the two stools at the little counter by my kitchen that serves as my dining table, desk, office, ironing board, and private tennis court, although, strictly speaking, I do not play a lot of tennis. I poured him a snort of gin I kept in the fridge for emergency gimlets.

"None for you?" Milo asked.

"Nah, I gotta hump up three hundred and eighty-seven steps to the Cheese's place and I haven't slept. I'm afraid I might lose my will to live if I have gin for breakfast. Drink up."

"You can take the cab," Milo said.

"Nah, no place to park it up there anyway." With that I threw Milo's keys on the counter.

I only had one ice tray, but it was going to have to do. I ran some water on the bottom of the tray and cranked the lever, then dumped the ice into my only dish towel and handed the bundle to Milo.

"What's this for?"

"Your eye, or your other eye, or your knee, or your head. Maybe you just switch it around until it melts. You wanna take a shower?"

"Nah, I just need this medicine to kick in." Milo slid the water glass across the counter and I poured him three fingers of gin. He worked an ice cube out of his ice pack, dropped it in his glass, and toasted me before sipping off the top, wincing when the gin hit his sore lip.

"I'll call Cookie's," I said. I had the number written on the wall by my phone. Cookie answered on the third ring, a voice that sounded like he was gargling with gravel.

"Cookie's Coffee." I hadn't seen Cookie in a while, as he stopped working graveyard over a year ago, citing that he'd had enough of drunks, actors, singers, hookers, and hustlers. The day crowd was cops and politicians, so it wasn't like he was meeting a better class of people.

"Cookie, it's Sammy Tiffin."

"Who?"

"Sammy. I come in with Lone Jones, Black guy, about twenty-eight feet tall."

"Oh yeah. Sammy. Skinny kid, walks with a cane."

"Yeah, not anymore. But that's me."

"Whaddaya want?"

"I'm looking for Doris. You heard from her today?"

"Who's asking?"

I thought I had just been through that, but instead of saying that, I said, "Milo. He's right here with me." I held the phone out. "Say hi, Milo."

"Hey, Cookie," Milo said.

"Yeah," said Cookie. "She called in sick for tonight. Said if a guy named Milo called, she's hiding out at her sister's in the East Bay."

I looked at Milo, held the phone against my chest. "Sister? East Bay?"

"Yeah, no idea where she lives," Milo said. "Is Doris okay?"

"Was she okay?" I asked Cookie.

"Yeah, she said to tell Milo she's fine, but she's not coming back to work until things get worked out with the Swede. I told her things better get worked out in the next two days or she's got no job to come back to. I gotta go, Sammy. Order in."

"Thanks, Cookie."

I told Milo what Cookie had said.

"I got no idea where her sister lives," Milo said. "No number, either."

"You think Lars knows?"

"Nah, she wouldn't go there if he knew. She can't lose that job, Sammy. We gotta do something."

"You aren't going to do anything for a day or two except heal up."

Milo looked over at my sad single bed. "I gotta get out of your hair."

"You're fine. I'll bunk at the Cheese's for as long as you need. There's some cornflakes and milk, some bread and butter. I'll bring by some groceries later. You can listen to the radio, read a book, get better."

"What about Doris? What about Lars?" Milo shuddered a little bit and sort of checked out for a second, his eyelids fluttering like hummingbird wings—like the ghost that ran the Milo machine had stepped out for a smoke and would be back in a second. He did that, had done that since I'd known him. It was a leftover from when he got blown up in Germany. And it was the real reason he was afraid of driving—that he might check out and wake up in flaming pieces under a train or something. We all acted like we didn't notice. Guys had come back from the war with a lot worse than five-second surprise vacations from reality.

I took the opportunity to switch out my lost-and-found peacoat for my wool overcoat, out of the closet.

And Milo was back. "What's the deal, you looking for snow?"

"Nah, I'm going to take your sawed-off with me and I don't think I can hide it in the peacoat. I had a tailor in Chinatown sew a sheath for my cane down the inside seam of my overcoat. Should work. Or I can maybe buy a newspaper and roll it up in there."

"Just leave it in the cab. Lock it. I do it all the time."

"Yeah, you don't have the kid around. Speaking of which, the kid has a key. You wanna hook the chain on the door after I leave so he doesn't come in while you're sleeping. If he gets hungry, just shove a bread-and-butter through the gap."

"Sammy, you don't mind me saying, you got some daffy ideas about kids."

"Fine, give him a bowl of cornflakes."

"That's not what I meant."

"I gotta go, Milo. I gotta get some shut-eye or I'm gonna fall down." I peeked into the hall before stepping out the door, in case there was an ambush waiting.

"Sammy," Milo said, "I ain't sure I got what it takes to blast Lars, even after he cleaned my clock. I never scragged a guy before. Sure, I ran over some Jerries with my tank during the war, but that's different. That ain't blasting a guy with a shotgun."

"Come out of there, you dirty pecorino!" the kid yelled from the hall.

"That's a cheese, kid," I said through the gap.

"No it ain't, ya liar. You're yellow. Yellow, I tell ya."

I bounced my eyebrows at Milo. "The kid would do it for two bits if we tell him Lars is a German spy. He's been after Moo Shoes as a Jap spy for years."

"But Moo Shoes is Chinese," Milo said.

"He's a horrible little kid," I explained. "I wouldn't hand him a fully loaded shotgun. Maybe show him how to load it, give him one shell, and drive away fast. Worst that happens, the kid splatters Lars and does a few years in reform school. Do him good."

"You do need some sleep, pal," Milo said.

"Yeah. I'll be back around four to shower and get a clean shirt for work. I'll bring some groceries. Anything else you want?"

"Nah, maybe a pack of smokes. Can I use your phone?"

"Yeah, whatever you need." I cracked the door. "Kid, you got any arrows out there?"

"Nah, Father Tony down at Saint Pee-Pee's took 'em away from me when I was climbing up to get the one out of the cow window, the rat bastard."

"Fine, I'm coming out. Be nice or I'm chucking you down the stairs again."

"You and what army, you stinkin' calzone!"

"Kid—oh, never mind."

And off I went to climb the 387 steps up Telegraph Hill to the Cheese's empty bed, where I fell in, face-first, overcoat and all, and slept like a corpse until hours later when I felt her soft lips brush my ear and whisper, "Hey, sailor, wanna get lucky?"

8

GHOSTS
OF
CHINATOWN

San Francisco, 1906

It took little time for the Ghee Sin Tong to realize that young Ho was complete shit as a hatchet man. First, he was so incompetent at swinging the hatchet that it was of no use except as a threat, and second, he kept losing his hatchet. The boss would send Ho and another hatchet man out to collect protection money from some vegetable vendor, and they would return with nothing but excuses.

"He needs more time," Ho would say.

"He will have no more time. Did you show him your hatchet?"

Then Ho's companion would rat him out. "He put down his hatchet when he stopped to pet a rat, and forgot it."

"A rat? What is wrong with you?" Ho spoke a regional dialect of Cantonese, and so much of what his tong brothers said sounded like nonsense to him.

"It was a virtuous rat and deserving of protection," said Ho. Much of what Ho said to his tong brothers sounded like nonsense to them because it *was* nonsense.

Then he and his cohort would both be punished, until no one would let themselves be teamed with Ho. No matter how small the job, Ho's sensitive nature would somehow betray him to the task, and no matter how many beatings he suffered, the bosses could not harden his heart.

When the Ghee Sin Tong went to war with the Ping Kung Tong over a stolen whore named Golden Peach, Ho was given his fifth hatchet and sent to the front of the battle line as a sacrifice, and while he did no damage whatsoever to the enemy, so wild was his flailing and screaming that the Ping Kung thought him quite insane and avoided engaging him at all, lest they catch whatever madness had infected him. Many fell on both sides that day, but Ho remained unscathed.

"*Well done, Catfucker,*" said the voice in Ho's head. "*Be so fierce that no one dare fight you.*" And with that, even Ho himself had to admit that he was probably quite mad.

While prevailing in battle gave Ho some respite from ridicule and won him a position in the dormitory kitchen, where it was thought he could at least do no harm, it wasn't long before he was dismissed for talking to turtles.

"They don't like being in the crates," Ho told the head cook, standing amid a room full of wandering, dinner-plate-sized snapping turtles.

"We keep them alive in crates so they are fresh when we cook them," the cook told him while doing an awkward dance step to avoid being bitten on the ankle.

"But they don't like it," said Ho.

"Do they like being made into soup?" asked the cook.

"Turtles don't talk about the future," said Ho. "Right now they are happy to be out of the crates."

"Get out of my kitchen, you loopy fucker," said the cook.

So Ho, devoted soldier of the Guild for the Protection of Virtue, was sent to the opium den to prepare the pipes and collect the vomit bowls set out near the head of each new smoker. He did well as a "pipe boy," since almost everyone in the opium den became dreamy and pleasant after a pipe, until one afternoon when one of the customers tried to bugger him, to which he objected by hitting the fellow soundly in the face with his hatchet.

"He was pulling down my trousers," Ho told his boss, an old man called Chin.

"Men here are lonely. You should have just sent him to the brothel," said the boss. "Or just let him and charge him a dollar. Now you will have to pay for a doctor to stitch him up or finish him off and feed his body to the pigs."

Ho was beginning to suspect that the Ghee Sin Tong was not about protecting virtue at all.

"I will fetch the doctor," said Ho.

"*Although,*" Ho heard the pigs say as he went by their pen on the way to the doctor, "*if you sprinkle a little five spices on that guy he will be fucking delicious.*"

After that Ho was sent to wash the whores.

In those days, the Chinese men in Big Town outnumbered the Chinese women twenty to one, and indeed, Ho passed his first year in the city having seen only two women who were not prostitutes: the wife of a man who sold joss sticks, who was very old and very ugly but who everyone agreed smelled quite nice, and a rather stern-looking white missionary woman named Dolly Cameron, but who everyone in the tong called the Boss of the White Devil's Daughters.

"Stay away from her, Ho," the boss said. "She steals our whores from us and converts them to the Jesus Tong. They become the White Devil's Daughters and interpret for her."

More nonsense, Ho thought. Why would a powerful brotherhood like the Ghee Sin, which had sent him and his brothers to war over a single whore, put up with some bustled white devil woman? Whores were one of the three bases of the Ghee Sin economic triad: whores, protection, and gambling (opium was only a small side business). The tong ran brothels on every street and alley in the north end of Chinatown, from the lavish brothels on Dupont and Stockton Streets, worked by beautiful women in Western dress, where Ho himself had lost his virginity at the expense of the tong, to the crib brothels in the alleys: rows of stalls barely large enough to accommodate a cot, where big-foot girls sold into slavery by their families in China for a song were kept, servicing up to a dozen rough men a night and locked in during their off-hours. The life expectancy for a whore in a crib brothel was three years.

Ho was sent to work at a crib brothel. It was his job to go to each of the stalls every four hours with a bucket of water, a bar of lye soap, and a cloth, and stand by while each of the whores washed herself. If a whore refused or was too weak to wash, he was to throw the bucket of cold water over her. Ho, the sensitive boy, was horrified by his new job and at first crossed his arms and said that he would not do it. His new boss said, "No more demotions for you. If you disappoint the brotherhood again, I will feed you to the pigs."

"*Oh no!*" said the pigs, the next time Ho passed by. "*That would be most unfortunate. But just in case, could you keep a couple of onions in your pockets?*"

The other voice Ho heard in his head, louder now that he was near the Ghee Sin clubhouse, said, "*Don't press them, Catfucker. You serve no one by getting yourself killed.*"

Catfucker? Catfucker? Had he not left his family and crossed an ocean, subjected himself to hard work, beatings, branding, and ridicule, to escape that dreaded moniker? Did it mean he had gone mad that it followed him as a voice in his head? A voice, he had to admit, that seemed to have his best interest at heart.

He stayed alive by performing his duties in the most humane way he could devise, without attracting attention. With his own money he bought a charcoal brazier, which he kept burning in the alley outside the stalls, and he set the metal buckets next to it so the water he took to the women was at least warm; then he would set down the water and turn his back while they washed. When an old man brought a bucket of cooked rice from one of the tong's dining rooms to feed the whores, Ho would add soy sauce, sometimes vegetables or spicy sausage, which he bought at one of the Chinatown butchers and cut up with his hatchet. He had to justify any kindness he showed the whores to the boss who ran the brothel, a fierce one-eyed warrior, as protecting their value to the tong. And even that was suspect, as their value was nothing after the tong recovered the five hundred dollars they paid to a slave trader who had bought a big-foot daughter from her family for half that, or even less if she was taken as payment for a gambling debt from an unlucky father. The boss stood at the head of the alley and collected a dollar from each of the patrons, while Ho would stand by a stall with an available whore, unlock the door, and let the customer in. If he was far enough from the boss so he would not hear, Ho would whisper, "Don't hurt her," and he would pat his hatchet. At most he would get a nod, and often the customer would not acknowledge him at all. Ho thought they might not understand his dialect, which happened often. They understood. Ho was a slightly built fellow, with only the wisp of a beard, but the Ghee Sin Tong carried with it the threat of great violence, and no whores were killed or badly injured on Ho's watch. His were the very smallest kindnesses, small enough to go unnoticed by the boss and so keep Ho alive, but just big enough so he could actually sleep when he went to his cot at night. At least until one of the whores forced him to be courageous.

It was a fine, sunny spring San Francisco afternoon, and a gentle breeze off the bay had blown the stink off the city. Ho was sitting on one of his wash buckets upturned, smoking a clay pipe, which was a habit he had only recently picked up, when one of the whores began to scream. It was not the yip of overzealous humping, nor the low, sustained wail of suffering, which he had learned to ignore, but the long, piercing scream of bloody murder.

Ho went to the offending stall and threw open the door, to find a stout white man in a planter's hat who had the whore bent over, her face against the wall, her arms twisted up behind her back, her shoulders almost popped out of their sockets, as he had his way with her.

"Let her go!" shouted Ho, and the white man didn't even look back. The girl continued to scream. Ho hated dealing with the white devils. Few of them came to the crib brothels, but those who did were always drunk and they were hard on the whores. Ho shouted again, this time saying one of his few English words, "No!"

"Get out of here, Chinaman," said the white man. "Or I'll kill this bitch."

Ho had no idea what the man had said, but the girl was still screaming and the man was still humping, so Ho pulled his hatchet from its loop on his belt and drew back. Thinking about how much it had cost him to have his last hatchet blow stitched up, at the last second Ho turned the hatchet and conked the john soundly on his hat-covered head with the flat of the blade. The hatchet was one made for cutting roofing shakes, so had a heavy hammer butt for pounding nails, which made it heavier than the lathing hatchets used by most of the Ghee Sin brethren, which captured the john's attention immediately. He dropped the whore and wheeled around wildly, striking out as he turned, knocking the hatchet out of Ho's hand. The john grabbed the front of Ho's shirt, but Ho backed out of the stall into the alley, pulling his attacker with him. The john's feet tangled in his trousers around his boots and he fell face-first into Ho, who was still trying to pry the john's hands off his shirt when the girl buried Ho's hatchet in the back of the john's head, right through the wide-brimmed felt planter's hat, and they all fell into a pile, halfway out into the alley.

The boss, drawn by all the commotion, had made his way down the alley from his station at the street. "What is going on here?" he shouted.

Ho and the girl looked up, the girl naked, still holding the hatchet, Ho pinned under the dead john, his face splashed with blood.

"Nothing," they said in unison. Ho managed a grin.

A few minutes later Ho and the girl sat in the stall, side by side on the wide wooden bench that served as a cot, the dead white man at their feet. The girl was wearing a flour sack, holes cut for her head and arms. The boss had run off to find tong soldiers to help with the body.

"What will they do with him?" asked the girl.

"Wait until dark, then take him away and feed him to the pigs," said Ho.

"Am I in trouble?" she asked.

"No worse than you were before," said Ho. "Wait, you can understand me?"

"We speak the same dialect," said the girl. "I am from—" Then she said the name of her village, which translated to Glorious Location of Various Weeds.

"Ieeee!" exclaimed Ho. "I too am from Glorious Location of Various Weeds!"

"I thought so," she said. "You are the one they call Catfucker, right?"

"No," said Ho.

And the voice came to him, "*Save this one, Catfucker. Save this one and save yourself.*"

"Are *you* in trouble?" the girl asked.

"Yes," said Ho. "I think I am."

Sammy

Eddie Shu was working the host podium at Club Shanghai when I breezed past the giant double Fu dogs by the door and up the red carpet to his station. Moo Shoes was wearing a red sequined sport jacket that made him look like a Christmas ornament that had escaped the big tree they'd just put up in Union Square. It was two thirty in the morning, but the place was jumping.

"What's the scam, Sam?" asked Moo Shoes, by way of a greeting.

"Nice jacket," I said.

"Belongs to the joint. MC was late. I had to introduce the first act."

"I need to talk to Uncle Ho," I said.

The cornet tootled reveille from the main ballroom and I looked past Moo to see four leggy Chinese dames half-dressed like Uncle Sam in short, striped satin shorts and plunging-neckline blue blouses begin to belt out a "Boogie Woogie Bugle Boy" that would knock all the socks off a centipede.

"Aren't there only three Andrews Sisters?" I asked. They were hitting the harmonies like champs.

"Yeah," said Moo. "We got four—superior Chinese version. Lois is the second Uncle Sam from the left."

"Wow, Lois can sing," I said. "In addition to being a biscuit of delicious aspect."

"Wait until they start tap-dancing," Moo said.

I noted that the Uncle Sams were all wearing sparkly Mary Janes, about four inches taller than Dorothy's ruby slippers, but with a similar finish (matching Moo Shoes's jacket).

"Do the Andrews Sisters even tap-dance?" I asked.

"Our girls gotta do more, sing better, dance better, show more leg, because they're Chinese. They gotta go that extra step to keep the nobs coming in."

"Well, they *are* impressive, Moo, but maybe they lose the white beards. Nobody likes a dame with a scruffy white beard."

Moo Shoes considered the quartet of Sams and nodded. "I'll bring it up tomorrow at the meeting. C'mon, step into my office." Moo nodded to one of the other hosts to watch the door and led me off to a lounge, lots of dark oak and red velvet, where the music was somewhat muted. We leaned against the bar like trail-tired cowpokes.

"Seltzer, rocks," Moo said to the bartender. To me, "Resting my liver. You?"

I gestured to the barkeep to bring two. "Driving. I have Milo's cab outside," I said.

"He waiting at Cookie's?"

"My place. Busted up," I said. So I told Moo Shoes about Milo getting pasted by Lars and how he was on ice at my place, about how Doris was hiding out in the East Bay, and how when I dropped off some groceries and smokes for him in the afternoon he informed me that there was not enough information in the songbird's history book to shanghai Lars.

"So just blasting Lars is completely out of the question?" Moo asked.

"Nah, Milo is not up to it, and Inspector Dunne has made it known that he has his eye on me because of the Pookie O'Hara rumor, so a blasting within my immediate circle might attract attention."

"Why don't we just ask Lone to pound Lars into meat paste?"

"I don't believe Lone would fare well with the gendarmes, either, being he is of the dark persuasion and a known associate of yours truly. Which is why I want to talk to Uncle Ho."

"Uncle Ho is a thousand years old and weighs maybe seven pounds. I think Lars can take him."

"No, I was thinking because he has lived a life in the underworld and has henchmen and whatnot, he could steer us in the right direction. Maybe even lend us a henchman."

"Ho doesn't have henchmen anymore. He doesn't even have a hench. Squid Kid Fang moved in on Uncle Ho's opium den."

"Already? But Ho's got to know a guy, right? He probably remembers shanghaiing guys in his youth."

"Maybe," said Moo. He cocked his head toward the ballroom and mimed conducting the last few notes of "Bugle Boy." "That's

Lois's last number. Let me get someone to cover the door and I'll grab Lois and we'll go look for Ho."

"Look for him? Can't we just call him? Maybe go to his place?"

Moo Shoes rolled his eyes at me like I had asked him to be pope. "I don't know where Ho lives. But I think we can find him."

◇◇◇◇◇◇

I've never driven a cab for a living, but as I sat in Milo's cab outside Club Shanghai, turning down nobs who were coming out with their dates three sheets to the wind and wanting a ride to Nob Hill or Pacific Heights, I could see the appeal.

"I'll double your fare," said one guy.

"I'll tip you twenty dollars," said a banker type, showing off for his date, a broad half his age.

"Nah," I told them. "I'm waiting for a guy."

Disappointment on a rich guy's face is like a little dose of Christmas morning, but I thought it was a shame Milo couldn't just steel his nerves enough to maybe wait outside one of the clubs at closing time for the highest bidder. Two fares a night would easily produce enough cabbage for a nice little crib for him and Doris. Of course, it was his busy time selling shots outside of Cookie's, but you have to sell a bucketload of shots at two bits a pour to make up for a couple of twenty-dollar tips. I was contemplating the sadness of it over a smoke when Moo Shoes popped the door and climbed into the backseat. Lois Fong, still in her Uncle Sam outfit, jumped in the front across from me.

"Hey, doll," I said. "It's a little chilly out for that getup. I can wait if you want to go in and put on some street clothes."

"No," said Moo Shoes. "She looks good. The outfit will help."

"Freezing my ass off," said Lois, who evidently did not think that the outfit would help.

"Help how? What kind of game are you running, Moo?"

"Uncle Ho's at Tall House." Tall House of Happy Snake and Noodle, the jook joint where Moo Shoes and I once had a side business selling poisonous snake urine to old guys to treat their sagging dragons. "I thought we could recruit a few driving school students."

"If you knew that, why didn't you just say so inside?" I asked.

"I thought you would say no," said Moo.

"Eddie, I'm cold," said Lois.

"Give her your coat to throw over her gams, you mook," I said to Moo Shoes.

"Yeah, you mook," said Lois.

Eddie squirmed out of his wool overcoat and passed it over the seat to Lois, who managed to curl up inside with just her Uncle Sam hat and eyes showing above a pile of tweed.

"Tall House of Snake and Noodle it is," I said. I threw the Checker into gear and headed down Grant Avenue to Bush Street, where I hung a U-turn and headed back the other way toward Pacific and Tall House.

"Moo Shoes," I ventured, "while I am flattered and privileged to be in the company of a lovely dame such as Lois, why is she piled up front with me?"

"I thought you could give her a driving lesson on the way."

"The chief instructor of your driving school does not know how to drive?" I looked at Lois. She shook her head.

"When was I supposed to teach her? We don't have a car," said Moo Shoes. "And she's our chief recruiter. I am the chief instructor."

"I'm the boss," said Lois.

"Right," I said. "Maybe tonight we just find Uncle Ho and you can borrow the cab tomorrow during the day and give her a lesson."

"Milo won't mind?" asked Moo.

"Nah, Milo is going to be out of action for a few days."

"And you're staying at the Cheese's place?"

"As far as I know."

"You should bring her along," said Moo. "I'll bet she could bring in some driving students."

"I am not bringing the Cheese as bait for the snake noodle nut-sack guys."

"No, the Cheese for *gwai lo* student only," said Lois.

"Enough!" I said, pouring calming oil on *shut the fuck up*. "There are no old white devil nut-sack guys that need to learn to drive, and if there were, I wouldn't know where to find them."

"The Cheese know," said Lois.

"She even knows how to drive, right?" said Eddie, hanging over the seat like a little kid now. "We could run two cars, four students each. Let's go pick her up. It's what, maybe ten minutes by car." Moo Shoes was power mad with the magic time travel of having a car in the city at two thirty in the morning.

"Nah, she's not home," I said.

"Not home? She hanging at Jimmy's Joynt with Myrtle?"

"I don't think so. I asked her to stay away from Jimmy's for a while after the second murder. But I checked at her place before I came to get you two and she wasn't home." I may have been a little power mad at having a car and facing the 387 steps up to the Cheese's place with no more effort than pushing the gas pedal.

"She out giving someone else the razzmatazz," said Lois, pronouncing the *r* as an *l* just to be annoying. "Some rich *gwai lo* with good job and future."

"She is not," I said.

"What second murder?" said Moo.

"You didn't hear? Frankie Fortuna, one of the drag singers down at Mona's 440, got scragged in an alley two nights ago."

"What they expect?" said Lois. "You dress like man, you make man mad, man kill you."

"You're wearing a beard, doll," I said.

Lois palmed her bearded cheeks and her eyes went wide. "Oh no, I am next!"

"You're not next," said Moo Shoes. "My grandma's got a heavier beard than that." To me, Moo said, "So that note to Jimmy Vasco really might have been from the killer? Maybe he changed his mind when he found out Jimmy carries a roscoe."

"Jimmy has a roscoe?" said Lois, pronouncing the *r* perfectly, just to be annoying. "I want a roscoe."

I didn't want to tell Lois that if she reached under her seat she'd find a twelve-gauge sawed-off roscoe all her own, because as much as I enjoy making a dame's dreams come true, she was Eddie's squeeze, and we had arrived at Tall House of Happy Snake and Noodle and two young mugs in suits and leather car coats were landing gut punches on an older Chinese gentleman of the cat-fucking persuasion.

9

DRIVING LESSONS

Sammy

There was a lot more tap-dancing involved in the shoot-out than I would have expected, but as it was, strictly speaking, my first gunfight, there were bound to be a few surprises.

"That's Uncle Ho," Eddie said as we pulled up.

I rolled right past them about four car lengths.

"Those Squid Kid's men," said Lois.

"I can't believe that's a real gangster's name," I said, popping my door. "Let's go."

"They can't see me and Lois," said Moo Shoes. "They'll recognize us, then we're goners."

"What if they recognize me?" I asked. "I'm in Chinatown all the time."

"They won't. You people all look alike," said Moo.

I left the engine running, stepped out of the cab, and said, "Fine. But if it's just me, I'm going to need backup." I reached down and pulled the sawed-off out from under the seat. It was one of the old type, a double-barrel with a hammer you cocked for each barrel and two triggers. Probably some farmer's hunting gun fifty years ago. "This goes badly, you two get out of here."

I started walking toward the two guys who were alternately punching old Ho and shouting at him in Cantonese. The old man just wheezed and tried to wave me off. Normally, I'd be a little hesitant to dust up with two guys, but they weren't that big, I'd been putting my time in on the heavy bag, and two and a half feet of vintage scattergun will do wonders for a guy's confidence. I pulled up about twenty feet away and cocked both hammers of the shotgun, then held it so the stock was against my hip. These mugs hadn't even looked up when the cab rolled up, probably because it was a cab, and they didn't look up now.

"Hey, fuckstick!" I called, as casual as a can of corn.

The guy closest to me turned, and was telling me to get lost over his shoulder, I guess, when he caught sight of the scattergun and his eyes went wide.

"Let him go," I said, and I tipped the shotgun a little bit, to show him I meant business, and that's when it went off with no little noise and fire and Squid Kid minion number one was blown backward off his feet into the wall three or so feet away.

"Well, that's a surprise," I said. The trigger had been filed so it went off if you breathed on it, and I guess I breathed on it. This was a very sketchy weapon. Someone could get hurt.

Squid Kid guy number two started digging into his car coat and got a snub-nosed heater almost clear of his buttons when I let him have it with the other barrel and he traced a similar path to that of his pal, slamming into the wall on the other side of the door and sliding down.

"*Gwai lo,* you dumb cocksucker!" said Uncle Ho, in perfectly pronounced English. I think that's what he said, anyway. My ears were ringing from the shotgun blast.

"You're welcome," I said. I broke the shotgun open and started to pull out the spent shells, then I remembered I didn't have any fresh ones, so I snapped it shut again.

I felt a hand on my shoulder and turned to see Moo Shoes

standing next to me. Lois was on the other side, sort of clicking her heels in place, out of nerves, I guess, but she was putting down a pretty good rhythm.

"Oh no," she said. "We sure fucked now. We sure fucked."

Uncle Ho seemed like the only one not in shock from the fracas.

"Quick, drag in alley." He gestured wildly at the two downed gangsters.

We all went for the closest guy, but Ho grabbed Lois's arm and barked something to her in Cantonese.

"What? What? What?" I said.

"He said to start dancing," Lois said.

She did.

San Francisco, 1906

"What is your name?" said young Ho to the girl he was locked in the brothel stall with.

"I am Niu Yun," she said. Ho knew it meant Girl of the Clouds and thought it a silly and pretentious name for a big-foot whore in a crib brothel. He was a product of his time and his village and thought giving value to a female beyond her ability to work and breed was silly. He once knew a girl called Exquisite Lotus who was traded by her father to a farmer's second son as a wife in exchange for two goats. *She should have been named Two Goats!* Ho thought.

"I am Bai Da Wong," said Ho. "But that is my paper son name. Really I am Shu Ho at home."

"Not Gao Mao Yow?" asked the girl.

"No," said Ho. "But you won't need to remember it, because when it gets dark, I think they will come and kill us."

"We should escape," said Niu Yun. "Run away and hide among the white devils."

"A voice in my head is telling me to do that," said Ho. "But I think I am just insane."

"From all the cat fucking?"

"No, because the voice has power. When they branded me it took away my pain." Here he pulled back his sleeve and showed her the brand the tong had given him.

The girl looked at him with a blank expression, as if she did not have enough information to judge his sanity, so she just said, "Yes," then slid off the bench and began to remove the dead man's boots.

"What are you doing?" asked Ho.

"I will need shoes if we are going to run. And his clothes will cover me. I can wear his shirt like a dress and roll the sleeves. His hat will hide my face."

"Run where?" asked Ho. "We are locked in, and when they come tonight, they will come with enough men so we won't be able to fight."

"Yes," said Niu Yun. "We are locked in a wooden stall made of clapboards. If only we had some way of chopping through them." She tossed her head at Ho's hatchet, still solidly buried in the back of the dead guy's head.

"*She's smarter than you, Catfucker,*" said the voice. "*Save her. Steal the dragon and run away.*"

"Stop calling me Catfucker!" Ho yelled to the voice.

"You really might be insane," said Niu Yun.

Sammy

Lois Fong was tap-dancing a snappy version of "On the Good Ship Lollipop" for the four old guys who had rushed out of Tall House of Happy Snake and Noodle at the sound of gunfire, while Moo Shoes and I dragged the second gangster into the alley near where the cab was parked and Uncle Ho directed all onlookers toward Lois.

Moo Shoes let go of the gangster's arm, and the guy gasped, then moaned.

"Hey, this guy isn't dead," said Moo, and I was going to retort with something clever and tough, but then the other guy moaned and started to roll over.

"Holy shit," I said. I couldn't see very well in the alley, so I ran my hand over the front of the first guy's car coat and my hand came up not bloody at all. But I felt a bump on his chest and reached in his jacket and pulled a snub-nosed .38 from a shoulder holster. Moo had stuffed the other mug's gun, a slim automatic, in his waistband.

"Shoot him again," said Moo Shoes. "Before he gets up."

"I didn't want to shoot him the first time."

"You want me to shoot him?" asked Moo. "I'm just a driving instructor. I'm not a killer."

"Clearly I am not a killer, either, as these mugs are distinctly unkilled."

"Yeah, if one of these guys gets an eyeball on me we're all goners."

My guy—the guy I had just disarmed—was trying to sit up, and I considered for a second conking him in the coconut with his own gun, but I'd been down that road before, and it is a lot harder to knock a guy out with a pistol than George Raft movies would lead you to believe, so I drew the sawed-off out of the long pocket down the front of my overcoat, where it had been swinging like a disinterested elephant's dong, took it by the barrels, wound up, and gave him the full DiMaggio to the side of his melon with the flat of the stock. He dropped with a thud.

"Now this guy," Moo said.

"Tie him up," I said.

"Hit him first."

"No, tie up my guy."

"With what? I'm not carrying rope."

"Use your tie on his hands, your belt on his feet."

"I like this tie. And this is my only belt."

I took off my own tie and tossed it to Moo Shoes. The guy on the ground moaned. I crouched down. "Hey, buddy, you okay?" I said. "Let me give you a hand."

He was still seeing birdies, but I pulled him up until he was sitting and got his arms down behind him so he could prop himself up. "Just like that," I said. Then I stepped back and swung for the fences again with the scattergun.

Moo Shoes had the other guy's hands tied behind his back with my tie and was standing up to admire his work. I pulled my Zippo out of my pocket and gave it a flick.

"You're going to burn the bodies?" Moo asked. "I don't know, Sammy, that seems—"

"Just getting a look." I played the lighter over the chest of the gangster. White powder and dents in his leather jacket, and a few specks of blood on his shirt, but nothing like the hamburger he should have been from catching a twelve-gauge in the breadbasket. "Rock salt," I said. "Milo's shotgun was loaded with rock salt."

"Fucking Milo," said Moo Shoes.

"Back the cab into the alley, Moo," I said. "Keys are in it. I'll truss this guy up. Give me your tie."

"I still like this tie."

"This guy comes to, he's going to be sore. You want him tied up or you want him to join Lois on the Good Ship Lollipop?"

Moo Shoes gave me his tie and his belt, forgetting he had the gangster's gun shoved down the back of his waistband, so he looked like he was shaking a heavy steel turd down his pant leg as he walked away.

By the time I had the gangster trussed up, his hands tied behind his back with Moo's tie, his feet with his belt, Eddie had the cab bubbling back into the alley. He jumped out, ran back, and unlocked the trunk.

"You could fit three or four guys in there if you packed 'em tight," Moo said, looking in the trunk.

"Milo says he could set up house back there if he wasn't claustrophobic," I said. "He says with some modification you could put a jukebox and a pool table in there. Here, grab this guy's feet."

Stilton

Across town, near the decommissioned naval shipyard at Hunters Point, Stilton was musing on the trunk space of the Chrysler New Yorker she was driving.

"We're gonna need to steal a truck," she said.

The Chrysler was loaded with scrap iron, from hydraulic cylinders to levers, gauges, and valves, to a heavy waterproof hatch that the girls had spent most of the night cutting off an abandoned ship, frame and all, and had moved into the trunk with a block and tackle. The Chrysler was riding on its axles, and even going slow, the back bumper threw up sparks against the tarmac when they hit a pothole.

"How'd you know where to find all this stuff?" asked Myrtle. They'd spent most of the night collecting the scrap at various buildings across the shipyard, which had shut down after the war.

"Well, I been meaning to tell you, Myrt, I kind of got a partner in all this, and he sort of tells me what I'm supposed to get and how to get it."

"A short partner," asked Myrtle.

"Why would you say that?"

"Because one day you show up with a shiny new Chrysler when I know you ain't got two dimes to rub together, and it's got pedal extensions welded on, which you promised to explain but never have. So I just figure you're stepping out on Sammy with a little fella. I get it. I think the world of Sammy, but he's going nowhere fast. A gal's got to look out for herself."

"No," said Stilton, looking away from the road to put an eyeball on her friend to see if she was busting her balls. "What? No, nothing like that. What?"

There was a beep from a horn behind them and Myrtle jumped in her seat. A red light started flashing and was playing across the rusted shipyard buildings around them.

"Oh shit," said Stilton.

"Make a run for it," said Myrtle.

"I can't make a run for it with all this junk. I'm barely making a walk for it." She didn't slow down.

"Well, I'll start throwing stuff out and you keep going."

Stilton kept the Chrysler creeping forward and started talking like an auctioneer making his case at the gates of hell: "Myrt, you know you're my best pal and I would never ask you to do anything that would hurt you. Right?"

"Yeah, right. Me, too."

Stilton checked the mirror. Just one guy in the cop car. "Well, as your best pal, I'm going to ask you to blow this guy. To save us."

"I don't know, Tilly, I'm not sure I'm any good at that kind of thing anymore."

"Ah, you don't have to do it, just pretend you're going to do it, and once you have his wanger out, fake a fit. No guy is going to expect you to go through with it once you're having a fit. He's got to let us go, then, once you're flopping like a chicken on the ground and he has his dick out, he can't take us in. Easy peasy."

"Well then, why don't you do it?"

The cop fired up his siren. Stilton checked the mirror.

"Because I'm kind of going steady with Sammy. Wouldn't be right."

"Well, I'm kind of going steady with Jimmy."

"I know. And Jimmy is the tits. But you're better at faking a fit."

"Well, that's true," Myrtle said. "I don't like to brag, but—"

"Great! I'll scream bloody murder when you start flopping." Stilton pulled the Chrysler over. "Unzip your coveralls, show a little skin."

"Fine, but as soon as you see his wanger, start screaming. Hey, if you're going steady with Sammy, what about your little fella?"

"Here he comes, look sexy," Stilton said, rolling down the window.

"Okay, but when this is all over, you need to explain about—" Myrtle shut up when the cop's face appeared in the window. He was military police, which surprised her, a young guy.

"Good evening, Officer," Stilton said.

Myrtle slithered across Stilton's lap and pushed up until her face was about six inches from the cop's nose. "Well hello, handsome," she said.

The cop stepped back. "Ma'am, what are you doing out here at this time of night? This is a restricted government facility."

"He called me ma'am," Stilton said, smacking Myrtle on the butt to make sure she was paying attention. "This jamoke called me ma'am. I'm twenty-five years old. You don't call me ma'am."

"He can call me anything he wants," said Myrtle in her best hot-to-trot tone.

The cop looked up and down the length of the car, then peeked in the back window at all the metal inside. "Hey, what is all that stuff? You need to get out of the car."

The cop took another step back and reached down and un-snapped his holster. Then there was a *zzzzdttt* noise, a blinding flash, and a loud pop, like a big flashbulb breaking.

Myrtle was blinded but smelled something burning. She blinked away the blue field that had filled her vision and saw a pair of smol-dering boots and a lump of molten metal that had been the cop's gun amid a pile of ash on the tarmac.

"Holy shit!" said Myrtle, on the edge of panic. "Holy shit! Holy shit!"

Stilton said, "Goddammit, Scooter, I thought we agreed there would be none of that."

"Wait, what?" said Myrtle. "Who's Scooter? What just happened?"

"I'll explain," said Stilton. "First we should probably sweep up that cop."

Sammy

There were four old Chinese guys in the backseat of the cab and Lois Fong was stretched out across their laps, the full Uncle Sam in tap shoes, translating what I was saying as I drove.

"We're going to take a left up here on Washington," I said, "so put on your blinker a hundred feet or so before you get to the corner."

Lois rattled off a string of Cantonese and I guess the old guys got it because I could see one of them nodding out of the corner of my eye. Eddie Moo Shoes was sitting in the front seat, leaning against the passenger-side door, holding one of the gangsters' guns on the old guys, whom he'd told he'd blast if they laid a hand on Lois, so they all had their arms folded against their chests like stiffs arranged for burial. One of the old guys said something and Lois ignored him.

"He say, 'Where is blinker?'" translated Ho the Cat-Fucking Uncle, who was sitting in the front seat between me and Moo Shoes and who smelled like dusty monkey butt.

"Moo," I said, "how long is this driving lesson supposed to go on?"

"I told them an hour for the first lesson."

"The first lesson?"

"Yeah, I sold them a package. You gotta get them coming back. Repeat customers, that's the jam, Sam."

"You want repeat customers, maybe you shouldn't have picked guys that look like a brisk wind would croak them." I paused, then changed to my driving instructor voice. "Stop at the stop sign. Look both ways. Signal right. Shift to first gear. Now give it a little gas, let off the clutch, and make the turn." Lois Fong translated.

"Nah, these old fucks are tough," said Moo Shoes.

The old fucks were talking among themselves and sounding like they might be getting worked up.

"What's up with them?" I asked.

"They want 'Good Ship Lollipop,'" said Lois. And before I could say anything, the wonder of initiative that Lois is, she started singing, and lying on her back across the old fucks, she put her feet up on the window behind me and started to do her tap-dance routine against it.

"Easy, Lois, don't break the window," I said.

"One of these guys gets a woody I'm blasting 'im," said Moo Shoes.

"Ah, ah, ah, Eddie, return customers," I said. "You know, 'The Good Ship Lollipop' doesn't sound half bad in Chinese."

"Cop," said Uncle Ho.

"What?" I inquired.

Uncle Ho pointed to a prowl car backed into an alley, lights off.

"Balls," I said. I checked the rearview. The cop was pulling out after us and his red light was on.

"Make a run for it," said Moo Shoes.

I was tempted, and if I had had Milo's knowledge of the city's streets I might have, but if I wasn't walking, I didn't know where I was going half the time, and the only way I'd lose the flatfoots would be to take a turn they didn't know about.

"I don't think Milo's cab is fast enough," I said.

"Well, pull over and come clean," said Moo. "We're not doing anything wrong."

"You mean other than running an illegal driving school in the middle of the night with a couple of Chinese gangsters tied up in the trunk that I shot with an illegal shotgun that is also on board?"

"Well, when you put it that way, it doesn't sound so good," said Eddie.

"Also heroin," said Uncle Ho, pulling a metal box out of his inside jacket pocket that presumably held some dream dust and a rig. I'd seen him use the same on Pookie O'Hara, putting the big cop down for several days before his demise.

"Why do you have heroin?"

"Business," said Ho.

I put on my blinker to pull over. I didn't pull over, but I put my blinker on.

"Okay, everyone, listen: Lois, I need you to sing 'The Good Ship Lollipop' in Chinese and tap-dance on the window for all you're worth. The rest of you mugs join in, and don't stop singing; that means you two, too, Moo Shoes and Ho. And whatever you do, do not say a fucking word in English. Not one."

And with that Lois broke into song and dance, joined by Eddie Moo Shoes and his cat-fucking Uncle Ho, and backed up by the four nut-sack guys, who joined in with a chorus that sounded like they were beating cats to death with ukuleles.

I pulled over, screwed my hat down on my coconut, flipped my collar up, then rolled down the window.

The cop, a portly mug of about forty, trained a flashlight on me, then peeked in the back, then looked at me.

"Sir, I don't know what's going on here, but I don't like it. You need to step out of the car."

"Look, buddy, I'm on the job. I'm working undercover for the Nun."

The cop raised an eyebrow. "The Nun?"

"You know who I mean. Head of vice."

"Dunne the Nun?"

"The same. You know how he feels about cross-dressers. Well, I got all these dames on the line, getting them to lead me to their hangout."

The singing continued. I think I was starting to lose the hearing in my left ear from the tattoo of Lois's tap shoes on the window behind me.

The cop played the flashlight over my crew again.

"These are dames?" he said.

"Every one. You can check their skivvies if you want. Three-articles law. Take a couple off my hands, maybe, and maybe they'll shut the fuck up with the singing."

"Well, that one in the Uncle Sam outfit isn't fooling anyone," the cop said.

"Take her off my hands, it'll strengthen my front."

"Let me see your badge."

"I can't. I show you my star, it'll blow my cover."

"I'd say your cover's blown, pal."

"Nah, none of them speaks a word of English. C'mon, take a couple of them off my hands; do the paperwork, would you? I've been listening to this squealing all night."

Then there was some pounding and male shouting coming from the trunk. Moo Shoes shouted something in Cantonese, which I guess meant "louder" because everyone sang louder. It didn't help.

"What's going on with the trunk?" asked the cop, stepping away.

"Die, *gwai lo!*" screamed Ho as he lunged across the front of me with the sawed-off and pulled the triggers, which did nothing at all. The cop leapt back at the sight of the shotgun, but recovered fast and started to draw his gat.

I dropped the Checker into gear, floored it, popped the clutch, and the Good Ship Lollipop screeched away into the night like a nightmare having its nuts twisted off.

10

FOG CITY FOLLIES

San Francisco, 1906

Young Ho chopped at the stall door with the bloody hatchet while the girl dressed.

Niu Yun tore a wide strip of cloth from her flour-sack dress and wrapped it around the dead john's planter's hat to cover the hatchet wound and most of the bloodstain. She had already made a dress of the john's shirt and belted it with his wide leather belt. She wrapped her feet in more strips of her dress and put on the john's cowboy boots. They were too big, but she would be able to walk, perhaps even run, with the padding.

"Look, Catfucker," she said. "My feet are bound like a proper beautiful lady's now. I can marry a man of means. Ha!"

Ho ceased his chopping for a beat and let his shaved forehead rest against the doorjamb. How could she joke at such a time, after what she had suffered? He squeezed his eyes tightly shut and tried to push back his shame—for what he had done to this woman and the others. He would never laugh again. He did not deserve to laugh, to smile, even.

"Hurry, Catfucker," said Niu Yun. She pried the hatchet out of his hand, pushed him away, and began chopping at the door by the latch. With four quick chops she was through it. She swung the door open, peeked out, saw no one in the alley. "Come, we must go,

Catfucker." She started up the alley toward Grant Avenue, pulling him by the sleeve, until he pulled back.

"No, not that way. They will come from that way," Ho said. "We should release the others first."

"No, we must go now or we can do no good but to die with them. We will go to the Boss of White Devil's Daughters, and she will save them."

They ran the other way down the alley, which led through a maze of smaller alleys, some so narrow they had to turn sideways, even past a pen of pigs that Ho didn't even know were there.

"*Don't forget the onions, you know, in case you don't get away,*" said the pigs in his head. "*But we're rootin' for you.*"

They emerged onto a busy street full of vendors, wagons, horses, and the occasional automobile. No one gave them a second look amid the flow of the crowd buying vegetables and meats, along the sidewalks.

"Where is *Sacramento Street*?" asked Niu Yun. She said the street in English, which startled Ho a bit.

"How would I know? I can't read their signs."

"I cannot read at all, but we learned the name of the street in the cribs. The girls whispered it between us. They said if you get away, you are to find the large brick house at *nine-twenty Sacramento Street* and any white devil would direct you. There we would find the Boss of the White Devil's Daughters and she would help us. We must go there, and she will go back and save the others. They say she is nine feet tall, and fearless."

"*No, Catfucker,*" said the voice in Ho's head. "*First you must steal the Rain Dragon from the brotherhood hall.*"

"No," said Ho. "First we must steal the dragon from the guild hall. A voice is telling me I must. I think it is the dragon."

"You silly man, there is no dragon. You are crazy with the pox. There are no such things as dragons."

"It told me to save you."

"Well, that is a wise fucking dragon," said Niu Yun. "You should definitely listen to that dragon."

Stilton

"Let him motorboat your boobs," said Stilton. "It's how his people say hello."

She was sitting on an upturned five-gallon bucket next to where Myrtle had fainted when she first saw the moonman. The moonman stood by the rhinoceros, which is what they had decided to call the thing they were building, blinking at them, froggy membranes coming down over his big black almond-shaped eyes like windshield wipers, then retracting somewhere into his gray lightbulb head.

"C'mere, buddy," Stilton said. She unsnapped the bib of her leather welder's apron, unzipped her coveralls, and beckoned for the moonman to come to her. He scampered forward, all three feet of him, and plunged his face into her cleavage, then proceeded to wag his mug back and forth and make a burble-tweeting noise approximating the sound of a happily drowning songbird.

"Aw, Tilly, don't let him touch you," said Myrtle, who had propped herself up on the floor where she had fainted. "He's touching you. Eww. Oh my God, he's just got his little face right in there. I think I'm gonna be sick. Eww."

"Relax, Myrt. He's doing the best he can. He can't really get a good motorboat going because he doesn't have cheeks. Or lips."

"He's touching you. Eww. His little froggy fingers—"

"Outside of my bra only. He's harmless."

"He incinerated a cop, Tilly."

"A military cop."

"Incinerated! Burned up. Turned the guy to a pile of ashes and boots."

"Yeah, I don't know what was wrong there. He usually doesn't leave the boots. Maybe his cow-blaster needs tuning or something."

"Where in the hell was he?"

"He's tricky. He gets around."

"I can't talk to you with that thing—"

"Scooter."

"I can't talk to you with that thing—Scooter—motorboating your boobs."

"Fine," Stilton said. She took the moonman by the head—a palm placed gently on either side where ears would be—slowed him down, then pushed him away. "It's nice to see you, too, Scooter." To Myrtle she said, "This would be so much easier if he had ears you could grab. I tried putting my fingers in his ear holes to pull him off, but he made it pretty clear that ear holes are off-limits."

"Good to know," Myrtle said.

The moonman whistled and clicked and turned to Myrtle.

"No fucking way, buster," she said. She folded her arms over her chest.

Scooter made a sad trilling sound, then turned, scampered over to the rhinoceros, and climbed in. Clanging and pounding sounded from inside.

"So," said Stilton, "you probably have some questions, huh?"

Lone Jones

No one was coming into the Moonlight Club at three in the morning, so Thelonius Jones abandoned his post at the door and went to stand at the end of the bar to listen to the songbird's last number of the night. She was doing a sultry version of Hoagy Carmichael's "The Nearness of You," and she was tired and had drunk too much and smoked too much so her voice was just a little raspy and Lone was sure she was singing just to him. He felt like there was a cord that ran inside of him from his heart to his loins that he hadn't known existed until her voice plucked it. She sang her outro and let the band wind it all down with a sleazy improvisation on the sax and some sizzle on the cymbals. She took her shoes off and carried them, fingers hooked in the straps, as she padded off the stage to the end of the bar where Lone stood.

"Hey, Secret," Della said. She'd been calling him Secret since he'd confessed about his ambition to be a Secret Service agent. Everyone in the band had had a good laugh over it.

"Miss Della," said Lone. He had been calling her *Miss* since everyone in the band had laughed at him about his ambition to be a Secret Service agent.

"Can I get a double Scotch, rocks?" Della said to the bartender, who scowled and hesitated before throwing some ice into a glass like he was trying to bludgeon a small invisible enemy in there.

"We ain't supposed to drink at the bar," Lone said.

The bartender set the drink in front of Della with a thud.

"We?" said Della, swirling the ice around in her drink. "You got a mouse in your pocket?"

"Colored folk," said Lone.

"I knew what you meant. Get you a drink, Secret. You think this cracker-ass bartender gonna tell you no?"

"Naw, Dave all right. I don't want to get no one in trouble."

"Ha! You in trouble already. You always been in trouble, you just don't know it. Like a fish don't know he wet 'cause he ain't never been anything else. But I know, Secret." She drained her drink and set the glass down hard enough to bounce an ice cube out.

"No, I ain't in trouble. You wanna come with me up to Cookie's? You already friends with everyone there."

"Secret, you can just go on out and use your special magic Secret Service powers to hail me a cab, 'cause you ain't getting any of this." She presented herself with a flourish, like she had just finished a particularly graceful ice-skating routine.

Lone said, "I ain't—"

"You don't think every club owner or talent booker or bandleader don't want some of this? And a lot of 'em think they got it coming. Think I owe them something because they let me sing and look pretty and bring people in to see the show and make them a mess of money. Well, ain't a night goes by I don't have to disabuse one motherfucker or another of that delusion, and tonight your night."

Lone took off his top hat and wiped his forehead with his palm. "Miss Della, I just—"

"Look, Secret, you a nice fella, and you ain't hard to look at, from a distance, so you look normal size, but this ain't for you. What you think gonna happen I go with you? I'm gonna live in a little house with you and your mama? We have a bunch of kids and I'll stay home and take care of them and your mama while you try to make enough money to buy them shoes?"

"I was just gonna axe you if you want to get a cheeseburger."

"Why don't you just find me a cab. I'm gonna go back and grab my purse."

Lone slunk out the front door and flagged down a cabdriver who he knew wouldn't mind giving a ride to a colored girl and held the door for Della when she came out.

"Thanks, dummy," she said, climbing in.

Lone pushed the car door closed, and when he turned to go back inside there was a young couple standing behind him, cringing at what they had just heard.

"Aw, she don't mean nothing," Lone said to them. "She just had a little too much to drink. Can I get y'all a taxi?"

He put the couple in a taxi, pocketing a nice tip the man gave him, then checked out with the bartender and started a slow slog out of North Beach, up over Nob Hill, and down into the Tenderloin to Cookie's, the taps of his shoes sounding out the sad clip-clop of a worn-out workhorse. When he walked into Cookie's, everyone shouted, "Happy New Year," and he found a bit of a smile had been hiding somewhere way back in his heart.

Before he had a chance to look around for his friends, Doris came whizzing by like a broad-bottomed streetcar and took him by the elbow. "Come with me," she said.

"Has Sammy and the fellas—"

"Nobody's here," said Doris. She pulled up at one of the booths by the front window. "Now sit," she said. "I'm going to buy you a meatloaf."

"But I was only—"

"And if you finish that, I'll buy you another, but you get comfy, because I need you here until the end of my shift, in case Lars comes in."

"But Miss Doris—"

"Cookie said he'd fire me if I didn't show up for my shift, so here I am," she said. She squeezed his biceps. "I never been so glad to see someone in my whole life."

No one other than his mother had ever said anything like that to Lone, and despite the fact that they had never had a previous exchange that didn't center on meatloaf or burgers, he would have taken a bullet for Doris right then.

"I'll look out for you," Lone said. "You gotta work."

"You're goddamn right I do. You want mashed or french fries?"

"I believe I'll have me some fries tonight," said Lone.

"Butcher's revenge!" Doris called to the cook. "Bury Bossy in frog sticks!"

Sammy

If you pick a fat cop you can get a good jump on him before he gets back to his car, so we were four blocks away before we heard the siren. I didn't know any side streets or alleys, but old Ho did. I zigged and zagged through Chinatown, sloshing the pool of Lois and the nut-sack guys in the backseat, then floored it through four lights on Stockton and, with four lanes to play with, slid around the corner on Broadway, headed south toward the tunnel.

Uncle Ho chattered something and Moo Shoes translated. "Take a right up the ramp just before the tunnel."

"There's no turn-off just before the tunnel," I said.

"Slow down, slow down, slow down," Moo said.

I did, and Moo was right, there was a turn-off into a one-lane, one-way street that immediately launched straight up through a bunch of Victorians perched on the side of Russian Hill like swanky vultures waiting to dine on the neon corpse of North Beach. Before you could say Joe DiMaggio, we were in the air over Mason Street, where we landed with a shower of sparks and the screams of Chinese guys old and young. The cab was still bouncing when I pulled into a blind alley, then stopped and killed the engine and the lights.

"Everybody down," I said, which wasn't strictly necessary, because none of the nut-sack guys was tall enough to be seen out the back window. And we waited. "You gotta keep your foot off the brake pedal or you give the whole game away with your brake lights," I told them.

One of the nut-sack guys said something in Cantonese and Lois translated. "He want to know if this going to be on driving test?"

"Yes," I said. "Tell him yes."

So we waited for about five minutes and no cops came screaming by behind us. In fact, there was no traffic at all.

When I was sure the coast was clear, I fired up the Checker, backed out of the alley, and proceeded across Russian Hill. Topping the hill on Mason Street, I could see the lighthouse out on Alcatraz sweeping the bay and I got a little case of the willies when I realized how close we'd come to a one-way ticket there. I headed down the hill toward the water, hung a right on Bay Street, and headed out to Pier 29, where I parked the cab behind Jimmy's Joynt.

"I'll be right back. I gotta check to see if the Cheese is here."

"What do you want us to do?" asked Moo Shoes.

"Traffic laws quiz?" I suggested. "I'll bet Lois could sing the stop signs off the traffic manual."

As I was walking in I looked back to see that someone had draped something out of the trunk and down over the license plate. I trotted back to the cab and peeked in.

"Moo Shoes, you slam something in the trunk?"

"Yeah, Milo had a blanket back there, so I draped it over the license plate after we tucked Squid Kid's guys in there."

"You know that's probably why that flatfoot pulled us over?"

"Yeah, it's also the reason he'll never find us through Milo's cab."

"Eddie is genius," said Lois.

I was thinking *jamoke,* but if a pal's squeeze wants to think he's a genius I am not going to bust his chops in front of her. There would, however, be a chop busting at some point in the future. Fucking Moo Shoes.

There were two broads working the door at Jimmy's even though it was pushing four in the morning and technically the joint was closed. They were both bigger than me and wearing suits better than anything I owned.

"We're closed," said the taller of the two, who was wearing a Stetson Stratoliner fedora with a little silver airplane on the hatband— also a nicer hat than any I had. *I'm in the wrong business,* I thought. *I could be a doorman. I'd even beat some sense into a guy with an enormous black rubber dong if it was part of the deal.* That was a sharp fucking hat.

"Nice lid," I said. "I'm a friend of Jimmy's, friend of Butch's— who was a stand-up dame. Glad you two are looking out."

"We're closed," the shorter one said.

"Fine, you haven't seen Stilton, have you? Blond, surprised hair—"

"Yeah, we know Stilton," said Stratoliner. They all knew the Cheese. "What about her?"

"I'm worried about her, what with the killer on the loose. I stopped at her place and she wasn't in. Look, you guys, I know that

Butch's favorite part of the job was pasting some guy who was bitter about his squeeze going over to the all-girl team, but I ain't that guy. I really am a friend of Jimmy's, and I really do need to talk to her, so could one of you hold me at bay with the wiggly wonder there under the podium, and the other can go tell Jimmy that Sammy Tiffin is here and maybe we can find the dame I'm crazy about."

They looked at each other, looked at me.

"You seen Myrtle?" asked the shorter one.

"I was hoping Stilton was with her, here."

"Sorry," said Stratoliner. "Go on in. Jimmy's at the bar. Sorry about the hard time."

I breezed past them. "You kidding? I'm glad you're on the job. Keep an eye on that cab I pulled up in, would you? I got two Chinese gangsters in the trunk who are going to be good and sored up if they get out."

"We'll keep a lookout."

"Thanks. If tap-dancing starts happening, let it go. Part of the plan."

I left them blinking and thinking. *You dames think you got weird? I'll see your big black dong and raise you a leggy Uncle Sam and the nutsack guys.*

Jimmy Vasco was sitting at the bar nursing something brown on the rocks and smoking a coffin nail in an ivory holder. She'd slipped out of her tux jacket and was just in shirtsleeves with French cuffs and ruby and diamond-crusted cuff links the size of cocktail olives. The place was nearly empty, just Mel the bartender doing her side work and a cocktail waitress dressed like a butler wiping down the tables and putting the chairs up. The lights were up halfway and there was a hazy dinge over the joint.

Jimmy gestured for me to take the stool next to hers and I did.

"You seen 'em?" she asked, by way of a greeting.

"Nah, thought they'd be here."

"This shit is getting old, Sammy."

"Yeah. I checked Stilton's when I closed up, nothing."

"Yeah, I been calling Myrt's all night. She said she and Stilton were going to work on a project."

"A project?"

"Yeah, like an art project or some daffy thing. Myrt was supposed to catch a ride here by two. We certainly didn't need to stay open. It's been a ghost town since the killing at Mona's."

"Even with the new muscle at the door? I'm surprised. I feel safe."

Jimmy snorted at my joke. "Well, it's the killer and the raid by Dunne the other night. It is not a good time to be out and about in Dyke Land, Sammy." She reached into her pants pocket, pulled out a folded piece of notebook paper, and threw it on the bar. It read TO JIMMY V on the outside in big block letters. "Take a gander."

I picked it up and unfolded it. It read YOU'RE NEXT, THIS TIME'S THE CHARM, same pen, same handwriting.

"Fingerprints?" I asked.

"Are you kidding? Someone tacked this to the back door before I came in this afternoon to do books, so first thing I call Central Station. They give me an on-duty detective, who tells me that Captain Dunne is handling the case and to call him, so I call the number he gives me. The guy at Dunne's number brushes me off like I'm reporting a cat up a tree. Hang on to it, they'll take a look at it when I'm in the neighborhood. Says if I get any more, be sure to call it in to Central again. There's nobody taking fingerprints. They haven't even been back since the morning they found Butch. So I call over to Mona's 440, and you know there's no love lost between me and the dame that runs that joint, Babe Bowman."

"Competitors?"

"We had a thing for a while."

"Oh," I said. "So what did Babe have to say?"

"She is still somewhat unhappy with me, but she did say that the cops haven't been back since Frankie was scragged. Did a few interviews with the staff and that was it. Didn't get names of patrons, nothing. Not that Babe would have given them any names. She's a bitch, but she would never rat out another dame. Thing is, they're not even looking for the killer. I think Dunne sees them as doing his work for him. A couple of dykes get killed, he does just enough to get it in the papers, our business goes to shit, he gets to call it a win, and no one important gives a shit if the killer is ever caught."

"What are you gonna do?" I asked.

"No, what are *you* gonna do?" Jimmy said. "I'm going to hire you to find the killer."

I laughed. I know it wasn't a laughing matter, but Jimmy was clearly yanking my chain. She wasn't laughing.

Jimmy just stared at me. Smoking. Waiting. After about an hour, probably, she said, "Well?"

"Jimmy, I would love to help you out, but I don't know anything about catching a killer."

"You got rid of Pookie O'Hara. You saved Myrtle and the Cheese. You got every nob on Nob Hill and Pacific Heights to leave you and your friends alone, and even the cops never gave you a second look. You might not know anything about catching a killer now, but I got the feeling you're a fast learner."

"I gotta be honest, Jimmy, I did not scrag Pookie O'Hara. That was just a coincidence—"

Jimmy put a finger on my lips, shutting my trap. "Let me stop you right there." She rattled the ice in her glass and Mel dove in the well, came up with some Irish, and poured it in Jimmy's glass. "First, you never gotta be honest; that's just a cliché used by people who are bad liars. And second, I don't care what happened with you and Pookie; I know he's gone and you did it. And third, I have a building up on Chestnut, a triplex, my retirement. You do this, you find this fuck, and the top apartment is yours and the Cheese's, rent-free, long as you want it. Plus enough cash to put some furniture in it. Big, bright, two bedrooms, view of the bay. I might even throw in my Ford. You can get your girlfriend a fucking phone, for Pete's sake."

It was the best offer anyone had made me since the first time the Cheese pulled off her dress, but while I could pour everything in *Mr. Boston's Big Book of Booze* from memory, and I had gotten pretty handy with an arc welder and a cutting torch at the shipyard during the war, I didn't know enough about investigating a homicide to lube up a ladybug. "Jimmy, I don't—"

"This fuck is going to try to kill me, Sammy."

"But why me?"

"Because you're my friend and you're not going to let that happen."

"Fuck," I said.

"Yeah," she said. "You want a drink?"

"Yeah. Irish is fine."

Jimmy signaled. Mel put it together.

I lit a smoke while I tried to think of something to say. It had become obvious to me through my top-notch detective work that it was not going to be *no*.

I said, "I don't know how to put a murder case together, Jimmy. Even if I catch this guy, the cops don't want him, the DA will do what the cops want, hell, even your note isn't evidence now that we've had our dirty mitts all over it. He'll never be convicted."

"Don't care. Not why I'm hiring you. I want him stopped. Gone. Disappeared."

"Killed?"

Jimmy shrugged. "It's a nice apartment, Sammy."

I looked to see if Mel had been listening; she hadn't. She was in the stockroom or the office or somewhere that was not in hearing range. "I got something I have to finish. And I can't quit my job."

"I can't lend you my heater," Jimmy said. "I'm gonna need it."

"I got a line on a couple."

"You can have the keys to the Ford as soon as I know Myrt is safe."

"Can you run by the Five and Dime and see if they're there? I'm in the middle of something."

"At four in the morning? Whatever it is, if the Cheese isn't with you, it's the wrong thing."

I thought about explaining what I was in the middle of, with all the fixin's, but instead I said, "I gotta finish giving a driving lesson."

11

SNATCHING LARS

San Francisco, 1906

"I'm going to need it to chop off some dicks," said Niu Yun, holding Ho's hatchet at arm's length away from him. They were standing in the middle of Stockton Street, which was very busy with people buying and selling, hawking and haggling. The hatchet was still bloody, although much of the blood had dried. People were beginning to notice.

"But you can't even tuck it in your belt without it showing," said Ho. "Let me carry it and if you need to chop off some dicks, I'll give it back to you."

A man driving a wagon drawn by two mules pulled up his team and shouted in Cantonese, "Get out of the street, you crazy woman!"

"See," said Niu Yun, "there's a dick needs chopped off already."

She stormed at the wagon, hatchet held high. Ho caught her by the back of her belt, swung her around, then dragged her backward up onto the sidewalk. She wheeled on him, hatchet first. Ho let go of her belt and the hatchet whizzed by where his wrist had just been. Ho thought it a good sign that she had only tried to cut his arm and not kill him like the john. "Fine, you carry the hatchet," he said. "But find something to wrap it in."

Niu Yun was not listening. She leapt up on the wagon beside the man who had just shouted at her. She grabbed the front of his shirt and brandished the hatchet over his head. "Tell me where Sacramento Street is or I'll chop your dick off." She said *Sacramento* in English, which was fine with the wagon man because that was how he knew it. He would tell her, of course, but he hadn't been this close to a woman in the two years since he left China, so he really hoped she wouldn't chop his dick off, because he was stalling, just stretching out the moment, pretending like he couldn't remember.

"Where?" she shouted, and she drew back with the hatchet.

Ho thought since Niu Yun was a big-foot girl, no one had taken the time to teach her how to ask directions. But because the village he came from was small and everyone there lived and died within a two-mile radius, no one there knew how to ask for directions, either, so he decided not to correct her.

The wagon man sighed. Ah, it was a fleeting moment, a flirt with the spice of danger, but he let it pass and pointed to the corner and the sign that read SACRAMENTO ST. "Right there," he said.

"Oh," said Niu Yun. She lowered her hatchet and jumped off the wagon. "Right there," she said to Ho, pointing with the hatchet.

Ho snatched a newspaper that was tumbling in the street and held it out to her. "Wrap the hatchet in this until you need it." She did.

They made their way to the corner and the few people who had stopped to watch an axe murder went about their business. Ho knew American numbers and searched for them on the buildings from the corner. There it was, right across the street. A hulking three-story brick building with an arched doorway, extending halfway down the next block. "There it—" Ho was about to point, but someone caught his arm from behind and he nearly shrieked.

"Don't move," came a female voice from behind him. "Back away from the corner before they see you."

Ho ventured a glance back. It was a woman, no taller than Niu Yun, but perhaps twice her age, dressed in men's clothes, with black trousers and slippers and a long black shirt like Ho's own. She wore a conical straw farmer's hat that covered her face. Her hair must have been tied up inside.

Niu Yun brandished the hatchet in its newspaper sheath until she saw it was a woman and tucked the weapon under her arm. "They are watching," the woman said. "I am one of the White Devil's Daughters—a translator for Miss Donaldina." She pulled them both into a crowd of men in front of a vegetable stand. "Look, they are at every corner of the mission. You almost ran into one."

Ho looked back and spotted one of his Ghee Sin brothers at the corner, facing the mission building. Another two steps and they would have passed in front of him. The woman led them back the way they had come and ducked into an alley just wide enough for the three of them to stand.

"You won't get in there today, maybe even tonight. They know one of their women has been taken. They will watch until she has been found." She tipped her hat back and looked hard at Ho. "And you, aren't you a Ghee Sin hatchet man, too?"

"I have his hatchet," said Niu Yun. "I'm going to chop off some dicks with it."

"First you have to stay alive," the woman said. "You won't get in here, but the mission has a farm where you can go. North. The village is called Eldridge. Outside of Sonoma. Say it in English."

They each tried several times to say "Eldridge" and she corrected them until they sounded like her. "Now say 'Sonoma.'" They said it until she was satisfied.

"There is a Chinatown in Sonoma. If you find it, go into the Chinese general store; they will direct you to Miss Donaldina's farm. Go north. You will have to cross the Golden Gate. See if you can get a ride on a fishing boat. There are a few Chinese fishermen with boats. They are afraid of the tongs. Maybe if you show them your hatchet and your brand they will take you. From Sausalito it is two, perhaps three days' journey on foot. Go north. Go now."

She turned to go but Ho heard a voice in his head, a shout, "*Stop her, Catfucker!*" He caught the woman by her shirt and pulled her back into the doorway. "Down," Ho said. And he crouched down and the two women joined him, as if they were playing some gambling game on the ground, just as two tong soldiers walked by. She would have walked right into them. Instead they were just three dark figures crouched in shadow among hundreds.

"*Now fetch the Rain Dragon, Catfucker,*" said the voice. "*Without the dragon you and the girl will be caught and killed.*"

"That is going to be difficult to explain," Ho said.

"What is difficult?" asked Niu Yun. "North. It's that way. I know that and I've been in a cage for—" She trailed off, grabbed the front of his shirt, and looked in his eyes. "How long have I been in a cage?"

Sammy

When we told them there would be no more driving lessons, because Milo needed his cab back, the nut-sack guys came up with a plan. It wasn't the cleanest plan, but here's how I figured it: Moo Shoes is always telling me how in the Chinese culture, elders are venerated and respected, and the only people more venerated and respected are the ancestors, so if their plan went to shit, the worst thing happens, the nut-sack guys get promoted to ancestors.

Eddie, Lois, and I sat in the front seat of the cab, parked half a block down from Doris's basement apartment in South Park, a very old San Francisco neighborhood that was mostly warehouses and factories. Uncle Ho and the nut-sack guys were working their plan. The gangsters in the trunk had been agreeably quiet since we had injected them with the frog juice. Mr. Ping, one of the nut-sack guys, owned an apothecary shop on Washington where we waited among the bear gallbladders and shark uvulas and a lot of other spooky-looking animal parts, while Ping put together a package with the right ingredients to poison the Squid Kids. (I still can't believe there's a gangster called Squid Kid.) Ping wanted to make a tea and have them drink it, but I predicted that waiting for guys to drink tea while trussed up in the open trunk of a cab might appear unsavory to any passersby, at which point Ho suggested they inject the tea with his heroin rig and Mr. Ping thought that was a swell idea, so the gangsters were now very much nighty-night or possibly dead. Uncle Ho's first suggestion was to shoot them with their own guns, put onions in their pockets, and feed them to the pigs, which was a problem, because where you going to get onions at five in the morning?

"He makes a tea out of frogs?" I said.

"Nah," said Moo Shoes. "The frogs are skinned and the skin is dried and powdered and he makes tea out of that."

"Oh, well, that's much better," I said, thinking, *That's not much better.*

"Here we go," Lois said, pointing down the block to a large blond guy lumbering up the sidewalk. Lars.

Two of the nut-sack guys, Mr. Gong and Mr. Ping, both dressed in business suits, were following Lars, waving like lunatics to their cohorts ahead, in case they missed the enormous Viking-looking jamoke wandering down a sidewalk that was deserted except for some random old Chinese guys who just decided to casually hang out in a strange neighborhood at the crack of dawn like they do. Mr. Lee, in a long black cotton shirt and trousers, was crouched behind a mailbox across the sidewalk from the apartment, and Mr. Chen, in a traditional silk coat and hat, red, was leaning against the brick wall at the top of the stairs reading a Chinese newspaper like you do. Uncle Ho was crouched in the stairwell that led down to the apartment.

When Lars reached the mailbox, Mr. Chen lowered his newspaper. Uncle Ho came up the steps with the sawed-off in hand and yelled, "Hands in the air or you die, *gwai lo*!" The shotgun was still loaded with the spent shells, but Ho didn't know that. He'd learned to cock the hammers since pulling it on the cop, so he thought the problem solved.

Lars, looking confused, raised his hands slowly, and that's when Mr. Lee came out from behind the mailbox and jammed the needle in Lars's ass. Chen threw his opened newspaper over Lars's face as the big Swede instinctively whirled to cold-cock whoever had just poked him in the butt, and he would have, if Mr. Lee had been a foot taller. As it was, Lars windmilled over his head and Misters Gong and Ping stretched Milo's blanket between them and threw it over Lars's head, almost.

I started the cab.

Lars brushed the blanket away and made for Misters Gong and Ping, at which point Uncle Ho fired the shotgun, which clicked, I guess. I don't know because at the time I was driving the cab up to the curb by where all this was going on.

"Not good. Not good. Not good," chanted Lois, in case we had missed that an enormous steamed-up Scandinavian longshoreman going berserk on a quartet of tiny old Chinese guys was probably not good.

Ho and the nut-sack guys were doing a pretty good job of staying out of Lars's reach, so Moo Shoes and I sat on either side of Lois, watching, each of us holding one of the heaters we'd taken from the Squid Kid's guys. (Moo says Squid Kid is pushing forty, and they still call him "kid." That's no way to run a criminal empire, whether you have a dragon or not.)

"You help," said Lois. "Help them."

I looked at Moo. He looked at me. We both looked at Lois, then out the window at Lars, raging.

"I think they're doing pretty good," said Moo.

Lois screeched something in Cantonese, which conveyed her sense of urgency, despite my not understanding a word.

"Fine," I said. I shrugged out of my overcoat and handed the gun to Lois. "If he doesn't go down in fifteen seconds, shoot him."

I climbed out of the cab and yelled, "Hey, Lars, your mother blows reindeer!" (I don't know, I was trying to say something that would set him on me. Swedish guys love their mothers, right? And Sweden's where they grow reindeer, right?)

It worked. He turned from chasing Misters Gong and Ping and came my way, waving his arms like a drunken bear. I ducked under his arms and gave him two quick shots to the ribs, heard his breath blast out of him, then danced away before he could grab me.

Lars reeled around like a surprised drunk, looking for me. I bounced up to him, ducked another bear swipe, and gave him a hard right to the solar plexus, which doubled him over, at which point Mr. Lee delivered a side kick to the big man's knee that sent him face-first into the concrete. Lars pushed up from the sidewalk, but before he could lift his head, Uncle Ho smacked him across the side of the head with the stock of the shotgun and the big man went down, still.

I looked at Mr. Lee, who was catching his breath from the exertion.

"Lee, you sneaky rascal," I said.

Mr. Lee grinned. "Kung fu," he said.

"You're welcome," I said. "Help me get him into the trunk."

The four nut sacks, Moo, and I gathered Lars up and stuffed him into the trunk on top of the Squid Kids. Mr. Ping checked all their pulses and gave me a quick nod before slamming the trunk lid shut. We all piled into the cab and I headed to the Bay Bridge. Mr. Gong had an import-export business and held a part interest in a ship with a Malaysian register that was docked in Oakland. A half hour later we were standing around a sturdy wooden crate big enough to ship a pool table in, with Lars and the two Squid Kids slumped in the corners. Before the crew (all Filipinos) nailed the lid on the crate, one of the mates, I guess, a guy in charge, anyway, approached Mr. Gong and spoke under his breath for a minute. Gong gestured for Moo Shoes to join him by the crate. I watched Moo dig into his pockets and hand the mate every bill he came out with, wearing a face so sad he might have been giving up his boyhood dog to the pound. The mate handed Moo a cloth sack, which maybe held beans at one time, then barked at the other crew. One of them put a two-gallon metal gas can in the crate and they started nailing it closed. Moo Shoes slogged back to me and the others and handed me the cloth bag. The ties and belts we'd tied the gangsters with were inside. I took mine out, handed Moo Shoes his, and we made our way back to the cab.

"He took all the money I made from the driving lessons to feed them until they get to Malaysia."

"What was in the can?"

"Water. Mr. Ping says they'll be out for a couple of days, but in case they wake up early, they won't die of thirst. They'll be in the middle of the Pacific before the mate opens the crate."

"Sorry, Eddie," I said. "But hey"—I punched him in the arm to cheer him up—"your driving school is out of the gate and galloping like a champ."

"Yeah, but I got these guys to pay in advance, and as of this morning I still got no car and Lois is going to be very sored up when she finds out I have given all of our cheddar for the care and feeding of hostages."

When we got back to the car and everyone climbed in, Uncle Ho fired off a barrage of Cantonese that had Moo Shoes breathless trying to translate on the fly. Finally Moo Shoes let the old man wind down before explaining.

"He thinks we made a mistake by leaving Squid Kid's guys alive."

"I thought we all agreed we weren't in that business," I said.

"But he has a point. If they're alive, even if it's weeks before they can reach Squid Kid, they're going to tell him who they were roughing up when somebody shot and drugged them. They might not remember you, but they'll remember Uncle Ho, and Squid Kid will find him and torture him until he gives up all of us."

"Did he really want to say all that in front of the nut-sack guys?"

"They know. They know that Squid Kid's men were beating Ho to get some information. They don't know it was about the dragon, but they know."

"Why didn't they help him?"

"Because they don't like him."

"Because he's a criminal?"

"You kidding? It was illegal for these guys to even exist in the States until four years ago. Chinese Exclusion Act of 1882. They were criminals just for being here, and half of them were probably in the fighting tongs, too. It's the history, with my grandpa spreading stories from the old country, the family, his reputation, spread long after Uncle Ho was already here. A bum rap."

"The cat-fucker thing?"

"Yeah, something like that. My people hold grudges even when they forget what they're over."

"I guess us finding that Rain Dragon thing isn't going to wash with the Squid Kid now, huh?"

"No," said Moo Shoes. "But Uncle Ho will still pay me, if he lives."

"So we have what, three, four weeks?"

"Unless those sailors just throw the crate overboard and keep my money."

"A guy can hope, I guess," I said.

◇◇◇◇◇

We dropped Ho and the nut sacks at the cable car turnaround at the end of California Street near the Ferry Building, where they could catch a ride into Chinatown, one or two at a time. I knew that all the cop had seen was that we were in a cab, no license plate, but we made a pretty memorable crew, and I didn't think it was a good idea to be seen together in town during daylight. The cop we had ditched would be off shift at eight and then things could relax.

Lois pulled off her beard and I gave her my overcoat to cover the rest of her outfit. She climbed out and kissed each of the nut-sack guys on the cheek, told each she'd see him at the next lesson. Then she went to Uncle Ho, put her arm around his shoulders, turned to the nut-sack guys, and said something in Cantonese, then kissed Ho on the temple and crawled back in the cab. As we pulled away, the nut-sack guys were all bowing to Uncle Ho and shaking his hand.

"What did you say to them?" I asked Lois.

"I told them that none of this happen without Uncle Ho tells me to."

"What did they say?"

"They say it is best driving lesson they ever have."

I whistled. "Lois, you are a stand-up broad."

"Ho is only one doesn't try to touch my butt. All night."

I didn't want to point out to her that Ho had been in the front seat and probably had enough class not to get handsy with his nephew's squeeze (unless she was a cat), because either way, it was a stand-up move on Lois's part.

We dropped Lois off in front of her building, an Art Deco hulk off Union Square where she shared an apartment with five other showgirls. But it was a nice building, outside of Chinatown, if only by a couple of blocks, and Lois was proud to live there.

"You can wear my coat, give it back to Eddie to bring to me at Cookie's."

"No, you take. Thank you." She slipped out of my overcoat, folded it, and handed it to Eddie through the car window. We watched as she walked into her building, much more slowly than necessary, in her red-and-white-striped satin shorts, blue sequined top, and tall sparkling tap shoes, way too slowly. Her doorman, who obviously had never seen Lois in her work clothes, was taken with a wave of patriotism and nearly popped an epaulet getting the door for her.

"She's a stand-up dame, Moo," I said.

"Yeah. Outta my league."

"You're pimping her, Eddie."

"I am not. She's the love of my life."

"Well, you're parading her around in front of old guys who would murder their many children to give her the razzmatazz and are willing to pay to look at her and think about it and you're collecting the money."

"Holy smokes, I'm pimping out the love of my life!"

"It would seem so."

"I'm peddling the ass of my heart's desire!"

I'd never seen Moo Shoes so distressed, and I'd watched him fail miserably at pistol-whipping a cop once. So I decided to throw him a rope. "But in your defense, you spent all the money to feed the hungry."

"Prisoners. Guys we kidnapped."

"You think they won't be hungry when they open that box? And she's gaining fans, you gotta admit that."

"Yeah, so I'm promoting her career, like."

"Absolutely," I said, glad I could make him feel better. "As a floozie," I added, because no one wants to see Moo Shoes too chipper at six thirty in the morning.

"Can we step on it to your place? I gotta take a leak."

So I did, and we were there in ten, and while Moo Shoes was draining his lizard, I helped Milo get his kit together and got him to the car.

The kid crawled out from under the front stairs as I was loading Milo in. I didn't even know there was a place under the front stairs, and I'm sure the landlord didn't, either, or he would have rented it out to some down-on-his-luck mug who still had two dimes to rub together.

"What happened, someone rough up one of your spy buddies to get the goods on that Nip cocksucker?"

"Chinese," said Eddie, who was climbing in behind the wheel.

"I'm going to Cookie's Coffee, kid. You want I should bring you a donut?"

"Nah, I want a cookie."

"They don't have cookies, kid. I can bring you a donut."

"Why do they call it Cookie's if they don't have cookies? What is that place, some kind of prostitute?"

"A prostitute is a person, kid, not a place." I didn't want to give him any examples.

"No it ain't. You're a stinkin' liar."

"Fine, no donut." I climbed in the car and we were back at Cookie's Coffee in the Tenderloin in fifteen.

Doris was standing outside in her pink waitress outfit and Lone Jones stood beside her in his full doorman's tux and top hat, like the world's biggest ringmaster waiting for the circus to pick him up at the curb. Before Moo even got it stopped, Milo was out of the cab ouching and wincing his way into Doris's arms. She was cooing and smooching him all over his bruised face and he was wincing and cooing back at her. I was watching Lone Jones watch them, first with a big smile, then with sort of a forlorn, sad look. I got out of the cab.

"Hey, Lone."

"Hey, Sammy."

"You okay, buddy?"

"Yeah. I stayed all night to keep an eye on Doris. She was scared that Lars fella might come here."

"She couldn't have been safer, pal. We could have used your help, but I'm glad you were here. You need a ride home?"

"No, I been sittin' all night. I think I'll walk, blow the french fry smell oft me. Mama will be mad she thinks I ate another strange meatloaf."

"All right, pal. Thanks for looking out for Doris."

"You're welcome. I look out for my friends. See you tomorrow?"

"Day after. I got a day off and so does the Cheese. We'll probably do something."

"Day after, then. See ya." The big man turned and started up the street toward the Fillmore, the taps on his shoes clicking out a slow "Happy Trails" rhythm.

I turned to Doris and Milo. "You kids get in. Eddie's going to drive you to your new place. A place for just the two of you."

Their faces lit up. I added, "Well, it's new for you two. It's actually Doris's old place."

"But what about Lars?" Doris asked as she helped Milo into the back.

"You're never going to see Lars again," I said, jumping into the front.

"Probably," Moo Shoes said under his breath as he started the cab.

"Probably," I said.

"But he isn't dead," I added.

"Probably," Moo Shoes said. Fucking Moo Shoes.

Milo and Doris snuggled in the back, Doris crying a little bit, tears of joy and whatnot.

"You guys are the tits," said Milo.

"I'm going to need to borrow the cab tomorrow," said Eddie.

"Hold up, Eddie," I said when I remembered. "I gotta go in and buy a donut."

Lone Jones

Lone Jones was surprised there was a light on in the parlor when he let himself into their little house. It was after 7 A.M. and well light out and Mama didn't waste the electric. "Mama, why you—" She was there in her rocker by the radio, holding her pocketbook in her lap, wearing one of her good church hats and her good church suit and her second-best church shoes (not the Sunday ones, the Wednesday night ones). "Mama?" Lone didn't expect her to answer, she was as still as stone, but he said it again, "Mama," and he went to her and fell to his knees and put his arms around her, the chair and all, and pressed his cheek to the front of her good long church coat, and sobbed.

12

FOG CITY AL FRESCO

Sammy

When I walked into my place the Cheese was lying on my single bed, naked, reading a book.

"Whoa," I said, more than somewhat surprised and no little pleased.

"Hey, Toots, where you been?" she said. "And before you answer, did you bring breakfast? Because things will go easier on you if you did."

"I got some ideas," I said, shamelessly ogling her charms and bouncing my eyebrows in an appreciative manner.

"Oh, this?" she asked, gesturing to her aforementioned charms, from painted toes to the towel turban on her head. "This is not for you. Well, it is, but that's not why I am *al fresco* at the moment."

"Pretty sure that means *outdoors,* doll. I have lived in this Italian neighborhood lo these many last two years and I have picked up some things." Yeah, it was a dumb thing to say, but no one is more heavily burdened than a guy who thinks he knows a thing.

"It means *in the cold,* smart guy, and I have also lived in North Beach since the war, and the only thing of value you have picked up is me."

"Strictly speaking, I don't think Telegraph Hill is in North Beach."

She grabbed the blanket from behind her and whipped it over

herself, then looked at her book. "Excuse me, I have to find out if Jack London gets this fucking fire started."

"I have a jelly donut," I said, pulling the jelly donut I'd grabbed for the kid from my coat pocket in its little sheet of wax paper.

She whipped the blanket back off herself. "You are the most handsome man I have ever met. I must give you the razzmatazz immediately or I shall surely perish of desire." She did a little wrist to the forehead of distress, as sometimes is seen by ladies in films who are anguished upon the moors or have just had their plantations burned up.

So I went to the bed and made to join her *al fresco,* which I'm sure she would have helped me with, but she was eating a jelly donut, which she finished at the same time that my boxers hit the floor. There followed much merriment and a good time was had by one and all, and after, when we lay there, catching our breaths, me sitting up, leaning against the wall, and her leaning back against me, I lit two cigarettes and passed one to her and said, "So, if not that, what is the reason you are *al fresco* at this time?"

"Because when I got here I was covered with grit and sweat, so I took a shower and I didn't want to get back into my dirty clothes."

"When did you get here?"

"About an hour ago. I wanted to surprise you."

"Consider me surprised. Where were you, that you were covered with grit and sweat first thing in the morning?"

"Working on a project. Myrtle is helping me."

"What kind of project?"

"I can't tell you."

"Why not?"

"Because it's for your birthday."

"My birthday isn't until June. It's November."

"It's a big project."

"Aw, you don't have to do that."

"Okay, I won't. So where were *you* all night?"

So I told her about our adventure, about Uncle Ho, the Squid Kids, the nut-sack guys, about Jimmy Vasco hiring me to find the killer, shanghaiing Lars, dropping Milo and Doris off at their new love nest, bringing me right up to the time when I walked in the door to be blinded by the beauty of the light of my life.

"*Al fresco,*" she said.

"Yeah, I think that was implied," I said. "And by the way, I am very glad to see you, but how did you get in?" I really had meant to give her a key.

"The kid," she said. "It's okay, he's helping with my laundry."

"Your laundry? Where is your laundry?" It was not a very big apartment and I would have seen a new pile of clothes.

"In the laundry room."

"Which is in the basement."

"Yeah, the kid showed me. My stuff is hanging up down there, drying."

"So you came back from the laundry room *al fresco*?"

"Yep."

"You could have put on one of my shirts."

"The kid made it a condition of letting me in."

"Aw, Stilton, this kid is only like nine, or eleven, or—doesn't matter—you could go to jail for something like that."

"What? I didn't flash the kid, he asked. Kind of demanded. Kind of wouldn't let me in if I didn't promise. You know what, Sammy, I can run a sixteenth-inch bead with an arc welder so smooth you'd think a jeweler polished it, and cut perfect gingerbread men out of a half-inch steel plate with a cutting torch. I can work a block and tackle, tap and thread bolt holes, and shoot rivets like a sewing machine, but none of that was going to open the door. This did." Again with the flourish. *Voilà,* as the French say.

"I'll kill him," I said. I had a gun now, the snub-nosed .38 I'd taken off one of the gangsters. I wouldn't even have to choke the kid till he croaked.

"Try it, ya stinkin' Fresno," said the kid, from right outside the door. "That dame's too lumpy, anyway."

"Hey!" said the Cheese.

I got up, threw a blanket at Stilton, grabbed her towel turban off the floor, wrapped it around my hips, and sallied forth to murder the kid.

I threw the door open. "Kid," I said, "you can't treat a dame like that. You especially can't treat *that* particular dame like that. And Fresno is a city."

"No it ain't. I helped her out, didn't I? She was gonna wait for you, but I saw that mug was following her, so I let her in and I waited for him. And I took care of him, didn't I?"

"Wait, what mug?"

"What mug?" said the Cheese.

"That mug that was following you. Didn't even see it coming. I was up on the porch roof, so I had a good shot. Dirty Nazi took my arrow with him. You owe me six bits."

"Wait, you shot a guy?"

"Got him right in the heart." The kid popped himself high in the chest to show where he got the guy. "It didn't kill him. But it got rid of him. He got in his car and took off."

"Wait, you shot a guy, a real, grown-up guy? I thought Father Tony took all your arrows."

"I swiped 'em out of the rectum where he bunks."

"Rectory."

"No it ain't."

"What kind of car, kid, a black Chrysler?"

"I don't know what kind. Big, red, only not red like a fire truck, but like, red-brown."

"Maroon?"

"You're a maroon!"

"No, that's a color, kid. Kind of a brownish red."

"Oh. Yeah, sure, maroon."

"Big guy? Black suit? Sunglasses?"

"Nah, skinny guy. Mustache. A hat."

"Everybody wears a hat, kid."

"You wanna see where I shot him? There's blood on the side-walk."

The kid just turned and went down the stairs. I went after him, trying to keep the towel wrapped around me.

"Kid, wait!" But he was already through the downstairs door.

"Right here, next to where his car was parked," the kid said from the street. "Come look. Blood."

This jamoke found a parking place right in front? In the morning? I went to where the kid was pointing.

"I don't see any blood." I looked up. The kid was gone.

"You were supposed to bring me a cookie," the kid yelled. He was inside the lobby. I heard the front door close, then lock.

"Oh, goddammit!" I said, almost losing my towel.

Chinatown, 1906

"You heard her, we need to go to the water," said Niu Yun. She looked up at Ho from under the dead john's hat, squinting so hard she might have been in pain. Ho realized it had probably been months, maybe years, since she had been in sunlight. He knelt down so she did not have to look up.

"We will go to the water, but first we must fetch the Rain Dragon from the Ghee Sin hall."

"The Ghee Sin hall? Can't you see they are looking for us? Why would you go there?"

"Because the dragon has told me to. And it is on the way to the water."

He didn't wait for her response. He took her by the hand and led her across Stockton Street and back into the alley from which they had come. They were both breathless and sweating by the time he pulled up at the end of a very narrow passageway between two buildings across the street from the Ghee Sin guild hall, which from the outside looked like any other storefront on Dupont Street.

"*Go, Catfucker,*" the dragon said to him. "*I will protect you.*" Ho had grown up in a Confucian society, under the Emperor and his vast bureaucracy, where order and obedience were valued above all, so he was used to being told what to do and doing it. It was why the people of Chinatown submitted so readily to the extortion and terror of the tongs, and why Ho was taking orders from the strange voice in his head.

"I'm going in," Ho said. "Maybe they will not notice me. But they will notice a woman. You stay here."

"What if they do notice you?" said Niu.

"The dragon says he will protect me."

"Fine, then leave me the hatchet." She still had the hatchet, wrapped in newspaper, so it might have been a fish shaped like a hatchet. "And point the way to the water."

"The water is that way." Ho pointed. "But wait here."

"Give me your money, too. In case the dragon forgets to protect you and I need to bribe someone to take me across the bay."

Ho dug into his pocket and pulled out three dollars, which was all the money he had. He handed it to her. "Wait here. Sit down, let your hat cover your face, like you're drunk."

"How long?"

"Until I come back."

"What if you don't come back?"

"Eldridge," he said in his practiced English. He started across the street, got halfway, then came back. "Niu Yun, if they kill me, I am sorry."

"Go," she said. "Go, go, go." She waved him away with her newspaper hatchet.

Off he went, thinking that if someone stopped him he would try to fight very hard so they killed him on the spot. He did not want to serve as an example to the other Ghee Sin brothers of what happened to someone who was disloyal.

The front of the guild hall might have been a reception lobby for a law office or a surveyor, as it had a high counter behind which one or two of the brothers usually sat. There was only one there today, and he appeared to be asleep. Ho slipped past him, through a hallway that led upstairs, where the bosses met and lived, and then through double doors, which were open to the grand hall where he had been given his initiation. The tables were moved to the sides and it might have been an empty dance hall but for the dais and altar at the far end, where joss sticks smoldered on either side of the dragon. Another of the brethren lay on the floor by the double doors, a stool overturned beside him.

"I told you, Catfucker. Now fetch the dragon."

He made his way around the edge of the room to the dais and peeked behind the curtains to see nothing but bare wall. There were two doors, one on either side of the dais, and he looked from one to the other, as if his death might come through either at any second, until the voice came again.

"Move, Catfucker!"

He went to the dragon, as black and shining as a sliver of night, checked to make sure it wasn't secured to the lacquered platform on which it stood, then wrapped his arms around it and lifted. It was lighter than he expected. Still heavy, but nothing he wouldn't be able to carry in a proper knapsack. Perhaps twenty-five or thirty pounds. But he couldn't just walk into the street carrying it. He was looking around for something to cover it with when he heard the footsteps at the other end of the hall. Niu Yun stood over the sleeping brother, her hatchet in hand.

Ho shook his head and tucked the Rain Dragon under his arm so he could wave her off. As quickly and quietly as he could, he made his way back across the room, but she was already poking the downed brother with her hatchet.

"Is he dead?" she asked.

"No, he's sleeping. Come away."

"He's not moving. He looks dead."

"He's snoring."

"You don't know how tricky they can be. When they bought me, they told my father I would work for a year and be free."

"They told me three years."

"I'm going to chop his dick off."

"That will probably wake him up."

She pushed the brother hard with her hatchet. "Maybe not."

"See if he has any money."

Niu Yun rifled through the downed brother's pockets and came up with a fold of bills. She held them up and grinned. "He has a gun."

Ho hurried forward and crouched. "I'll take that." He didn't want to spend the rest of the day trying to keep her from *shooting* men's dicks off. He stuffed the revolver into his waistband and stood. "Let's go."

In the front Niu Yun took the money from the counter man, then held her hatchet high as she pushed him off his stool. He thumped to the floor but didn't wake up.

"Find something to cover the dragon," Ho said.

She searched under the counter and came out with a long red-and-gold silk tablecloth, probably for covering the counter during ceremonies. In a moment she had unfolded it, then doubled it twice and tied it, forming a loop of about an arm's length. She threw the loop over his head, making it a sash, and said, "Give me the dragon."

Ho hesitated. Would the dragon approve of being carried by a big-foot woman? "*Give it to her, idiot!*" said the voice in Ho's head. He gave it to her.

She tucked the dragon into the folds of the tablecloth, the sash, and slung it under his arm. With the wide band of silk distributing the weight, it was an easy carry. "How did you know to do that?"

"Peasant girl," she explained. "Let's go. To the water."

"To the water," Ho said. He followed her out the front door and into the street.

Sammy

No one likes to go into work on his day off. I mean, when I worked in the shipyard or the warehouse, I never showed up on my day off for a little recreational welding or forklift driving. But a bar or a restaurant is different. If you go in on your day off, the food is cheap or the liquor is free, and since Sal flew off to Douche Bag Valhalla on a burning DC-3, the saloon wasn't awful during the day if you didn't mind the gloom and pervasive despair. But you never know when you might get called to work because of an emergency. I'd manufactured a lot of emergencies in the last year. I was just lucky that Bennie had no life, so he had been able to cover for me. You don't want to volunteer you're available to work by being at work, because bars, like restaurants, are emergency factories. But there was something at Sal's that I needed, and I didn't know where else to get it: a moldy, wet-brained old homicide detective. So I untangled myself from a sleeping Cheese in the early afternoon and made my way down the street to Sal's to learn how to catch a killer.

I came in through the back door and beckoned Bennie from the far end of the bar. The stools were about half-full of day drunks and a couple of businessmen who had decided to drink a long lunch at a low-rent dive. Smoke hung over the bar like the specter of a dead dream.

"Hey, Sammy," Bennie said, lumbering up to me. "I thought you were off today. Mrs. Sal called and said she'd be in a little late." Mrs. Sal, the late owner's wife, who covered the bar on my nights and Bennie's days off, was called Maria, and that's what we called her to her face, but she was always "Mrs. Sal" when referred to between us.

"No, I'm off. Just taking care of something, Bennie." I spotted Fitz on a stool at the far end of the bar by the front door, where he'd been when I last saw him, at least until I knocked him off it. I kind of hid behind Bennie, which wasn't tough, because he had shoulders like an offensive tackle. "What's the skinny on Fitz? He still sored up about me knocking him off his stool?"

"Nah, doesn't remember any of it except I took him home and tucked him in. I told him he fell off his stool and hit his head."

"Good man." I patted him on the shoulder, went through the back pass-through, and came around the customer side of the bar to the empty stool beside Fitz. "Hey, stranger, how you been?"

"Sammy Tiffin. Hey, did I ever tell you that whoever took care of Pookie O'Hara did the world a favor?"

"Yeah, you mentioned it once, Fitz." The old man was looking around my face, the way a drunk will do when he's trying to recognize you but doesn't trust his own senses. Maybe Fitz was having memory mirages of the guy who smacked the shit out of him a few days ago. "Hey, I got a problem, and you're the only one I can think of can help me with it."

"Me? Kid, I got no money."

"No, not money. I need some of your street smarts." I decided to just spill it. "I need to figure out how to catch a killer."

Fitz opened his eyes all the way for the first time since I'd met him—like I had said his magic wake-up word. "What, you trying to cover your ass for Pookie O'Hara?"

"No, Fitz, I didn't scrag Pookie O'Hara. I'm talking about whoever iced the two dames from the drag king clubs."

"They think that's the same guy?"

"I have reason to believe it is."

"Not much about it in the paper. I didn't know the neighborhood. I wouldn't have even known they were dykes."

"Yeah, well, both were killed late at night, outside of the clubs where they worked. First one was a doorman, the second an entertainer."

"Not like the paper to let the lurid details go." Fitz was on full alert now. It was like twenty years had dropped off him. "Do you know who's running the case?"

"That's the thing: Dunne the Nun pulled the case off of homicide. And I know some people at the clubs who say they aren't investigating because Dunne doesn't think killing a couple of lesbians is worth looking at—that he thinks it's a way to close down the clubs without lifting a finger, so he's not lifting a finger."

"I hate that sanctimonious fuck. Not his job to judge the victim, it's his job to catch the killer."

"Which is why someone has hired me to do it."

"You got a PI license I don't know about, Sammy?"

"Nah, but I know people, and this guy thinks I'm the one to look into it."

"Look, kid, if they *had* arrested a suspect, and you *were* a PI working for the defense, you *might* have a chance putting a case together, they'd have to give you access to the investigation, but without a card and a client, you're shit out of luck."

"That's why I came to you. I need expert help."

"Are you blowing smoke up my ass, kid?"

"Is it working?"

Fitz laughed until he triggered a coughing fit. Bennie brought him some water. When the old man recovered, he said, "Kid, the first thing you do in a homicide investigation is secure the scene, which you can't do. Then you secure the evidence from the scene, which you can't do. Then you establish a pool of suspects and weigh the evidence against the suspects. Which I assume you don't have."

"I have none of those things. But let's say a guy wanted to get a bunch of suspects in the pool. Where would he get them?"

He shook his head like he was amazed by how much I didn't

know about crime investigation, but what he didn't know is I had only revealed the tip of the baby toe of the giant that was all the stuff I didn't know. I didn't want to dazzle him, being as he was ancient and fragile and a good dazzling would probably finish him off, so I said, "Well?"

"You have to talk to the victim's family, friends, lovers, enemies—especially their enemies—people where they work. You got to find motive. Find out if they owed anyone money, or if anyone owed them money."

"And what if I already know the motive?"

"What, you think that because both these dames were dykes you're done? They were dykes last month, too, weren't they? Why weren't they killed then? There's a hundred just like them in each of those clubs each night, right? Why these two? Find out what they have in common besides they liked the ladies. You don't even know if they were killed the same way, do you?"

"Nah. Butch, the victim from Jimmy's Joynt, got hit in the back of the head with a blunt instrument, as they say, but I don't know how the dame from Mona's got it."

"I heard ice pick," said Bennie. He was polishing glasses down the bar a ways.

"Ice pick where?" asked Fitz. "In the gut, in the eye, in the heart? And how many times? It can take a lot of pokes from an ice pick to kill someone."

"I heard one time, back of the neck," said Bennie.

"Confident," said Fitz.

"Where'd you hear that?" I asked Bennie.

"In here, some guys talking at the bar."

"What guys? Regulars?" I asked.

"Nah, never saw them before."

"They look like cops?"

"They didn't try to drink for free." Bennie shrugged like that told it all.

"They wouldn't if they were working," said Fitz.

I thought about it a second. "But if they were working and didn't want anyone to know it, why would they talk about a murder within earshot of Bennie?"

"Well, look at him," said Fitz. "Doesn't look like he could scrape together enough brains to butter a cracker. They probably just talked past him like there was a dog in the room."

"Christ on a crutch, Fitz, you have got to stop talking about people like that. Someone's going to stop your clock."

"Let 'em try." Fitz patted his jacket where his .38 hung in a shoulder holster. I tried to imagine an old geezer getting ready to leave the house every day to come to the bar for his breakfast. Doesn't shower or clean the soup off his shirt from last night's supper, but slings on a roscoe in a shoulder rig so he can talk ugly to random strangers.

Behind the bar the phone rang and Bennie picked it up and announced, "Sal's." Then he looked at me. "Just a second, I'll check." He covered the mouthpiece with his palm. "Sammy, you here? She says it's Della from the Moonlight Club."

I jumped up, ducked under the pass-through, and took the phone from Bennie. "This is Sammy," I said.

"Sammy, this is Della, the singer. We met the other night."

"Of course, Della, what can I do for you?"

"I'm at Thelonius's house. Sammy, his mama died this morning, maybe last night. We were rehearsing at the club when he called in sick. He's in a bad way and gonna need a friend. I got a gig to get to and I don't want to leave him on his own."

"I'll be there as soon as I can, Della. Half hour tops. Thank you." I hung up and announced to Bennie and Fitz that I had to go.

Fitz said, "I'll make some calls, Sammy. I still know some guys on the job—one that works down at the morgue."

"Thanks, Fitz. You know where to find me." I ducked under the pass-through, grabbed my coat and hat, and was in the wind.

13

ESCAPE

Songbird

Della didn't know why she went to Lone Jones's house when she heard about his mother, yet she called a halt to rehearsal on the spot and asked the trombone player to give her a ride to the Fillmore. When she arrived, the parlor was full of old Black church ladies clucking and sniffling into lace hankies and a pastor who was speaking softly to Lone, who sat on the sofa, holding his head in his hands, his knees up by his ears. The rug below his face was damp with tears.

"Reverend," Della said softly, and he looked up at her, not hiding his surprise that she was both young and dressed in street clothes, with brown wool slacks and a simple cotton blouse. "Excuse me, my name is Della Washington. I'm a friend of Mr. Jones and his mother. Thelonius and I work together at the Moonlight Club."

The pastor stood and took Della's hand in both of his. "Pleased to meet you, miss. I'm Pastor Cole."

Lone looked up slowly, surprise replacing sorrow on his face for a moment.

"Reverend," Della said, "I know you and the ladies are a comfort and strength to Thelonius, but I know the owner of the club, and he will fire Lone if he doesn't show up to work tonight, and I'll bet anything he hasn't slept." She put her hand on Lone's shoulder. "Have you slept, Lone?"

He shook his head.

The pastor puffed up a bit. "The man's mother just passed; they wouldn't dare fire him. Why, I—"

Della reached out and squeezed the reverend's hand. "He's the only Black man working in a club in all of North Beach, Reverend. They don't need an excuse to fire him. You understand."

"Yes I do, child. Yes I do," he said. He patted her hand.

"So you'll help me with the ladies?"

"Of course."

In five minutes each of the church ladies had delivered her condolences to Lone along with a promise to drop a little something by tomorrow.

"C'mon, Lone," Della said, nudging him. "You got to get to bed. I wasn't lyin' to the Rev. They will fire you."

"But Mama dead," Lone said. "I wasn't here for her and she just up and died. Was in that chair, like she was fixin' to go to church."

"You don't know that nothin' would be different you was here, Lone. Now get up and get your ass to bed. You don't gotta be at work until eight, but you *got* to be there then." She pulled him to his feet, or pulled at him until he decided to get to his feet. She pushed him, herded him really, out of the parlor and toward the back of the house, pushing on different parts of him to see if she could get one part to go and maybe the rest would follow.

"Where your room?" He nodded and drifted in that direction.

"Where you mama at?"

"She's down't the funeral home. The reverend had them come get her. I should be there with her."

"No, baby, she with Jesus now. You should be right here, sleeping. Now sit down." Lone sat down on the bed and she took off his shoes and his socks, then unbuttoned his shirt, took it from him and hung it on a hook by the door, then took off her own and hung it over his.

"But I don't—" Lone started to say, but she shushed him, a finger on his lips, and pushed him back on the bed. She took off his pants, then her own, then climbed on top of him, because there was no space left on the bed, and pulled the chenille bedspread up over both of them. She shushed him again, then kissed the trails of his tears.

Later, when she answered the door and let Sammy in, she held her finger to her lips to signal he stay quiet. "He's sleeping. He has to be at work at eight o'clock sharp tonight. You get him there. And make sure he shower and put on a clean shirt. That man smell like meatloaf."

"I will," Sammy said. "Thanks, Della."

She nodded, tucked in her blouse, and grabbed her purse off the hall tree where she'd put it when she came in. Sammy stood aside, watching her. She said, "Yeah, I know, I smell like meatloaf, too. Nobody like a smart-ass, Sammy."

"Just don't break his heart, okay?"

"His heart is as broken as it can get. I just wanted him to know all the love didn't leave the world with his mama. And now you here, you'll remind him again when you wake him up."

"I will," Sammy said.

"Don't you let him be late, Snowflake."

"I won't, Songbird."

She rolled her eyes at him and headed out the door.

Sammy

Grief was streaming off Lone like stink off a cigar, but I got him to work, doing his job, even if he moved in a daze, pure habit and muscle memory. I saw it during the war, with widows who lost their guy, like some kind of ghost took them over, took care of the details of their lives, their kids, their jobs, got them through the pain with a functioning numbness. I saw it with my mother when my brothers, Judges and Second Samuel (long story), were killed, except she crawled into a gin bottle for comfort, and as far I know, never came out. I left after my foot healed enough to find out the service wouldn't take me.

Della promised she'd get Lone home after work and I trusted her. Strange dame. You ask me yesterday, I'd say she wouldn't have given Lone the time of day; today she steps up for him like a champ. The Moonlight Club was only a block and a half up Broadway from Mona's 440, so after I got Lone installed at the door, it was time for me to start my career as a homicide detective.

There were two gorillas in a Dodge parked in front of Mona's in a no-parking zone. As if their bored mugs and rumpled suits weren't enough to give them away as cops, squatting in the no-parking zone with impunity cinched it. From no more than a glance I could tell these were the cops who had been staking out the counter at Cookie's the other night, but they clearly were not recognizing me.

I strolled up to the door and tipped my hat to the two broads working there, neither one of them as butch and brawny as the ones at Jimmy's Joynt, one even wearing a skirt, but the door at Mona's wasn't down a hall from the club like it was at Jimmy's, so anyone pushing through would be met with a crowded room. I was surprised there was anyone on the door at all at eight thirty on a weeknight.

"Good evening, ladies," I ventured with a tip of the hat, flashing a smile that had been compared to a sunny day in the park. (Only by the Cheese, but it had.)

"Beat it, tough guy," said the skirt, who obviously did not care for sunny days in the park. "We're not playing to the tourist trade tonight."

Which was weird, because down the street at Finocchio's, the male drag joint, they depended on the business of couples and tourists coming in to gawk. I wondered if Dunne was busting the drag queens' chops with everyone else's.

So I dropped the only name I had. "I'm here to see Babe."

"Babe?" said the dame in slacks. "Never heard of him."

"Well, you wouldn't have, would you. But if you meet someone called Babe Bowman, tell her I dropped by with a tip on Frankie's murder. Condolences, by the way." I took off my hat and put it over my heart, out of respect for the dead.

"The cops already been here. They're still here," said the skirt.

"Fine. I'll just be on my way," and I was, replacing my lid, doing a dancer's pirouette (on my good foot), then soft-shoeing away like there was a drummer on a sizzling brush snare playing me off.

"Wait," said Skirt. "What's your name?" She signaled for Slacks to go ask someone inside.

"Sammy Tiffin," I told her.

"Well, you ain't a cop or you'd have badged your way in, so what's your line?"

"Private," I said.

She nodded to Slacks, who disappeared for a second and was back before I could light a smoke. Skirt stepped aside and waved me past. "Babe's at the far end of the bar."

The interior of Mona's was like any small club if you went in during the day: badly lit, sparsely populated, and smelling like sour booze and cigarettes. Except Mona's wasn't closed. The place was a ghost town, two couples at tables at opposite corners of the room, a dark stage with a vacant runway, and one sizable dame sitting at the opposite end of the bar. The bartender was the only one who looked like she'd come to play, a tall forty-something dame in full black-and-whites, a vest, garters on her sleeves, and hair pinned up and back so she might have been smuggling a blackjack or a turd at the back of her head. Somewhere over in a dark corner by the stage someone was tinkling out a helpless version of "Stardust." I nodded good evening to her as I went by and walked up to the broad at the end of the bar, who was looking over a calendar gridded out as a work schedule. She was maybe fifty; hair dyed black, short and combed into a pompadour; a body built for moving furniture. I tried to imagine her with Jimmy Vasco and blew a fuse. I'd try not to think about it later.

"You Babe Bowman?"

"The one and only. Josie tells me you know something about Frankie's murder. Spill it."

"I have a few questions first."

"You're a private dick, right?"

"That's right."

"Can I see your license?"

"It's in my other jacket."

"That work for you? Ever? Because I've been in the liquor business as long as you've been alive, kid, and it's never worked for anyone in one of my joints."

She had a point. Every kid I ever asked for ID said they left it in their other jacket, or pants, and when I sent them to get it, never came back.

"I'm not licensed. An interested party has hired me to look into Frankie's murder."

"Who?"

"I can't tell you. Let's say it's a family member."

"Frankie didn't have family. None that gave a rat's ass about her, or would have anything to do with her, anyway. There's a lot of that in our tribe."

"I've heard that. I'm sorry about Frankie. I hear she was a swell dame."

Babe shrugged. "What do you know about her killer?"

"You first?"

"Fine, one question."

"Do you know anyone who would have a reason to hurt Frankie? Bitter girlfriend, someone she upstaged in the show, anyone?"

"Nah, like you said, Frankie was a swell gal. Got along with everybody here. The other performers loved her. She'd step in for whatever they needed, sing harmonies, dance partner, a good sport. Paid her bills, didn't gamble, that I know of."

I started to ask another question but Babe stopped me, finger in the air, and said, "Nope, your turn. But I'll give you this: the cops never asked as much."

"Really? Do they not let flatfoots go to the pictures? That's the first thing you ask."

"Yeah, you don't ask if you don't want to know. They're not interested in catching Frankie's killer. Just shutting us down."

"I saw the pair of plainclothes holding down that Dodge out front."

"Yeah, they're about as inconspicuous as a tire fire. The Nun says he stationed them there to keep us safe, but they're just here to keep our customers out. The kind of gals who patronize a place like this aren't always excited to share their, uh, preferences." She tapped the schedule with the eraser of her pencil. "I'm just trying to figure out how I'll keep my staff in beans and weenies until that heat comes off."

"Maybe if I can find the killer it all gets better."

"It's still your turn. You got in the door saying you knew something."

"I know that whoever killed her might be looking to put a hurt on the club owners."

Babe stopped looking at her schedule and gave me a squinty eye. It would have been more effective if she'd been looking up from under the brim of a hat, or if she'd had a cigarette in her pie-hole and the smoke were streaming in her eye, but she didn't have either of those things, so she just sort of looked like one of those sour-faced little kids in the W. C. Fields movies. "Well, your killer is going to have a hell of a time finding the owners of this joint. They're a white-haired couple that lives up in the hills in the East

Bay, and neither one of them has set foot in the place in years. Who are you working for? It's that little shit-box Jimmy Vasco, isn't it?" Babe got up off her stool. She was bigger than she appeared when sitting down and not angry. "Get the fuck out of my place," she said.

I backed away, holding my hands up. "Hey, Babe, look, we want the same thing. Jimmy wants the same thing. She lost someone, too."

"You think I didn't know Butch? Oh, I knew Butch. Butch was how I found out Jimmy was a lying little tramp."

Well, that was new information. I felt like this investigation was going great, and if I stayed away from her, I could probably get a couple of good shots in on Babe before she knocked me out. "Fine then," I said. "But if you remember anything about that night Frankie was killed, give me a call. I'll leave my card at the door." I was going to need to get some cards made.

"Get out, and tell that little shit Jimmy Vasco I hope she's next!"

I backed out the door, said my adieus to Skirt and Slacks, scampered across the sidewalk to the Dodge parked there, and jumped into the back. "What's the buzz, fuzz?" I said, as cheerful as a sack of parakeets.

Young Ho

"You are a shit gangster," said Niu Yun.

Young Ho showed the fisherman his gun and told him he needed to take them across the bay to the north.

"No," said the fisherman. He spoke Cantonese, although a different dialect than Ho, but "no" was pretty clear.

"I don't think he understands me," said Ho.

"He sees you have a gun," said the girl. "I think he understands."

Niu Yun took the newspaper wrap from her hatchet, because surely it was her hatchet now. "Well, I suppose I will have to chop his dick off."

Ho shrugged at the fisherman. "I am sorry, my friend, but all day she has had her mind set on chopping off someone's dick and I no longer think I can talk her out of it."

"You will have to kill me before I will let you do that," said the fisherman, who scrambled to the far end of his boat.

Niu Yun looked at Ho. Ho looked at Niu Yun. Niu Yun shrugged. "It might take a few whacks. I was lucky that first time."

"First time?" asked the fisherman.

"When she killed the white devil with her hatchet earlier today," Ho said.

"I will take you," said the fisherman. "But I will only do the sailing. You must do the rowing out and into dock."

Ho nodded. He held the girl's hatchet while she climbed into the boat, then handed it back to her, shoved the boat out, and jumped in.

"Now row out," said the fisherman. "I can't put the sail up here."

Ho made a great show of picking up the oars and moving them around and nearly conking Niu Yun and the fisherman each on the head, and came quite close to tumbling into the bay. Niu Yun pushed him down on one of the three seats. She fit the oars into the oarlocks and began rowing.

"Which way?" she asked the fisherman.

"Out," he said, pointing away from the shore.

I know "out," she thought. *There are more directions than just "out." I have not been in a cage so long that I don't know a fisherman who needs his dick chopped off when I see one.*

When the boat was well clear of the shore, the fisherman shooed Niu Yun to the front of the boat with Ho and shipped the oars.

"Did your father not teach you how to row?" Niu Yun asked Ho.

"I am from a landlocked village. There was no need to row."

"I, too, am from a landlocked village, but I know how to row."

"Perhaps you were not regarded by your family with the disdain of a second son."

"They sold me into sex slavery."

"You rowed very well," said Ho.

Ho threw up three times before the fisherman had sailed two of the four miles to Sausalito, and Niu Yun joined him the second time, even though she had no food in her stomach to spew.

"We are going against the wind. Tacking," said the fisherman. "It will take a long time and be rough. But coming back will be fast."

"*The great and wise Rain Dragon will help you, Catfucker,*" said the voice in Ho's head. It was loud now with the dragon in the sling around his neck.

Ho didn't want the fisherman to think he was mad, so rather than tell the dragon to be quiet, he slapped it through the silk, then waved his hand as if it had been burned, because he had just slapped a stone statue.

Then it began to rain—a torrent of rain. The wind came up from behind Big Town, and they were driven before it, the sailboat bucking in the waves and the fisherman doing all he could to keep the boat right in the squall.

"It will go fast now," said Niu Yun.

"The Rain Dragon is helping us," said Ho.

"Bail!" shouted the fisherman.

Indeed, the water in the boat was over their ankles and rising, causing the boat to pitch even more in the waves. The fisherman pulled a canvas bucket from under his seat and threw it to Niu Yun. She bailed out one side of the boat with the bucket and Ho did his best on the other side with the fisherman's hat. When the fisherman dropped the sail he shouted, "Row! You row!"

They fitted the oars into the locks and each took an oar, rowing at the direction of the fisherman, who was squinting into the rain. Ho looked behind them as he rowed, and when lightning flashed he saw something massive, coiling and rolling in the water behind them, larger than the island they had passed that the fisherman called *Alcatraz*. He lost his grip on the oar and nearly went over backward in the boat, but Niu Yun caught him and pushed him back up. When lightning flashed again, the dragon was gone. At the dock Ho climbed out, the Rain Dragon in the sash dragging against the dock and nearly pulling him back, but he found his feet and Niu Yun threw him a line. Ho lashed the boat to the pier, then pulled Niu Yun and the fisherman up onto the dock, where they all fell, breathless and shivering.

"Did you see it?" Ho asked Niu Yun.

"What? I can see nothing in this," she replied.

"*I see you as you actually are, too, Catfucker,*" the dragon said in his head.

14

TATER
AND
TOOTS

Sammy

"Who the fuck are you and what the fuck are you doing in our car?" asked the passenger-side cop. He had a nose like a potato and the back of his neck, below his hat, looked like he was smuggling sausages in a pouch back there.

"I was just going to ask you the same thing," I said. "But it turns out I don't care."

"Look, buddy," said the driver, whose features were as sharp and lean as Potato Nose's were round and doughy. I made Sharp Face to stand north of six-four, the way his hat brushed the roof of the Dodge. "I'm going to give you to three to get out of this car and we'll write it off as a drunken mistake."

"Wait," said Potato Nose. "I saw this guy go into Mona's fifteen minutes ago. What were you doing in there, kid? Tourist? Thought you'd get an eyeful of some lady-lovers?"

"Yeah, something like that. And maybe catch a killer, since you mugs are just sitting out here on your duffs holding your dongs."

"That's it, buddy," said Potato. I was starting to think of him as Tater. "Let's see some ID. You don't like the way we do our job, well, we just got us a suspect. You know that, right, kid? Half the time the guy who shows up at the scene asking questions is the killer, right?"

"Let me make a note," I said. *I should really get a notebook,* I thought. And I don't mind that he called me kid, despite probably not being ten years older than me. Guy calls you kid it means you might go to him sometime for guidance, or a loan.

"ID," said Tater.

"I am Thrushcross Grange Heathcliff, of the Boise Heathcliffs," I said, without even a hint of an English accent, because I was trying to sell it. And I *am* from Boise, so would be credible if they asked any geography questions. Also, it seemed very unlikely that either one of these shit stacks had ever read *Wuthering Heights.* "And I left my ID in my other jacket."

"Get out of the car, pal," said Tater. "So I can cuff you and put you back in the car to take you downtown."

"Or just get out of the fucking car," said the far more reasonable Sharp Face.

"I got a clue on this murder. I'll show you mine if you show me yours."

"Fine, buddy, spill it," said Tater.

"What am I, some kind of sap? You're not going to show me yours."

"But we might not take you downtown and put you in the tank with a bunch of drunks who will puke on you," said Sharp Face.

I had spent several nights in the drunk tank during the war. It was a credible threat. "Fine, I think I know who the killer is going after next."

"And how would you know that?" asked Sharp Face.

"A little bird told me."

"A little dyke bird called Jimmy Vasco?" said Tater, and he laughed in that way that a guy laughs right before he sucker-punches you.

"Yep, you got me," I said. "Well, I'll be off." And with that I jumped out of the Dodge and scampered down Broadway, ducked between Mona's and the next building, and ran like a scared bunny up some stairs to Vallejo Street, where I waited. And nothing.

They weren't coming after me, and even if they did, there was no way Tater would make it up the stairs without having a heart attack. I needed to get to Jimmy's Joynt quick, and I didn't relish hoofing it all the way out to the Embarcadero, so I headed down Vallejo back to Grant Avenue and three blocks later I was stepping up the red carpet of Club Shanghai, where Moo Shoes was holding up the host's stand when I arrived.

"What's stinkin', Lincoln?" said Moo, by way of a greeting.

"Moo, I need the keys to the cab. It's here, right?"

"Found a parking spot over on Kearny. I'm never moving it."

"Moo," I said, giving him the business look.

"Put some gas in it," Moo said, fishing the keys out of his pocket.

"I will, but I only got two bucks. That's why I didn't take a cab."

"Why, why, why," said Moo to the ceiling. "Why are we poor? Are we not bright?"

"We are as bright as stars," I said.

"Are we not talented?"

"Goddammit, Moo."

"Fine." Moo dug into his pocket and came out with a five-spot. "Here, put some gas in it. Lois and I have a driving lesson tonight after hours."

"Already? Wow, you two *are* bright and talented," I said as I backed away.

"Sammy, before you go . . ."

I paused. Moo Shoes suddenly seemed very serious for a guy who a minute ago was lamenting being talented but poor to a god unknown.

"We have to go to Locke. One of the nut-sack guys, Mr. Chen, called here earlier." Eddie looked around, made sure no one was in earshot. It was early yet; the place was slow. Probably most of Moo's helpers were still setting up. "Squid Kid knows something happened at Snake and Noodle last night. He doesn't know what, but he knows he sent two guys to find Uncle Ho, and now his guys are gone and so is Uncle Ho. He's going to start leaning on people."

"What good is going to Locke going to do?"

"Uncle Ho thinks that the only way he isn't blamed is if he brings Squid Kid his dragon."

"Until Squid Kid's guys reach Malaysia and get to a phone or a Western Union office."

"Let's cross that bridge when it's a bridge," said Moo Shoes.

"When? Locke? When?"

"Tomorrow?"

"I have to work tomorrow, and solve a murder, and you have to sleep, or did you forget you're giving a driving lesson tonight?"

"Yeah, but this one shouldn't take as long because we won't be shanghaiing anyone. Can't you get Bennie to cover your shift? Or Mrs. Sal?"

"Moo, I need the money. I only have two bucks. And this was supposed to be date night with the Cheese."

"I'll have some money. There's money in Locke if we find Uncle Ho's dragon."

He had me there. "I'll see what I can do. I'll try to get the cab back to you by midnight."

◇◇◇◇◇◇

An hour later, when I got to Jimmy's Joynt, there was a surprising amount of available parking on Pier 29 out behind the club. (It took an hour because I picked up a couple of fares, who, if I may say, were very cranky indeed about a guy who mostly walks the city not knowing which streets are one-way. I was beginning to understand Milo's distaste for driving a cab.) Anyway, Jimmy's parking lot looked like a ghost town, with maybe five cars in all, one of them being Jimmy's own pearl-black Ford coupe, and two that gave me the willies as soon as I saw them: a black Chrysler New Yorker, such as the G-men who tried to ice me and the Cheese had driven, and a big maroon Packard with all the trimmings, parked near it. What I didn't see were any cops staking the place out. I parked close to the door and sat watching the two land yachts for a minute behind the reflections on the cab's windshield. There was someone sitting in the Chrysler, just a silhouette, but I couldn't see who it was or if they had the look. Had the feds found us? I didn't have the .38 we'd taken off the Squid Kid's guy with me, but the empty scattergun was still under the seat. I didn't want to go toe-to-toe with a couple of feds on a bluff, and I figured I'd used up my direct-approach luck by jumping in the Dodge with the two SFPD undercovers. For once, I figured I'd play it cool and just go about my business like I wasn't being watched. Maybe Jimmy would have a line on the feds and know who was driving the maroon Packard. Could be a coincidence, right? And if it was the guy the kid had seen this morning, the arrow sticking out of his chest would give him away.

I pulled my hat down to cover my face and got three steps out of the car before I heard a wolf whistle from the direction of the Chrysler and a dame's voice saying, "Hey, Toots, why don't you shake that moneymaker over here!"

I turned. I looked. I saw the Cheese hanging out the window, surprised hair tied up with a bandana, coveralls, and a lipstick grin that would dazzle a dead man. I had never been so glad to be mad in my life.

"Don't call me Toots," I said, walking out to the Chrysler.

"C'mere, you, you know I love smoochin' you when you're sad."

"I'm not sad."

"Well, you haven't talked to me yet, have you?"

"I'm sorry I broke our date night to go find the killer."

"Ah, you'll make it up to me. I got something to do anyway. I'm here to pick up Myrt."

"It's ten o'clock at night. You're not going out on the town like that?"

"Nah, we're Wendy the Welders tonight." She put her arm out the window, pulled her coverall sleeve up, and flexed her biceps. "Wanna feel my muscle?"

"Always."

As I got closer to the car I could see she was sitting in sort of a frog position, not like you'd normally sit in a car. Nevertheless, I smooched her mercilessly and then handed her my handkerchief to wipe the smeared lipstick off us.

"So," I said, lighting a smoke, sharing it. It was that good a kiss. I said, "So, the car?"

"Yeah, nice, huh?"

"Looks a lot like the Chryslers those G-men drove."

"Looks *just* like those, huh?"

"And I can't help but notice that the pedals have extensions on them and you are sitting with your knees up by your ears."

"I thought you liked that."

"Not when you're driving, doll."

"Well, the welding work on the pedals is first-rate, I can tell you that. Jump in. I'll show you by dome light."

"This is the car you fixed up for the moonman," I said. She'd done it on her own. We'd inherited the car from a couple of G-men who were trying to kill us in a motel outside of Petaluma when the moonman vaporized them. Yeah, moonman. Also, Pookie O'Hara's stiff was in the trunk at the time, having been previously ventilated by the G-men, I presume. But the moonman also vaporized that. Him. The stiff. So we brought the Chrysler to the city and the Cheese borrowed the arc welder from Bert's Garage on Hyde, welded some extensions on the pedals so the moonman could drive, then off he went, rolling into the sunset. We hadn't seen him for five months.

"Yeah. It just showed up parked on Telegraph Hill, down from my place. Keys in it. It's like Scooter brought it back as a thank-you gift."

"But you haven't seen him?" I don't know why I was less worried about the moonman than I had been about the feds. Maybe because it felt like he had been on our side. Also, he was only three feet tall.

"Nope. But I kept the Chrysler on the down low because I didn't want to give away your birthday surprise."

"I guess that's good. But you shouldn't be sitting out here alone in the parking lot. There's a killer on the loose."

"It's okay, I brought your gun." She held up the snub-nosed .38 and sort of waved it around like she was gonna blast a circling mosquito.

"Hey, be careful with that thing. You know what you're doing with it, right?"

"Sure, my pop taught me how to shoot his old Webley revolver he brought back from England after the Great War. But I won't have to use it. You're gonna catch the killer and take me off to Monterey for a romantic weekend with your killer-catching money."

"That's the thing, doll: I'm not doing so well on the killer catching. I went by Mona's 440 to interview some suspects and witnesses and whatnot, and no one there will talk to me. I had trouble even getting in the door. That old cop, Fitz, says if I don't have a suspect pool I won't find the killer."

"Heck, I can interview your witnesses and suspects," she said. "Lesbians love me. My best friend is a lesbian. Here she is now."

I turned to see Myrtle, also in coveralls, coming out the back door of Jimmy's Joynt. Strictly speaking, Jimmy's doesn't have a front door, but the entrance and the exit through the back hall are on the same side. She was coming out the exit that didn't have two tough-looking dames guarding it.

"Hey, Myrt," I said.

"Hey, Sammy. Oh no, look at this car I stole and loaned to Tilly without her knowledge."

"I told him," said Stilton.

"Oh," said Myrtle. "Sorry, Sammy. I did not steal this car."

"She was afraid she'd given away your birthday surprise we're working on," said Stilton.

"Yeah, happy birthday, Sammy," Myrtle said, climbing into the Chrysler.

"It's in June," I said.

"Yeah, I meant happy early birthday. Well, we better get going."

Stilton fired up the Chrysler. "I won't be out late. Work in the morning."

"Come by my place when you're done, doll. No matter what time. I'll leave the door unlocked." I really needed to get a key made for her.

"You got it, Toots," Stilton said.

"And sorry about date night."

"I'm fine, you just gave me the razzmatazz in the middle of the morning like the landlord, right? Bye." And she pulled away.

"Wait, what?" I said, but she was already driving the black dreadnought down the pier like a giant frog pilot with surprised hair.

I pinched the bridge of my nose to squeeze back a headache I felt coming on, then headed inside. I stopped to chat up the door dames and asked the one with the Stetson Stratoliner if she'd seen who drove the maroon Packard.

"Oh yeah," said the door dame. "Thin brunette with a bob. Can't miss her. Pulled up a couple of minutes before you."

"Thanks." I tipped my hat because it was all I had to tip and eased into the club.

So it wasn't the guy the kid shot with an arrow. There was a chance, I figured, that there might be more than one big maroon car to be found in Fog City.

The place wasn't as dead as Mona's had been, but nearly so. There was maybe a half-dozen couples, some of whom I recognized— probably local dames down from the bay side of Telegraph Hill. Jimmy was on her perch at the bar, paying close attention to a thin dame in a gray herringbone suit, cut closer than any guy would wear, and not a wool herringbone, but rather silk or something shiny, and no camisole or blouse underneath, just a stripe of bare skin to her navel, like the first time I saw her, the night Butch was killed. Her eye shadow was as black as a silent film star's.

"Hey, Sammy," Jimmy said. "Meet my new friend—" She paused to let the thin girl fill in. I guess they were *really* new friends.

"Nora," said Nora. "Charmed, I'm sure."

She wasn't. She offered me her fingertips to shake like she'd found me in a rat trap and was prodding me to see if I was still alive.

"Sammy," I said. "Sammy Tiffin."

"Sammy works for me," Jimmy said.

"I do? Oh, right. Anyway, nice to meet you, Nora. You're just the person I was hoping to run into."

"Oh yeah, and here I thought we just met."

"Yeah, I saw you in here the night Butch was killed. You were the last one in and the first one out after the raid. I just wondered if you saw anything."

"Anything like what?"

"Like was Butch at the door when you came in?"

"Yeah, she offered to take my coat."

"You were only wearing a coat, right?"

"Yeah, go figure."

"And she was gone when you left."

"Yeah. Shame. I missed saying good-bye."

I thought of the Argentine backbreaker she'd put on Mel the bartender on her way out. Butch probably wouldn't have minded that kind of good-bye.

"Nothing else? Nobody else?"

"You mean other than a shitload of cops? Nope."

"And that's your Packard parked outside."

"Yeah. You need a ride? I can have the bartender call you a cab."

"No, I'm covered, thanks."

Nora snagged the cigarette, holder and all, out of Jimmy Vasco's mouth and took a deep drag off it, then put it back where she'd found it as she blew smoke out at me. "I gotta go, Jimmy. I'll be seeing you."

I expected her to lay a smooch on Jimmy like she had Mel, but she just sort of faked a soft punch to Jimmy's chin and slinked away.

"Bye," Jimmy said weakly. I'd never seen her nonplussed before. Nervous, frightened even, but never stunned. After the girl was out of sight, Jimmy came awake and noticed I was there to ruin her evening. "So why are you here, other than to ruin my evening?"

"Doing what you hired me to do. What's the story on Nora?"

"Just met her, like you. She wasn't here ten minutes."

"Yeah, she seemed to have a different effect on you than she did me."

"Kid that age's got no business having that much self-confidence."

"She's got more going on than she lets on. For one thing, money. She's driving a new Packard, and I don't even know what that suit she was wearing was made out of, but I can tell you it was made *for* her."

"Yeah, I noticed. She was wearing a tennis bracelet you could cut glass with. No dame ever bought *herself* a diamond tennis bracelet, I don't care how much cabbage she's shredding. I was going to try to find out what went on between her and Dunne that night he called off the raid, but you came in to charm her and she ran like a cat on fire."

"Yeah, sorry. But I need to know who you told about the notes from the killer."

"Besides you guys from Cookie's, the Cheese, and Myrt, no one else."

"The cops?"

"Of course the fucking cops. It's a murder."

"Uh-huh, well, I just talked to two vice cops, and from the way they acted, the whole vice squad thinks it's a big joke."

Jimmy shrugged. "We know they're dragging their feet on the case. Maybe they know a lot more than we do. Maybe they know who did it and they're covering for them. Or they just don't care."

"They don't. That's the only thing I found out at Mona's. The cops didn't even ask about Frankie's personal life, anyone who had it in for her. Nothing. I'll work on finding out more on that end. And I have a guy looking into the physical evidence. I'll talk to him tomorrow."

"So, did you meet Babe?"

"She sends her regards."

"Yeah, fuck her, too."

"I need a couple of things. I need some money for expenses, and I need to know about Butch's personal life. You know, anyone had a beef with her, jilted girlfriend, I don't know, you tell me."

Jimmy pulled out a roll of bills that would clog a toilet, peeled off five twenties, and held them out. "That do it?"

"For now, yeah."

Jimmy pocketed the roll. "Butch didn't really have girlfriends so much as she had one- or two-night stands. A lot of them."

"So Butch was a slut."

"See, Sammy, men are like dogs. They will hump anything or anyone that lets them."

"And women are like, what, swans?"

"Swans? What? Yuck. No? Women are also like dogs, but they're like female dogs; they know sex has consequences. They think a little bit more about it before jumping in."

"So Butch was a dog?"

"No, she was a slut. I just wasn't comfortable with *you* saying it. But as far as I know, Butch always left things friendly. I mean, sometimes a one-night stand would loop around for an encore performance and you don't want to close that curtain."

"What about you? You have a history with Butch?"

"Why would you ask that?"

"Because you, too, are a slut?"

"I will shoot your fucking eye out, fuckstick."

"So not a slut?"

"Oh no, I'm a slut, although I have reformed my ways. I just wasn't comfortable with you saying it. No, Butch and I never even had a one-night stand. Not my type. But I don't think one of Butch's exes would want to hurt her. Why you busting my balls?"

"Nothing, something one of the cops said. And Butch didn't know Frankie?"

"Not that I know of, but I'll ask around. See if they have anyone in common."

"Thanks. And thanks for the doubloons. I'll call you when I find out more."

"Or just come back."

"I might. I might need to borrow your car."

"You know where it is."

"Watch your ass, Jimmy."

She patted her jacket pocket, which was heavy with her Walther. "Always do, doll."

I touched the brim of my hat, grinned, turned, and walked out wondering why it seemed like every woman I knew was lying to me.

And why they were so bad at it.

And why were they all packing heat?

Well, that, I actually knew why.

But why did it bother me that dames were calling me *Toots* and *doll*?

15

LAWYERS, MUGS, AND MONEY

Sammy

I checked in with Lone Jones, who might have been one of those mechanical characters on one of those goofy German clocks for all the light in his eyes, but he said he was okay and Della said she'd see that he got home. I slipped Della ten from my expense money to buy him a meatloaf at Cookie's, which, if I was a true pal, I would have done myself, but then again, a true pal is not going to get between a guy and a delectable doll who is trying to help him, so I bid my adieus and told Lone to call me if he needed anything.

I dropped the key to the cab off to Moo Shoes at Club Shanghai and pocketed a handful of the fortune cookies they keep in a silver bowl on the bar in the lounge for laughs. Club Shanghai got through the Great Depression and the war selling Chinese cheese, and they were leaving no cheese unchurned.

"Locke, tomorrow," said Moo Shoes. "Get your shift covered."

"I'll see what I can do. Maybe take your driving lesson to another neighborhood tonight. That cop might have an eye out for you."

"Already the plan, Sam. We are touring the boppin' burg of Colma tonight."

"City of stiffs?" Colma is where San Francisco moved all of her dead back at the turn of the century because they were stinking up the joint and driving down property values and where we're still sending them today.

"Should be quiet and flatfoot-free."

"You are an ace businessman, Eddie. Ding my ling at Sal's tomorrow. I'll be there during the day. I got to see a guy. Hey, I was thinking, anyone know you're Uncle Ho's nephew?"

"Nah, not that I know of. The beauty of the family disowning him *and* me, you don't exactly brag about your opium-selling, cat-fucking great-uncle. Why?"

"Tommy 'Squid Kid' Fang," I said. "Stay cool, fool."

I was beat, so I decided to squander some of my expense money to grab a cab home. While I was waiting for one to show, I cracked one of my fortune cookies.

The Dragon's demand shall be your destiny, it said, which I immediately took to mean I had picked up a defective cookie, so I threw the shards in the gutter and cracked a second one.

You waste cookie, white devil, Dragon will bite you in the ass.

I threw that one down like it was on fire. I needed sleep. I waved at the next passing cab like I was drowning and the cabbie must have sensed my desperation because he pulled a U-turn and rescued me. I was home in five. I didn't see the big Chrysler when we pulled up, so the Cheese wasn't back yet. I had a few questions. Not murder investigation questions, but questions about how you explain a government Chrysler showing up out of nowhere and what's with all the sudden welding. I mean, I was a welder in the shipyards during the war, too, but I don't yearn to return to it.

I left the front door to the lobby unlocked when I came in. The kid was curled up like a dead bug in front of my door. It wasn't particularly cold out, and I didn't want the Cheese to trip over him on the way in, so I picked the kid up by the back of his overalls, carried him down the stairs, and set him in front of his ma's door. I put my last two cursed fortune cookies on the floor in front of him because breakfast is the most important meal of the day, my ma used to tell me.

I stripped off my duds and did a free fall into the sack for a nap that lasted until sometime later, when the Cheese woke me up with a kiss on my eyebrow. She was naked and smelled of soap and toothpaste and was crowding her way onto the single bed.

"Move over, ya lug."

"What time is it?" I mumbled.

"Not that late. Go back to sleep."

"We gotta get a bigger bed. A bigger place. For both of us."

"Don't worry about it, Toots, I ain't going anywhere."

"But the landlord crack."

"I was yanking your chain. I do the dishes in my underwear a couple of times a month with the curtains open and he accidentally forgets to collect half the rent. It's a bargain. Go back to sleep."

"Okay," I said. I was wide awake and she was snoring on my shoulder.

◇◇◇◇◇◇

At eight in the morning, with only one drink in him, Fitz, the old murder cop, was as sharp and springy as a fresh Gillette blade. I was not. I asked Bennie to put on a pot of coffee.

Fitz flipped open a reporter's notebook. "The coroner gave me the skinny. Walked in on him boning a corpse once and didn't say anything, so he owes me. So here's what I found. The first broad, Natalie Melanoff, drowned, probably knocked out and dragged to the edge of the pier. Salt water in the lungs. She had blunt-force trauma to the back of the head. The wound was square, and it fractured her skull in a way that makes it look like it was a brick. Would have knocked her out for sure, though. It's not like Dunne was going to send divers down under Pier 29 looking for a brick. But thing is, you don't plan to kill someone with a brick. That's a weapon of opportunity. No defensive wounds, no bruises, nothing. She never saw it coming.

"The second one, Francine Fortuna, got an ice pick up through the first vertebra to the brain. Probably dead while she was standing. No murder weapon found, so the killer took it with them. Again, no defensive wounds. It's possible whoever did it just found an ice pick somewhere, but let's face it, an ice pick isn't a found weapon. And you gotta aim it to turn off someone's light like that. You try to kill someone with an ice pick by just stabbing them, you're going to be there awhile. You gotta pop them twenty, thirty times usually if you're going for the body. This Francine woman didn't bleed out, she was shut off. That one I'd say was planned, maybe not her specifically, though. Maybe the killer just knew he was going to kill *someone,* maybe he didn't know who when he left the house, but someone. Frankly, if they both weren't dykes working at drag king clubs, I'd say there was no connection between the two murders."

But Fitz didn't know about the note to Jimmy Vasco. He was evidently the only cop, present or past, who didn't. "He?" I asked.

"Yeah, had to be a he. Dames don't do sick shit like this. Not even junkies or psychos."

"Wait, so you walked in on the coroner having sex with a corpse?" The coffee was just kicking in. I was starting to notice stuff.

"No, Christ, where'd you get that? No, nothing weird like that. He was cutting the bones out of a corpse. With a fillet knife. What's wrong with you?"

"Right. Sorry. I'm new at this." Because filleting a corpse was not weird, but bonking one was? I had a lot to learn about murder copping.

Fitz looked at me like I'd shit on his shoes. "Okay, what'd you find out in your interviews?"

"Butch was a slut."

"Natalie Melanoff?"

"Yes, Natalie is—was—Butch."

"Well, did she have any enemies? Did she piss off a lover? Did she know the other victim?"

"Don't know. I don't think they knew each other."

"What about Francine?"

"Her family doesn't talk to her."

"Did her family tell you that?"

"No, her boss did."

"That means nothing. You gotta talk to the family. What else?"

"She was a stand-up dame who got along with everyone."

"So you got no suspects?"

"Nope."

"Nobody who saw either of them on the night they were killed?"

"Well, one was an entertainer, and one was a doorman. A lot of people saw them."

"Anyone pissed off?"

"There was a guy who had a beef with Butch not long before Dunne raided the joint. Thin guy with a pencil-thin mustache, late twenties, early thirties. Dressed like a nob."

"Find that guy. That's your first suspect. Who was the last to see Natalie—er, Butch—alive?"

"Dame called Nora. Young, pretty, oodles of noodles. Was driving a Packard and wearing a diamond tennis bracelet. I talked to her."

"And?"

"Nothing suspicious. Butch being Butch."

"Well, the coroner puts the time of death right around the time of Dunne's raid. You said three in the A.M., right?"

"Yeah. But I don't think this Nora dame conked Butch with a brick and threw her in the drink, then came in for a little dancing."

"Nah, she's probably clear, but talk to her again, see if she remembers anything."

"I'll try. Hard to get a handle on her."

"Try harder. Frankly, kid, with vice working murder cases, and the way Dunne is dragging his feet, you're the only hope these two women have, because the SFPD is shoving these murders under the rug. They didn't even look for bloodstains at the Melanoff scene. You have to honor the victims, Sammy. You're their advocate. You can't bring 'em back to life, but you can bring 'em justice. You gotta do better."

Fitz looked more alive than any time I'd ever seen him. Five thousand drunken mornings ago, he'd probably been a hell of a detective.

"I'll do better, Fitz. I got a plan."

The phone rang and Bennie grabbed it on the second ring. A drunk at the bar yelled that if it was his wife, he wasn't there. It wasn't his wife and he was always there. Bennie covered the mouthpiece and looked at me. "Law office, Sam? You want to talk to a lawyer?"

"What's the lawyer's name?"

"Stoddard."

"Balls," I said. "Yeah, I'll talk to him."

◇◇◇◇◇

The last time I'd been to the offices of Alton Stoddard the Third I punched him in the mouth and then pulled Jimmy Vasco's heater on him, and I was only half hoping it would go differently this time. The firm of Stoddard, Whittaker & Crock was in a bank building down on Kearny Street among the other towers of commerce where nobs kept and moved their money and looked down on the rest of us.

I didn't even have to get the down-the-nose stare from the elevator guy dressed like the dictator of a small island nation, with epaulets and enough gold braid to rig a small ship, to know that I had no business being there. So what business did I have there? Alton Stoddard the Third had offered me a C-note for fifteen minutes of my time and that was several times my going rate, so I agreed to meet him. There was also the chance I might get to bop him in the beezer and I felt like this time I might be able to knock him out.

Instead of the disapproving matron in tweeds meeting me at the elevator as before, there was a gorilla in a cheap suit who wanted to frisk me before he'd let me even talk to the receptionist.

"Mr. Stoddard insisted I pat you down before letting you in," the gorilla said.

"For another Jackson I'll let him do it himself," I said. "I'm not easy, but I'm cheap."

The gorilla didn't laugh, but just started at my ankles and went up.

"Or you can do it for nothing," I said. "Because I like you."

When he was behind me, checking under my arms for a shoulder holster, the gorilla said, "Was up to me, we'd send you out of here in a basket." Which is not the kind of thing you expect to hear at a top-shelf law firm. When he found out what I had told him at the start, that I wasn't packing, he said to the receptionist, "He's clean."

She was a forty-something fancy librarian and part-time whip-and-chain specialist (probably) in silver cat glasses, behind a half-moon granite desk that looked like it would be swell for serving drinks off of to mourners at a funeral or maybe checking folks in at a hotel for the dead.

"Don't get up, doll," I said, waving for her to keep her seat. "I know the way."

"Mr. Tiffin, you can't just go in there," she said, rushing after me.

"But I can, and in the meantime, you can put your monkey back on his chain so he doesn't fling poo at the clients."

I skipped down the hall to Stoddard's office (I really did know the way, and I really did skip), opened the door, stepped in, then stepped aside, stuck out my foot, and watched the gorilla and the madame tumble through the door and into a pile on a very nice Persian rug.

"What the fuck, Alton?" I exclaimed. "What kind of clown show you running here? I've got a good mind to take my business else-where!" The gorilla came up ready to swing, and I bounced back a step, dukes up. "You're gonna wanna rethink that move, Giggles, unless you want to be eatin' mashed bananas for the next month."

"Out!" said Alton Stoddard the Third. Giggles and Miss Priss scrambled to their feet and vamoosed, closing the door behind them. Alton Stoddard the Third: tall, thin, maybe sixty, balding, Ben Franklin specs, the look of a guy who just licked a lemon.

"Alton," I said, the very picture of congeniality, crossing the walnut-paneled room big enough to hold a hockey game in, with my arms wide. "Buddy!"

Yeah, I know I was playing it broad and loud, but see, thing is, nothing scares rich guys more than poor guys unbound, and nothing stirs up their carefully constructed sense of control like a little chaos. For all his starch and polish, I knew that Stoddard had had people scragged, and the only thing keeping him from adding me to the list was his fear of what me and my network of unseen lowlifes would do to him. I needed to keep him jumpy.

"Mr. Tiffin, won't you have a seat?"

"Don't mind if I do, but I'll need that C-note you promised before we proceed."

He looked disgusted that I would bring up something as gauche as money, but he got over it fast enough to pull a Franklin from his wallet and hold it out to me like it was a swath of leprosy. I took it and slid into one of the chairs in front of his desk, then held the bill up to the window light and snapped it a few times, making a show that I didn't trust he didn't print it in the basement.

"What's your line, Frankenstein?" I asked, to signal I was ready to do business.

"I beg your pardon?"

"Why did you call me?"

"Fine, I'll get right to the point. Mr. Tiffin, my daughter, Olivia, is missing—has been missing for more than a week, and I need you to find her."

"I'm sorry to hear that, Alton, but that sounds like a problem the cops could help you with. How old is she, anyway?"

"She's twenty-three. Still lives at home, although we seldom saw her there, even before she went missing. The police are involved in a limited role."

"Then why me? I don't have any experience finding people. Once, when I was a kid, I lost my little sister for two days, and it turned out my mother had just sent her to the liquor store for some gin. Man, for a seven-year-old, that kid could drink."

Stoddard did not give a hot squat about my little sister.

He said, "Believe me, I have other resources, but I contacted you because of your assurance that you were connected to the man on the street."

I only gave him my assurance of how well connected I was as a way to threaten him, but hey, he remembered.

"True, I get around."

"And you are connected with a scene that my daughter has been exploring of late."

"What scene would that be?"

"The cross-dressing scene. Drag kings and lesbians in particular. She's simply trying to embarrass me and her mother."

"How do you know I'm connected with that scene?"

"I had you followed. My men saw you at one of the establishments known for that kind of thing and they presumed you were headed to another when they lost track of you in Chinatown with that Cheese woman."

"You didn't call her *that Cheese woman,* did you?"

"I believe you introduced her to me as Dorothy Gale. I've since learned that wasn't her real name."

"Well, her real name isn't *that Cheese woman.* What kind of ratty detectives are you hiring, Alton? The woman wears a name tag at work, for fuck's sake."

"I will speak with my detectives."

"If you have a team, why don't you have your detectives find your daughter?"

"My detectives are all men."

"I am also a man."

"Allegedly," said Alton, looking like he'd just scored a big touchdown in a water polo game or whatever game rich guys play.

"How'd your mouth heal up after the last time I popped you, Alton?"

"I will give you a thousand dollars if you find her, and a hundred dollars a day for looking until you find her," he said, wisely moving along and preserving his dental work.

I tried not to whistle or otherwise indicate that I was about to cave like a meringue mine shaft.

"I'll find her," I said, like I would actually find her. "I'll need a recent picture and a retainer."

"I thought the hundred dollars was a retainer."

"Alton, what kind of lowlife scumbag cheaps out on finding his darling daughter?"

"Two hundred?"

"And a picture," I said.

Stoddard lifted up his leather desk blotter and slid out a five-by-seven photo, then handed it to me over the desk. "That was taken about a year and a half ago. It's the most recent photo I have."

It was a picture of a young dame, fresh as a spring day, in what looked like an Easter dress, except there were a bunch of young nobs in caps and gowns milling around in the background. I plastered on a poker face as best I could. "Good-looking kid," I said. I slid the photo in my inside jacket pocket and made for the door. "I'll give you a call as soon as I find out anything."

And I was out of the law offices like someone had rung the fire alarm. Even in the frilly dress and no eye shadow, the brunette bob and the Louise Brooks points to the corners of her mouth were distinct. Olivia Stoddard was the dame who had introduced herself to me at Jimmy's Joynt as Nora.

A lot of what had gone on with the cops over the last week started to make sense.

16

HARD-BOILED CHEESE

Stilton DeCheese, Private Eye

Name's DeCheese, Stilton DeCheese. I was working a double murder undercover in a drag king joint on Broadway called Mona's 440, trying to shake a few trees to see if I could get a killer to drop. I pulled the gig from a tasty little piece of talent called Sammy Two-Toes, who I'd been giving the razzmatazz in my spare time. I'd borrowed the kid's Stetson wide-brimmed fedora so he could feel like he helped, and a blue pinstripe suit from Tommy Vasco, a pal of mine who owns a club on the Embarcadero that caters to the lady-lover crowd. The suit was a couple of sizes too small, so I had to take the pants off to drive, but where I was going, that would only help. I wore it over a lace camisole so sheer it might have been woven by spiders that didn't care if you could see their boobs.

The place was slower than the ladies' room line on nickel beer night, but that would give me a chance to chat up everyone before the show started. Sammy had fronted me a little of his cookie jar money to oil up a few Bettys if that's what it took to loosen their tongues, but I didn't mind slapping them around a little if it was called for. Or requested. I was packing Jimmy Vasco's little Walther .380, which was as cute as a bug's ear and only somewhat more deadly, but I'd promised Jimmy I wouldn't shoot anybody unless they were really asking for it, so she also gave me the clip and showed me how to load it. I'm a wheel-gun dame, myself—give me six coming fast and loud out of a limey .45 revolver that will knock over a buffalo any day over a little Kraut automatic that would really sore a mug up if he found out you'd shot him with it before it jammed. But borrowers can't be bitchers. And besides, the bulge of a revolver would have ruined the lines of my outfit.

I spotted a sturdy-looking doll sitting at the bar nursing a martini the size of a birdbath and took a seat next to her. She had shoulders like a piano mover and a face that looked like she used to be a bulldog before she grew into her awkward stage, but she smiled sort of sideways when I rolled up.

"Hey, doll, haven't seen you around here," she said.

"Nah, I'm new," I said. "I'm Tilly." My pal Myrtle always says she's new. Just like in waitressing, she says, they give you a break if you tell them it's your first day.

"Babe," Babe said. "Welcome to Mona's, Tilly. I run this joint. Can we buy you a welcome-home drink?"

"I don't know, am I home?"

"You bet your sweet ass you are, doll," said Babe.

If Babe had different plumbing I'd have called her a hound, but it didn't much matter since there wasn't enough room in these tinhorn pants for the two of us. "Sure, pour me something cheap that goes down easy," I said.

Babe gulped a little, which was a good sign, and ordered me an old-fashioned. The bartender, a short, skinny blonde with a figure like a ruler, didn't think I saw her roll her eyes at Babe when she went to fetch it, but she was rolling them like a cable car on the Hyde Street hill. This wasn't the first time she'd seen this particular show.

I pulled an SFPD inspector's badge out of my jacket pocket and plopped it down on the bar. "So who do I have to lick to get some fucking murder clues around here?" I said.

"They teach you to run an investigation like this at the academy?" asked the bartender as she set my drink in front of me.

"Don't bust my balls, Toots, I'm new," I said.

"I didn't know SFPD even had any women inspectors," said Babe.

"I'm undercover."

"Then why did you slam your badge down on the bar first thing?" asked the bartender.

"Look, I'm asking the questions here. If you dames make me cry I'm gonna start shooting people, so shut the fuck up and answer my questions, unless you want the gorillas in the Dodge outside to live there forever."

"That's why you're here?" asked Babe. "So they can go somewhere else?"

"Yeah, the department said you wouldn't talk to a guy, so they promoted me."

"Went right for the cream of the crop, did they?" said the bartender.

"What's your name, wiseass?"

"Bev."

"Bev what?" I pulled my notebook out of my jacket pocket. Not the pocket with the gun. The other one. Pencil from behind my ear.

"Beverly Shaffer. With two *f*'s. Is that an order pad?"

"It's what we use now."

"Top-notch police work," said the wanting-to-be-punched-in-the-chops Beverly Shaffer.

I said, "So if we're on a stakeout we can put our lunch order on it and give it to a kid to go get sandwiches."

"Yeah, yeah, yeah," said Babe. "Bev, why don't you go restock your bar before the rush."

"There's not going to be a rush, as long as those cops are parked outside."

"Then why don't you go stock your bar so I can help the inspector here with her investigation and the cops will go away and maybe there *will* be a fucking rush?"

"Yeah, Bev," I said. Then as Bev went away all huffy, I said, "Thanks, doll, this won't take long."

"Shoot," Babe said.

So I did. I had some notes on my order pad. "The night Frankie was killed, anyone unusual in here?"

"Unusual like broads dressed in guys' duds, or unusual for here?"

"Unusual for here."

"Not that I can remember, and I've been trying to remember. It was a good night. Frankie had a good set. There was a young doll dressed very femme, satin hostess PJs and Veronica Lake blond wig, flirting with Frankie all night. Looked like it might get under Frankie's skin for a minute, but she came through like a pro. Didn't even stay for a drink after her set."

"Kind of dark during a show. How'd you know it was a wig?"

"You could see her brunette sideburns sticking out. It was so bad I thought she might be one of the skinny guys from Finocchio's down the street running a game on us."

"Was it?"

"Nah, she was pure filly. I got an eye for these things."

"You said sideburns, you mean like this?" I pulled the picture Sammy had given me out of my pocket. The badge and order pad pocket, not the gun pocket.

"Yeah, like that. That one in the picture's a little more fresh-faced, but the haircut could be the same."

"Seen her since?"

"Nope. But she left that night not long after Frankie. And she left alone, ditched her date."

"What do you mean?"

"The blonde wasn't alone. She was with another broad all night, but she left alone."

"Did you tell the cops, I mean, us, about that? The first cops that questioned you."

"No one questioned me until now."

"So I might not be a bad detective after all, huh?"

"You're a better cop than you are a dyke."

"What are you talking about? Lesbians *love* me!"

Sammy

If the Cheese thought I was going to send her to a murder scene undercover without looking out for her, she had another think coming. I told her I was working my usual shift at the bar, but I called in another favor from Bennie to cover me and threw him some of my expense money so he was making double time, but I couldn't keep calling on the kid like that. Making him work double shifts for days in a row just might be what would send him on a bender that could be his last.

I borrowed Jimmy Vasco's sweet little Ford coupe and found a nesting place just around the corner from the black Chrysler, which was parked in one of the few pullouts on Telegraph Hill, maybe a block from the Cheese's little tunnel of love—which is what she'd started calling her apartment after we met, because it had been a crawl space at one time and the owner of the building had a crew dig out a space big enough for some furniture, a bathroom, and a little two-burner cooker and a sink. Rent was low and evidently even lower if the Cheese did dishes in her underwear with the curtains open, which made me want to punch the guy's lights out, but the Cheese forbade it on account of she made an agreement and she was a stand-up dame.

She came out about eight, like I figured she would, and climbed in the Chrysler. She was wearing one of Jimmy Vasco's pinstripe suits but it fit her quite a bit more snugly than it had Jimmy—in a good way. She also had on a wide-brimmed Stetson fedora like the one I used to have, and a pair of men's black-and-white wingtips, not unlike those of Eddie Moo Shoes, and even with her being a knockout in most all ways, they were ridiculous.

I followed her to Mona's, where I parked far enough down Broadway to keep an eye on the front door, but not so close I'd attract the attention of the two flatfoots still standing guard in the Dodge.

The Cheese breezed past the door dames like I knew she would. I smoked and went through my notes while I waited. Yeah, I'd started making notes. The Cheese had given me an order pad and a pencil from the Five & Dime and threw a kid's tin sheriff's badge in the bag as a joke. Wiseass.

She was out in forty-five minutes, which was forty minutes better than I'd done, and I followed her to Jimmy's Joynt, where I had to stay back a bit because it's on a pier and because I was driving the boss's car. But no one was watching. That's the thing, why was no one watching? They were all over Mona's like ugly on an ape, but the other drag king club where a dame got scragged and they're ghosts? Since talking to Alton Stoddard the Third, of course, I knew the gorillas at Mona's were no more trying to catch a murderer than the cops who had been hanging out at Cookie's Coffee that night had been. They were looking for Stoddard's daughter, and not doing a very good job of staying out of sight. But Olivia Stoddard had been here at Jimmy's just last night and there wasn't a cop in sight. Why?

Then, when the Cheese came out, a half hour later, with Myrtle, wearing coveralls and a ball cap, I figured out why. I was parked all the way at the end of the pier, facing the city, but I could also see Piers 27 on one side and 31 on the other. When Stilton drove off the pier, some headlights came on over at Pier 31 and the car headed toward the Embarcadero. Someone, probably cops, had been watching Jimmy's from the next pier. With binoculars maybe. The cops fell in behind the Cheese at the Embarcadero and I fell in behind them. If they'd been watching last night when Olivia Stoddard, aka Nora, was at Jimmy's in the Packard, why hadn't they snagged her then?

I followed the cops about a block back as the Cheese went up Broadway and took a left on Grant Avenue into Chinatown. This must have been where Stoddard's guys had lost the Cheese in Chinatown, and the mooks must have thought Myrtle in her coveralls and ball cap was me. I was kind of offended. I'm a slim guy, but I'm not Myrtle slim. No wonder Stoddard hired me if that's the quality of shamus he has on the staff.

The Cheese took an abrupt right on Washington, and by the time I reached the corner of Grant and Washington, I could see her taillights disappearing down an alley to the left. Just as the cops got to the corner a beam of light came out of the alley, as thin as a thread, and went right through the front of the cops' car, sending up puffs of smoke on both sides. If I'd blinked I would have missed it. The cop car rolled to a stop in the alley. I drove by, trying not to look or attract attention to myself, but there were a couple of very distressed hats in that car. I took a left on Stockton, then floored it to catch up with Stilton coming out of the alley. I kept a block and a half back, until I could just see her taillights. I had a pretty good idea of what had knocked out that cop car and I didn't want any part of it.

She jumped on Third Street and took it all the way out along the waterfront until she bailed onto side streets of the Hunters Point complex of warehouses, factories, and railroad yards, where I'd worked for most of the war. It was a ghost town now, not even the odd hobo or wet-brain wandering among the corrugated steel buildings.

The Cheese pulled into a spot in front of a big building that looked like it was probably used for fabrication—there were rails leading into forty-foot-tall doors. Something big went in or came out of that building. Myrtle jumped out and went in through a normal dame-sized door, and in a second, one of the forty-foot doors was sliding aside. Stilton pulled the Chrysler into the building and the door closed behind it. They'd done a pretty good job of blacking out the windows, but when the lights went on inside you could trace a line of light around the doors.

I parked the Ford in front of a building across the street, a good hundred yards away, and hoofed it over. I was pretty sure the navy still patrolled this area, and if they stopped to check out the Ford, I didn't want them looking for the owner where the Cheese was doing whatever she was doing.

I was just about at the door when some headlights raked across the open space, headed my way. I jumped through the door and pulled it shut before they got to me.

"Sammy!" called the Cheese, who had no pants on.

"Sammy!" exclaimed Myrtle, who had on coveralls, so I guess, pants.

"*Tweet, beep, zip, zip, worrfle, oot!*" yeeped the moonman, who was climbing out of the trunk of the Chrysler (sans pants).

Stilton ran to embrace me and I let her, as I am highly vulnerable to a dame I'm crazy about who is not wearing pants, but I was still looking over her shoulder from the moonman, to Myrtle, to the thing they had been building, to the moonman, and so on. I'd seen a moonman before, presumably this very same moonman, since he seemed to know me, but I'd never seen anything like the metal—machine, I guess, occupying much of the floor space. The Cheese finally let me go and turned to face the thing.

"Do you like it?"

I was going to answer that it was the best one of those enormous fucking metal things I'd ever seen, but at that point the moonman was running toward me, his arms wide, making various cheeps and beeps of excitement.

Myrtle said, "You just gotta let him motorboat your boobs, Sammy, then you'll be his best pal. It's how his people say hello."

"Um," I said.

The moonman paused in front of me, arms still wide, waiting, evidently, for me to return his embrace or let him motorboat my boobs.

"I know it's weird at first," said Myrtle. "But you get used to it and it makes him so happy."

I took one of his little froggy fingers by the tip and gave it a friendly shake. "Nice to see you, too, Scooter."

He scampered back over to the Chrysler to retrieve something the Cheese and I called his cow-blaster, because when we first saw him use it, that's what he was doing. A collection of batteries and wires and an old cornet, plus some crystals he sort of spooged out of his froggy fingers.

"Well, you ruined your birthday surprise," said the Cheese.

"Doll," I said, "you know how much I love for you to take off your pants and lie to me, but there's no need now, you've built a giant steel"—I gestured at the thing because I didn't have a word for what it was—"and why do you have no pants on?"

"Can't drive in Jimmy's pants. Too tight." She waved a flourish at the steel thing like a model presenting a washing machine in a magazine ad. "We called it the rhinoceros for a while. Then the armadillo. Now we call it—Myrt, what are we calling it now?"

"The fucking thing," said Myrtle.

"The fucking thing," said the Cheese. "We think Scooter is having us build him a rocket ship so he can go home."

I walked closer to the thing. It was a good two stories tall and twice as long, made of one-inch plate steel it looked like, which was pretty light for building warships but seemed pretty heavy for something that was going to fly. There were a lot of sharp fins and rollers around the perimeter of it, all sweeping toward the tail.

"You dolls have done a first-rate job welding this thing together. It's got to weigh tons."

"Yeah," said Myrtle. "We got real good with a block and tackle, and this building has rails and cranes built in. They used to build the bridges for ships in here, then lift them onto the ships in one piece."

"Looks like there's a lot of machining besides welding." I looked at the Cheese. "You know how to do that?"

"We've gotten pretty good. Scooter finds stuff and tells us where it is to bring back, and he does a lot of fine cutting with a modified cow-blaster. Like a table model."

"How does he tell you? He's still just beeping and chirping, right?"

"He shows us," said Myrtle. "Like suddenly I just have a picture in my head of what something looks like and where it is."

"Yeah," said the Cheese, running to a drafting table set up to the side of the workshop. She pulled a big drawing off and brought it to me. "Down to the millimeter."

It was an incredibly detailed mechanical drawing of some bit of machinery I didn't recognize.

"You drew this?"

"Yeah. Pretty good for an amateur, huh? Inspired."

"Where'd you learn to draw like this?"

"Well, I learned to read blueprints in the shipyard during the war, but this stuff just kind of comes to me. Sometimes I don't even remember drawing it."

"Yeah, like the welding," said Myrtle.

"Let me get this straight: you dolls are welding and drafting and machining and whatnot, and you don't remember doing it?"

"Ah, that's nothing," said Myrtle. "That used to happen to us all the time when we were going out during the war."

"You were blackout welding during the war?"

"Nah, but you know, you can get pretty hooted up when guys are buying you drinks to defeat the Nazis and whatnot."

I tried to get my head around it. I'd gotten to be pretty good at welding and cutting steel when I was working in the shipyard during the war, but nothing like this. This was way, way beyond my abilities.

"And Scooter's modified cow-blaster, that's what he drilled that cop car with?"

"I guess. He's been messing with it, working out the bugs," said the Cheese.

"Bugs?"

"Well, he kind of semi-vaporized a military cop," said Myrtle.

"*Semi*-vaporized?"

The Cheese had stripped down to her panties and a camisole and was pulling on her coveralls. "Yeah, there were parts of him left. We think the cow-blaster was on the fritz."

"What parts?"

"Like his boots," said Myrtle. "And, uh, his feet. And a lump of metal that used to be his gun."

"And did you get rid of those?" I asked. "Chuck 'em in the bay or something?"

"We're not barbarians, Sammy!" exclaimed the Cheese. "We put them in a hatbox and buried them. We even said some words over them. Well, Myrtle said some words. I was a little nauseous from packing the hatbox."

"Like what kind of words?"

"You know, funeral stuff, like forgive us, Jesus, for letting a moonman burn this guy up with his cow-blaster."

"I'm not sure that's normal funeral stuff."

"Yeah, I was trying to sugarcoat it a little. It was horrible. That guy probably had a wife and kids or something. It wasn't something we planned. In fact, we had a plan where Myrtle would pretend she was going to blow him, then when the guy had his wanger out, she was going to fake a fit and then we were going to blackmail him for trying to take advantage of an epileptic and everyone lived happily ever after."

"I'm gonna take a flier and guess that plan didn't come to you through inspiration from Scooter?"

"Nah, we didn't even see where Scooter's shot came from. There wasn't room for him in the trunk," said the Cheese. She was shaking the wrinkles out of Jimmy's jacket and tried to hang it on the drafting stool. The jacket got upended and stuff fell out of the pockets: a gun, a badge, an order pad, a lipstick.

"Oops," said the Cheese, gathering the jacket jetsam.

"That's a real SFPD inspector's badge, right?"

"It's Pookie's," the Cheese said. "I grabbed it off the lawyer's desk when you were punching him that time. Don't be mad. Are you mad?"

"You sent me in to question witnesses with a toy badge and you had this?"

"I thought you'd be mad if you thought I was keeping a secret from you."

"Uh-huh," I said as I gestured grandly to the enormous fucking machine in the room, which, no matter how I turned my head, appeared to be breathing. No, it was steel.

"Good point," said the Cheese. "But I got the skinny on the victim. That Frankie dame. And what I could about Butch."

"Are you trying to change the subject?"

"Look, you're the one who's getting paid to catch a killer, buster. I'm just trying to build this, this—"

"Dragon?" I provided.

"Hey, now that you mention it," said Myrtle, stepping back, hip out, stroking her chin, "it is starting to kind of look like a dragon."

"With really short legs," said the Cheese. "A squat dragon."

"Don't insult our dragon, Tilly. If Scooter wanted a tall dragon he'd have given us plans for a tall dragon."

"Whaddaya say, Sammy?" said the Cheese. "You wanna do a little welding, operate a little dangerous machinery, have moonman plans projected into your noggin? Huh? Huh?" She did a couple of those horse clucks with her tongue, like she was trying to get me to gid-dyup.

"I'm a little out of practice, doll, thanks." I suppose I was more than somewhat relieved that the reason for the Cheese being distracted wasn't her seeing another guy, but trance welding.

"Sometimes when you come out of it, your butt hole hurts a little, too," Myrtle blurted out.

"Myrt!" the Cheese Myrted.

"Well, it does. You got to admit it."

"Then I will absolutely pass," I said.

"We could climb into the dragon and do the razzmatazz," said the Cheese. "I've never done that."

"That you remember," said Myrtle.

17

THE RAIN DRAGON

Petaluma, California—April 1906

Since he had brought the storm and appeared to Ho in the bay, the dragon would not shut up. He was in Ho's head like a nagging ghost.

"*North, Catfucker. Go north! If you can't go faster, kill a man and steal his horse,*" said the dragon.

"I will not kill a man and I will not steal a horse," Ho said aloud.

"Have you gone mad again?" asked Niu Yun. They were walking along a dusty road outside of Petaluma, California, two days after they had crossed the bay to Sausalito.

"No, I'm not mad. I don't even know how to ride a horse."

"You sit on it and it goes," said Niu Yun, as if it were the most obvious thing in the world. She had never ridden a horse, either. "But no one asked you to."

"The dragon did."

"If the White Devil's Daughters are going to take us in, you will have to stop saying crazy things."

"I will if the dragon stops saying crazy things," said Ho.

Now that they were across the bay safely and had been on foot for two days, Ho wished he could leave the Rain Dragon behind.

It was getting heavy, and it had started to vibrate, ever so softly at first, but more as they moved north. Even Niu Yun admitted she could feel the vibration.

"Perhaps we should bury it and come back for it later," said Ho.

"If you bury me I will make the girl chop off your dick with her hatchet."

"Perhaps I'll carry it a bit longer," said Ho.

They had spent the first night in a boathouse in Sausalito with the fisherman, who had shared a fish and some rice they bought from the man who owned the boathouse. The next night they slept in a hollow, under blankets they bought from a white man with a mercantile wagon, along with a canteen, a pot, and enough salt pork and rice to last them for the journey. Because they were Chinese, he would not sell them a knife, so Niu Yun prepared their food using her hatchet.

On the third night out of the city they reached the town of Sonoma and slept in a shed behind a shop where the Chinese shopkeeper fed them a hot meal for a dollar and gave them directions to Eldridge, which he assured them was only a short walk from town. That night the dragon was vibrating so violently that Ho put it outside the little shed, still wrapped in the red-and-gold tablecloth, and they slept for several hours, until they were startled awake by a huge thunderclap.

"Go now, Catfucker," said the voice in Ho's head. *"Go north now!"*

The cracks between the boards of the shed lit up blindingly bright, and the thunderclap came in that same instant, the boom like it was right on top of them, and they leapt into each other's arms in terror, then pushed each other away, her because she had vowed that no man would ever touch her again, and him because he didn't want to get his dick chopped off.

The lightning and thunder came again, but they could hear the Rain Dragon buzzing outside the shed.

"Now, Catfucker!"

Ho opened the shed door and the buzzing seemed to be coming

from inside his head. "We have to go to Eldridge now, Niu Yun. The dragon demands it. Now."

"It's the middle of the night and it's dark and you're mad."

A lightning bolt hit so close to them they could feel the heat and they were blinded and deafened by the blast.

Niu Yun blinked and put her fingers in her ears to see if she could clear them. "I think we should go now," she said. She slung the dragon around Ho's neck and shoulder, then threw his blanket over his other shoulder.

"What?" said Ho. He was blinking bright spots away from his eyes, but he could see her pointing.

"Go that way. There's a road." In a second she'd made a sling out of her own blanket and was carrying their supplies and her hatchet in it.

The lightning and thunder stopped. There was no wind and no rain, no sign that there had been a storm or that there would be one. They followed the road, worn deep with wagon wheel ruts, into rolling grassy fields, dark from the spring rains but dotted with wildflowers that shone under the moonlight like soft little stars among the shadows of small live oaks here and there.

The dragon stopped buzzing and Ho relaxed just a bit, took a few breaths of peace, but then the dragon's voice started in his head again. "*Why are you so slow, Catfucker? Do I need to raise a river to wash you along the road? Faster, Catfucker!*"

"The dragon is very excited," said Ho.

"It is good it wants to go in the same direction we are going," said Niu Yun.

After a mile or so, the dragon was speaking quickly in a dialect Ho didn't understand, fiercely, as if he was angry, but not so loud, as if he was muttering to himself.

"Why do you think the dragon wants to go to Eldridge?" asked Niu Yun. "I know why we want to go there, but why would a dragon want to go to a farm full of rescued girls?"

"I don't know. I didn't even believe in dragons until three days ago."

"I saw it," said Niu Yun.

"Saw it?"

"In the water, when we were rowing, I saw it. I told you I didn't, but I did. I have been afraid many times since I left home, but seeing the dragon was a fear that felt as if I had been hollowed out, that I would keep inhaling with fear until I burst."

"Awe, I think," said Ho. "I peed. A little. It was better when I just thought I was mad, or being guided by an ancestor. Now, a dragon is real in the world and I have seen it and I do not know what to do."

"Do what the dragon tells you to do," said the dragon.

"Did you hear that?" asked Ho.

"What?" said Niu.

"Nothing, we must go faster."

And they did, exhausted as they were, for Ho had not set foot outside the ten-block area of Chinatown for two years, and Niu Yun had been in a cage for that long, so neither had been ready for this very long walk, yet they picked up their pace, stumbling at times in the dark, toward whatever the dragon was leading them to.

In another hour the sky began to glow with the dawn and they could see the hills lightening around them. They came to a cross-roads where a clapboard sign pointing one way read SANTA ROSA and another, marking the way they were headed, read ELDRIDGE, but since neither could read the English characters they stood for a long time, catching their breath.

"The sun will rise on that side of the hills," said Ho. "So that is east. This will be north." He waved in the direction the Eldridge sign pointed. The road here was parallel to a narrow river that still ran fast and high with the spring thaws coming down from the Sierras. In the morning twilight Ho could see tall brick buildings, some lights in the windows across the river to his right, then a very narrow road through a fence to his left, and a small fishpond near which cattle were calmly grazing.

"That way," said Ho, pointing across the bridge to the buildings in the distance. He took one step and the Rain Dragon trembled violently against his hip.

"I meant that way." He took a single step toward the pond and lightning cracked the sky above them and thunder shook their ribs.

"I don't know which way!" Ho screamed at the clouds. Niu Yun had crouched by the side of the road with her arms over her head as if she were shielding herself from the falling sky.

"*You have arrived,*" said the dragon.

Lightning fired across the sky all around them, and above them clouds began to swirl. Ho crouched beside Niu Yun and threw his blanket over both of them.

The sky whirled in a widening dark circle, lightning flashing at its edges, and the rain came down on them as if there were no space between the drops. The ground began to shake, then undulated, as if they were on the back of a great serpent. Even from a crouch they were knocked flat to the wet ground. Ho shielded his eyes against the rain and looked up. Above them the sky was filled with the great shining coils of the Rain Dragon, its edges defined by the lightning firing there. He tapped Niu Yun's leg and shouted her name. She opened her eyes enough to see him pointing to the sky, and her mouth fell open in awe. The coils of the Rain Dragon, slipping over each other like the gears of a huge machine, now filled the sky to the horizon. The ground jolted and Ho heard a screeching from where the cows had been grazing. The pond was draining, something sucking it away, and in a few seconds it was gone, just a gaping crevice in its place. Cattle were swept down like leaves into a river. Then out of the sky came the dragon's head, the eyes green, as bright as lightning, diving toward them, the great maw like a cityscape of teeth, each a church tower, which would surely consume them—them and everything they could see. The dragon's whiskers snapped back into the sky, lightning at their tips. Ho could look no longer, but reconciled himself to his death. He put his arm around the girl, held her tight, and waited, bracing for the end, two tiny humans clinging together beneath power eternal. Niu Yun's fingers dug into his shoulders so hard he thought they might draw blood, but he was grateful for the pain because it meant he was not alone.

But the dragon did not gobble them, did not take a bite of the earth. It tucked its great horns and whiskers, pulled its lightning-green eyes back into its head, and dove into the crater where the pond had been. Ho peeked out from under the blanket to see the body of the dragon going by vertically, like a train diving into the ground, the tail still seemingly miles into the sky. Seconds passed, a scraping sound like a thousand shovels being plunged into sand as the dragon uncoiled and disappeared into the hole, the tail whipping away a stand of live oaks as it plunged out of sight.

And for a second, it was quiet. No thunder, no rain, not a cow lowing in the distance, not a bird calling on the wind. Absolutely still. Ho lifted the blanket and looked at Niu Yun, who dared to look up.

"Are we dead?" she asked.

"I don't think so," said Ho.

"If he can do that, I don't know why we had to carry him on foot for four days," said Niu Yun.

She stood. He stood. They looked around. Then they were both knocked off their feet as if the earth were a rug that had been ripped from beneath them. Ho clung to the grass as if he might be tossed into the air, and after several seconds of the shaking and the waves he felt his gorge rising, like a whole voyage's worth of seasickness had visited him in a single jolt. A great geyser of smoke exploded into the sky out of the crater where the pond had been, then it snapped shut like a crocodile's mouth, sealing the crater as if it had never been there. When the shaking stopped, he vomited until his stomach was empty, and Niu Yun did the same. Perhaps a minute had passed since the dragon had dropped from the sky, but it seemed like hours—like it would never end. Niu Yun held tufts of grass like a baby monkey clutching its mother's fur.

"Is it over?" she asked.

"I don't know," said Ho.

"*For now,*" said the dragon in Ho's head. He looked to the fallen dragon statue that had spilled from its tablecloth nest and was sticking in the mud, a completely ridiculous piece of carved black stone.

"Water?" asked Niu Yun. She held out the canteen. Ho took it, rinsed his mouth, spit, then took a drink and handed it back. She did the same routine.

They sat there and watched the sun come up over the hills to the east, both afraid to stand up, just drinking water and staring. Ho would begin to speak, then catch himself, because nothing he would ever say would be anything but insignificant drivel, and he knew it before he said it. After perhaps an hour, two women came over the hill from the north in a wagon pulled by a single horse. As they got closer, Ho could see that they looked Chinese, although their clothes were Western.

When the wagon pulled up beside them, the woman holding the reins called, "What are you doing here?"

Before Ho could speak, Niu Yun blurted out, "We are looking for the White Devil's Daughters. A woman at the mission in the city sent us."

The woman's expression softened. Her companion was looking at the crater where the pond used to be and seemed to be in shock herself. The driver said, "You escaped from one of the brothels?"

"Yes," said Niu Yun.

"Who is he?"

"He helped me."

Ho climbed to his feet, steadied himself, and bowed. "I am Shu Ho, from the Glorious Location of Various Weeds, Guangdong Province."

"What do you want?" the driver asked.

The rising sun was behind the woman's head, and when Ho raised his hand to shield his eyes, his sleeve slipped down his arm, revealing the Rain Dragon brand on his forearm.

"You are Ghee Sin Tong?"

"Not anymore."

"You have to go away. There has been a terrible tragedy at the farm. Buildings have collapsed. You must leave."

Niu Yun jumped up and stood beside Ho. "He helped me."

"You can go up to the farm. They will need the help, but he cannot stay."

"You go," Ho said to Niu Yun. "I will leave."

"Return to your tong brothers," said the driver.

"He can't go back," said Niu Yun. "He betrayed them to save me. He stole their dragon."

"He can't stay here. There is a Chinatown on the east side of the bay. The tongs leave them alone. There is an agreement. You will be able to find work there. Were you a farmer in Guangdong?"

"Yes," said Ho.

"There is work for farmers in Locke. Can you say that, 'Locke'?"

Ho tried to say it and failed miserably. She made him try again.

"Go due east, not back across the Golden Gate. It will be three or four days on foot. Now go."

Ho picked up the Rain Dragon and slipped it in the silk sling, now coated with mud. "I will go."

Niu Yun gathered their supplies and packed them into her blanket sling, then went to Ho and held out the sling so he could duck into it. "Don't tell them what you have seen," whispered Ho. "They will think you are mad."

"I don't believe what I have seen," said Niu Yun. Suddenly she wheeled on the driver. "Let him stay. He is sturdy and he sacrificed his own safety to help me."

"No," said the driver. "Donaldina will not stand for it."

"Then I am not going to stay, either," said Niu Yun.

"Suit yourself," said the driver. "Go to Locke with him. There will be work there, and they probably have not seen a Chinese woman in a long time."

"I will," said Niu Yun, as if it were a threat.

"Go, then," said the driver. "I have to go to town and get supplies. There is much to be done. Go to Locke. Say it."

"Locke," said Niu Yun.

"Again, say it."

Niu Yun said it.

"Go with God," said the driver. She snapped the reins and the wagon rolled off.

"Wait," Ho called after them. "What is that place with the tall brick buildings there? Is that a town?"

"That is a hospital for feeble-minded children," the driver called back. "They don't want you, either." The wagon rolled away.

"*Locke*," said Niu Yun, taking the sling with their possessions from Ho and hanging it over her own shoulder.

"We are learning so many new English words," said Ho, as bright as the newly risen sun.

Stilton DeCheese, Private Eye

I knew he was a going-nowhere mug with a pretty face and a headful of broken dreams, but he knew his way around a dame's naughty bits and he'd get out when you were finished with him or cook breakfast in the morning if you asked, which are the kind of qualities I like in a guy. Sammy Two-Toes pulled up on me on a job I was doing for a short guy in gray, and I told my pal Myrt, who was helping me, to take the client and amscray while I brought Two-Toes up to speed on the murder case. (His name wasn't Two-Toes any more than mine is DeCheese, but if you want street cred you gotta have a good *nom de guerre,* as they say in fucking France.)

"So," I said, "according to Babe Bowman, Frankie did all her flirting on the stage. Outside of the club she lived like a librarian, so she wasn't on the make the night she was scragged."

"And Butch was a big flirt and a slut, according to Jimmy V," said doll-face McBonk.

"Right. So no connection there. But the night she died, there was a dame in a Veronica Lake wig flirting Frankie's shorts off, and Babe says she could see the brunette points of this doll's real hairdo showing underneath. Like a flapper bob."

"Alton Stoddard's daughter?"

"You can count on it. And when Frankie left after her set, the Stoddard frail followed her out."

"So she was there the nights both dames were murdered."

"And get this: Babe said she had a date. An older doll Babe had seen her with before. They never came in together, but they'd met up there before."

"Any idea who this dame was?"

"Nah, I talked to the bartender and the door dames, and they knew her by sight, but not her name. Said she usually came in late, trying to stay on the down low. Sat in the corner, in the dark. Never came up to the bar to get a drink. But the bartender said she'd been coming in on and off since before the war ended. She called her a war bride."

"Like your mother?" Sammy asked.

"Nah, not like my mother; she was a real war bride. In the lesbo scene, it refers to married dames that used to come into the lesbian clubs when their men were overseas. Let them get out of the house or have a drink after work if they were pulling shifts in the shipyards without having to fend off horned-up sailors on leave. Some of them either started batting for the all-girl team or found they just liked the hound-free atmosphere and kept coming in after the war. So the bartender, Bev, thinks this war bride could be the Stoddard dame's sometimes squeeze, despite being old enough to be her mother."

"Maybe it is her mother; ever think of that?"

"Not unless she smooches her mother with lots of tongue and no little grab-ass."

"Maybe not."

"My guess is, you find this older dame, you find Stoddard's daughter, pass Go, collect two hundred dollars, and maybe solve a murder."

"Collect a couple of grand and expenses and maybe get an apartment for me and my best gal."

"Yeah, I know, I was being poetic, ya mook. Why you bustin' my balls here? What I'm saying is you gotta find this war bride."

"You got a description? Car? Anything."

"Yeah, I was getting to that. Wait, were you looking at my ba-zooms while I was talking?"

"Nope," he said, innocent as a new lamb on its first frolic.

"You're lying like a rug."

"Yes, I am."

Yeah, well, I can't help it. The kid is a charmer, and the way he smiles when you catch him running a game on you, I just want to throw him down and give him the razzmatazz until he barks, so that's what I did. I filled him in on the details when we came up for air.

"I'll get back on the case soon as I can," he told me, basking in the afterglow and so forth, "but I gotta go find Moo Shoes's dragon tomorrow."

Fucking Moo Shoes, anyway.

18

NEVER STEAL HAM FROM WHORES

Sammy

Eddie Moo Shoes was losing a fight with a road map and he wasn't even going to get to the second round if I didn't pull over to help him.

"Why is this road so wiggly?" said Moo. "There's nothing out here to go around. No buildings. Hardly any trees. There's no reason for it to be so wiggly."

I steered Jimmy Vasco's Ford onto the shoulder, put it in neutral, and set the brake. "The reason it is wiggly, Moo, is because the road is running along the Sacramento River, which would be that wiggly wet thing to our immediate left." I don't think Moo Shoes had been out of San Francisco more than a half dozen times in his life, and most of those had been to Oakland, so he'd been a little jumpy since we'd driven into the farmland of the Sacramento River valley.

I eased the map out of Moo Shoes's hands and backfolded it until there was just enough to track the next few miles of our route. "This," I said, pointing to a spot on the map, "is where we are now. And this"—I pointed to the small grid of streets marked *Locke*—"is where we are going."

"How do you know that? How do you know this is where we are? We aren't marked on the map."

"See that bridge ahead?" I asked, pointing ahead of us to a small bridge over the levee. "That is this bridge here." I pointed to a spot on the map. "So we must be here."

"So that's Locke, right over there. Just right there." Moo pointed across the levee, where there was a tiny village of clapboard buildings that looked like a cross between an army barracks and a western cowboy town.

"Yes." I handed him the map. "You know, you should maybe have Lois teach the navigation in your driving school."

"Yeah, at least my squeeze isn't sneaking out at all hours to allegedly make me a birthday present." Then under his breath he added, "Because you know that's not what she's doing."

I had not told Eddie about the return of the moonman or the little project the Cheese was really working on. If the G-men who had been after the moonman before ever returned, the less Moo Shoes knew, the better for him.

"I'm pretty sure it is. She was naked when she told me about it, and it is a well-known fact that a dame cannot lie to you when she is naked."

"It is sad being your pal, Sammy, because if you were not a pal and not broke most of the time, it would be a joy to exploit your naivete for financial gain."

"If I was not broke most of the time, I would hide my filthy lucre by drawing a map showing clearly where I keep it, safe in the knowledge that you would never be able to find it. This, by the way, is Locke. Right here. Where we are." And we were *there*, as much as four streets, each one block long, with simple wooden buildings, no gingerbread, no stained glass, just a lot of signs written in Chinese characters, can be *there*. I turned off the Ford and set the brake.

"Now, we just ask around about a dragon statue Ho the Cat-Fucking Uncle left here forty years ago?"

"Uncle Ho said to ask at one of the brothels about a woman called Niu Yun."

"*One* of the brothels? *One* of them? This town probably only has one telephone and they have more than one brothel?"

"Uncle Ho said they had three, maybe four, but he doesn't remember which one."

"You probably have to sign up to make a phone call. Make an appointment."

"So we just need to ask someone where the brothels are."

"They probably only have one nickel for the phone. You have to ask if you can use it when you make a call," I said. "*Oh no, sorry,*" I said in my perfect imitation of a guy who lived in a town you could throw a baseball across. "*Thirsty Jim bought a Coke with the nickel, so no one can make a call until we go to the city and get another one.*"

"We should get out and walk," said Moo Shoes.

I got out—considered bringing the heater, then decided against it. I tucked it under the front seat. The sidewalks, where there were sidewalks, were wooden. We walked up one street and down another, seeing almost no one at all except for shopkeepers, bartenders, and the very occasional old guy just sitting in a chair on the sidewalk, all Chinese, all giving us the hairy eyeball. There were three general stores, three restaurants that looked like big cafeterias, four gambling houses, five bars. One of the general stores had a gas pump. There were no brothels. At least there were no buildings that had signs that said BROTHEL. Moo Shoes had been reading the signs as we walked along, and except for ESSO on the globe over the gas pump and COKE on the side of a cooler at the general store, there wasn't anything written in English. I wondered why Uncle Ho thought a *gwai lo* was needed for this particular job.

As we were finishing our complete tour of every street in Locke, which took about fifteen minutes of less-than-brisk walking, I said, "What kind of daffy burg has four blocks of nothing but saloons, gambling houses, restaurants, and four whorehouses?"

"A daffy burg without dames," said Moo.

He was right. I think I saw one woman through the window of

one of the restaurants. Everyone else was guys, most of them old. "And we only have a dame's name as a clue?"

"This place was built by Chinese workers after they built the railroad. Uncle Ho said it was just a swamp, a river delta. Chinese guys built all the levees, all the roads, raised all the farms that would grow fruit. But they didn't bring women with them from China. They came here to work, to make their fortune, and they lived *here*. They spent their buck a day on gambling and whores, or at the restaurants and bars."

I whistled, thinking about the scope of it—all the levees and raised plots of land and causeways and other engineered stuff we'd driven through to get there—and that it was all done by Chinese guys with shovels and wheelbarrows, no tractors, trucks, or bulldozers? It made my back hurt to think about it.

"We need to ask someone where the whorehouses are, Moo. And by *we*, I mean you, because I don't think my ten words of Cantonese are going to cut it."

"*Egg foo yong* is not Cantonese."

"My *seven* words of Cantonese are not going to cut it."

"Fine," he said. He ducked into the next gin joint we came to and bellied up to a bar that looked like it might have come around the horn on a sailing ship, which was the case with a lot of the bars in Fog City, too, including the one at Sal's, so I figured we were in a legit house of spirits, although the guy behind the bar looked like he was aspiring to become one of the nut-sack guys pretty soon. Ancient, is what I'm saying.

Moo said some nonsense to the bartender and asked me what I was drinking. I told him nothing, and the bartender set a shot of Old Tennis Shoes in front of each of us.

"I said 'nothing,'" I said.

"I'm becoming a customer," said Moo. Then he fired out what I guess was a bunch of Chinese pleasantries, which ended on an up note, which I took as Moo Shoes asking a question.

"He wants to know why we want to know where the whore-houses are."

"Did you tell him the normal reasons?"

"I did. He doesn't believe me."

"Tell him we're looking for a dame."

"I told you, I told him that."

"No, that specific dame. Tell him she's your, uh, I don't know, auntie."

Moo Shoes launched into a compelling and heart-wrenching story about finding his long-lost auntie Niu Yun—I heard the name—and the guy just listened. At the end he said four syllables, then walked through a door to the back.

"What, what, what?" I asked Moo.

"He said I am a liar."

"Yeah, but that's not all."

"No, that's all he said."

"No, I mean, yes, you are a liar, but you have many other talents as well."

"Thank you."

"Navigation not being one of them."

"Let it go, Sammy. This is not going well."

The guy came out of the back room and said something to Moo Shoes. Moo downed his shot. Then the old guy gestured for me to do the same, and was pretty urgent about it. I make it a policy, as a professional, to drink Old Tennis Shoes (or Old Tennessee, as the uninitiated call it) only when I am near broke or when nothing else is available, because it often causes me to end up in dice games or the company of unsuitable women, sometimes both. But Moo Shoes was buying, and technically, we were looking for unsuitable women, so I downed my shot.*

I had no sooner finished that noise everyone makes after

---

* Old Tennis Shoes is also the brand that Milo pours out of the trunk of his cab, since it comes in affordable one-gallon jugs and fifty-five-gallon oil drums.

downing a shot of Old Tennis Shoes, a mix between a gasp and a sigh, than three Chinese mugs of respectable size came through the front door and took positions behind me and Moo Shoes.

The bartender said something to Moo. Moo translated, "He says to go with these guys."

"Did you bring your roscoe?" I inquired.

"I did not," said Moo. "But I have my wallet in my jacket pocket and might be able to bluff us out of here."

"We speak English," said the largest of them.

"Fancy that," I said, the very picture of congeniality and good-will toward mugs of all nations. "I was just discussing with my good pal here that I have mastered over ten"—Moo coughed—"*seven* words in your own mother tongue."

"Come with us," said the large guy.

"Lead the way, my good man," I said.

The big guy led the way and the two other guys, who were of average height but had shoulders that looked like they knew their way around slinging hay bales or buckets of potatoes (I'm from Boise, we really only have potato metaphors), followed. I thought I might be able to take one of them—two if I got in a lucky punch and stopped one's clock early—but I wasn't sure Moo could hold up his end. Unless one of them pulled a heater, it was always an option, and from the looks of them, work shirts over work pants, they weren't rodded up, so I decided to go along to see what I could see and not start swinging until the bell rang.

The muscle led us to the end of the street and a three-story house with absolutely nothing of note about it except a wide covered porch with a couch on it and a sign in Chinese characters over the red double doors.

"What's it say?" I asked Eddie.

"Wa Ting Shan Fong," he said.

"Oh, thanks, Moo, I'll be completely prepared for whatever fate

awaits us through those red doors now that I know that." Fucking
Moo Shoes.

"Slow your roll, Joel, I was getting there. It means Flowery
Arbor Mountain Booth."

"Doesn't really need a sign, does it? I mean, you look at this
oversized cracker box without so much as a geranium in the window, sitting on a flat-as-a-flapjack river delta, and what immediately
comes to mind?"

"Flowery arbor mountain booth?" Moo ventured.

"Exactly."

The guy in front opened the door and stepped aside, revealing
a foyer with a red Persian rug and a golden dragon statue such as
are often seen in chop suey joints in Chinatown. It opened onto a
parlor done up in much red velvet and red mohair couches going
bald on the arms, such as one often finds in cathouses and the lob-
bies of haunted hotels.

"Sit," said the big guy. "Wait."

So we sat. We waited. A half hour went by. An hour. We saw
not a soul.

"Were we supposed to take a number?" Moo asked.

I peeked into the other rooms. No one. I said, "A guy who used
to come in the bar told me once that if you go in someplace and
they don't pay any attention to you, then start stealing stuff. They'll
either start paying attention or you'll have something for your time."

"Wise. What business was that guy in?"

"Thief, I think."

"Maybe we check in with someone and go get some lunch?"
said Moo.

"Maybe we go looking for the kitchen and see if we can find
lunch, huh?"

So we did. We soft-shoed it through what must have been a dining room and another sitting room, went by an office with no one

at the desk, and finally found a swinging door behind which there was a pretty good-sized kitchen, unattended. Moo Shoes went for the icebox right away.

"Hey, there's a whole ham in here."

"I think there's a saying about whorehouse ham."

"Do you know what it is?"

"Nope, pull that rascal out."

Moo lifted the ham out and put it on the counter. I found a bread box where there was a new loaf waiting. "Look for mustard," I said.

"Got it," said Moo Shoes.

I found a butcher knife in a drawer and sliced some bread, then slid the knife to Moo Shoes, who went after the ham like an axe murderer at a debutante ball. Moo Shoes stacked the ham on the bread, and he was about to slather on some mustard when a tiny Chinese broad who looked about a hundred years old came through a door at the back of the kitchen waving a hatchet and screaming. A spry hundred.

Moo was through the swinging door in a flash. I grabbed the sandwiches and followed, past the office, through the dining room, the sitting room, the parlor, by the dragon in the foyer, and out the front door. Moo Shoes bounded off the porch, and I was about to follow, but a woman's voice behind me said, "You'll want to hold the door shut."

I turned. There was a dame of about forty in a slip, redhead, sitting on the couch, smoking a cigarette.

"She won't chop the door," the porch broad said.

"Hold the door, Moo," I said.

"You hold the door," said Moo Shoes.

"I can't. I'm holding the sandwiches."

Moo pulled the door shut and held the double knobs, which began to rattle. The tiny hatchet dame was yelling much Chinese through the door.

"She seems steamed," said the porch broad.

"Yeah. We were just about to pay her for the sandwiches, but she didn't give us time to explain."

"You can pay me," said the porch broad.

"You want a sandwich?" I asked her, holding one out. "Mustard!" I bounced my eyebrows in the manner of a guy who really thinks mustard is the tits.

"Nah, still finishing my breakfast," she said, holding up her cigarette. "That's five bucks for the sandwiches."

"That seems a little steep." At the Five & Dime lunch counter they wouldn't go for more than a buck fifty, and that would include two Cokes.

"Oh, did you not want the blow job? Comes with them."

"Nah," I said. "Just the sandwiches will be fine."

"Okay, two bucks then."

I handed her one of my sandwiches to hold while I dug in my wallet for the two bucks, which I traded her for my sandwich.

"So, that it, then? We don't really have much of a lunch crowd at a place like this, you know."

"Nah, we're looking for something," I said. "Sure you won't have a sandwich?"

"Stop trying to give my sandwich away!" said Moo Shoes.

"You can't eat it," I said. "You have to hold the door."

"Hang on a second," said the porch broad. She went over to the door, got right up next to Moo, and shouted something very sternly in Chinese. The rattling and shouting on the other side of the door stopped.

"What'd she say?" I asked.

"She was saying that she was going to chop our dicks off with the hatchet," said Moo.

"No, I meant our gracious hostess," I said, nodding to the porch dame.

"I told her to shut the fuck up and get back to work, we were doing business," the dame said.

"Oh," I said. "So, you're the boss?"

"During business hours," she said. "We're not really open this time of day. Most of our clientele is working on the farms around here during the daylight hours."

"Right," I said. "So, we were looking for something and someone who might help us find it."

"Yeah, who and what led you here?"

"Well, three guys led us here when we mentioned a woman named Niu Yun, but we're really looking for a statue that an associate lost in this town a long time ago. We've been hired to recover it. He figures it might be at one of the—"

"Brothels," said Moo.

"Well, I've never heard that name," said the redhead. "But I can ask around. What kind of statue?"

"It's a black dragon, about yea big." I held the sandwiches apart to signify yea big.

"Never seen anything like that. I can give you a deal on that golden dragon in the foyer. Thirty bucks."

"Is that with—"

"No, a blow job is extra with the dragon. Look, buddy, you seem like a nice fella. I'll call around. I got a boss in the city I have to answer to before I let anyone rifle through the house looking for a statue. I'll ask about this doll you're searching for, too. You got a number?"

I handed the sandwiches to Moo Shoes, pulled out my order pad and wrote down my name and number, tore off the sheet, and handed it to her. "It's a bar I own," I said. "If I'm not there you can leave a message for me."

"Sure thing," she said, looking over the number. "Is this an order pad?"

"My cards are at the printer," I said. "Thanks for your help."

"We'll give you five hundred bucks for the black dragon right now," said Moo Shoes.

"What?" I said. Fucking Moo Shoes.

"Even if I knew where it was, I'd have to talk to my boss," said the porch dame.

"Well, you have my number, doll," I said.

Moo handed me my sandwich as we walked away.

"What was that?" I asked.

"Uncle Ho gave me a grand to offer for the dragon."

"And you're just telling me about this now?"

"That dame was holding out on us," he said. "She might have given us the dragon for free. If you'd known we had the money you would have led with that."

"I am very uncomfortable negotiating with a dame in her under-wear," I admitted. I *would* have offered her the money. Fucking Moo Shoes. "Why do you think those guys at the bar brought us here?"

"I think the bartender recognized the name. I think Uncle Ho is also holding out on us."

"*Two-Toes! Where is the Catfucker?*" someone said to me. I hate it when people call me Two-Toes. "Who said that?" I looked around.

Moo Shoes had a mouthful of ham sandwich and looked at me like I was nuts.

Locke, California—April 1906

It took five days to get to the town of Locke—five days sleeping outside of towns and villages, sometimes just in a field. Finding their way from one Chinatown to the next, getting directions and buying supplies. Five days of walking during the day, shivering in the cold at night huddled together under their blankets. Five days and not a word from the dragon. After what they had seen at Eldridge, with every day they didn't hear they rested a little better, despite the rough conditions.

"Maybe we should leave the statue here," said Niu Yun one morning outside the town of Vallejo, after they had slept under an oak tree.

Ho set the dragon on the ground and began to walk away, then stopped. "I don't think so. The dragon told me to save you. I think it wants to stay with you."

"You are mad," said Niu Yun.

"We both saw the Rain Dragon come from the clouds and dive into the earth. We both are mad now, I think."

"Fine, bring it," said Niu Yun. "Stupid dragon."

"*You're a stupid dragon!*" said the dragon.

"He says that—"

"I don't care," said Niu Yun. She stomped away. Ho followed after her. He hadn't realized what a relief it had been to not hear the dragon's voice in his head for a while.

When they reached Locke, the streets were alive with men scurrying here and there, carrying bundles of clothes, some leading donkeys pulling wagons, possessions piled high. Men carrying everything they owned, without a place to live. One man ran up to them as they plunged into the crowd. "There is no place to stay," he said. "Did you hear, Big Town burned? Chinatown is gone. Everyone is looking for shelter." Then the man seemed to notice through her borrowed clothing that Niu Yun was a woman, and he stopped talking and just stared.

Another man joined him, gawking, then a third.

"Is she your wife?" asked one man.

"I will give you forty dollars for her," said another.

"She is my wife," said Ho. "And I will shoot anyone who touches her." He pulled up his shirt to show his gun.

"After I chop off their dicks," said Niu Yun, who brandished her hatchet.

Interest waned quickly and the gawkers moved on to looking for food and shelter again. One very old man tottered up to Ho and said, "There." He pointed to a big house with red double doors at the end of the street. "Take her there. They will know what to do."

They paused in front of the house with the red doors and Ho read from the sign over the porch: "Flowery Arbor Mountain Booth."

"You're making that up," said Niu Yun. She couldn't read and did not trust men who could, or men who couldn't, for that matter. "This place is none of those things."

"I have a little money left. Perhaps we should go back to Exalted Pavilion of Blissful Rice and Chicken Feet down the street and have a meal first?"

"Just go," she said.

Ho walked up to the double doors and was about to knock when he noticed one of them was ajar. He pushed it open. Inside he saw fine carpets and furniture and a glorious statue of a golden dragon.

"What do you want?" came a woman's voice in Cantonese. She stood in the middle of a parlor wearing an austere cotton dress and apron, a servant, it seemed—perhaps sixty years old. Beyond her a half-dozen white women lounged on divans and in chairs, smoking and looking bored.

"A man in the street told us you could help us," said Ho. He didn't like the look of this place and he didn't like being in the presence of so many white devil women.

"Follow me," said the Chinese woman.

They followed her through the parlor, then another sitting room, then into a room with a desk where an older white woman wearing spectacles on her nose looked up from some papers she had been working on. She said something in English to the Chinese woman, who said to Ho, "What do you want?"

Ho heard a scuff of shoes behind him and looked back to see two large Chinese men standing there.

"I need to find a place for this woman," said Ho. "The White Devil's Daughter told us to come to this town."

The Chinese woman translated, then the white woman spoke at length.

"We do not have Chinese whores," said the Chinese woman. "All our whores are white or Indian. It is an agreement we have with the tongs. We run no Chinese whores in Locke and pay our tribute and they leave us alone. We have no place for her. Sell her somewhere else. There are many Chinese workers who would pay for her, but she can't whore in Locke."

Ho looked at Niu Yun and shook his head as if to say, *Please be quiet and don't talk about chopping off dicks right now.*

He took a gamble and pulled up his sleeve, flashed the brand of the Rain Dragon on his forearm. "I am of Ghee Sin Tong, and this woman is under my protection. Our agreement remains and you should have no Chinese whores, but you must find a place for this woman."

The white woman looked perplexed as the Chinese woman translated, but both their eyes had widened at the sign of Ho's brand. After some time, the white woman spoke at length and the Chinese woman translated.

"We honor our agreement with the Ghee Sin, and we will never run Chinese whores, but we will find a place for this woman, but as she cannot pay her way, we would ask that you pay for her upkeep."

Ho dug into his pockets and pulled out what remained of the money they had taken from the brothers at the guild house: twenty-seven dollars. He put it on the desk. "This is for her up-keep. And she must never be put to work as a whore or there will be swift action by the tong."

The white woman sneered at the crumpled bills and said something abrupt to the Chinese woman.

"It is not enough. This will barely keep her for a month. There are many who have no place to go. There is no room for a big-foot woman that we cannot whore."

Ho suspected the last part was not something the white woman had said.

"I will work," said Niu Yun. "I can cook and clean. And I can tend pigs and chickens if needed. I am from a farm and I know how to work hard."

"No," said the Chinese woman. "I do the cooking and cleaning here."

"Wouldn't you like to rest?" asked Ho.

"No," said the Chinese woman.

"I have this," said Ho. He unslung the Rain Dragon and set it on the desk with a thump. "This is a talisman from the Ghee Sin. It is our patron protector. If ever you should have a dispute with the Ghee Sin or any other tong, give them this and they will grant you a favor. It must be so. But you must never tell anyone you have it until it is time to redeem it. Ever. It must remain secret. In exchange, you need only give this woman shelter and a chance to earn her way." As if on cue, the dragon's green eyes flashed and the two women looked at each other with fleeting expressions of panic.

Ho realized that fear was his best approach. He lifted the front of his shirt and showed them his gun, then looked at the Chinese woman and said, "I can make a vacancy for her here, if that is the problem."

"And I will chop your dicks off," said Niu Yun to the men behind them.

"Not now," said Ho.

"Sorry," said Niu Yun.

The two women spoke at length in English and finally the Chinese woman said, "She may stay. There is a closet behind the kitchen where she can sleep. We will honor our agreement with the tong."

"And she must never be sold or whored out, and no one from Big Town must know she is here," insisted Ho. "Or the wrath of the tong will come down on you."

The Chinese woman nodded and translated. The white woman nodded in turn.

Ho looked at Niu Yun. "You will be safe here. If they treat you badly, you know what to do."

She smiled and patted her hatchet. "Where will you go?"

"I don't know."

Niu Yun lunged for the bills on the desk, grabbed one, and handed it to Ho. It happened to be a five-dollar bill. "For your food."

The other two women did not protest. Ho nodded and took the bill.

Ho leaned in close to Niu Yun so only she could hear him. "I am sorry."

"Good-bye, Catfucker," she said.

19

MABEL'S
ON POST

Sammy

When I got back to the city and checked in at Sal's there was a message waiting for me from Mabel. Just *Mabel*, and a number. Mabel is the preeminent nookie bookie in Fog City, and Mabel's on Post Street the foremost cathouse in the greater Bay Area.

"She said it was important," Bennie said.

"She called herself?"

"It was a dame, sounded like she was large and in charge."

"That's her," I said. I made the call. A guy answered on the first ring. I told him who I was and Mabel came on the line.

"Sammy, we need to have a natter."

"At your service," I said.

"Not on the phone. Dunne the Nun might have my line tapped—you hear that, you no-dick, lowlife, flatfoot piece of shit?—excuse my fucking French, sweetheart. Can you drop by the *casa*?"

"I'll be there in twenty," I said.

I was there in twenty. Mabel's was a massive Victorian mansion on Post Street that had miraculously survived the earthquake and therefore had a lot more stone in its construction than most houses in the city, because masonry hadn't fared well during the quake. Of course, wood hadn't fared well in the fire after the quake. It was a wonder we weren't all living in asbestos tents in these modern times.

On the street, two SFPD plainclothes were staked out in a black sedan as inconspicuous as a grizzly bear in a donut shop.

Mabel's was set back off the street, with a marble walkway lined with boxwoods trimmed in the shape of bullets, or maybe gumdrops, depending on how you were feeling that day. I skipped up the sandstone steps and walked into the lobby, where I was met by a linebacker-shaped fellow in butler togs.

"Mr. Powers," I said, flashing him a smile of recognition and bonhomie that I bring to all my interpersonal business.

"Mr. Tiffin," said Mr. Powers, with equal parts goodwill and intimidation. "Pleasure to see you again. Are we rodded up today?" (Firearms are not permitted on the premises during business hours, which are all of them.)

"We are not, Mr. Powers," I said. "I have ventured out sans roscoe today, as I anticipated your fine joint would be under scrutiny by the gendarmes."

"Today and every day," said Mr. Powers. "So constant is their presence of late that management has considered sending a complimentary cocktail out to the gentlemen."

"Of the Molotov variety?"

"That very blend has been suggested."

"Excellent choice."

"Go on in, Sammy. She's by the bar."

I tipped my hat to Mr. Powers, then entered a capacious parlor outfitted with various fancy furniture festooned with floozage* in silk of all shapes and sizes, all looking very bored indeed. All the nail filing and gum cracking sounded like firecrackers in a sawmill. I tipped my hat all around, saying "ladies" as they perked up at my

---

★ *Floozage*: an arrangement of floozies.

presence only to be disheartened when Mabel said, "Settle down, he's not here for you."

Mabel stood at the bar in the corner, a statuesque broad of many curves, smoothed somewhat by time but no less compressed into a green sequined evening gown with buckets of bosom spilling out the top and a fountain of red hair splashing down over it all. She was smoking a cigarette in a long ivory holder. Behind her, a bartender, a skinny mug about my age in black-and-whites with garters on his sleeves, was trying to look busy and failing spectacularly. I'd only been in Mabel's a few times, but even of an afternoon, I'd never seen it so bereft of customers.

"Hey, handsome," she said. You could be the mayor of Uglytown and she'd greet you the same way and make you believe it.

"Hey, doll face," I said.

"Madame Doll Face to you. Can I buy you a drink?"

"Thanks, miles to go and whatnot. What can I help you with, Madame Doll Face?"

"Right down to business."

"I heard that's how you like to do things."

"I suppose I do. So, I take it you saw our crossing guards out front?"

"Kind of hard to miss. Courtesy of Captain Dunne?"

"They been there for a month. Not three shifts a day, but you don't know when they're going to be there and when they're not. He didn't just bust up the joint and take the girls away—we have too many friends in high places for that—so he made it visible, put those mugs out front in plain view. Our more distinguished clients didn't want to be seen coming in and out, but our more distinguished clients also tend to be rolling in simoleons, so we were sending girls out to them at various destinations. Even made an arrangement with a couple of cabbies to see that everyone got to where they needed to be. So then the heat starts following the girls wherever they go, and that hurts business. Even our high rollers don't want the law having a record of hookers meeting them here and there. It's like Dunne has turned the vice squad into a bunch of divorce peepers. Thing is, I got no angle on this guy. Some of my best customers are cops—they get a discount, for fuck's sake—but I got something on each of them. Even Pookie O'Hara, douche bag that he was, could be worked. You always have an angle on a crooked cop, but this Boy Scout, I got nothing."

I kind of wished I'd had that drink. I had a feeling I knew where she was going and I did not think she was going to like what I was going to say. "It's tough, Mabel. Everyone in the fun business is feeling the pinch. I don't know what I can do about it."

"Well, I wish you could send him on vacation to the same place Pookie went—"

"Mabel, I didn't scrag Pookie. I know people think I did, but—"

"Kid, Powers saw him outside in your rumble seat, beat up and gacked to the gills on something, and that was the last time anyone saw him anywhere, so spare me the innocent eyes and the 'little ol' me' speech. That's not why I called you."

"You don't want me to scrag Dunne?"

"It would be nice. Don't get me wrong. I would be very pleased if that happened, so I don't want to talk you out of anything, but the Mother Superior put himself smack in the middle of a supply and demand problem, so that problem will take care of itself before long. He's pissing off a lot of the wrong people. I called you because you are looking for a dragon, I know where it is and who's got it, and I know how you can get it."

I probably gulped. "You do?" I said, trying to pretend I wasn't surprised.

"I do," said the madam. "Yeah, that place in Locke is mine. The hookers in Locke have been white going back to the turn of the century—an agreement with the old fighting tongs. So, I can see to it you get your dragon, but you are going to have to do a favor for me, and it's a big one, but I think you're up to it."

"I'm all ears."

"I need to throw a Christmas party, like I do every year, sixty miles north of here, and I need to get all of my girls and the house staff to it, and back, and none of those cops outside can ever know they were gone."

I whistled and looked around at all the dames lounging in the parlor, smiled, and made like I was tipping my hat, even though I was holding my hat and not wearing it. "Ladies." Hat tip. "Hey, doll." Wink. "Looking good there, red."

To Mabel I said, "How many dames you got?"

"Thirty. Staff of six, bartenders and maids. Four security guys. Call it forty altogether."

"This place got a back door?"

"Garage underneath where servants entered and they used to make deliveries when this place was a private residence. But you can see it from the front."

"You tried leading them on a goose chase? Sending a couple of dames off as decoys and sneaking the rest out when they follow the rust rabbits?"

"Rust rabbits?"

"Mechanical hares that greyhounds chase at the dog track. I got a buddy from Florida with a gambling habit."

"I like it," she said, handing her cigarette holder to the bartender, who butted it, reloaded it, and handed it back to her, then stood ready with a lighter. "But yeah, we tried drawing them off, tried to catch them on a shift change, even tried sending coffee with a laxative out to them. They got radio cars. Before one leaves they call another one. After that they wouldn't take the coffee with the knockout drops."

"Your staff goes home from work, don't they?"

"Yeah, they leave them alone. Look, not a lot of people know I do this party, but somehow Dunne got wind of it and he doesn't want it to happen, despite that it's barely even against the law."

"And you think I'm the guy that can figure this out. Me? A bartender at a dive bar in North Beach. Why?"

"Because you're clever, Sammy. I knew that the minute I met you. You got some stones on you, too. I saw how you went up against Pookie and the Bohemian Club, and you came out scot-free. And most important, you're about to owe me a favor, and I love a guy that owes me a favor."

I nodded. "And when is this party supposed to happen?"

"It's gotta be December first. The only time the venue will be open."

"That's four days after Thanksgiving. I might be able to use that. Where's the venue?"

"The Sonoma Hospital for Feeble Minded Children, in El-dridge."

"You're yanking my crank, Mabes."

"What, feebs like Christmas, too. Feebs fucking love Christ-mas. Can you do it?"

"Let me ponder it." I liked that Mabel thought I was clever. Reminded me of my dear mother, who had occasionally given me the same compliment. Always when she was pretty sauced up, but it was nice just the same.

"You do this, I'll make it worth your while, but better than that, I'll be your friend. I'm a good friend to have in this town, Sammy."

"I guessed that, Mabel. You haven't ever solved a murder case, have you?"

"Made sure a couple never got solved. That helpful?"

"It might be." I put my hat on. "I'll be in touch. Nice to see you."

"Yes, it is. Don't wait long, sugar. I got a ticking clock over here."

"Right. As soon as I figure it out."

"That's when you'll get your dragon."

Stilton DeCheese, Private Eye

I was staking out a drag king club called Jimmy's Joynt on the wharf, and I'd borrowed some looser pants from Jimmy so I didn't have to shed them when I was driving the Chrysler I borrowed from a friend of mine from out of town. He's a little guy and has pedal extensions welded on, which make it hard for a normal-sized dame to drive without looking like she's winding up to give birth. I don't bust his chops about it; we were all little once.

I was looking to accidentally on purpose run into a thin frail called Olivia Stoddard, who goes by Nora on the street. Her daddy is a gold-plated nob lawyer who's more connected than Western Union, and he wanted to get a line on her before she got canceled by whoever was murdering Fog City dykes, or at least that's what he claimed. I don't care why he wanted to find her, she wasn't working that hard not to be found, so I guessed he wasn't going to handcuff her to a radiator and beat her until she couldn't drool her own name—his money was good and the drinks were going on expenses. I took the job.

I'd only been at the bar for an hour or so when she came in. I'd already asked Jimmy Vasco, the owner, to take a powder if Olivia came in, because for a little dame Jimmy uses a lot of oxygen and I might need a little breathing room to work.

"You just gonna pull a roscoe on her and make her come along with you?" Jimmy asked me.

"Nah, I figure I'll charm her into giving herself up, or at least letting on where her papa can find her."

"Then can I have my gun back? I'm a little jumpy with the death threats and whatnot."

"Sure," I said. "The safety of our clients is our number one concern." I pulled the Walther out of my jacket pocket and held it out to her.

"Don't just hand me a heater over the bar in front of everyone." She snatched the roscoe out of my hand and pocketed it.

"Why? The more people that know you're rodded up, the less chance someone's gonna punch your ticket with an ice pick, kid."

"Kid? I'm at least twenty years older than you."

"Yeah, but you'd never know it to look at you."

"Oh, spare me the butter job," she said. "I don't care what Sammy says, you're more ham than cheese." But she laughed and straightened her tie a little like she was feeling younger every second, which is one of the many reasons lesbians love me: I know the right thing to say.

"And you've got a figure that would make a dame feel like she's sittin' in soup," said Jimmy.

"What?" This daffy dame was talking to my inner monologue.

"You're saying your private dick narration out loud, Stilton. You're cut off." She called to Mel, the bartender, "Hey, just lime and soda for this one for the rest of the night."

Jimmy could be a vicious bitch if you got on her wrong side, but she was seeing my best pal Myrtle and I was under orders to string her along until Myrt got the combination to the office safe.

"Still saying it out loud. I'll be in my office if you need me."

She sauntered off like she'd just had the pleasure of starving a few orphans and was celebrating the good times.

"Shut up, Stilton," Jimmy said.

Anyway, the Stoddard dame came in a little after that. She was wearing a black suit over a red silk camisole with some kind of white flower in her brunette bob. I don't know if she was going for butch or just confused, but she slid onto a stool down the bar and started putting the flirt on Mel the bartender, who was also tall, thin, and androgynous, and the two of them looked like they might have escaped from the cane-and-top-hat chorus of a Busby Berkeley musical set in a town where they'd never discovered sandwiches.

I scooted down the bar and slid into the seat next to the Stoddard bird. "Hey, doll, buy you a drink?" I said. It's what guys always say to me. I don't know how to pick up a dame.

She held up the glass that Mel had just set in front of her and winked. It looked like a gin and tonic, what with the lime and the fizz.

"Yeah, I knew that. I thought I'd wait until you ordered to offer and save a little money."

She laughed. She had a nice laugh. The kind of laugh that made you want to take her to a Marx Brothers movie, buy her a Coke, and watch her shoot it out her nose. "I'm Nora," she said. She held out her hand to shake.

"Tilly," I said. "Tilly DeCheese." I took her hand and shook it by the fingertips like guys do sometimes so they don't crush your dainty hand, and you let them so they don't feel your calluses from hammering rivets and bending steel stock.

"DeCheese?" she asked.

"It's French," I said.

"Then wouldn't it be *Le Fromage*?"

"It was, but those fucks at Ellis Island made us change it." I was beginning to see why Sammy got sored up at me sometimes. Nobody likes a dame that's smarter than them.

"I like your flower," I said, nodding to the white blossom in her hair.

"Thanks. It's a carnation."

"Oh yeah," I said. "I like Carnation canned milk in my java sometimes. My pop used to say only sissies take milk and sugar in their coffee."

"Works for me," she said, giving me and then the joint a once-over. "Hey, Tilly, this place is a graveyard. You want to get out of here, go somewhere fun? I know a place. You'll love it."

This broad was pretty confident I was going to go with her. I mean, I'd just met her, and I was probably too corned up to be driving, especially with the cops watching the place, and she had been on the scene at the time of a couple of murders—of dames dressed in drag, like I was. What did she think, I was some kind of easy sleazy? Some kind of pushover?

"You bet!" I said. "I love fun."

"Let's go," she said. She threw some bills on the bar, winked good-bye to Mel, then took me by the hand and pulled me up the ramp, past the door dames, and out onto the pier.

"Look, Nora, I've had a few too many to be driving."

"That's swell. I'll drive," she said, heading to a maroon Packard. "Jump in."

"Where we going?" I asked. Like I was just going to take off with her, no gun, my only backup hiding in the trunk of the Chrysler, and not tell anyone where I was going or when I was coming back? Ha! Not bloody likely, as my dear limey ma used to say.

"You'll see," she said. "It'll be an adventure."

"I *love* adventure," I said. This frail was worth a grand plus expenses. Letting her drive off into the night would be like throwing money out the window. I shot a glance over to Pier 27 as we pulled away and, sure enough, some headlights came on and someone started heading toward the Embarcadero in parallel with us. She hung a left and so did the car at Pier 27. When Nora cut up Broadway, the car that had been with us took the turn, too, and so did another one that looked familiar behind that one.

"What's so interesting back there?" Nora asked.

I guess I was up on my knees on the seat looking out the back window. "I think you picked up a tail, doll."

She laughed. "Is it a Packard like this one?"

"Nah, a Dodge, I think."

"It's just cops, then. Nothing to worry about."

We were headed into my usual stomping grounds. As she passed Mona's 440 Nora said, "You ever been to Mona's?"

And just like that she pulled up to the curb and set the parking brake.

I fell back on Myrtle's lesbian strategy. "Nah, I'm new," I said.

"I thought you looked a little soft around the edges."

"Really?" *Soft? I could snap your skinny neck like a pretzel.*

"That's okay," she said. "I *like* soft around the edges." Then she slid over on the seat and kissed me, hard and long and with no little tongue, and because I was drunk and undercover, I kissed her back. I kept thinking, *Would I kiss this dame for a thousand bucks?* And the answer evidently was yes. But then I thought, *Would I get murdered for this dame, even for a thousand bucks?* and the answer was *Not on your life, sister.*

She reached over me and pulled the door handle and we both got out on my side. I started toward Mona's and she grabbed my hand.

"No, doll, that's not where we're going."

Sammy

"I hope we'll be seeing more of you, Mr. Tiffin," Mr. Powers said as I was leaving Mabel's.

"It seems like that will be the case, Mr. Powers," I said. "Will you be in attendance at the Christmas party?"

"I will be serving that evening and attending to security matters as they arise."

"So she is really going to take thirty hookers to a hospital for feeble-minded children?"

"They don't call it that anymore, but Mabel gets nostalgic around the holidays."

"Powers?" I said. I gave him the raised eyebrow of incredulity, which is akin to my eyebrow of *Are you shittin' me?*

"It's nothing." He shrugged, great square shoulders rising like the spans of a drawbridge. "You should work at this place for a while. Some of the kinks these guys pay for would cinch your sack up. Some of them as specific as an exacta bet."

"But with fewer horses, right?"

Mr. Powers rolled his eyes. "Good night, Mr. Tiffin."

"Good night, Mr. Powers."

I drove crazy, parked double, and was at work only a little over an hour late. Bennie was wiping down the bar the way you do when you want someone to imagine he is grinding your face into the bar. Yeah, my face.

"You got a message," Bennie said.

"I'm sorry, Bennie, I got held up."

Bennie ignored me, went to the pad by the phone. "Jimmy Vasco called. Just a few minutes ago."

"Thanks, Bennie."

I shed my jacket and hat and hung them in the back. Tucked my tie in my shirt and went to the phone. Dialed Jimmy's Joynt. The bartender answered and put Jimmy on in a tick.

"You called?" I said.

"Sammy, the Cheese is down here at my bar in drag, quaffing gimlets like she's fighting off scurvy. Says she's working a case. Look, I have been hooted up as much as the next dame, from time to time, but she is rodded up and I don't want her driving Myrtle to their secret birthday project. I'm going to go get my gun from her, but after that, this is a Sammy problem, which I would like Sammy to solve."

"Aw, hell, Jimmy, I'm on the clock at the bar, and I've already had Bennie working doubles for me for the whole week. Can't you just keep her there? Cut her off or let her drink until she passes out? I'll come get her after my shift."

"She's wearing my clothes, Sammy. I don't want gimlet barf on my clothes."

"Keep her there. I'll be there as soon as I can."

I rang off and turned to Bennie. "Pal?"

"No."

"But—"

"No."

"I'll give you"—I dug in my pocket and looked at my remaining expense money—"a hundred and eleven dollars."

"No."

"And thirty-two—thirty-three cents?"

"No. I got a date."

"You do not. You don't have to lie, Bennie. I've been a heel. I know it."

"I have a date, and I've had to reschedule three times to cover for you."

I felt like I'd showed up for second-grade show-and-tell with a sack of drowned kittens. I peeled forty bucks off my expense money. "Here, Bennie. Dinner and whatnot."

"I'm not staying."

"I know. Take it, go."

"You're supposed to cover my shift in the morning. You agreed to it when I covered you last night."

"I'll be here," I said. "Go, before I have to kick you out for ma-lingering."

"I don't know what that means." He took the bills. "You don't need to do this."

"Penance," I said. "I almost went to seminary."

"Okay, thanks," Bennie said. "Bye."

"Have fun, kid." I waited for him to get out the door, then went to the phone. If I just closed the bar and it got back to Mrs. Sal, I'd probably lose my honored position as the guy who pretends to own a dive bar in North Beach. And it *would* get back to Mrs. Sal. On the other hand, if I didn't go remove the Cheese from Jimmy's, well, there was no limit to the ways it could go bad. Moo Shoes was working. Lone Jones was working. Most everyone else I knew was a drunk or couldn't be trusted with other people's money. I checked my little slip of numbers by the phone and dialed Doris's apartment.

An hour later I was handing the bar keys to Doris. "This is my night off," she said.

"How's Milo?"

"He's still healing up. Still not ready to drive."

"You can close up at one. No need to stay open later."

"I'm throwing everyone out at midnight."

"Or midnight is good, too."

There was a ticket on Jimmy Vasco's Ford that I was going to have to add to my expenses. I was getting used to having access to a car and I was thinking about asking Jimmy to throw in the Ford when I caught the killer. I hit the Embarcadero in five minutes flat and was moving slow up to the turn onto Pier 29 when I saw the maroon Packard pull out. No question the Stoddard dame was driving, and the Cheese was in the passenger seat, looking back to see if anyone was following. Someone was. Someone besides me. I saw a big sedan in my rearview pull out of Pier 27 behind me. I dove the Ford into an open fire lane like I was parking and let the sedan go by. A Dodge, black, standard SFPD plainclothes issue. Tall mug driving. I didn't get a look at him. When he was a block ahead I pulled back onto the street and followed.

The Packard turned at Broadway with the Dodge right behind, and five blocks later the Stoddard dame parked the big Packard like a champ and climbed out. The Dodge found a spot another block down and I pulled a U-turn and parked across the street. It was a club block. I could see Lone Jones at his station at the door at the Moonlight Club a block up. Then Finocchio's, the drag joint; the Green Room, blues; then Mona's 440, with a couple of smaller bars in between. And that was just one side of the street.

Then Olivia Stoddard laid a lip-lock on the Cheese and for a second it looked like the Cheese was giving as good as she was getting. I was a little nonplussed, as was the tall cop who had crawled out of his Dodge and then taken up a station of holding up a wall while he waited for the dames to dismount. Then they broke the clinch, and before I got across the street, Stoddard had led the Cheese by the hand into Finocchio's. About that time, I got a good look at the cop, and him at me. I scampered the rest of the way across and fell in beside him.

"Captain Dunne, fancy meeting you here," I said, cheerful as a chipmunk full of cashews.

"Tiffin," Dunne said, not looking at me, just striding on, like if he ignored me I might fall down a manhole. "What are you doing here?"

"Same as you, following the Stoddard girl. Daddy told me he had other resources. That you, Captain—you a resource?"

"That's none of your business. And what you mean, Daddy? Alton Stoddard is having you follow his daughter?"

"Nah, just to find her, so I'm in the money, it looks like. Unless you decide to snatch her out from under me. That what you're going to do? Put the cuffs on her, smack her around a little? Throw her in the cruiser and take her downtown?"

He stopped walking and turned to me. "How long have you been following her? Do you know where she's staying?"

"Nope. About ten minutes, including parking the car."

"What do you plan to do?"

"Keep an eye on her, follow her to where she's staying, then let Mr. Stoddard know where she is. You think Stoddard will go get her himself? Climb down from his tower? Or maybe send two gorillas along with her wet nurse to retrieve her?"

"Her wet nurse?"

"Yeah, that's how rich kids do, right? Their wet nurse stays with them until they marry, like in *Romeo and Juliet*."

"What do you know about *Romeo and Juliet*?"

"Mother was an English teacher. So, you just going to waltz into Finocchio's after keeping surveillance on them for a week and not expect them to react, maybe stop the show, maybe hustle certain regular customers out the back? But you've got a guy on the back, right? You're not out here by yourself, a captain, head of vice, following a poor little rich girl?"

"We don't have this place under surveillance."

"Just the drag *king* joints? But you've had a car sitting on the street half a block down. I've only been detecting for a week and I know that it would make more sense that they were watching this place from half a block away, like Jimmy's Joynt on the wharf, than watching Mona's from right out front. So I'm sure *they* think they're under surveillance. Anyway, good luck. I say a lone cop hitting the door at this point, I give it ten seconds before everyone in the joint knows you're there."

"What are you getting at, Tiffin?"

"What I'm getting at is, you scream cop. The cheap suit, the wrinkled shirt—you can get those pressed for two bits in Chinatown, by the way—the scuffed shoes, the freakish height. You might as well be carrying a sign that reads COP. But if you show up as part of a couple—the kind of fellow that often shows up here—well, they just might show you to a dark table in the back and you can keep your eye on the Stoddard dame."

"I'm not calling for backup," said Dunne.

"Why, Captain, you've got backup right here." I threaded my arm in his and put my head on his shoulder, while staying ready to give him a right uppercut to the chin if he reacted wrong. "I'm going to be your date."

Out of the corner of my eye I caught another maroon Packard parking up the block. What were the odds?

20

RETURN TO BIG TOWN

Locke, California—April 1906

The last thing the dragon said to Ho was, "*Go back to Big Town, Catfucker. Become a son of the white devils. Wait until I call.*" So Ho trod off toward the city, eating cherries and strawberries he found in orchards and fields tended by Chinese farmers along the way. After the first day he began to see the streams of people coming from Big Town: Chinese, whites, and Spanish, all of them with looks of shock and despair on their faces. Many were carrying all of their possessions on their backs or, if lucky enough, tied to a horse or a mule.

One Chinese man grabbed Ho as he passed him on the road. "Why do you go this way? Big Town is gone. Piles of bricks and ashes." Ho pulled away from him and kept on. In the hills above Berkeley, when he could first see the bay, and San Francisco smoldering in the distance, the tent cities began to appear. Many Chinese had set up camps and the stench of too many people living closely in too small a space with too little water was tall in the air. He bought some rice from a man who had managed to escape with a fifty-pound sack, who also gave him water from a bucket to cook it with. He slept under his blanket in the camp and in the morning made his way down the hills to the shore of the bay.

What was left of Oakland was full of terrified, wide-eyed people who had escaped Big Town and continued to come. Boats, wagons, and trains dumped their human cargo and then left nearly empty, so Ho was able to find a place on a ferry for half a dollar. They landed at the edge of what had been the Barbary Coast, just blocks from Chinatown, and as soon as his feet touched the shore, Ho could hear the pigs. Fewer of them, but they knew him. *"There is one alive under the bricks. Can't you smell him?"*

Ho walked paths through rubble that had once been the streets of Chinatown. What he smelled was a pervasive stench of horses that had been crushed under fallen buildings and were already beginning to rot. *"By the old opium den,"* said the pigs in his head. *"He is alive."*

Here and there a few Chinese were trying to dig into the rubble, but most of the movement in the streets was firemen, policemen, and soldiers, brought in to stop any looting, although Ho could see that little of value had escaped the fire.

He located the alley where the opium den had been, and the pile of bricks that had once been the building it was in. *"Yes, that's it. He's in there,"* said the pigs. *"Listen for him."* Ho dug through the rubble, brick by brick, for an hour. Policemen came by at one point and stopped him. A Chinese man with them interpreted.

"Are you looting?" asked the interpreter.

"No," said Ho. "I am digging for someone I know. I think he is down here."

"He is dead. Everyone is dead or has run away."

"I am not running away," said Ho. "Tell them I am just trying to find a friend." No one in that building would have actually been Ho's friend, but he was a sensitive fellow and thought that if he could save someone who was buried alive, he should do that.

The interpreter told the policemen, who moved off. The interpreter stayed for a moment.

"You are from Guangdong Province?"

"Yes," said Ho. "The Glorious Location of Various Weeds."

"The white devils are trying to make us move Chinatown to

Hunters Point. Far from business and the rest of Big Town. The merchants of the Five Companies want to build it back here before they can do that, while they are still confused and cannot blame us for the earthquake. Will you help?"

"Yes," said Ho. "I have nowhere else to go."

"Good. The city hall burned down, and with it all the birth records. There are desks and counters set up in the streets, where they are making new documents. Go there. Tell them you were born here, but grew up somewhere else. Somewhere they won't know, like Macao. Give them a Chinese name and the date of birth for your age. There will be Chinese interpreters there to help you. Do not let them turn you away. You are an American citizen today."

"I am?"

"You will be."

"Why are you helping me?"

"Because the earthquake did not destroy Chinatown. The white devil police set dynamite to many of the buildings here. To stop the fire, they said. But they only destroyed more buildings and caused new fires. Chinatown fell at the hands of the white devils."

"But you are helping them?"

"Am I? I just kept them from shooting you for looting. I have saved many this way because I speak their language. Now, go get your papers."

"I will. I have some more digging to do."

"Your friend is dead," said the interpreter.

"We shall see," said Ho.

The interpreter ran after the policemen and Ho began to move bricks, one by one, tossing them away into a pile, not knowing where he was digging to, but trying to judge from where he remembered the entrance to the opium den to be. "*Call to him, you nitwit,*" said the pigs. "*He is alive and he will hear you.*"

Ho dug until well into the afternoon; his once work-hardened hands, softened by preparing opium pipes and washing whores, were bleeding when he stopped to eat the rest of his rice, which he had formed into a ball and stored in the sash fashioned from his blanket, as Niu Yun had taught him. While he was eating he heard the voice. "I am here. I am here." It was weak but not far from him.

He tore the sleeves from his shirt and made crude mittens to cover his hands and set about digging again, calling back to the man under the bricks. In an hour he had uncovered a hand, then, under a beam that had fallen and protected the buried man, a face. He pulled the man out of the rubble to a flat spot, dusted him off, and made him drink water. It was Chin, his old boss from his days in the opium den.

"How did you know I was there?" asked old Chin.

"I heard you calling," lied Ho. "Are you hurt?" Ho looked for blood and broken bones, and although the boss was scraped and bruised and very dirty, it appeared he would live.

"I hurt everywhere," said Chin.

"That beam saved your life," said Ho, pointing into the wreckage.

"*If he doesn't make it,*" said the pigs, "*remember who your friends are.*"

"I don't even know where you are," said Ho.

"I'm right here," said Chin. "Do you have dust in your eyes?"

"Yes, yes, I do," said Ho. "See if you can stand."

"I will, but first, right next to where I fell when the building collapsed, there is a wooden box. You may have it. For saving me."

"I have nowhere to go," said Ho.

"There is money and opium in the box. A lot of opium. Take it. And find some pipes. You know how to prepare them. There will be men who come to clear this rubble and build Chinatown again. They will want to dull the pain."

"But the tong?"

"No Chinatown, no tongs. Take the opium, but give me a little of the money."

Ho did.

Sammy

The guy sitting on the Cheese's lap had enough bazooms to smother a medium-sized monkey. He was singing a Mae West song and evidently really, really wanted the Cheese to *come up and see him sometime,* and she was giving every indication that she was going to do just that. I don't think I'd ever seen the Cheese laugh that much, and it was all I could do to keep from busting out myself watching her, but I held my tough-guy mug in deference to my date.

A couple of minutes before, a skinny guy in an evening gown, a blond wig, and eyelashes that looked like epileptic tarantulas had sobbed out that he was "Falling in Love Again" in a Marlene Dietrich German accent that was thicker and sillier than anything Marlene had ever dreamed of, while grinding on the Stoddard dame and, at one point, licking her eyebrow. The drag queens were working the whole crowd, but when Stilton and Olivia Stoddard sat right on the aisle dressed like drag kings, the queens had the best foils they'd ever found. No one was going to get sore, no one was going to get embarrassed and storm out, no dame was going to wonder about the preferences of her man, and no guy was going to worry that if he laughed his date would think he was a pansy. So Stilton and Olivia became the second set of stars of the show.

"You know," I said to Dunne, "there's nothing better than watching someone you're crazy about laugh. Unless it's watching someone you're crazy about laugh while they're giving you the razzmatazz, don't you think?"

"That's not the way you talk to a policeman, Tiffin," said Dunne, scowling at the entertainers. "And *that* is repugnant."

"Harmless fun," I said.

Captain James "the Nun" Dunne did not think so, apparently. He couldn't have been more uncomfortable if he'd been sitting in a bucket of hot nails, which made the show even better for me. We'd gotten our table in the dark corner, and when we were seated

I warned Dunne not to get handsy in the dark, at which point I think he really considered bopping me in the beezer.

I tsked him. "Tsk, tsk," I said. "You don't want to blow your cover."

When the waitress, a slim guy in fishnet stockings with fabulous gams, showed, I said, "I'll have a vodka gimlet and Captain Dunne of the SFPD vice squad would like a Shirley Temple. And don't spare the Shirley."

Dunne audibly growled at me at that point, which is very unprofessional behavior for a professional law enforcement fuckstick.

"Relax, Karloff, I got this," I said, rolling some bills off my dwindling expense wad.

He did not relax. For a guy who seemed to want an entire city to control itself, he was not an ace at self-control. When he took off his hat I could count his pulse on the vein throbbing in his forehead. I mean, he was watching some guys dressed like dames singing to some dames dressed like guys (one of whom I am highly fond of) and you would have thought he was watching war crimes. I would have given two-to-one odds he wouldn't do anything in his capacity as head of vice, but it was less than even money he might just ventilate me on a personal note if I kept busting his balls.

I kept an eye on the door for whoever had arrived in the Packard matching Olivia Stoddard's to show up, but no one had darkened the door for fifteen minutes, and I hadn't gotten a good look at the driver because I'd been trying to shadow Dunne. Coincidence?

Between sets, when the waitress came by I signaled for two more, even though Dunne hadn't touched his first Shirley.

"So," I said, "if you're not grabbing Olivia Stoddard for her father, are you liking her for the drag king murders? She was at the scene of both of them."

"So were you. Maybe we like *you* for the murders. Mr. Stoddard mentioned we should keep an eye on you."

"I was with Jimmy Vasco when Butch was killed, and I was working until two in the morning the night of Frankie's murder—there's a hundred witnesses who can put me at the bar, and that many saw me at Cookie's until the wee hours." I *wish* I'd had a hundred customers that night, but what did this jamoke know? "In fact, your own guys saw me at Cookie's until about four. The two you had staking out a coffee place? For what?"

"I wouldn't count on them as alibi witnesses," Dunne said.

"So, your high moral standard evidently only applies to dress code and sex, I guess. Still pretty squishy on the old corruption front, huh? I get it. My own priest has a gambling habit."

"You're a Catholic?"

"No, but I keep a priest on retainer in case I need some emergency absolution."

"I could take you in right now," Dunne said.

"Then you'd have to explain what you're doing here, wouldn't you? And what *are* you doing here? Because it's not to bring in Olivia Stoddard."

"How do you know I'm not finding her for her father, like you are?"

"Well, for one, you've got a squad of what, twenty cops, staking out drag clubs and whorehouses and you haven't found her, or if you've found her, you're not doing anything about it. And she's not doing a great job of hiding, is she? I've found her twice, and I'm a bartender working with a squad of one waitress. You could have had her picked up a dozen times. So, no, you don't want to pick her up, and you're here by yourself, in the same room as her, and you haven't gone to a phone to call Alton Stoddard the Third."

"Neither have you," said Dunne.

"Good point," I said. "Keep an eye on her, would you?" I could see from our cozy corner table that there was a pay phone down the hallway to the left of the stage. I got up and headed back. Something

Mr. Powers had said had been bugging me since Dunne had arrived at the club, and it kept looping back and biting me in the ass. I dialed Mabel's number and Mr. Powers picked up on the second ring.

"Hey, Powers, it's Sammy Tiffin. I need to talk to Mabel and it's kind of urgent."

The madam came on the line in two ticks. "That was fast, slugger. I like fast. In my business, fast is a blessing."

"Mabes, Mr. Powers said something to me about everyone having a certain kink. You got anyone who maybe has one of the girls dress up like a guy, maybe roughs them up a little?"

"Does this have to do with the event we discussed?" she asked, still being careful in case her phone was tapped.

"Yeah, let's say it does. Does it ring a bell?"

"Discretion is my business, Sammy."

"It's about the drag king murders, Mabes. If it's a cop, they already know."

"Well, fuck those mugs, anyway. Yeah, there's one guy. A nob lawyer. Had very particular tastes, too. Had to be a pretty girl dressed butch. I had to eighty-six him. He hurt one of my girls. Not bad, but bad enough he needs to get his jollies somewhere else. Named Stoddard."

"Alton Stoddard the Third was slapping dames in drag around?"

"Fourth," Mabel said. "Alton Stoddard the Fourth. They call him Four."

"Holy shit. Thanks, Mabes. I'll call about the other thing soon." I hung up.

The drag queen dressed as Marlene Dietrich was hustling by and I smiled and waved him down. "Hey, doll, great show. Can you do me a favor?" I started scribbling a note to Stilton to have her meet me by the phone. Now.

"I vant to be alone," said Marlene, still marginally in character.

"Swell. That's Garbo, by the way. But could you give a note to that blonde in the guy suit and Stetson you've been playing off all night?"

"Oh, you know Tilly?" said Marlene, three octaves higher, breaking character completely. "She's the tits. But, sweetheart, she and her gal pal just vamoosed."

"Thanks," I said. I dashed down the hallway onto the club floor. Stilton and Olivia Stoddard were gone. So was Dunne.

By the time I got outside, the maroon Packard was disappearing down Columbus Avenue and Dunne was trying to pull a Y-turn to get turned around to go after it. The other Packard was gone from where it had been parked, and for all I knew, that was the one Dunne was chasing. Amid the screeching tires and the oncoming drivers yelling, Dunne was able to get around the corner. I climbed in the Ford and fired it up, but before I even got to Columbus, the Packard came roaring out of Grant Avenue, taking a left onto Broadway right in front of me as the oncoming traffic screeched and swerved to miss her. Oh yeah, it was her. I could see the Cheese's head thrown back laughing as they slid around the turn. Daffy broad.

I shifted to second and stayed about half a block behind them, but Olivia Stoddard was not sparing the horses and that dame could drive. I heard more screeching and honking behind me and checked the rearview to see Dunne's big Dodge blasting out of Grant onto Broadway behind me.

The Cheese knew this neighborhood as well as I did, so I had a pretty good idea where Olivia Stoddard was heading: the little turnout just before the Broadway tunnel. Sure enough, her brake lights lit up and she managed to get the big Packard off Broadway and then back parallel with it, headed up Russian Hill (which the Broadway tunnel went through). It was the very same way we'd evaded the cops the night of the Nut-Sack Driving Lesson and Shanghai Adventure.

Decision time for me: let Olivia Stoddard get out of my sight, or let Dunne chase them somewhere and pull them over someplace with no witnesses. After watching him nearly melt down at Finocchio's, I thought it would be better to let the Cheese take her chances with Olivia. I wished she was packing Jimmy Vasco's Walther, though.

I pulled into the little turn-off and stopped, blocking it completely. I lit a smoke, rolled down the window, and smiled at Captain Dunne, who was stopped, with no way to get up onto Russian Hill without either turning around and going back a block, or going through the tunnel for a mile. He honked. Several times. I waved and pretended to be having trouble with the gearshift. Were cops the only ones who didn't know about the tunnel turn-off?

After what I thought was sufficient time for Olivia and the Cheese to be well on their way, I put the Ford in gear, backed up a few feet, then slowly and carefully pulled back out onto Broadway. Dunne revved it into the little turn-off and headed up the hill, where I'm sure he came to realize he had no idea which way Olivia Stoddard had turned at the top. I would have given five-to-one odds that I did.

Less than ten minutes later I was pulling onto Pier 29 and I could see the taillights of the maroon Packard as it turned to go behind Jimmy's Joynt. I rounded the corner to see Stilton leaning in the window of the Packard, smooching the bejeezus out of Olivia Stoddard. She looked up when my headlights swept them, grinned, and waved like a lunatic. The Packard pulled away.

The Cheese ran over to the Ford.

"Hey, gorgeous, where you been?" she asked. Her lipstick was a clown-sized smear.

"Get in, doll. We don't want to lose sight of Olivia."

"We're fine," the Cheese said, pulling her order pad out of her jacket pocket and holding it up. "I have her address."

◇◇◇◇◇◇

The sunrise came through the Cheese's front window like a flaming hangover brick. She opened one eye, then pulled the covers over her face.

"What's the story, morning glory?" I said with the good cheer of a guy who knows he had much less to drink than his squeeze. I tried to pull my arm out from under the Cheese so I could reach the little double-burner cooker to start the coffee. "Move, move, move, light of my life. I will prepare breakfast in bed to fortify you through your day."

"I hate you, your family, and everything you stand for," said the Cheese from under the covers. I managed to stretch enough to grab my pack of smokes off the counter, shake one out, and snap a kitchen match to light with my thumbnail. She sat up, leaving the sheet draped over her head like she was haunting me, and snatched the cigarette out of my hand. My right arm, which had no feeling at all up to that point, stung like I'd grabbed a hot wire. I sort of waved the whole appendage around, but it remained wiggly and out of control.

"You gotta get a bigger bed, doll." I lifted the sheet with my living hand and pulled it back so she didn't set it on fire with her cigarette or her breath.

She squinted, one eye open, testing it. "When you pick up your reward from Stoddard today, why don't you go buy me one."

"Not today, doll. I have to open the bar for Bennie. Used up all my favors."

"You could just call it in and have him send the cash over."

"You kidding? I'm not giving him his daughter's address until I'm holding hard cash in hand. I don't trust that mug as far as I could drop-kick him."

"Yeah." She opened her eyes. "Ouch, ouch, ouch. I must have gotten pretty hooted last night, huh?"

"A little bit," I said, trying to be sympathetic, not smug. "You put on a show at Finocchio's, then got in a car chase and smooched the lips off of Olivia Stoddard." I was a *little* smug.

Her hand went to her mouth like she'd just said something embarrassing. "Oh, baby, that was nothing, you gotta believe me. I was just playing the part. You're my one and only."

"You made that pretty clear after we got back here, so I'm letting you off the hook."

"Oh, good." Then she caught a glimpse of the little alarm clock on the kitchen counter. "Shit! I gotta get to work. Do I smell like gin? I was supposed to meet Myrtle last night at Jimmy's to go work on your birthday surprise. And did we catch the killer?"

I replied, "You weren't drinking gin, so no. I know it's not my birthday surprise, so you don't have to keep saying that, and no, we did not catch the killer, but I think I might have some clues. Also, I too have to get to work, and I need to go home and shower first, because I smell like you barfed on me."

"Oh no, did I barf on you?"

"No, doll, I just smell like it. And so do you." I kissed her on the forehead, stepped over to the shower pan she had on the opposite side of her little kitchen counter, and turned on the hot water. "Jump in. I gotta go. You want breakfast?"

"Nah, I'll have Phil make me a bacon at work. Thanks."

"A bacon? One bacon?"

"Turn on the coffee and go away. I am finished with you and now you are annoying."

"You're cranky in the morning."

"Begone!"

The dame is nuts about me.

21

ROLLING CALLS

Sammy

An hour after leaving the Cheese's place I was showered, shaved, and setting up shots for the morning drunks who were coming up the block in a march of the undead to drink their breakfast. Some of these guys, like Fitz, had been doing this since long before I was a bartender, and how they were still alive was a mystery. I put Bennie's bottle of watered hooch in the well for their second round.

Fitz was first through the door. "Kid, where you been?"

I signaled to him that I had a shot set up for him away from the door, where he usually sat, and he doddered down the bar grumbling like there was a running tugboat moored in his chest. He climbed on the stool and downed the shot, then coughed. And coughed. And coughed soul-wrenching, eye-watering, there's-going-to-be-a-lung-on-the-bar-any-second coughs. I poured a glass of water and set it in front of him. And he coughed. When he finally stopped coughing and gasped for air a couple of times, then blinked the tears out of his eyes, I held my pack of smokes out to offer him one.

Then he laughed and coughed some more, but I thought, *Well, if this old fuck dies, at least he had a last laugh*. Down the bar the rest of the undead were going through similar rituals, although a couple had learned in their old age to sip, rather than gulp and gasp. The joys of working the day shift in a dive bar.

"So where you been, kid?" Fitz said, tapping on the shot glass for me to hit him again.

I poured him a shot of the iced tea and Old Tennis Shoes diluted mix. "I don't work days, Fitz. I been on the case."

"You got a suspect base?"

"I do."

"And?"

"It's the San Francisco city phone book."

"You'll need to narrow that down, kid."

"Winnowing. I like to think of it as winnowing."

"Well, I called an old buddy of mine, retired from the LAPD a few years back, got the skinny on Dunne the Nun. Turns out he hasn't always been such a Goody Two-shoes. Dunne worked vice out of L.A., too. Fell for a working girl, which happens with vice guys. Anyway, he marries her, then he wants to get her out of the life, away from the influences, so he moves to San Fran right before the war, gets full rank and benefits transferred, which big departments will do. Cheaper than training someone up. Anyway, the war breaks out, he signs up, but he's really too old for combat, so they give him a commission and he runs MPs in Europe and North Africa for the duration. Comes home, he's working for Pookie O'Hara, so his puritan tendencies, if he had them then, were held in check."

"What about the wife?"

"Don't know. He's still with her as far as I know. I guess she sat out the war here in Fog City. But a hooker is a hooker. No way a guy who is stepping on every whore and horse player in town is going to want his crew to know his old lady was a working girl. You can use that, right?"

"Maybe," I said. Then the phone rang. "'Scuse me, Fitz."

It was Moo Shoes. "Sammy, I called your place last night. You weren't there."

"I was at the Cheese's. I'm here now," I said. "Covering Bennie's shift."

"I just got a call last night from Mr. Ping, the apothecary store."

"Dried armadillo dongs and whatnot?"

"That's the guy. Anyway, Snake and Noodle had a visit from a couple of Squid Kid Fang's guys last night. They were pushing around some of the nut-sack guys. Somehow the mugs we shanghaied got to a phone or a radio or something and Squid Kid knows they were jumped at Snake and Noodle. He's blaming Uncle Ho. He wants his dragon, now, or a hit goes out on Uncle Ho."

"Won't he put a hit on Uncle Ho anyway?"

"Probably, but Uncle Ho thinks giving him the dragon might slow him down."

"I'll make a call and get back to you. Can you get Milo's cab to go get the dragon? I had to leave Jimmy Vasco's jalopy at the club." (I wasn't going to try to explain how I got to the Cheese's place the night before and how I'd let her drive home hooted because of the weird pedal extensions on the Chrysler.)

"I'll see what I can do. I'm at my apartment."

I rang off. Even if I could pull it off, I'd have to get Mrs. Sal to cover my shift. I'd wait to call her to make sure I needed her. I hated to do it, it being only a little after seven in the morning, but I dialed Mabel's number.

"Whores!" answered the dame.

"Is this Mabel's?" I asked.

"Yeah," she said.

"Why didn't you say that? What if I was selling encyclopedias or something?"

"Then you'd know right away you had the wrong number, wouldn't you?"

"Good point. Can I talk to Mabel? This is Sammy Tiffin."

"She's sleepin', and I ain't gonna wake her up. You got a message?"

"Could you have her call me at Sal's? She has the number. Tell her it's really important."

"Sal's. Got it. You think *floozies* would be better? You know, to answer the phone with."

"Nah, *whores* is more professional. A floozie might just be an enthusiastic amateur. How about *courtesans*?"

"Oh, I like it. Classy. Sounds fuckin' French. Okay, 'Sammy at Sal's.' Bye."

She keeps it up, she'll be working in a law office any minute. Speaking of which, it was too early to call Stoddard. I refilled all my drunks and called Mrs. Sal. She answered on the second ring, which surprised me.

"Maria, it's Sammy, down at the bar. I got a family emergency."

"Don't lie, Sammy. Mama hates it when you lie."

What a coincidence. Sammy hates it when you refer to yourself as Mama, I thought. "Fine, I gotta go pick up a stolen dragon and deliver it to the Squid Kid or he's going to scrag Moo Shoes's cat-fucking uncle."

"Family emergency it is, then. Can you hold it for an hour? Give me a chance to put my face on?"

"Thanks, Maria."

I had just enough time to water my drunks and take their money before Moo Shoes called back.

"Doris took the cab and didn't come home last night and Milo wants to know what you did with her."

"I didn't do anything. The place was locked up like normal when I got here this morning. I thought when she said she was closing at midnight it was because she had a shift at Cookie's last night. Did he try calling there?"

"He said last night was her day off."

"Hey, she could have kept the bar open until two at least then."

"Not really the point, Sammy. Think you can get Jimmy Vasco's Ford for the day?"

"I'll try. Stay by the phone."

So now, evidently, I was going to call everyone who had ever told me never to call them in the morning. I dialed the number at Jimmy's Joynt, which I knew rang in the back office, and Jimmy had a little apartment dressing room thing hidden off her office where she spent most nights, unless she was at Myrtle's. I let it ring. And ring. And ring.

"Are you fucking kidding me?" shouted Jimmy.

"Jimmy, it's Sammy."

"Are you fucking kidding me, Sammy? It's"—I could sense her looking around for a clock, or her watch, or something to give her an idea of the time, since there were no windows in her secret crash pad—"fucking morning. Why are you calling?"

"I need to borrow your car."

"I will shoot your other eye out."

"It's important. I think I have a line on the killer."

I could hear a lighter click, a deep inhale, like she was resolved to be awake for a minute. "What line?"

"Not sure yet. But can I borrow your car?"

"Yes. How long? What for? Never mind. Yes. Is Myrt with the Cheese? She didn't come home last night."

"Probably at the Five and Dime. Did you call there?"

"No, I didn't call there. I was sleeping until someone just woke me up by letting the phone ring for an hour."

"You should unplug your phone when you're sleeping."

"Yeah, I would have, but my girlfriend didn't come home last night."

"I'm sure she's fine. I'll call over there and let you know. Can I come get the car, in an hour, say? I'll probably need it all day."

"Yeah, I'll leave the keys on the visor. Don't wake me up."

"Even if I find Myrtle?"

"Fine, wake me up if you find Myrtle."

"Jimmy, one thing. Which cops did you tell about those death threats you got? The notes? Dunne himself?"

"Yeah, not that he gave a shit."

"After the first one, or both?"

"I showed the first one to Dunne, then one of his grunts looked at the second one. Didn't take it. I didn't get his name."

"Okay, thanks."

I hung up and dialed the Five & Dime. The Cheese answered after half a dozen rings.

"Murphy's." Murphy's was the real name of the Five & Dime. Well, Murphy's Five & Ten Cent Store. Nobody called it that.

"Hey, doll, it's me."

"What's cookin', good-lookin'?"

"You sound better."

"Coffee, aspirin, and clean living. What's the fad, lad?"

"Did you get that from Moo Shoes?"

"Yep. Fucking Moo Shoes."

"Is Myrtle there with you?"

"Yeah, she's dragging worse than I was. She and Doris were working on your birthday surprise last night. Myrt wandered into Sal's late, looking for me. Recruited Doris to the cause. Myrt was steamed at Jimmy. Saw her flirting with Olivia Stoddard before I came in."

"That dame gets around."

"She's all right. She's not your killer, though."

"No? How do you know?"

"She's scared—for all her sass, she's scared. Hey, did you know that Doris wired Liberty ships during the war, over at Sausalito?"

"I did not. Is Doris there?"

"Nah, went home. Hey, I gotta go, hon. Order up."

"Fine, tell Myrtle to call Jimmy at the club. And let it ring."

"Gotcha, bye."

So I found both Doris and Myrtle in one phone call. I felt like this detective thing was working for me.

"Hey, who do I gotta blow to get a drink around here?" said Fitz.

"That would be me," I said. I topped him off with Tetley and Old Tennis Shoes. "You can owe me," I said.

The phone rang.

"Sal's," I said.

"Sammy, you goddamn dummy," said a doll's voice.

"Sorry, wrong number," I said. I hung up, topped off my wet-brains, and had circled back to the well by the time the phone rang again.

"Sal's," I said.

"Sammy, you goddamn dummy. Don't hang up. It's Della."

"Hey, Della."

"Where the fuck you been? Lone been checking at Cookie's ever' night and you ain't there. Hey, you ain't even supposed to be working now. I was just calling to leave a message."

"I been busy. How's Lone?"

"Well, he sad, dummy, how you think he is? His mama's service is tomorrow—noon at Union Baptist on Webster. You better get your dumb ass there and bring your dumb-ass friends. He supposed to be your friend. Don't you leave him blowing in the wind."

"We'll be there."

"You better," she said. She hung up.

I checked on my drunks. They seemed happy, but I topped them off on the house.

The phone rang. I picked up.

"You got my girls answering the phone 'courtesans' now?" Mabel asked.

"It's classy," I said.

"Sounds like a donut shop."

"Classy donuts," I said.

"What's so important, Sammy? Your phone's been busy."

"Mabes, I'm going to need you to do me a solid."

"That's disgusting, Sammy. What did they teach you guys in Europe? You want that kind of thing, you are doing business with the wrong cathouse."

"It means I need a favor, Mabel. Hepcat jazz talk."

"Oh, okay. Sorry. What do you need?"

"I need you to let me pick up the dragon early, before your party. The person that wants it is dropping the hammer and someone's gonna get scragged if I don't deliver the dragon statue in a hurry."

"You got an angle on my party?"

"Yeah, I think I got something figured. You really want to take thirty hookers to a hospital for the feeble-minded?"

"They'll be dressed like elves, Sammy. Don't make it sound weird."

"Right. Of course."

"For Christmas."

"Yeah, that's even better. So, the dragon? Could I get it today? We'll pay."

"Yeah, I already talked to Locke about it. They had some conditions, though."

"I thought it was your place."

"I'm not in charge of the antique sales. Do you know a guy called the Catfucker?"

"I might," I said.

"Well, you have to take him with you to Locke or they're not letting the dragon go."

"I can do that."

"And Sammy?"

"Yeah?"

"There's no cat fucking in my places. I won't stand for anyone being mean to animals. Or too friendly. If that's the kind of thing you want, you need to find a different cathouse."

"But—" I couldn't help it. I knew I shouldn't, but I couldn't help it. "It's right there in the name."

"It's just a name, Sammy. You know what I mean. You can call it anything you want."

"House of Courtesans," I suggested.

"I'll call Locke and tell them you're coming, smart-ass."

"Thanks, Mabel. And hey, for the next couple of days and nights I need you to open the shades at your place. Have the girls dance around, be seen all day and night."

"That's not usually something we go for, that showing off for the cops."

"It's part of my plan."

"Sure, I can do that. They'll hate it, but they ain't in charge. Bye."

I hung up, poured for my drunks, and called Eddie Moo Shoes.

"What's the sign, Clementine?"

"Eddie, that is no way to answer the phone. And by the way, that phrase you use about doing someone a solid? There is certain company you can't use that in."

"Why are you awake?" said Moo. "Why are *we* awake? This side of morning blows goats."

"You'll want to temper your talk of goat fun around Mabel's crew, I just learned. Anyway, I got Jimmy's Ford for us. Mabel says we have to bring Uncle Ho with us to Locke or it's no dragon. Can you get hold of him?"

"He gave me a number. He's not going to like it."

"If he wants the dragon, he has to be there. It's going to be tight in the front seat of that coupe with the three of us. Tell Uncle Ho to bring a coat. We'll put him in the rumble seat."

"We can't put my venerated uncle in the rumble seat."

"Well, he sits on the door, then. He smells like dusty monkey butt."

Moo did not defend his uncle's odor, because he knew it was true. "Milo called. Doris came back with the cab. She was out all night with the Cheese's pal Myrtle. You want I should get it?"

"Nah, too much runaround. Already got a line on Jimmy's Ford."

"I have to be back in time for my shift at the club."

"I'm supposed to be working a double today, too. It's an hour and a half each way. We'll be fine."

"There's too much day when you get up in the morning," Moo Shoes whined. "How do they do it? Citizens?"

"Suckers," I said. "You notice everyone is in a really foul mood in the morning? I don't recommend it. Look, I got another errand to run. I'll pick you up in front of your place in two hours. Get Uncle Ho there."

"He'll be there."

I hung up, turned to water my drunks, and one of them, Frank I think was his name, fell off his stool.

"He dead?" I asked.

The old guy next to the fallen slipped off his stool and checked his pulse. "He's okay."

"You can't pour for us that fast," said Fitz. "You're gonna kill someone."

"Sorry," I said, holding the bottle of T&T up in query.

"Sure, I'll take a topper," said Fitz.

An hour later I'd parked Jimmy's Ford outside the offices of Stoddard, Whittaker & Crock on Kearny Street and went right to Stoddard's floor without calling ahead. Maybe I'd get through without a frisking this time, but just in case, I left the .38 under the seat of the Ford. I had Olivia Stoddard's address written on a sheet from the Cheese's order pad in my jacket pocket.

The receptionist looked up at me in horror when I came off the elevator, which was an improvement, because she did look this time. She was tweedy and officious, but she had some chopsticks pushed through the bun in her hair, which I guess was supposed to convey a sense of fun or was something she could use to defend herself against a charging chow mein in an emergency.

"I'm here to see Alton Stoddard the Third," I said.

"Do you have an appointment?"

"You know I don't, but I'll bet he'll see me. Tell him Sammy Tiffin is here with what he asked for."

She did some dialing and button pushing and whispering and came up with "He'll be about five minutes, if you'd like to take a seat." She gestured to some very nice leather office chairs sort of off to the side. It wasn't really a waiting room to speak of, more like a fancy Nob Hill version of the area at the police station where they handcuff suspects to chairs while they wait for their mug shot.

"I'll go on back," I said. Chopsticks stood up like she was going to stop me and I gave her the look as I passed that Lone Jones called his "chile, please" look, meaning please don't trouble yourself because you know your efforts will be futile.

I blew by another tweedy doll at a desk and burst through the door of Stoddard's office to surprise him and a young guy in shirt-sleeves and suspenders, standing over him at his desk. The younger guy was thin, had receding hair, slicked back, and looked familiar to me, but I couldn't place him.

Stoddard said, "Mr. Tiffin, you were asked to wait."

"Yeah, sorry to interrupt while you're talking to your slaves, but I got a full day today. You want what I have or not?" I held up the order sheet with Olivia Stoddard's address on it.

"Associates," Stoddard said. "Not slaves. Associates."

"Yeah, according to him, right, buddy?" I said to the thin guy, grinning and bouncing my eyebrows.

He did not smile back. In fact, he looked pretty annoyed.

Stoddard closed the folder they were looking at and said, "Give me five minutes."

Thin guy turned and made his way around the desk. As he did I saw a red spot on his shirt just below his left collarbone, leaching out from under his blue suspender. Right where the kid thinks the heart is.

"Toodles," I said to the thin guy. Then, just as he reached the door, I said, "Four."

He turned to look, waited.

"Never mind," I said. I waved him on, then put the order slip back in my pocket. To Stoddard I said, "Look, Mr. Stoddard, I just wanted you to know I'm really close. Almost had a line on your daughter last night, but she slipped away. Another day, two tops."

"You could have just told that to the receptionist or my secretary."

"Personal service," I said. I looked for Alton Stoddard the Fourth on my way out but didn't see him. I couldn't remember where I'd seen him before, but I knew he'd followed the Cheese to my place that day and got an arrow in the chest for his trouble. I really wished the Cheese hadn't given Jimmy Vasco back her Walther before taking off with Olivia Stoddard. I needed to swing by the Five & Dime before I picked up Moo Shoes and make sure the Cheese was sufficiently rodded up and tell her that we weren't getting a new bed. At least not today. I had a nasty feeling that Stoddard hadn't hired me to find his daughter at all. He'd hired me to put me in Dunne's suspect pool.

22

FLOWERY ARBOR MOUNTAIN BOOTH AND METAL DRAGON

Locke, California

Old Ho did not want to come to the Flowery Arbor Mountain Booth. He did not want to go to Locke at all. In fact, on the drive over, he suggested several times that he would rather just go to Squid Kid Fang and get murdered than go to Locke, so afraid was he of seeing the Rain Dragon again. After the first half hour, when they were barely out of Oakland, he was asked, sternly, to ride in the Ford's rumble seat, and while the car was distinctly quieter after that, it still smelled of dusty monkey butt for the rest of the drive.

The boss, a tall redhead who had chosen the professional name Misty, greeted them in the foyer and introduced herself, although Eddie Moo Shoes and Sammy had met her before when she was off duty, and had come to think of her as the "porch dame." She was more fully attired now in her work clothes, a black satin evening gown with an extravagantly plunging neckline and a slit up the leg that traversed her right hip. She led them into the parlor, where a trio of professional women were lounging on the furniture in lingerie, reading magazines, and cracking their gum so rapidly it sounded like a small popcorn machine or perhaps a typing pool might be working behind the curtains somewhere. The professionals perked up upon their entry and Misty waved them off. "Not here for you, girls," she said. The girls resumed reading and cracking.

To Sammy and Eddie, who held Ho between them like a prisoner, which at that point he was, Misty said, "Mabel called, gentlemen, so if you'll have a seat, we'll see you get your dragon. But there were some conditions."

"We understand," Sammy said.

"*Good, Two-Toes, you brought the Catfucker,*" a voice sounded in Sammy's head, and he jumped as if he'd been stung by a bee. Old Ho clamped on to Sammy's knee because he had heard the voice, too.

"I am not the owner of the dragon," Misty said. "I'm just facilitating this arrangement, but the owner has some conditions. They want to meet with the one of you called the *Catfucker* first."

"That's him," said Eddie Moo Shoes, throwing a thumb at his uncle.

"If you'll come with me, Mr.—" Misty paused, waiting for Ho to fill in, which he did not.

"Shu," Eddie said.

"Mr. Shu," Misty said. "If you'll come with me."

Sammy and Eddie lifted Ho to his feet and shoved him ahead a few steps.

"*Catfucker! My old friend. Come here.*"

Ho followed the redhead up the stairs, down a long hall past many doors, to a door at the end, which she opened and held. "Go on in, Mr. Shu. I'll be downstairs when you're finished."

Ho inched forward, ever so slowly, trying to peer into the room before entering it, wondering how long it would take him to dash down the stairs and out the front door, or if his dashing-down-the-stairs days were past and he might just tumble down the stairs and break his neck, and how that would be fine, too.

"GET IN HERE, CATFUCKER!"

Ho stepped in and Misty closed the door behind him. In a small library with a fireplace, paneled in oak and trimmed out in brass, stood a small, very old Chinese woman.

"Catfucker," she said. "I thought you were dead."

"Soon, I think, Niu Yun. I am in trouble."

"With the tong?"

"In a way. The tongs are not the same," said Ho. "I am glad you are not dead."

"Where did you go?"

"I went back to Big Town. It was destroyed."

"I know. How did you survive? How did the tong not kill you?"

"The fighting tongs never recovered after the earthquake. Anyone who remembered me was killed or left Chinatown. Except my boss at the opium den. I found him and dug him out of the rubble. He gave me money and a big ball of opium. When Chinatown was rebuilt, I started a business, kept it going. I survived."

"If they didn't remember you, why do they still call you Catfucker?"

"It followed me. After the fire I was made a natural-born citizen at the city hall—well, at a table where the city hall used to be. All the records had burned. You just had to tell them your name and where you were born in America and they gave you a birth certificate. A true paper son. So after I made some money, I brought my brother over from China, and because he was a blood relative to a citizen, he has been able to stay. He brought his wife and children. My grandnephew brought me here today. He is a good boy. His girlfriend, a great beauty, is the most famous tap-dancing driving teacher in all of Big Town. I hope to help him to marry her. Anyway, my brother gave me the name Catfucker when we were children. He told everyone here."

"After so long? That is cruel."

Ho shook his head. "The shame was deserved."

"So you *did* fuck that cat? I always suspected, because you were mad."

"No, not because of a cat. Because of how you and the other women were treated. How I abandoned you here. It is my shame. I am sorry, Niu Yun."

Ho hung his head. Niu Yun went to him, took his hand gently, and patted it.

"You saved me, Ho. You did not abandon me."

"But you are still here, at this brothel, after so many years."

"But I have never been a whore. I have had a life. A good life. I have worked here, cooking and cleaning, doing the laundry. I have a house in town. I married a man. A good man. A farmworker. He died. I have two children, a boy and a girl. They both live in Seattle with their families. I take the train to see them at Christmas. Do you know the white devil holiday of Christmas, Ho? It's the tits."

"I know it," said Ho. "It is the time when the Jews come to Chinatown to eat. There is much prosperity, but I think it needs more firecrackers and dragon dancers to be a real holiday."

"Yes, more firecrackers." Niu Yun smiled. "So, you are here for the dragon?"

"Yes, but I don't think it will do me any good. I am only doing it so the grandson of a tong boss, a gangster, will spare my family. I think he must kill me now. To save face."

"*Nonsense, that slimy Squid Kid mug won't lay a hand on you,*" said the dragon.

Ho started, looked around.

"He talks about you all the time," said Niu Yun.

"What do you mean, he talks about me all the time? You can hear the Rain Dragon?"

"I could always hear him," said Niu Yun.

"Why didn't you tell me? You made me think I was going mad."

"You knew we both saw him. We both know how Big Town was destroyed."

Ho stumbled and Niu Yun caught him by the arm and guided him into a heavy wingback leather chair by the fireplace.

"You could always hear him?" Ho asked, as if mumbling in a dream.

"*Dames are tricky, what are you gonna do?*" said the dragon.

"I will get you a drink," said Niu Yun. She went to a bar cart with crystal bottles of brown liquid. She poured an inch's worth into a glass and brought it to Ho, made sure his hands were steady around it, and padded away behind a big desk at the end of the room. She opened a lower drawer, lifted out a lacquered box, and set it on the desk.

Ho gripped his drink so hard he began shaking as Niu Yun opened the doors of the box. There it was, the black dragon, its green eyes glowing now as Ho had never seen them.

"*Voilà!*" said Niu Yun, in perfect fucking French. "I also have your hatchet, if you want it back."

Ho stared at the dragon and the fear, the panic, slowly drained out of him. He smiled. "Did you ever get to chop off any dicks?" he asked.

"No, but you just got here," said Niu Yun.

The Rain Dragon said, "*You two are warming my heart over here. Now send up that* gwai lo *cocksucker Sammy Two-Toes.*"

Stilton DeCheese, Private Eye, Shop Foreman

Milo was pretty surprised to find out that three dames he knew were building a spaceship for a moonman at the old shipyard at Hunters Point. I personally thought it was a bad idea for Doris to bring Milo to see Scooter's rocket ship, on account of him being dramatized by the war, but nobody asked me.

"Holy shit," Milo said, standing in the doorway, looking back and forth, up and down, at the steel dragon. "Holy shit," he repeated.

"Pretty spiffy, huh?" said Doris. "You ain't seen nothin' yet, snookums. Wait until you meet the pilot."

"Holy shit," Milo said.

Myrtle and me had come to the warehouse right after work to get an early start and because Myrtle didn't want to go home, as she was sored up at Jimmy for flirting with Olivia Stoddard. I got her calmed down a little bit after I told her that Olivia was hiding out and was probably going to get murdered, but then she got a little testy when I mentioned that I had been smooching Olivia only the night before.

"I hate that dame," said Myrtle. "First my girlfriend and now my best pal. My feelings are hurt, Tilly. I thought if you were going to go that way you'd at least come to me first, so I could help guide you."

"It's not like that, Myrt. I was just playing a part. Besides, I was pretty hooted up. I don't remember it completely."

"Holy shit," Milo said.

"We need to help Milo," I told Myrt. We both went over to him, patted his shoulders, rubbed his back, said stuff like "it'll be all right" and "there, there" and whatnot. Doris pinched his butt and bit him on the ear a little bit, so he finally stopped saying "holy shit."

"So you dames built this? All of this?" He started walking around, looking close at stuff.

"Yup," said Myrt, "with a little help from—"

"Not yet, Myrt," I said. "I started it and then brought Myrtle in a few days ago."

"It's huge," Milo said, looking at one of the dragon's claws. "How'd you machine stuff this size? How'd you *lift* stuff this size?"

Myrt said, "Well, there's this little—"

"Not yet," Doris said.

"What the hell is it?" said Milo. "I mean, I know what it looks like, but it can't be that, because something like that doesn't exist. How does something like this exist?"

"Maybe now," said Doris.

"Scooter," I called. "Could you come out here, please?"

The heavy hatch on the dragon's back made a whirring noise opening up. Scooter popped his little lightbulb head out and made a chirping noise.

"Holy shit," said Milo. "I thought he was gone."

Milo knew about Scooter. He'd helped us get rid of the government guys they sent after him back in June, but he'd never actually *seen* Scooter. The little guy slid down the side of the dragon and landed on his little froggy feet.

"You gotta let him motorboat your boobs," Doris said.

"It's how his people say hello," said Myrtle.

"It is their way," I added.

Milo looked like he was getting a case of the willies.

"Back off, Scooter," I said, waving him back. "Milo needs some time."

Scooter whistled and chirped and was off to the drafting desk to do one thing or another.

"How?" Milo said. "It's so big." He kept looking at the dragon, then giving the side-eye to Scooter.

"We're champs with a block and tackle," said Myrt. "There's also a crane in here. They built ship bridges here."

"And we have a big diesel forklift we stole from one of the other ship bays," I said.

"And also, we don't always remember how we did stuff," said Myrtle.

"Yeah, there's blackouts," I said. "Sometimes you're sort of out for whole shifts and all of a sudden you're wearing a welding helmet and there's a new piece on the dragon."

"Does your butt hole hurt when you wake up?" asked Doris. Then to Milo she said, "Last night was my first time, so I don't know what's normal."

"Wait, wait, wait," said Milo. "You mean that little monster put you dames in a trance and you built this thing and don't even remember doing it?"

"Kind of," said Myrtle.

"It's okay, we're inspired," I told him. "We're using the skills Uncle Sam taught us but nobody wanted us for."

"He just wants to go home, Milo," Myrtle said. She looked over to Scooter. "Scooter, show Milo your sad face." Scooter turned on the work stool and his face had exactly the same expression it always had, a blank, black-eyed stare, but he did make a sad whistling sound. "See, he just wants to go home."

"Plus, Milo, look at this fucking thing," I said. I did the big wave, the big presentation, the big "look at this fucking thing" flourish.

So he did look. Little Milo (because he is kind of short, not Scooter short, but kind of short) walked all around the dragon, climbed up on it, asked me a lot of questions. A few I could actually answer, but for a lot I told him to ask Scooter or look at the drawings.

"How's it powered?" he asked.

"I don't know, rockets?"

"I don't see any rockets."

"Invisible rockets?"

"Did you build some invisible rockets?"

"Possibly. Hey, want to see the plasma cutter?"

"What the fuck is a plasma cutter?"

"It's this thing like a cutting torch, only it will cut really big pieces of metal. Like a ray gun, only not for blasting cows and stuff. More a focused beam. Scooter designed it. I cut those big-ass claws with it."

"How do you know it's called a plasma cutter?"

"That's what I wrote on the plans I drew."

"While you were in a trance?"

"Really makes the workday zoom by. I wish I could do that when I'm working the lunch counter."

He had climbed up the side on the little ladder indents I'd cut in with the plasma cutter (which I remember). He looked really close at how thick the walls of the dragon were at the hatch. "Stilton, there is no fucking way this thing is going to fly."

"Sure it will."

"It must weigh, I don't know . . . the biggest thing I ever went up against was a Tiger tank, which was fifty tons, and this thing is three, four times that size. It's got to weigh two hundred tons."

"Yeah?" I said. "Are you saying my dragon is fat? Because listen, buster, this is a great fucking dragon. This dragon—"

"No, your dragon is the cat's PJs, Stilton. I'm just saying I don't know how it's going to fly." He climbed down in the hatch and I followed him in. Inside, the dragon could seat maybe a dozen people if we had built chairs, but there had only been one seat on the plans, with a lot of levers and glass screens and stuff around it. "And I don't know who is going to fly it," Milo said.

"What do you mean? Scooter's going to fly it. He's going to fly it home."

"Look at the seat, the controls. This things has pedals, levers, all placed for the pilot to reach them. Like in a helicopter or a tank."

"Yeah?" I said. Fucking Milo, criticizing our dragon—excuse me, our *FAT* dragon.

"Scooter won't be able to touch the pedals, he won't be able to reach the levers, I don't think he will even be able to see those top gauges and screens."

"Well, we'll put a pillow in. Poor guy doesn't have a butt. That metal seat will be pretty uncomfortable without a pillow."

"It's not going to work," Milo said. "You built this to fit a human pilot."

"I don't know, Milo, maybe he gets bigger in space. Scooter can do some weird shit." I climbed out of the dragon and down to the warehouse floor. I didn't like it, but Milo had made a good point. I mean, we *had* built an enormous, heavy machine for a creature from another planet, and we had no idea what it did or how to make it do whatever it did. But in the past, when I'd asked Scooter stuff like that, when we were working on the dragon, I would suddenly just know the answer. Usually, in the morning, there would be a drawing on the table that explained what I needed to know.

I said, "Scooter, goddammit, who is going to fly that thing? The seat is the wrong size for you, and we are going to need to fix it."

He whistled and hopped off the stool, then sort of bounced around the warehouse taking us each by the hand and leading us over to the drafting table. Milo had climbed down off the dragon, and when he joined us, Scooter gave him an especially enthusiastic whistle with a couple of clicks I hadn't heard him make before. He peeled off a big blueprint-sized sheet of drawing paper and made a delighted trilling giggle sound. It would have been cute as shit if I hadn't heard him make that same sound once right after he disintegrated a couple of federal agents with his cow-blaster.

Milo stepped up and gave the drawing a once-over. "Holy shit," he said.

"Oh, that's helpful," Doris said. "Let me look at it. I can read a blueprint."

"Uh-huh," Milo said.

"What's that?" Doris said, tracing a curved line with her finger.

"Oh shit," said Myrtle. "That would be the curvature of the Earth."

"It looks like a topo map, maybe, except not from above," said Milo. "I can read a topo map, and I've never seen anything like this. Geological, maybe?"

I looked. There was an inset drawing, a map, plotted on three axes, and drawings of the gauges on the pilot console at each of the changes of direction or attitude. "Holy shit."

"It doesn't fly," said Myrtle. "It digs. That's the bay. The route is going under the bay."

There was another inset drawing in the upper left corner showing the dragon itself, a cutaway view. "What's that in the pilot seat?"

I asked. Scooter had never drawn anything like that before. Hadn't had me draw anything like that before.

"That's me," said Milo.

Scooter made the delighted trilling sound.

"I think he drew your cabbie hat really well," said Myrtle.

"It looks nice," said Doris. "Handsome."

Sammy

Moo Shoes and I sat in the parlor, across from the floozies, trying not to make eye contact. We had smiled, nodded, said hi, and so had they, and once we were all sure there was no further business to be done, we might as well have been strangers in an elevator.

"So really," Moo Shoes said, "by letting the Cheese dress in drag and work the case, you're kind of pimping out the love of *your* life."

"Not going to bite, Moo Shoes," I said. Fucking Moo Shoes.

"Want to go car shopping with me tomorrow? I got a newspaper to look for cars in the classifieds." He held up the paper.

"Do I want to drive you around to look at cars tomorrow? No, because I will be at Lone's mama's funeral, and so will you. And *that* is a racing form and doesn't have classified ads for cars. And furthermore, and I cannot stress this enough, shut up." The harlots were looking.

In a minute I heard creaking on the stairs and looked to see Uncle Ho coming down, followed by the tiny Chinese woman who had chased us with the hatchet. The old broad headed toward the kitchen. Ho came to us. He wasn't carrying a statue.

"Where's the dragon, Ho?" I asked. "They have it, right?"

"Yes," Ho said to me, for once not pretending he didn't understand. "You have to go get it, *gwai lo*. I am sorry."

"You're sorry I have to go get it, or you're sorry for calling me white devil?"

"The dragon want to see you. I'm sorry. I thought you would be safe."

I always thought old Ho might be a few egg rolls short of a combination plate, but I hadn't seen him quite this daffy since we hired him to help catch a black mamba we lost track of during a previous business venture. He was really trying to talk to me in English, but was so jumpy he gave up and started talking in Cantonese to Moo Shoes, who translated.

"I wanted to bring a *gwai lo* because I didn't think the dragon could speak English. I knew you would be able to hear him, but I thought you would be safe."

"Ask him how he knew I would hear the dragon," I said to Moo. I was sort of getting the willies, because I *had* heard the dragon, and that spooky bastard could definitely speak English.

Ho talked. Moo translated. "He says that the rats told him. The rats you brought to him to catch the mamba with told him you were a good guy, sensitive to creatures' voices."

"I'm getting testimonials from rats? Fine. So I should go upstairs and get the statue?"

Ho nodded, talked, Moo translated. "He says you have to do whatever the dragon tells you to do or it will be very bad."

"Fine. I will follow instructions." I got up and headed up the stairs. Daffy old guy, anyway.

"The door at the end of the hall," Moo Shoes called after me.

When I stepped through the door at the end of the hall I don't know what I expected, but what I saw was an oak-paneled den with a fireplace such as nobs like Alton Stoddard the Third stand around while they smoke cigars and snift brandy and otherwise discuss fucking up the lives of working mugs. There were two big leather wingback chairs facing the fireplace, and although I couldn't see who was in it, one of them was occupied, and whoever he was, he had a long black tail with a barbed spearhead tip.

"Come in, Two-Toes," he said.

Meanwhile, Downstairs

After a while Niu Yun came out of the kitchen and joined Eddie and Ho in the parlor while they waited for Sammy. The harlots fidgeted. Although Niu Yun cooked for them and was generally very kind, treating each of them like a favored niece, she did have a tendency to fly into tirades of angry Cantonese over who knew what, and she was never far from that fucking hatchet.

To Eddie she said, "Your uncle tells me that the tong grandson will kill him, even if you bring the Rain Dragon."

Before Eddie could answer, Ho said, "She is a silly washer-woman and so many years in the brothel have made her crazy."

Niu Yun regarded the old man, then said to Eddie, "Did he tell you I have a hatchet for chopping off dicks?"

"No," said Eddie. "You know each other? Are you the one that asked we bring him here before we could get the dragon?"

"Yes. Is it true, do you think this gangster will harm Ho?"

Eddie glanced at his uncle, then quickly away. "He's pretty steamed. We shanghaied two of his guys, and the only one he knows to blame is Uncle Ho."

Niu Yun smacked Ho on the thigh. "Well, you fucked the dog on that one, Catfucker," and she cackled like a sea witch that had just sucked the life marrow out of a young sailor. She calmed herself and said, "He can stay here with me."

Ho started to protest and she shushed him. The hatchet was implied.

Eddie shook his head. "Honored Auntie, Squid Kid has many men working for him. I think they will find my uncle, even hidden here."

She said, "This fuckstick is called Squid Kid? Ho, you will not be killed by someone called Squid Kid." To Eddie she said, "Not here. You say this Squid Kid is the grandson of a tong boss? He believes in the old ways enough that he wants the dragon returned? He will not come or send men here. The tongs are forbidden. It has been so for half a century. I have a house with an extra room, and I have plenty of money for food. Ho can work the garden and talk to the pigs. Do you still talk to the pigs, Ho?"

"My nephew does not know about that," said Ho. "But I do think it is better if I don't go wherever you take the Rain Dragon. That would be a disaster for Big Town. I thought if Squid Kid just killed me the danger would pass."

"It is settled, then," said Niu Yun. "You will stay here with me, and work the garden, and talk to the pigs, and when you go to sleep, I will chop your dick off with my hatchet."

"What?" said Eddie.

"Ha! Joking," said Niu Yun. She grinned like a Fu dog eating demons. "And no one calls it Big Town anymore, Ho."

Ho began rocking in his chair. It was not a rocking chair. "I don't know why you—"

"Because it is my turn to save *you*, Catfucker."

"You have to stop calling me that, though," said Ho.

Niu Yun cackled. The harlots smoked and read their magazines and for once were glad they couldn't understand a word the old woman said.

Meanwhile, Upstairs

I have seen eighty-year-old Chinese guys pay twenty bucks a scoop to slurp poisonous snake urine in their noodles. I have seen Lone Jones hit a guy so hard he forgot his own name for two days. I have seen a space alien rise from the dead out of an ice machine, eat a whole pack of peanut butter cheese crackers, then blast two cows into ash with a thing he built out of parts from a junk store and a crystal he spooged out of his finger. I have seen some shit. I am not easily startled. But I startled myself more than somewhat when I screamed like a terrified little girl upon seeing the dragon.

I needed a moment to reflect, I thought. I needed a moment

to assess the situation. So, still screaming, I grabbed the doorknob to open the door and the dragon's tail shot across the room and slammed it shut.

"Okay," I said, deciding instead to lean against the door, casually digging my fingernails into the oak, until the dragon's tail receded.

"Sit down, Two-Toes. I won't hurt you, you fuckin' mook. I'll overlook the scream, because frankly, pal, that mess was embarrassing."

He turned in the chair, looked back at me. The size of a middle-weight fighter now, he was gleaming black, like his scales were made of black glass or oil. His eyes glowed green and were awake and alive and present, not like some reptile that had to taste the air with its tongue to know you were there. He had long golden whiskers and golden fins lining his limbs and back, curved and as finely edged as knives. He would have made a great statue to sit in the lobby of a chow mein place if you didn't mind the kids screaming and the dames fainting all the time from the terror.

"Sit down or I'll make you pee yourself," said the dragon.

"Huh?" I replied.

"I'm the Rain Dragon. Water is my element. I could make you wet yourself. You'd be uncomfortable. So sit down."

"What?"

"I could also grab your bowels with my tail and snap you inside out. Which would also be uncomfortable."

I sat down. "I thought you were a statue."

"Don't try to comprehend me, Two-Toes. I am a magical crea-ture. I can manifest in myriad forms."

"I'm supposed to take you to a gangster."

"And you will. I'm counting on it. Those dames build the Metal Dragon?"

"Yeah. You know about that?"

"I know everything. My people know everything."

"Then why'd you have to ask?"

"Nobody likes a wiseass, Two-Toes. When those monkeys came

into my cave to play, I did not breathe sentience into them so I would have to take shit from you."

"You made mankind?"

"Yeah. It was a Wednesday. I was bored. Since then we've all been keeping an eye on you bums to see how you do. Now turn your back while I change. I don't want to break your little mind. We need to blow this pop stand."

23

STILTON DECHEESE, PRIVATE EYE

Stilton

If I'd known I was going to run into the killer, I would have worn a different dress to the funeral. I picked my white with the big red polka dots because it's cheerful, and I figure people can use that at a funeral. I wore a nifty little red pillbox hat with a net for grieving and being mysterious, but it looked like a drowned hobo compared to the hats the church ladies were wearing, which were all kinds of arrangements of feathers and flowers and fur and net, so each of them looked like she was carrying a little parade float on her head. Pretty fancy, is what I'm saying. So I hid in the back with Sammy, Milo, and Eddie Moo Shoes, and we said Hallelujah, Amen, and Praise the Lord right along with everyone, half a beat late, so by the time Lone stood up, we were all pretty scrunched down in our seats pretending we were too grief-stricken to move.

After a while the pastor talked about what a swell broad Mrs. Jones was, and how she blessed us with her fellowship, and then he introduced her loving son, Thelonius. Lone stood and walked to the podium, wiped the tears from his eyes, and said, "My mama use to say, 'I don't see ugly, Lone, all I sees is beautiful souls wearing suits that don't fit.' And as I look out on all y'all, I want you to know that it don't matter how bad your suit fit or how ugly you think you are, you probably all right, especially if you got you a nice hat."

There were a few amens but mostly people looked uncomfortable, especially the ugly people. Before Lone got out another word there was a claw in my arm and I looked up to see a very fierce-looking, very pretty dame, who was whispering, "Come with me." She was looking at Sammy. "Talkin' to you, dummy," and Sammy gave me the sign that it was okay by letting her drag us out the back of the church and through the doors onto the sidewalk.

"You got to help that boy, Sammy, or he gonna fall apart."

Sammy said, "Della, Stilton. Stilton, Della. Della is a singer at the Moonlight Club. Stilton is my girlfriend." I was rubbing my arm. That dame had some nails.

Della said, "Charmed," like she meant "annoyed." Then she said, "Look, Sammy, my gig is up at the Moonlight. I booked a new gig in Chicago. I'm leaving tomorrow, and I haven't told Lone yet. I need you to be around when I do."

"Sure, Della," Sammy said. "What am I gonna do?"

"Be his friend. Be someone who cares about him, like I was when his mama died. Buy him a meatloaf."

"I will. We will," Sammy said.

"You better, because I don't think you want that man going dark on you. Buy him a meatloaf. Be his friend. They's a reception after this in the basement, then he's all yours. Now give me a hug." She hugged Sammy like she meant "annoying." She turned to me and offered her hand. "It was nice meeting you, Stilton. You know this man is a bartender, and not even in a nice bar? He's got no future."

"I don't have any future, either. We're perfect for each other."

"Good luck to you. Bye." She walked away, and she was good at it. "Buy him a meatloaf, Sammy," she called over her shoulder.

I looked at Sammy. "I don't know if a meatloaf will fix it."

"But she's right. I have to help him. Get him to work, keep him moving. Can you talk to your friend at Finocchio's?"

"I got it, doll. Leave a light on for me."

"It's broad daylight."

"Where I go, the dark follows," I told him.

He snorted. The bum. He said, "Be careful. I'm working to-night. Come into the bar when you're done."

"I'll try. I gotta go to the warehouse, too."

I smooched him through my veil, and was off to find the Chrys-ler, which I'd parked a couple of blocks up. I didn't see the killer then, and I was checking. I was at Finocchio's on Broadway in ten. They were closed, of course, but they had a little box office in the front and I tapped on the glass with a nickel until an angry face popped through the curtains inside.

"What?" said mad five-o'clock-shadow guy. "We open at seven, first show's at eight."

"Is Billie here? He told me to stop by. Tell him Tilly." I should have taken off the hat so he could see my wide-eyed surprised look. "Sorry my hat is mysterious," I said. "I was at a funeral."

He came around and let me in. "Down that hallway to the left. I think Billie is sewing his costume."

I went down a hallway of dressing rooms, doors open, until I saw a skinny guy hand-stitching some padding into something with se-quins. He looked a lot less like Marlene Dietrich than before.

"Billie?"

He looked up, brightened up, jumped up, and squealed. "Oh, Tilly, you came in. I didn't think you would." He took my hands and kissed the air on either side of my face, then stepped back. "What have we here? Bright, perky, scandalously out of season, a little change from the gabardine and fedora the other night."

"I been at a funeral," I said.

"For a clown? I love it! Sit, sit, sit. We'll talk while I sew. You want some coffee or something?"

"Nah, thanks. Look, Billie, you said if I ever needed anything, come to you. Were you just saying that for the show?"

"Maybe? What'd you have in mind? Before you answer, I'm broke. Okay, what did you have in mind? Before you answer, can I borrow that dress and hat and what size are those shoes?"

"Yes, yes, size seven."

"Drat. It's always the shoes. What do you need, kid?"

"I need thirty drag queens, convincing ones, all shapes and sizes, who can dress straight, too, for a whole night."

"Oh my, that's a lot of drag queens. Is it a party? Will there be cocktails? Will there be dancing? A lot of girls draw the line at dancing. It's the fucking shoes. Does it pay?"

I tried to figure out what the best answers to his questions would be, and still be kind of true.

"We're trying to fool the vice cops who have been busting everyone's balls. It might pay, probably not a lot, but I'll bet I can get you guys into some really slutty outfits."

"How slutty?"

"Professionally slutty."

"Will you throw in the polka-dot dress and the hat, *pour moi*?"

"You know it."

"Well, since the other night the cops have been camped out front during business hours. We're probably just a couple of shows from having them pull that three-articles check like they do at the girls' club down the street. Okay, doll, I'm in. I can probably make that happen. When?"

"Monday night."

"Wow, two days? Wow. But we *are* dark on Monday. Sure, you got a number?"

I wrote down the numbers at Sal's and at Sammy's apartment. "You can leave a message at the first one. I'll give you a call, see how it's going. I have the number here. And oh." I dug into my purse and pulled out a paper bag I'd filled up at the Five & Dime. "This is for you."

"*Moi?!*" He took the bag and peered in. It was full of lipsticks, mascara, eyeliner, powder, and other stuff I'd picked up at the store before leaving. "Fabulous."

"It's just cheap dime-store stuff," I said.

"Sweetheart, my whole look is cheap dime-store stuff."

He reached in and pulled out a metal and plastic tube he didn't recognize, I guess. "Is this lipstick?"

"No, doll," I said, snatching it out of his hand. "That's a shotgun shell. Must have gotten in the wrong bag. Any more in there?"

There wasn't. (They keep the shotgun shells by the toys at the dime store, not the makeup. No idea how I mixed that up.) We kissed the air by each other's faces and I hit the bricks.

I was headed to the address in the Mission to deliver another friendship package I'd put together before I left the Five & Dime today. I wasn't two blocks away from Finocchio's when I spotted the maroon Packard in my rearview. Well, I couldn't very well go see Olivia and deliver my friendship gift with her creepy killer brother following me, and I knew it was him, not her, because of the hat and the height. I hung a left into the Tenderloin, which is a neighborhood I know more than somewhat, and looked for the right spot to lose my tail.

I slowed down. The Packard slowed down, fell back a block. And who tries to tail you in a big maroon Packard with powdered-donut whitewalls? There it was, a narrow alley I could barely fit the Chrysler down, but light at the end of the block. I pulled in as slow as if I was pulling into my own driveway and crept forward, keeping my eye on the rearview. The Packard turned in behind me so I went until I found a little wide spot between buildings where they keep trash cans and orphans and stuff, and I stopped and put the Chrysler in park. It has fluid-drive automatic transmission, which is the tits when you're driving on the hills in San Francisco—no clutch—but also when you want to stop and take your foot off the brakes without having the thing roll away.

It took me a second to get the shotgun loaded. I knew the basics (my dad taught me to shoot), but the lever that breaks the breech open was a little tricky. Finally it worked and the sawed-off broke open. I dropped two twelve-gauge shells into the chambers and snapped it shut. The hammers were hard to pull back, too, but I guess that's to keep farmers from accidentally shooting themselves when they're climbing over fences and stuff, which I saw a guy do in a movie once.

I had the .38 that Sammy had given me, but ever since he'd told me about blasting Squid Kid's guys off their feet with rock salt, I'd been itching to give the scattergun a try. Doris had brought it to the warehouse for Myrtle, because of Jimmy getting death notes and so forth, but Myrt had left it in the Chrysler saying it didn't fit in her pocketbook and she didn't have a car. I thought I'd give it a whirl.

The Packard was creeping up and when he was, oh, about fifty feet behind the Chrysler, I fixed my dress, which rides up when I am driving in frog position, and started walking at the Packard. And he just kept creeping up. "Hey, you stupid son of a bitch, don't you see what this is?" I waved the sawed-off around a little, like I was demonstrating it for the curious housewife who wants a little leisure in her housekeeping day, like the magazine ad says. Although I think that's an ad for washing machines or vacuum cleaners or something. Anyway, he evidently did *not* see what I was carrying, or, and this is what I like to think, he was stunned by my sunny polka-dot frock and red hat, in November. So I let loose with both barrels.

Sammy

We were all camped out in a booth at Cookie's, watching Lone Jones cry into a meatloaf like he was trying to wash the ketchup off it.

"I wish Doris was here," Milo said. "She always knows what to do."

"She brings him meatloaf," said Moo Shoes. "She's not a miracle worker."

I checked my watch. We'd buried Mama, Della had broken the news that she was leaving, and we had three hours to get Lone pulled together enough to get him to work so he didn't lose his job. If he lost his job, everything else would go. And I had to get to my job, too. I went to the pay phone by the restrooms and called my apartment.

"What?"

"Kid, why are you answering my phone?"

"It's what you pay me for. You got a message?"

"No, I don't have a message. I'm calling."

"It's still gonna cost you two bits, you stinkin' struffoli."

"That's a dessert, kid."

"No it ain't."

"Look, kid, I need you to run down to Saint Pee-Pee's and tell Father Tony I need him to come to the bar tonight when I'm working. There's four bits in it for you."

"Why don't you call him yourself, you lazy cocksucker?"

"Because the phone doesn't ring in the church and I have to leave a message with the secretary at the rectory, and I can't leave the message I need to leave with her. So would you just go do it?"

"A buck."

I wasn't wishing that Stoddard the Fourth had ice-picked the kid, but would it have been so bad if he'd tied him up in the laundry room for a week or so? "Fine, a buck," I said. "Tell him I have a tip on a horse."

"What's the horse?"

"Not on your life. Go now."

"You're out of gin."

"What the fuck are you doing drinking my gin?"

"I didn't. I took it for my uncle Cassius. He gave me two bucks."

I wasn't going to ask if his uncle was a Roman general, because he is a horrible little kid and that's what he wanted.

"Fine," I said. "Go find Father Tony."

"Fine," he said. "And cornflakes."

"Buzz off, kid," I said and I hung up.

When I got back to the booth, Lone was eating and Moo Shoes and Milo were watching him. "All right, you guys. I'm going to need at least two of you to drive on Monday night. It's maybe an hour and twenty each way."

"I don't drive," said Lone.

"I can't," said Milo. "That's the day we launch the thing, and Scooter wants me to drive."

"*Let the pilot drive the dragon,*" said a voice in my head. The dragon statue, which he'd reverted to, was in my apartment, but I could still hear the bum. No wonder Uncle Ho didn't want to go to Locke. "I suppose by *pilot* you mean Milo," I said aloud. Lone stopped eating and looked at me. Moo and Milo looked at me. "What?" I said. "It's a non sequitur. My ma was an English teacher. You learn this stuff."

"Uh-huh," said Moo Shoes.

"What I meant to say was, you're telling me this now? Do you even know where you're going? How long it's going to take? If you're coming back?"

"I sort of feel like I do," said Milo. "I stayed at the shipyard working out the controls, I think, and, well, now I just know. Either way, we gotta get the—uh, thing—out of there soon. Like two shakes soon."

"Why?" I asked. "It's been there for months. A few more days won't make any difference."

"Yeah, there hasn't been an enormous hole in the wall of the warehouse for months. Only since this morning. Turns out it doesn't just dig, but also there are two very impressive beam things that fire out of the nostrils that sort of, not really burn, sort of *dis-*

appear stuff. And this morning Doris fired them off and now there's a dragon-sized hole in the wall."

"Don't you mean a *thing*-sized hole in the wall?" asked Moo. "Since we're being sly." Milo had filled Moo Shoes in on the metal dragon.

"Yeah, so we hung some tarps over it, but there's a thing-sized hole in the building."

"No, just say dragon," I said. "When were you going to tell me about that?"

"As soon as I remembered it, which is now."

"I can drive," said Moo Shoes, bright as a hummingbird sipping uranium. "I should have a car by Monday night."

Uncle Ho had paid us for finding the Rain Dragon, even though, strictly speaking, he wasn't going to get his business back, but the money was burning a hole in Eddie's pocket. I just wanted to get a bigger bed for the Cheese, maybe a phone. I wasn't giving odds on getting Jimmy Vasco's reward for finding the killer. And I figured I'd found the killer.

I leaned my elbows on the table and held my head in my hands, Shirley Temple–being-cute style, just for a second. I said, "You guys ever think that we are just puppets being pushed around by forces greater than us, who are just busting our chops for their own amusement?"

"Nope," said Milo.

"Not a chance," said Moo Shoes.

"Evil Jesus?" asked Lone Jones around a bite of meatloaf. "Nah."

"Absolutely," said the Rain Dragon in my head.

"Swell," I said. I caught a flash of green out the window and suddenly we all turned to watch a tarted-up blonde go by with an obvious and appalling lack of foundation garments under her dress. The Cookie's Coffee Irregulars all turned and tracked her progress, even Lone, who stopped weeping for a moment.

"Gotta be a pro," said Moo Shoes.

"Gotta be," said Milo.

"It's four in the afternoon," I observed.

"Well, y'all better decide how you feel about her because she comin' this way," said Lone.

And she was. She did. She caught us looking and winked, then walked right up to the table, stood next to Moo Shoes, who was sitting on the outside next to me, and said, "Scooch."

Moo scooched.

"I seen you at Mabel's," she said, looking at me.

"Only in a professional capacity," I said.

"Yeah, me too." She extended her paw. "Ruthie. Charmed, I'm sure."

I shook her hand, and introduced everybody all around, who all shook her hand.

I said, "Ruthie, didn't the cops give you trouble, coming down here?"

"Oh, they followed me. Four in the fucking afternoon? They might be outside right now, for all I know. I needed to get out, get some air, thought I'd grab a burger. Saw you through the window. You know, friendly face in a storm."

"Any port in a storm?" Milo ventured.

"Whatever," Ruthie said. "Can you guys get a waitress over here? They seem to have missed my entrance."

Lone waved to the daytime waitress, his fork still in hand, and she started our way.

"So," said Moo Shoes, "you going to the big party on Monday?"

"You betcha. My third one running. Wouldn't miss it. Way the fuck out in the middle of nowhere."

"Sonoma," I said.

"Whatever," she said. "Hey, you guys know the story, right? Why Mabel has a Christmas party in the Drooling Ward?"

Lone said, "Nope," and verily "nope" was repeated around the table.

"Let me order a burger and fries and I'll tell you," she said.

And she did.

Stilton DeCheese, Private Eye

So I let loose with both barrels, and I don't mind saying, two short barrels of twelve-gauge shotgun is a lot of loud, and it bucked quite a bit as well, although I held on. Hurt my wrist a little, but I held on. On the other side, the windshield of the Packard just exploded, and the back window and one of the side windows spiderwebbed. There was a chrome swan hood ornament that no longer had any wings, the hood was pockmarked here and there, and behind the wheel, sitting up now, was one surprised Alton Stoddard the Fourth. He wasn't shot, it didn't look like, but his nice white shirt was starting to polka dot with red, as was his face, from flying glass, I'd guess.

So there he was, white and red polka dots, and there I was, red and white polka dots, and both of us out of season. Well, I was mortified and so was Alton Stoddard the Fourth.

"Alton," I said, but it was like I was talking underwater, because my ears were still ringing, "we know you're the killer, so you should probably stop following me because you're going to keep getting shot until it's no longer necessary. And if the cops show up here in a second or two, that's exactly what I'm going to tell them." I shrugged as if to say, *So what do you want to do, doofus?*

He said something back, but I couldn't hear him, because, you know, but he didn't back up, so I said, "Fine, stay right there." I went back to the Chrysler, threw the shotgun on the seat, grabbed the .38 out of my purse, and started walking toward the Packard again. Alton decided then that he should probably back up and go seek medical attention or something, but in any case he definitely decided to back up, fast, and took out a couple of garbage cans on the way out of the alley.

I climbed back in the Chrysler and did a couple of tricky turns through the neighborhood to make sure I wasn't being followed by a Packard with a wingless swan on the hood, then headed to the address Olivia Stoddard had given me.

It was a little Victorian in the Mission near Sixteenth and Market, mostly Spanish neighbors, a few Irish here and there, all working stiffs—the last place you'd look for a hoity-toity Pac Heights nob dame. There was a detached garage out back where I'd bet there was a maroon Packard hiding. Olivia answered on the second knock, but just peeked out through a security chain.

"Hi, Tilly," she said. "I can't let you in right now." She glanced over her shoulder. There was someone in there with her.

"You okay, kiddo?" I said. She was maybe two years younger than me, but now that I knew her brother was killing people, I felt protective, like a big sister who got drunkenly smooched by her little sister and now feels really weird about it. "Blink if you're okay. Because I am rodded up and will blast anyone who is messing with you. I just shot your big brother, by the way."

"Four? You shot Four?"

"He's fine. Fucked up his swan, though. Anyway, I brought you this." I held out a brown bag from the dime store, which was not doing a good job of concealing the shotgun at all. "It's a sawed-off shotgun."

"I can see that."

"Do you know how to use it?"

"I've shot skeet at Father's club."

Okay, now I didn't want to give her Milo's shotgun, but I was sort of committed to the move. I looked around, realized no one on the street could see me. I pulled the shotgun out of the bag, broke it, dropped in two shells out of the bag, and snapped it shut. "Okay, see these hammers? Pull them back to cock it, but don't do that until you're ready to shoot or a bad guy is coming up the stairs. Each of these triggers fires a barrel. I don't know which is which, but I don't think it matters. I would recommend one at a time, because my wrist hurts like crazy from shooting your brother both at once. Got it?"

She nodded.

"How come you didn't call the cops?" I asked her. "He's the killer; he's looking for you. He came to my guy's house, too. Why did your brother come to my guy's house, Olivia?"

"You have a guy?" She seemed hurt.

"For fuck's sake, Olivia! Not the fucking point."

Olivia shushed me, closed the door to unhook the chain, then opened it and stepped out on the porch, holding the door behind her. She was wearing slacks and a silk blouse, simple and girly, not what I expected from her. "Look," she said in an urgent whisper, "I can't explain it. My brother was following me, which is why I'm holed up here. I had eyes on you before I met you at Mona's. I saw you coming out of Jimmy's Joynt, all butched up in coveralls and boots with your skinny girlfriend. So I followed you. You were in that big black car, I don't know what it was. I lost you in Chinatown. Four was following me, I guess, and thought I had something going with you."

"What if you did?"

"It's complicated. He's really horrible. I'm sorry, but you have to go."

"You don't care if I call the cops, then?"

"You think they don't know? My father is a very powerful man. He doesn't approve of—of how I am."

"But he's okay with your brother murdering people and terrorizing you?"

"Please go, Tilly. I'm safe here."

"Well, you are now," I said. I handed her the shotgun and turned.

"I like your dress," she called after me.

"Yeah, I used to, too," I said, too softly for her to hear.

24

THE WHEELS ON THE BUS

Sammy

I was pouring Father Tony a Bushmills Irish on the house, so already he was a little suspicious.

"So you want to borrow the church's camp bus and you don't want me to ask what you're going to do with it?"

"Yes. The purple bus. For one night," I said. "When you won't be using it."

"Lavender bus. What will you be using it for?"

"And," I said, "I will go to the track with you and stake you to a hundred bucks on your bets."

"And what will you be using the bus for?"

"A short trip. You won't even notice it's gone."

"Sammy, lying to a priest is a sin. But the sanctity of the confessional is inviolate, so tell me: What are you going to do with my bus?"

"Very short trip," I said.

"Who are you taking on a very short trip on my bus?"

"Thirty drag queens."

I could see that Father Tony didn't expect that. He pushed his glass across the bar. I poured him a double.

"But," I said, "I don't think you should judge. I mean really, have you ever seen the way you guys dress to give Mass?"

Nothing. Just sipping.

"The pope?" I continued. "Have you seen pictures of the Holy Father giving Mass? Really? The hats? Look at the fucking hats, Father Tony."

"Are you saying that the pope is a transvestite?"

"I judge not, Father, lest I be judged. And it's for a Christmas party for the disabled."

"You want to borrow my bus to take thirty drag queens to a Christmas party for disabled children."

Children was his word, but I allowed it. "Yes, indirectly."

"Where, *directly,* are you taking them?"

"To a whorehouse. But we *are* taking a bunch of people to a Christmas party for disabled children. For the children, Father." He was the one who brought kids into it. There might be kids. I didn't know.

"*Who* are you taking to the party?"

"Thirty hookers."

"You are using my church camp bus to take thirty drag queens to a whorehouse, and take thirty whores to a party for disabled children."

"They prefer to be called courtesans," I said.

"You are taking a busload of disabled *courtesans* to a party?"

Don't let anyone tell you that Irish whisky doesn't have magical properties. I poured him another double, and went in for the close.

"Two hundred bucks at the track. I'll drive."

"Bless you, my son," Father Tony said.

Stilton DeCheese, Private Eye, Shop Foreman

We didn't know, exactly, where Scooter was having Milo take him, but wherever it was, he was taking a shitload of peanut butter cheese crackers. Cases of them. We'd stacked them in the back of the metal dragon, along with some jerry cans of water, some salt, potassium, and a few other chemicals we had to order through the pharmacy at the Five & Dime. (Scooter had left a list. In my handwriting, but it was his list.) I guess they were moonman vitamins.

"You figure out where this thing is going?" Doris asked Milo, who was doing a last-minute thing with his wee bucket, which is something he insisted on putting in the dragon before he left.

"North, once I get to depth," said Milo. He was looking at the weird map Scooter had drawn.

"What's depth?" I asked.

"Looks like about two hundred feet, but after I get across the bay—under the bay—it goes deeper."

"I don't think you should go," said Doris. She'd been saying that since Milo realized he was supposed to drive the dragon, but he kept brushing her off.

"Look, doll, I'll be back before breakfast on Tuesday morning. It will be like you worked a shift at the diner."

"Yeah, but when I work my shift at the diner I can look out the window and see you there. You're not two hundred feet underground with a goddamn moonman."

Milo pushed the buttons that worked the metal covers over the windows, which were the eyes in the front and a few portholes down the side. There were covers like that over the lights around the dragon, too.

"Why does it need lights if it's in the dirt?" Milo asked. He was being really careful to check Scooter's diagram before pushing buttons after Doris disintegrated the side of the building. "Here goes," he said. He pushed the big button he said was power.

We expected loud, like a train or a big truck firing up, but what we got was a low, quiet whir as a lighted turbine thing (that none of us could remember building) started turning at the base of the dragon's short tail. After a few seconds it pulsed.

"Okay, everybody out," Milo said, checking his watch. "Except Scooter."

Scooter whistled sadly and hopped back to his stack of cheese crackers.

Myrtle looked at me. I looked at Doris. Doris looked at Myrtle. We all looked at Milo.

"We're staying," Doris said. "I'm not sending you off to never see you again."

"Scooter wants us along to say good-bye," I said, although how I knew that was mysterious.

"He's not coming back," Myrtle said.

Scooter whistled and hopped over to us and burbled Doris's boobs in celebration.

"I promised Sammy it was just me," said Milo. "I wouldn't let you dames on board."

"Yeah, so did I," I said. "He'll get over it."

"We're probably all going to die," Milo said.

Only this morning, Sammy had said, "Look, doll, I don't want you on that dragon. Milo doesn't know where it's going, and whether it's space or to the center of the Earth, I don't want you on it. Okay?"

"Okay," I said. "I want to go to Mabel's Christmas party."

"Not a chance. There's going to be gangsters there. Squid Kid is picking up the dragon right near there."

"That's the dumbest thing I've ever heard of," I told him. "Bringing gangsters to a Christmas party."

"I'm not. The dragon insisted that we turn him over to Squid Kid in Eldridge, so Moo Shoes got Mr. Ping, from the Shark Parts and Dried Bear Dongs Store, to contact Squid Kid to arrange it. Turns out the old guy's been paying protection to Squid Kid for years."

"You ever feel like there are forces messing with us without asking?" I said. It had been bugging me.

Sammy said, "All the time. I was just sayin'—"

"Like you trying to be the boss of me?"

"I couldn't bear it if anything happened to you," he said. "That's all."

"God, I hate it when you're sweet like that. I'll be fine. I'm tough. I shot a killer just Saturday."

"What?" he said.

I guess he hadn't seen that coming. So I told him the whole story, from blasting Four to giving the shotgun to Olivia.

"You gave her Milo's shotgun? What if she's as wacko as her brother?"

"She's not. She's just a kid trying to be someone her family doesn't want her to be. And her brother has some very weird stuff going on. Olivia says the cops already know he's the killer and aren't doing anything because of his father."

Sammy just stood there, like he was trying to think it all through, then he said, "You should have shot him better."

"Goddammit, Sammy, do I come into Sal's and tell you how to do your job? I'm new at this. If you want Four shot better, then go shoot him yourself."

"You're right," he said. "I'm sorry. I just worry."

Then we made up and I promised that I wouldn't go to Mabel's party and I wouldn't get on the metal dragon and I wouldn't go near Olivia Stoddard or her killer brother, and he promised to get me a new bed and phone and maybe a new place where we could live together with a future and it would be swell. And we made up the way we always do.

So I felt a little guilty as Milo pulled the lever that started the dragon digging. Then came the big noise as the four talons started tearing the hell out of the floor and the dragon descended, straight down, level, for a couple of minutes. It paused for a second, then Milo worked some controls and we started forward, level. I guess the nostrils were clearing the path, because things smoothed out considerably.

"Anyone else think this is a really, really stupid thing to do?" asked Myrtle.

"Oh yeah," said Doris.

"Absolutely," said Milo.

"This thing rides great!" I said.

The moonman chittered and whistled like a parakeet at a seed party.

SFPD Vice—Stakeout, Mabel's Courtesan and Elf Emporium

It turned out that staking out various dens of iniquity such as drag clubs, lesbian bars, and whorehouses could get pretty boring if you weren't actually looking to arrest anyone, even if you switched up stakeout venues with the other guys. For one thing, there really wasn't much day work, so everyone was working the night shift and was getting tired and cranky.

"Be a presence," the Mother Superior had told them. "Our goal is to defer the activity, stop the customers, the johns, the fags, the dykes, from making their disgusting lifestyles habit, and if you see the subject, Olivia Stoddard, or anyone associated with her, call it in."

Flint and Holcomb, veteran cops both, had drawn the Mabel's on Post Street stakeout, which had been a complete snooze until a couple of days ago, when the whores decided to open all the shades.

"I had no idea whores danced so much," said Flint. "And I've been working vice for ten years. Did you know whores liked to dance this much?" He was a wiry guy with a face like a hatchet and a five o'clock shadow no matter the time of day.

The whores had been dancing nearly all night long, and while at first it had been interesting, it was starting to get monotonous.

"You ever miss the days when Pookie ran vice?" asked Holcomb, a going-to-seed-at-forty-year-old who had his suit cleaned only once a season, and so often smelled of BO and mothballs. "I mean, he was an asshole, but if you had a stupid assignment like this, at least you could go inside every now and then and knock off a free piece. This 'being a presence' is for the birds."

"Hey, hey, hey, what's this?" said Flint.

A lavender school bus with the logo SAINTS PETER AND PAUL'S—SALESIANS OF ST. BOSCO pulled right up in front of Mabel's.

"There's a Saint Bosco?" asked Holcomb.

"Patron saint of chocolate milk," said Flint with the authority of a guy who had only seen the name Bosco on the side of a chocolate syrup can.

"That explains that holy cow on the front of the church," said Holcomb. It did not.

The bus started to unload a bunch of guys dressed in suits and ties, hats, a lot of them in sunglasses despite its being dark. A whole line of them. Every one was carrying some kind of gym bag or paper grocery bag.

"Are we supposed to do something?" asked Flint.

"I don't know," said Holcomb. "They're church guys, right? Not on our list? I mean, I thought us sitting here plain as day was supposed to be a deterrent for people like church guys."

"Well, I'm writing it down. Six ten P.M., observed—did you count how many guys got out of that bus?"

"Call it forty."

"Observed forty church guys, male, entering Mabel's," said Flint as he wrote.

"Hey, the driver is still sitting back there. I'm going to go bust his balls."

Holcomb climbed out of the Dodge and limped back to the lavender school bus, not sure which leg to favor because both his feet were shot from walking the beat and now his back was shot from sitting too much. Flint watched him in the rearview until he got bored, then he started watching the dames inside, who were dancing with the church guys now instead of each other.

Holcomb returned. "Guy's fucking Chinese. Doesn't speak a word of English."

"Ah, fucking Catholics will take anybody," said Flint.

"Hey, I'm Catholic," said Holcomb.

"Then you see my point," said Flint. "His license check out?"

"Looks legit. Eddie Shu. Probably added the American first name at DMV because they couldn't spell the Chinese one."

"Probably," said Flint.

"Thing is, there's another guy stayed on the bus. The biggest colored guy you ever saw, wearing a Santa suit."

Flint shrugged. "I don't think we are being a presence by rousting a guy in a Santa suit." He waved it off. "You know, these Catholic guys are pretty good dancers."

So they watched the Catholic guys dance with the hookers for a while until the big front door opened and out came a statuesque redhead in a red satin evening gown with a white fur collar and cuffs, escorted by a broad-shouldered guy in a tux.

"That's Mabel," said Flint.

"And that's Powers, the muscle, or butler. I don't know what the fuck he does, but he's always there in the lobby."

Mabel stopped about five feet away from the car and waited.

"What should I do?" asked Flint.

"Well, roll your fucking window down, you mook."

Flint did.

"Gentlemen," Mabel said.

Holcomb was straining to see her around the roof of the car and his partner.

"I'm sorry to not afford you eye-to-eye contact, gentlemen, you are welcome to get out and stand, but if I bend over I will likely fall out of this dress, and *you* can't afford that."

"What?" said Flint.

"Mr. Powers is going to escort me to a girl in the Marina who sands my corns off. You are welcome to follow if you sense anything untoward is going on, but we should return in about ninety minutes if you don't. Mr. Powers will be happy to provide you with the address, in case you lose sight of us."

Flint looked at Holcomb, who shook his head. "No, ma'am, we're good," said Flint.

"See you in a bit. Powers, this is our ride."

A pearl-black Ford coupe pulled up and Mr. Powers helped Mabel in, then crawled in himself and they were off.

"Write that down?" asked Holcomb.

Flint said, "I'm not writing down that Mabel left to get her corns sanded and we decided not to follow. Or do you want to follow and call in a backup to watch the church guys so we can follow her?"

"I hate this gig. I just want to bust a dice game or roust a street-walker."

"Be a presence," Flint said. They sat in silence, watching the dancing, until one by one it was only hookers again in the windows, and the big front door opened and the guys came piling out, a line of them, all of them with hands on their heads, holding their hats, talking as they walked to the bus.

"I guess that's it," said Flint.

"I guess they just came to dance," said Holcomb.

"Maybe it was a mission to save those dames' souls."

"By dancing?"

"You know Catholics, they do some goofy shit," said Flint.

"Hey!"

The bus fired up and took off.

"I'll write that down," said Flint, trying to change the subject.

"You know," said Holcomb, "I don't think that visit was wasted. These dames are better dancers now than when the church guys showed up. Maybe it was a lesson."

"Should have taught them about putting on their makeup," said Flint. He grabbed the binoculars off the seat. "Even from here some of them look like clowns. I mean, I know they're whores, but how about some restraint, girls."

"Whores," said Holcomb. "Whaddaya gonna do?"

Locke, California

"It's for you," said Niu Yun, holding out the phone. "It's your nephew."

Ho was still surprised that Niu Yun had a phone, and more surprised that Eddie had the number.

"Hello, Eddie," said Ho.

"Uncle Ho, I just wanted you to know that we are turning the Rain Dragon over to Squid Kid tonight."

"You must be very careful," said Ho. "Leave it somewhere and have him pick it up. Don't let him see you. I don't trust him."

"Well, Sammy is giving it to him. I'll be there, but not close. We are handing it over in a little town up by Sonoma."

"What town? What town are you going to?"

"Eldridge. I've never been there. Sammy said the dragon insisted. He's doing this daffy thing like he thinks the dragon is talking to him."

"You silly boy, the dragon *is* talking to him. You mustn't let the white devil take the dragon to Eldridge. When I was young the dragon made me take him to Eldridge. You must not take the dragon to Eldridge."

"It's fine, Uncle Ho. We have another job right by there. The woman who hired us goes there every year. There's a hospital for disabled kids or something."

"No! You must stop him. You must not take the dragon there."

"Why? You did, and look how well you're doing. I gotta run, Uncle Ho. I have to go pick up a bus I'm driving. I just wanted you to know Squid Kid was getting his dragon."

"The last time the dragon went to Eldridge it destroyed Big Town," said Ho, but the line was dead. Eddie had hung up.

Ho looked to Niu Yun. "The white devil is taking the Rain Dragon to Eldridge."

"Oh no!" said Niu Yun. "He can't do that."

"He is doing it. How far do you think it is from here to Eldridge?"

"Four, five days, just like before when we went. Maybe longer, since we are old."

"What about by car?"

"Oh, by car?" Niu Yun scanned the ceiling as if doing the calculation. "I don't know, maybe two hours. Maybe less."

"Can you get a car?" Ho asked.

"There is one at work I can use. I don't drive. Can you drive?"

"I have had one lesson," said Ho.

"We need to go to Eldridge," said Niu Yun.

25

CHRISTMAS, NOW, THEN, AND DOWN

Sammy

I don't know what I expected the Sonoma State Hospital, which used to be called the Home for the Care of Feeble Minded Children, to look like, but this wasn't it. First, it was huge, a whole campus, like a small town or a college, with large brick buildings that actually looked like hospitals, or courthouses, then a lot of smaller buildings of all shapes and sizes, from shops and garages to large houses, and all around them lawns and gardens and block after block of streets, all in this little valley surrounded by mountains with a forest of live oaks and pines, the odd redwood, all of which I could see by the bright moonlight.

Mabel told us there were six thousand people there, including staff and patients. They had their own general store and post office, their own phone system, even their own fire department, complete with an engine. There was no gate or guard post to check through to get in, although there were some low buildings near the entrance and Mabel said that was where we'd want to have our meeting with Squid Kid Fang.

"I don't want that bum on the grounds. They put people here to keep them safe and that guy sounds anything but safe."

Mabel directed me to the first of a row of brick buildings that looked like the big houses you see around colleges. "They're group homes," said Mabel. "The more advanced patients that can get around help take care of the droolers. We're having the party in this one here."

Mabel led the way in, and the door was answered by a nice woman with red curls going gray whom Mabel introduced as Nurse Stacy. "So pleased to meet you," she said, and I got the feeling that this broad would have made a great kindergarten teacher and could probably make everything okay for a kid who was missing his mom or made pee pants in class. She was in normal street clothes, slacks and a green-and-red blouse, I guessed for the occasion, but she had a stethoscope around her neck and those white shoes worn by nurses and other dames who spend too much time on their feet.

"How's he doing?" Mabel asked.

"He's good. He's having a good day," said Stacy.

She walked us into a big parlor, a ballroom by most standards, which was decorated with Christmas stuff, garlands and tinsel from stem to stern. There was a twelve-foot Christmas tree in the corner with all the fixings, and under it two big red sacks with presents spilling out. All around the room were the patients, fifty or more, but the room could have held a hundred easy, and when Mabel walked in they all cheered and those who could clap clapped, and one guy with tiny arms rang some jingle bells like he was summoning the spirit of Christmas its own self.

They weren't all kids like I expected. Some were older than me, as old as Mabel, I guess, while some were probably little more than toddlers, but they were all shapes and sizes, and I mean *all* shapes, some with twisted little bodies curled into wheelchairs with enormous noggins propped on specially fitted padded cradles, while others had linebacker bodies with heads no bigger than a softball. Some were walking, even tending to the ones who couldn't move. Others stared vacantly and rocked. There was laughing among them, and lots of smiles, although some of them had mouths shaped like I had never seen before, cleft palates so open it was like staring into their heads. Along one edge the hospital had set up cradles and beds for patients so malformed they couldn't even be propped up, even with the most clever wheelchair. There were more patients with giant heads there, and all of them looked young, like kids. There were more with tiny heads who might have been children or very old, you couldn't tell, and many with withered limbs or no limbs at all, others with no eyes, or milky globes that never blinked.

Standing there in the arched doorway, taking it in, I found I'd forgotten to breathe, and while I didn't realize it at first, tears were streaming down my face and dripping on the hardwood floor.

Powers put his hand on my shoulder and squeezed it. "Take a minute. Look at them looking at her. You're doing a good thing here, pal. This ain't sad."

I looked. And they were all basking in the vision of Mabel, the redheaded Mrs. Santa, as she sashayed through the room, smiling and blessing every one of them with joy, hugging the ones that knew her and asking after them, brushing her fluffy white fur cuffs over the faces and arms of the ones who couldn't move, laughing with them, waiting patiently for those who could to struggle out "Merry Christmas," helping them if they needed it. And after she had given attention to every person in the room but one, she went to him, a guy in a wheelchair, wasted away from years of not moving on his own, his head at a permanent tilt as he stared off into space. He had dark hair, receding, but someone had cut and combed it nicely, and he was wearing a crisp plaid shirt that smoothed over his bony frame. He might have been thirty or eighty, although I guessed somewhere in between.

Mabel stopped by him, bent, and kissed him gently on the eyebrow, causing all the other patients to ooh and aah like they were witnessing something scandalously naughty; then she leaned her head against his and just held it there, eyes closed.

The Story Ruthie the Hooker Told That Day in Cookie's Coffee

"How Mabel comes to work in the business, I do not know. Every hooker has a story how she enters the business, which is hers alone to tell, and Mabel does not enlighten me. In fact, the story how she comes to throw her Christmas party among the feebs comes to me thirdhand and from unreliable sources, but do not let that fuck up your Christmas spirit.

"It is the tall end of the Prohibition and Mabel, who is still quite a dish at the time, is turning tricks out of a speakeasy down off Union Square run by a guy called Black Jack Bukowski, who receives this nickname not because he is dark of hair and beard, but because in his days before his adventures in liquor and hookers, he works as a collection agent and often employs in his duties a lead sap, or blackjack, with which he is known to crack arms, legs, and heads and especially cheekbones, with great skill and brutality.

"So it comes to pass that Black Jack begins to procure some of his spirits from a bootlegger by the name of Emerald Ed Mahoney, who has a connection with some Canadian gents who sail down from British Columbia with a boatload of Canadian whisky every fortnight, which Ed claims, having passed through his hands, is genuine Irish, although no one cares, as it is Prohibition and citizens will drink disinfectant as long as it has enough alcohol content on which to get sufficiently hooted.

"But upon his repeated visits to Black Jack's nitery, Ed sees and takes a shine to Mabel, and she to him, for although he is a bootlegger and general ne'er-do-well, he is quite handsome and not short in the charm department, either, and Mabel, as is known by one and all, is not only a dish, but has moxie out the wazoo and the auxiliary backup wazoo.

"Well, there is much playful banter and flirting between them, despite the only barrier to their congress being a few bob and a door to one of the back rooms, but they pretend such is not the case, until one evening Black Jack intercedes to suggest that the two should take a turn around the park together, so to speak, and that Mabel's fee will be discounted from the next whisky delivery, thus keeping their budding romance from becoming a business transaction.

"Well, the two lovers jump at the suggestion, and before long, Emerald Ed is not only handing over his entire shipment of spirits gratis but begins to accrue a substantial amount of debt to Black Jack as well. Mabel and Ed are so smitten that they are spending every free moment together and some moments that are not free at all, and as the weeks run into months, there is talk of Ed taking Mabel away from the business and the two settling down together to a life of rum running and domestic bliss, although where Ed gets the idea that Mabel can keep house is beyond me, as I have seen that dame try to fry bacon and eggs once and we were lucky that there was not severe bodily injury or loss of life.

"Anyway, as the year-end approaches, Ed says that he wishes to take Mabel out to a Christmas party he throws every year, the location of which he will share only upon her arrival, as the event is dear to his heart and a surprise, but she will need to take the night off, and he will be happy to compensate Black Jack for her time if there is any protest. Well, Mabel is thrilled with the prospect, and even purchases a Christmas-themed frock for the occasion, but when the night of the party rolls around, Black Jack Bukowski informs Emerald Ed that his account is badly in arrears, and before Mabel can leave the premises, Ed will have to bring accounts current, which Ed cannot do, as he is currently more than somewhat skint due to the party expenses.

"Determined not to let Black Jack ruin the Christmas spirit with his penchant for filthy lucre, Mabel conspires with several of the other girls to slip a mild-to-fatal narcotic into Black Jack's Ovaltine, and when he slips off to Never-Never Land, Mabel, resplendent in her Christmas dress, departs for the party, waving to all the girls who send her off as if each will catch a bouquet to be the next one out the door.

"Mabel is very excited to attend this party, since she sees it as the gateway event to her and Emerald Ed's new life together, but much to her surprise, Ed does not pull up to a ballroom or club venue, but instead leads her into a place in the outer Mission called Saint Francis Home for Little Angels, which Ed says is an orphanage for Irish kids, which is named for Saint Francis of Killarney and not Francis of Assisi, for which the city is named, that Dago fuck (although no one ever hears of Saint Francis of Killarney, so Ed may have been somewhat misinformed). So, before entering, Ed changes into a Santa suit which complements Mabel's red-and-white dress perfectly, and they enter the venue to great cheers, applause, and other accolades from each and all of the parentless mick waifs.

"Well, Mabel is beside herself with joy and cries many mascara-streaked tears while helping Ed hand out presents to the orphans, then sits on his lap basking in the Christmas cheer as the evening passes and the treats and refreshments are served to the delighted waifs, all of it set up and paid for by Emerald Ed (although none of his specialty spirits are served, to cut down on knife fights among hooted orphans). Mabel has never seen Ed so happy. He tells her this is something he does every year, as he came up in an orphanage himself, and looked forward every year to when Santa would come and give each kid their own personal potato to cherish and care for until such time as it was boiled or stolen by rats.

"They depart the party at the end of the evening and Ed suggests that they retreat to his apartment in the Castro, where he lives among the other bog trotters of the city, and there they should celebrate the spirit of Christmas with a nightcap and some Yuletide razzmatazz. But little do they know, Black Jack Bukowski has since come to, and is more than somewhat sored up about having been slipped a Mickey by his own star attraction, and furthermore, he knows the location of Emerald Ed's flat, and he is waiting in the bushes when they pull up. And as they proceed up the walk, arm in arm, Black Jack jumps out of the bushes and says thus, 'No one welshes on Black Jack Bukowski,' and before Ed can protest being accused of being Welsh, Black Jack pulls a .32 revolver and lets one loose right in Emerald Ed's coconut, thus spoiling the Christmas spirit and splattering the sidewalk with no little blood and brain matter.

"Well, much to everyone's surprise, Emerald Ed survives, although with greatly reduced capacity, as he is only able to sit up in a chair and be fed by spoon while staring sideways at the wall, so if he is not a vegetable, he is certainly little more than a meaty entrée. And as Ed has no known relatives, and Mabel has returned under protest to the employ of Black Jack Bukowski, Ed's care is remanded to the state, and he is sent to the drooling ward at the Sonoma Center for the Care of Feeble Minded Children.

"Later, it turns out that Black Jack Bukowski meets an untimely end by accidentally ingesting a jeroboam of strychnine while accidentally holding a pillow over his own face until he stops kicking, rest in peace, but from that day unto this, never does a Christmas pass that Mabel does not ferry all of her employees from the business she inherited to what is now called the Sonoma State Hospital, where she throws a barn burner of a Christmas party for all the feebs, one of whom is Emerald Ed Mahoney himself, who lives there to this day, and whom she sits with through the evening, knowing he is smiling in his heart, even if he is only drooling in his fruitcake in the room."

Stilton DeCheese, Private Eye, Dragon Navigator

"Go that way. What are you, blind?" I said to Milo as I pointed to the diagram on the map Scooter had drawn.

Scooter whistled to agree and Milo turned the dragon until the needles on the instruments matched the diagram.

"I'm used to driving by landmarks," said Milo. "It's not like I can roll down a window."

He had a point, but the guy had been a tank driver in the army; he probably couldn't roll a window down there, either. I'll have to ask someone if you can roll the windows down in a tank.

We'd been going for about two hours and it was pretty smooth all the way. It was so smooth we didn't regret that we hadn't put in extra seats, but after the initial excitement it was more than somewhat boring and we had to chat and tell stories and talk about where we might be going so we didn't think about being hundreds of feet underground in a sealed can.

"What about lava?" asked Myrtle. "When we run into some lava we're goners, right?"

"Smegma," Doris said. "If it's under the surface, it's smegma. It's only lava when it comes out."

"What if we run into molten smegma?" asked Myrtle. "I really wish we could look out the windows."

"Nah," said Milo, "we're only six hundred or so feet underneath the surface. You have to go miles down before you reach molten smegma. But just in case, don't open the window."

All of a sudden Scooter started bouncing and pointing and sort of going crazy.

"I think he wants something, Milo," I said.

Milo looked at the chart and pulled back some levers. The churning of the claws stopped and all we could hear was each other breathing and the turbine thing humming in the background.

"We're here," Milo said.

Scooter bounced around the controls, hitting switches and turning dials.

"What's he doing?" I asked Milo.

"He's turning on all the exterior lights and—"

Before Milo could say what was what, all the covers over the windows started to fold back. We ran to the eyeballs in the front and looked out.

"We're not buried," said Milo.

"But we're inside of something," said Doris.

"It's a cave," I said. It looked like a cave, with some shiny, glass-looking mineral ahead reflecting the lights of the metal dragon.

Scooter hopped over to the hatch and hit the button.

"No, Scooter!" Myrtle screamed. "The smegma!" She dropped to the floor and covered her head, which I guess is from a drill she learned in school, but we didn't have that drill at my school, so I sort of snort-laughed at her.

Scooter bounded toward the hatch and crawled through. Milo ran to the hatch as if to catch him, but he was too late. The little guy was through. Milo stuck his head out and looked around. "It's okay, you can breathe."

"But?" said Myrtle.

"No smegma," Milo said. He climbed a little farther out of the hatch. "Holy shit," he said.

I ran to the portholes on that side, but I couldn't see what Milo was seeing.

"Holy shit," Milo said a lot quieter and a lot slower. "Goddammit, Scooter," he whispered in that furious whisper voice your mom uses to get you to shut up in church when you're a kid.

Milo looked back at us, put his finger to his lips for us to be quiet, then gestured for us to follow him out of the hatch. Doris was the first out after him, and as soon as her head was fully out and she looked around she said, "Holy shit." Milo shushed her furiously, so she said it again a lot quieter and climbed on out. I could hear her going down the stairsteps. It was my turn and I paused like they had when I first poked my head out and looked around.

We were inside a cave, a chamber of some kind, so big I could just make out the ceiling and the walls on one side. It was the biggest inside place I'd ever been in, bigger than I'd ever even seen in a picture. The ceiling had to be twenty stories high. But that wasn't what they were holy-shitting about.

I climbed down the steps and joined Milo and Doris and just looked at it, which took some time. "Goddammit, Scooter," I said.

Then Milo jumped in, doing the hissing, angry whisper at Scooter: "Goddammit, if you are going to read our minds and put things up our butts to put plans in our heads—don't whistle like you don't know what I'm talking about. You can give these dames instructions to build that fucking thing"—he threw a thumb over his shoulder at the metal dragon—"down to the millimeter, and you don't mention this—this fucking thing?"

Scooter whistled, but quietly, and he didn't seem sorry. Then Myrtle poked her head out of the hatch and screamed like she was on fire. We all dove to the cave floor and assumed the molten smegma defense pose, but after a second we looked up.

It hadn't moved.

The metal dragon's lights lit up the cave like a candle in the middle of a pitch-black room, and what we could see, besides that we were in an enormous cave, was that also in this cave was a dragon, a huge, enormous, fucking monstrous, rust-colored, smooth-as-glass dragon. So huge that even with the light of the metal dragon, the edges of its back disappeared into darkness. And after I shushed everyone, you could hear it breathing—or maybe snoring. It was curled up; its tail, circling the chamber in front of us, had been the shiny thing we'd seen when Scooter opened the eye ports of the metal dragon. In one of the dragon's back claws there was a white, I don't know what, a vessel, I guess, that was easily as big as the metal dragon, which made the brown dragon a hundred times bigger. Milo was right: Scooter should have said something.

I realized I had forgotten to breathe, looking at it, and finally I gasped, like I'd come up from a deep dive. Awe, I guess.

"Goddammit, Scooter," Myrtle said, evidently having recovered enough to realize why the rest of us were mad.

Scooter whistled and clicked, but it sounded far away. And it was. The little guy was hopping toward the white thing.

"No, Scooter!" Milo scream-whispered, and he took off after Scooter. The floor of the cave was smooth and covered with a fine dust, which was all over us from our defense dive, and Scooter was kicking it up as he hopped. Doris took off after Milo, whispering angrily for Scooter to come back, so Myrtle and I looked at each other, shrugged, and headed after them, catching up to Doris in a tick.

Scooter was heading for the white thing in the dragon's claws, and the closer he got, the more urgently we whispered, but he was ignoring us, and he had a good fifty yards on us and we weren't going to catch him before he got to the white—I don't know—egg. It wasn't shaped like an egg, but the dragon was protecting it like it was one.

When Scooter was about twenty yards away from the egg, it lit up and a door opened in the side of it, a ramp extended, and Scooter walked up it and into the ship. Well, *now* we knew what it was.

"Back," Milo said. "Back to the dragon. Back to the dragon." He turned and was running full-out toward the metal dragon.

"Aren't we supposed to follow Scooter?" Myrtle asked as Milo went past her, puffing now as he ran.

"Nope," I said. I grabbed her and pulled her back until she turned around and was running beside me and Doris, who had been bringing up the rear but was now pulling ahead of us, running for the metal dragon.

Milo helped Doris up the cut-in steps. "Go, go, go," he said. "I don't want to be in this cave if he wakes that thing up."

Milo gave me and Myrtle each a hand up. We scurried up the steps and crawled headfirst into the hatch, then we turned and pulled Milo in.

"Doris, that whole line of buttons, the hatch and the window shields," I said, pointing.

"Leave the eyes open," Milo said. "I don't want to steer into that thing's tail and piss it off."

"The chart, Milo," I said. "This cave isn't the end of it. This is just a waypoint."

"Fucking Scooter," Milo said.

26

SANTA IN THE DROOLING WARD

Sammy

The party really took off when Santa and his elves arrived, and not just because Santa brought hookers and liquor, although that helped, too. The elves came in first and framed an arrival ramp for Santa, like a chorus line in one of those musical numbers from the thirties, but instead of a presentation of guys in top hats, it was a bunch of pointy-eared whores in candy-striped stockings, although it was no less grand. Mabel had put "Jingle Bells" on the record player and several of the elves were armed with bandoliers of jingle bells as well, so it couldn't have been more festive if Tiny Tim had won the game in the bottom of the ninth by hitting a grand slam with his friggin' crutch.

Santa entered through the archway and between the colonnade of elves with a booming "Ho, ho, ho," but despite the volume, his spirit wasn't in it. Lone Jones hadn't laughed or smiled since his mama died, and no amount of meatloaf could fill the hole left in his heart. Although we had tried, and tried, until Cookie himself came out of the kitchen and eighty-sixed meatloaf to Lone in person, something we'd never seen him do.

"Kid, you're cut off," Cookie had said, patting the front of his apron for a cigar that would never be there because his doctor and his wife had conspired to ruin his life. "I lost my liquor license in

'32 because I overserved some mugs against my better judgment and they drove off a pier. I'm not gonna lose my meatloaf license."

"There's a meatloaf license?" Moo Shoes asked.

"Shut the fuck up, Moo Shoes," Cookie said. "You a lawyer all of a sudden?"

"I understand, sir," said Lone.

After Della had finally told him she was leaving, it took all our efforts to get Lone to work, and Moo Shoes even hung around the Moonlight Club for an hour to keep an eye on the big man until he had to leave to cover his own shift. It was Moo's idea to try to cheer Lone up by letting him play Santa.

"Think of how happy you'll make all those kids, Lone. This will be better than being a Secret Service agent. You won't even have to pretend to be white."

"I kind of will," said Lone. "Santa's beard is white."

"The fuck do I know?" said Moo. "I'm Chinese."

I know for a fact that Moo Shoes's mother goes to the Chinese Methodist Church on Stockton Street and he grew up celebrating Christmas from the jump. Fucking Moo Shoes.

So we almost got a smile out of Lone while we were telling him about all the joy he'd be bringing to the little kids, but now— behind the beard and red hat, and a Santa suit so big it had to be sewn together by elf whores—as he glanced around the room at all the twisted, broken smiles, he had the look of being purely overwhelmed. He needed someone to shake him out of it the way Powers had done for me—that hand on my shoulder and voice in my ear reminding me that I wasn't there for me. I started to make my way over to Lone, sidestepping some elves, but Mabel spotted it before I did, and after a quick smooch on Emerald Ed's forehead, she joined Santa and took his arm with a smile wide enough to fill the room. How she knew to start dancing, I don't know, but she did. She put Lone's arms around her and led him on a jingle-bell twirl around the room. The elves followed behind, and the patients, those who could, followed behind them.

Pretty soon the elves were dancing with the patients, and with each other. Powers took Mabel on a whirl to a Bing Crosby song, and Nurse Stacy got an armload of Santa and danced him from patient to patient, introducing them to him, and Lone said "Merry Christmas" to every one, and blessed their hearts just the way his mama would have, and before long Santa wore a smile of genuine joy.

A lot of them weren't kids, and they knew this giant in a Santa suit with the pillows stuffed in his coat and the shiny black tap shoes wasn't Santa, but every one of them wanted him to be, and Lone felt it.

I took one of the elves for a turn around the floor to "Good King Wenceslas," which is not a toe-tapper to dance to, but she was a good sport.

"You smell nice," I said to my dance partner. "Christmassy."

"Pine-Sol, just a dab behind the ears," she said. "Mabel made a rule: you can smell like pine, peppermint, or cinnamon, but no perfumes. 'Christmas don't smell like a floozie,' she said."

"I don't know, when I was a kid I dreamed of a Christmas filled with floozies."

"Really?"

"Visions of sugarplums danced in my head."

"Aw. That's sweet. It's never too late, you know."

"Nah, Christmas is for kids. But the pine scent is nice."

"Thanks. I'm glad I went with the Pine-Sol. Debbie went with the peppermint oil—she put some downstairs to freshen up a little, then she went running around the house wailing like her snatch was on fire."

"I will make a note of that for next Christmas," I said. "Let's dance over this way. I want to hear what Nurse Stacy is saying."

Lone had danced to the side of one patient in a high crib, a girl, you could tell by the hair, but she had no arms or legs, and her eyes were clouded and sunken, her other facial features small, crowded, like a child's doll that had been melted. She wore a nightgown that might have been a man's T-shirt.

"This is Angie," Stacy said. "Hi, Angie." Stacy very gently passed the back of her hand over Angie's cheek. "She can't see or hear us. Her eyes and ears never developed before she was born. She's twenty years old. Go ahead, you can touch her face, her head, just be very slow and gentle."

Lone touched her hair with the tips of his fingers. "Do she like it?"

"I think so. She's inside there, but she doesn't have words to put to the things she experiences. We just don't know. We know she likes the sun on her face."

"How you know that?"

"She smiles. We take her out in the sun for a little while every day if it's nice. She smiles."

Lone was looking at Angie like he was trying to solve a math problem with his heart.

"Can she smell?"

"Yes. We see her respond to smells. She'll smile and breathe deeper if she likes it. She'll crinkle her nose if she doesn't."

Lone reached out and grabbed my dance partner by the back of her elf frock and pulled her over.

"Angie, smell this ho. She smell like Christmas, darlin'."

Angie smiled, a crooked little smile, and so did Lone. "Thank you, miss," Lone said to the elf.

"Don't mention it, Santa. Merry Christmas."

"Merry Christmas to you, sweetheart." To Stacy he said, "So she can't hear this music, she don't know this party is here for her?"

"I don't think so. She probably smells the smells, feels the air as people pass by."

"She can feel the air move? You think she can feel vibration?"

"Yes. Some of our deaf patients can feel the vibration of the music by putting their hands on the speakers of the record player." She pointed to two adult patients who were doing just that across the room.

"Can I pick her up?" asked Lone.

"I don't know, Santa, she's very fragile."

"How 'bout you teach me how to pick her up."

So Stacy did that. I backed away and so did my dance partner. There was a semicircle of elves forming around Santa and Stacy and Angie as Stacy showed Lone how to support Angie. Lone pulled the pillows out of his Santa suit and threw them on Angie's cradle, then held her in his arms and began to dance with her face against his chest. "White Christmas," and Lone was humming the song as he moved, slowly and gently, everyone in the room giving him a wide path, and it went on like that, for song after song, with Lone humming deep and low, his eyes closed or staring off, and Angie, her little cheek against his chest, feeling the vibration, the movement, the loving arms around her, smiling.

"Not what I expected," said Moo Shoes from behind me. I turned to see him wearing a reindeer costume, a sprig of mistletoe hanging from one of his antlers. He was holding a drink. "This place is huge."

"Mabel says there are six thousand people here, patients and staff. They even have their own machine shop where they make the special wheelchairs for each patient. A farm, orchards, livestock— this place is like a small, self-contained city."

About that time, Lone danced by holding a boy with an enormous head but a tiny, withered body, his bones, as delicate as a baby bird's, showing through his skin. The boy could see and hear, unlike Angie. His eyes tracked the other dancers and a tiny hand tapped out the rhythm against Lone's chest, yet the big man still hummed the melody when he wasn't saying "Ho, ho, ho" and "Merry Christmas" to the other partygoers.

"They're going to call from those buildings by the entrance when Squid Kid gets here," said Moo Shoes. "They have their own phone operator."

"Yeah, Mabel told me. The dragon is stashed in the rumble seat of the Ford."

Moo looked at his watch. "Shouldn't be long now. You packing?"

"Nah, the Cheese has the snub-nose and she gave Milo's shotgun to Olivia Stoddard. Jimmy took back her Walther."

"I've got the automatic I took off of Squid Kid's guy," Eddie said, patting the waist of his reindeer suit, which buttoned up the back.

"I figure if it comes to a shoot-out, we're going to lose."

"Yeah, but he won't be able to torture us to give up Uncle Ho. I called him, told him we were doing the handoff. He went bananas about doing it up here. Said something awful happened back in olden times when he came here."

"You don't have to be there for the turnover," I said.

"Yeah, I feel like I should be, though. I kind of brought you in on this job."

"Apparently, according to the dragon, none of us had any choice in this. He's running the show."

"When this is over, will you stop talking like that? It's spooky and makes me want to put you away in the nut hatch."

"If you're coming, you may want to change before the meet. Your antlers look goofy."

"Says the guy who hears voices from statues."

"Fair point."

We watched as Lone took a seat by the Christmas tree and Mabel fetched presents out of the big red bags and handed them to Santa, who read the card, ho-ho-hoed, and merry-Christmassed, then the patient held up their hand if they could, or one of the staff identified the recipient, and one of the elves delivered the package and helped unwrap it if the patient couldn't do it themselves. There were perhaps a hundred patients at the party now, many brought over from other group homes since we'd arrived, but everyone got a gift. The presents were small: socks, a knit hat, a toy for a kid, a snow globe, a lamp that turned and projected aquarium fish swimming around the room—a gift for a woman who couldn't move at all, but could see—nothing expensive, but each picked special for the patient. Angie got a mink pompom on a wand that the staff could tickle her face with. It was pretty clear that Mabel had put a lot of time and effort into talking to the staff and putting the presents together.

I heard a phone ring in another room and tensed up. I waited. One of the elves came out from the direction of the kitchen and sort of sidled up to me. "They're here," she whispered.

"Moo," I called to Moo Shoes, who had gone to the bar to get a drink. He looked up and I tossed my head in the direction of the front.

Five minutes later Moo Shoes was in the passenger seat of the Ford and I was headed for the front gate. It was a good half mile from the rest of the facility, across a bridge, which was good. If things went pear-shaped, none of the patients or Mabel's people would get hurt. We'd stationed one of Mabel's security guys at the gate in a hospital staff coverall. He was supposed to make the call when Squid Kid arrived, then scram.

"He's likely to be pretty sored up. Mr. Ping told him if he wanted the Rain Dragon he needed to be here."

"Remember, we know nothing," I said. "We're just delivery boys for Uncle Ho. He's safe and we don't know anything. Got it?"

The "gatehouse" was really just a two-bay garage with a small office attached, which was used as an information booth to direct arrivals and deliveries. There was a map of the whole facility next to the entrance road. Two guys in suits were trying to look at it by the headlights of one car and there was another one parked by the garage.

"Didn't we say one car?" I asked.

"That's a roger, dodger," said Moo. "A gangster who doesn't follow instructions? I'm shocked, shocked, I tell you."

"Moo, this guy okay with his nickname? This isn't like your uncle Ho, who everyone calls Catfucker all the time, but he never tells me not to call him that, then he loses his fucking mind if I mention it to him?"

"Nah, he gets it from his grandfather. When Tommy Fang was little his grandpa took him fishing. Grandpa looked away for a second and when he looked back the kid was munching on a mouthful of bait—squid. So Grandfather Fang starts calling him Squid Kid. I'd go with Mr. Fang, though, to be safe."

"I think the *safe* ship sailed when we shanghaied two of his guys."

I pulled up in front of the second garage door, got out, and leaned against the Ford. I lit a smoke like I had all the time in the world. Eddie got out of the other side. I could see his antlers over the car roof. Fucking Moo Shoes.

"They're going to kill us, aren't they?"

"Yup," I said. I felt strangely calm, not rattled or afraid. Curious. Moo Shoes seemed pretty chilly for a fellow in a reindeer outfit.

One of Squid Kid's suits was holding open the door to the office, bowing like he was saying *after you*. So away we went, inside. The door guy patted both of us down while another guy stood by the cars, presumably ready to draw and fire if either one of us got tricky. He said something to Moo Shoes in Cantonese.

"What? What? What?" I asked.

"He said my antlers are stupid."

He had a point.

"Gentlemen, gentlemen," I said as I nodded to each and every one.

Inside was one of those metal desks you find on military bases, that look like they could take a two-inch artillery shell unscathed.

Sitting on the corner of the desk was a lean Chinese guy in a black suit with gray pinstripes, a blue-gray fedora with a silver dragon on the band. Tommy "Squid Kid" Fang, I guessed, because the other two guys in there were standing in the corners like they were covering the room.

"Where's the dragon?" Squid Kid asked, no accent at all.

"I got it, Mr. Fang," I said. "I just wanted to make sure everything was copacetic before I brought it in."

"This isn't an exchange. I'm not giving you anything. You just give me the dragon and you walk out of here alive."

"Maybe," said the guy in the corner closest to the garage, brown suit, not as nice as Squid Kid's. He snickered.

I grinned at the guy. "That poker face why you're not in charge, or you just too good at boot-licking to move you up?"

He looked really steamed and started to reach into his jacket for his gat. Squid Kid shook his head and Brown Suit dropped his gun hand to his side.

"*Stall, Two-Toes,*" came the voice in my head. "*Stall.*"

"So," I said. "All of this is because of your grandfather? Head of one of the fighting tongs?"

"Ghee Sin Tong," Squid Kid said. "What do you know of it?"

"*Hall of maintained justice,*" said the dragon.

"Hall of maintained justice," I repeated. This dragon would have been great to have had on tests as a kid.

Tommy Fang pushed his fedora back on his head, raised an eyebrow. He had a scar through the eyebrow, probably from a hard punch or a sap, not a knife, since it didn't extend to his cheek or up his forehead. "What do you know about it, *gwai lo?*"

I was going to answer, I really was, but there was a squeal and a crash outside—I mean, right outside. Followed by shouting in Cantonese and a fair amount of car doors slamming.

The two goons guarding the room looked at Squid Kid, who tossed his head, giving them permission to go check things out. They got to the door just as Uncle Ho was thrown through it. He landed in a pile in front of Squid Kid, who pulled his feet up for a second lest the old Chinese guy splatter on his shoes. Next, one of the outside guys came through holding the old dame from the whorehouse in Locke, who was squirming around and cursing like a sailor. (You could tell it was cursing, even though it was in Cantonese.) The guy holding her by the arm was holding a hatchet up with his other hand.

"This old broad tried to brain me with this."

"They smashed into one of our cars coming in. The Olds," said the other outside guy.

Uncle Ho looked up to me and started chattering a bunch of Cantonese at me. Moo Shoes, by habit, translated.

"You must take the Rain Dragon away from here. He cannot be here. Quickly, take him and go. The last time he made me bring him here he destroyed Big Town."

Squid Kid said something to Ho.

"No one calls it Big Town anymore," Moo Shoes translated.

"*Calm yourself, Catfucker,*" said the dragon inside my head, but I could tell that Uncle Ho and the old dame could hear it, too, the way they cocked their heads as if listening. "*I am here.*"

The phone on the desk rang.

Everyone looked at everyone else. Squid Kid nodded to Brown Suit to get it. He did, looked around, back at Squid Kid. "She wants to talk to someone named Sammy."

I raised my hand. Squid Kid nodded for me to take the phone, said, "Hold it so he can listen."

I took the phone and held it so Brown Suit could also hear. His cheek was maybe two inches from mine. I kept my eyes on Squid Kid, but I said, "You know, you're a very attractive man," to Brown Suit. He was horrified, which is kind of what I was going for.

"Sammy?" came Mabel's voice through the phone.

"Oh, hi, doll, we got a situation percolating here. What's the skinny?"

"My housekeeper just called from my place in the city. The cops thought there was something fishy going on and came to the door. One of the drag queens spilled the beans and told them what was going on. They're on their way here."

"How long?"

"She said it took a while before they let her go so she could call. An hour—hour and ten. We're going to wrap it up. I won't have Christmas ruined by the Mother fucking Superior."

I covered the mouthpiece with my hand. "Captain Dunne of vice," I explained to Squid Kid, out of courtesy. Then to Mabel, "Okey-dokey. We'll wrap things up here, too. Merry Christmas."

I hung up the phone.

Uncle Ho resumed his chatter, this time in English. "No, the Rain Dragon must go away from here. Wickedness will bring his wrath again. He will become larger than a mountain and dive into the earth and Big Town will be destroyed again—"

He went on, but Squid Kid backhanded him in the mouth. "That's it," he said. "You." He pointed to me. "Go get the Rain Dragon right now or Liu starts hitting people with that hatchet."

"Chop off their dicks!" shouted the old woman, which did not seem particularly helpful.

Squid Kid looked to the guy holding her. "Are the cars drivable?"

"Crushed the rear wheel well in against the tire on the Olds. I don't think so. The Buick is fine."

"We'll all go in one." To me: "Go, *gwai lo*—the dragon. Now!" To Brown Suit: "Go with him."

I winked at Brown Suit as I headed out the door. "Alone at last."

He drew his gun.

27

BE CAREFUL
WHAT YOU
ASK FOR

Sammy

I had the Rain Dragon statue in a surplus messenger bag I'd stashed in the rumble seat of Jimmy Vasco's Ford. I wished I'd remembered to put a roscoe in there with it, but I hadn't, and Brown Suit wasn't going to let me get close enough to swing the dragon around to conk him, although as heavy as it was, it would definitely have cracked his coconut. Ah, hindsight.

I led him back into the office.

"Take it out, put it on the desk," said Squid Kid.

I did as he ordered, peeled the messenger bag off the heavy black stone and set the statue in the middle of the desk. Uncle Ho began muttering, incoherent in any language. Squid Kid looked at the statue, walked around the desk, hefted it, and turned it around as if looking for some kind of trademark. He looked up to Brown Suit, the only one with a gun drawn, and said, "This is it. Kill the old man."

Moo Shoes pulled the automatic out from under his antlers and shot Brown Suit high in the shoulder, about the collarbone, spinning him around and causing him to drop his gun. Moo had stashed the auto under the hood his antlers were stitched to, then cinched down the drawstring. Everyone had been looking at the Rain Dragon and not watching Eddie scratch his head. Fucking Moo Shoes.

One of the outdoor guys reached into his coat for his gat, but before it cleared his jacket there was a sizzling *POP,* and his head rolled off his body and hit the floor while he was still standing in a fountain of his own blood. Behind him in the doorway stood the Rain Dragon, the one I had seen in Locke, his spade-tipped tail dripping blood, poised to strike again.

Squid Kid dove under the desk. The old woman screamed and huddled into a ball. Old Ho draped himself over her as a shield. Brown Suit tried to pick up his gun with his good hand—the dragon's tail struck him in the middle of the spine and exploded out of his chest. The other two goons were both dead while still standing, before either could clear their guns; one had lost a hand to the dragon's tail as it blasted into his chest.

Moo Shoes wisely tossed his gun into the corner, then put up his hands, I guess to show the dragon he was unarmed. He'd been sprayed head to toe with blood, as had the whole room, and he was blinking as if that would make it all go away. Uncle Ho peeked back over his shoulder, surprised to be alive. The old woman was whimpering.

I'm not sure why I wasn't completely horrified by it all. I guess I'd figured I was gonna get croaked from the jump, so I was feeling a little relieved. I'd also seen the Rain Dragon in this form before, although not with so much gore dripping from his tail.

I pulled a hankie out of my back pocket and wiped the blood spray from my eyes. I said, "Mr. Fang, you'll want to come out from under that desk. And I cannot stress this too strongly—do not be holding a gat when you do. The Rain Dragon you requested is here."

There was a shuffling and Squid Kid pulled himself up above the edge of the desk and took a good look at the dragon for the first time. The dragon would have been perhaps eight feet tall if he weren't curved, standing on hind feet, and while his tail was currently only six feet or so long, I had seen it bolt across the room more than twenty feet. When the dragon spoke you could see rows of white teeth as long as my little finger, needle sharp. In the front were four long fangs. His forked tongue darted out every few seconds and sniffed the air around his snout. I thought, with that tongue, it was weird he didn't speak with a lisp, but I didn't want to bring it up and make him self-conscious.

"Shoot him, Squid Kid!" shouted Ho. "Before he destroys the city!"

"Well, your loyalties went to shit pretty quickly," I said to Ho.

"You don't know, *gwai lo*. Because I am wicked and he will again take revenge on the city."

The dragon laughed. (Yes, it was disturbing to hear.) "First," he said, "Squid Kid is a fucking stupid name for a gangster. Sit down, Squid Kid."

I looked at Moo Shoes. "See?" I said.

"And second, Ho, you are not wicked and Big Town was not destroyed because of you. You were spared because you helped this woman who is also sensitive to us. Big Town was destroyed as an accident of passion. When you saw me in that form, that size, diving into the earth, I was going to find congress with my lover, the Earth Dragon. What followed destroyed the city. An accident."

"Wait, wait, wait," I said. "Are you telling me that the 1906 earthquake that destroyed San Francisco was caused by dragon razzmatazz?"

"He will do it again," said Ho. "He will grow and go there again."

Squid Kid was in a wheeled office chair, looking like somehow he might make a break for the door.

"Tommy," I said, "look around. Your pals are decorating this room. I mean, as far as I'm concerned, give it a go, but think it through."

Squid Kid settled down to just looking like he was going to go into shock.

"You," said the dragon to Squid Kid. "You wanted to return to the ways of the tongs? Even when the Catfucker saved this woman last moon—"

"Forty-one years ago," I said.

"Time is different for dragons," said the dragon. "Even then the tongs were corrupt. The Immortals put the dragons in the service of the Triads and so the tongs after them to preserve virtue. You have not been virtuous. You threaten this old man, take his business, charge merchants for protection from your own evil. You are not virtuous, and we are creatures of virtue."

"You destroyed a city doing the razzmatazz," I said.

"Give it a fucking break, Two-Toes. I'm going somewhere with this," the dragon said. To Squid Kid he said, "Go now. Return the business to the Catfucker, and never threaten him or do him or anyone else harm. If you do, I will know, and I will come for you. Do you believe me?"

Squid Kid nodded, then said, "*Hai,*" *yes* in Chinese.

"Go," the dragon said. He picked up the head of Squid Kid's henchman, his talon nearly encircling it. "Take this with you, to remember me by."

"*Hai,*" Squid Kid said.

"Who has the keys to the Buick?" asked Moo Shoes, who seemed to be recovering from his shock and accepting the reality that he was going to live, and that dragons were real. And they talked. He'd found a clean spot on the inside of his reindeer suit sleeve and wiped the blood from his face.

Squid Kid pointed to what was left of Brown Suit. Moo Shoes went to the corpse and dug into his jacket pocket until he came up with the keys. He threw them on the desk. "Can you drive yourself?" Moo Shoes asked. "Because I can give you a few starter tips if you need them."

"He is a very good driving teacher," said old Ho.

Squid Kid didn't answer, but snatched the keys off the desk and headed for the door, slipping and nearly falling on the bloody floor. The dragon's tail shot out to block his way.

"Take this." He held out the head. Squid Kid reluctantly grabbed the hair of his goon's head and took it from the dragon. "Do you still want the statue?" asked the dragon. Squid Kid shook his head. The dragon pulled back his tail and Squid Kid slip-slid out the door.

I looked to the dragon. "Do you need to dive into the earth and destroy the city again?"

"No, I cannot take that form yet. I am still exhausted from the last time. I need to rest."

"It was forty-one years ago."

"Wait until you are eons old, Two-Toes. It takes time. I will return to the Earth Dragon, but I will wait here for my ride."

We heard the Buick fire up outside and peel away.

I shook out a smoke and lit it, gave one to Moo Shoes, offered one to the dragon. "You smoke?"

"Only after sex," he said.

"Jeez," I said.

"Dragon joke," said the dragon.

I heard sirens in the distance. Dug the keys to the Ford out of my pocket.

"Moo, take them and take the Ford back to the group home." I nodded to Ho and the old lady. "Mabel and the girls should be ready. Get everyone on the bus and get out of here. Go right at the road, north, toward Santa Rosa. You'll come out on the highway back to the city."

"What about you?" Moo asked.

"Leave the keys in the Ford. I'll follow. I'm going to wait with the Rain Dragon for his ride. Oh, and either take that automatic you had or wipe it down. Same with the hatchet."

"My hatchet," said the old lady.

"Take the hatchet, and them, and go."

Moo gathered his gun and the hatchet, helped the old lady up, and took one of her arms while Uncle Ho took the other to steady her across the slick floor.

At the doorway Ho turned to the dragon. "I don't want my business back."

"Go with Niu Yun," said the dragon. "You did not deserve the punishment you took on yourself. You were brave and virtuous, not wicked. Go."

"Okey-dokey," said Ho. They went out into the night.

The sirens got closer. I went outside and the dragon stood beside me, watching the red lights from the cruisers reflecting in the sky. Moo Shoes went by in the bus. Some of the elves waved as they passed, thinking, I suppose, that the creature standing next to me, the color of black glass speckled with red, was some kind of Christmas costume, but when I turned to say something about it, the dragon wasn't there. The bus turned right out of the entrance and headed away from the approaching red lights.

"*You'll want to move away from here, to the other side of the bridge, Two-Toes.*" The dragon's voice in my head again.

I did as I was told and scampered back to the other side of the bridge, perhaps a hundred yards from the entrance, then stopped, waited, and heaved, because I smoke and I hadn't been putting my usual time in on the heavy bag every day.

Not a minute later the first couple of police cars pulled in, sirens blaring, lights flashing, and, seeing the wrecked cars at the entrance, figured, I guess, that that's where the trouble was. Those cops jumped out of their cars and ran into the open office and a couple of seconds later one of them came back out and started barfing. Two others ran out to the road and waved the rest of them in. In another minute there were ten cop cars and at least twice as many cops milling around the garage.

"You don't want any part of that," the Rain Dragon said. He was standing right beside me again. I think I jumped about four feet.

"Don't do that."

"Did you get the statue?" he asked.

"No, I thought you *were* the statue."

"No matter. We are magical beings. We are eternal. We take many forms. That was just one."

I felt a vibration in my knees, then a rumbling that threatened to drown out the sound of the sirens, then about fifty yards ahead of us, to the right of the road, the ground rose and exploded in a sort of reverse crater. Bright lights cut the sky and the metal dragon crawled out of the earth. As impressive as it had been in the shipyard, it was absolutely amazing when it moved, and I had seen a lot of amazing shit lately to compare it to.

"There she is," said the Rain Dragon. "She is a dish."

"She's a machine," I said.

"We are magical creatures, Two-Toes. We take many forms."

"I thought the moonman directed them to build that."

"Silly monkey, you think that we can only influence humans? The gray one will receive his reward as well."

The metal dragon made a loud grinding noise, its great claws tearing furrows in the earth as it headed toward the hospital entrance. The lights from the eyes played across the cop cars and that, along with the noise, drew the attention of some of the flatfoots who had taken a moment to get some air or do the rainbow yawn after witnessing the carnage.

Some were just frozen, watching what appeared to be a creature the size of a building ambling toward them, eyes glowing, but as it approached, some broke for their cars, only to find that their colleagues had blocked them in. When it was evident that the metal dragon wasn't going to stop, some drew their weapons and started firing, the bullets not even making a dull ding on the dragon. The dragon took off the corner of the garage as it turned, Milo evidently trying to avoid destroying the hospital's road, but then he went straight at the cop cars, slowly enough that I could tell he was giving the cops time to clear the cars, and they did, some trying to get into their cruiser, then abandoning it as the dragon crushed the vehicle in front of them. The screech of tearing metal replaced sirens that died like smothered mosquitoes when the metal dragon stepped on them.

A crowd of cops were running back down the road the way from which they'd driven, but one last cruiser started and was backing away. It almost reached the other cops. Dazzling beams of light shot from the dragon's nostrils and completely disintegrated the front of the Dodge—engine, wheels, and all—and what was left of the car skidded to a stop in a trail of sparks. Four cops jumped out and ran after the gang of cops heading down the road.

"Milo seems to have gotten over his fear of driving," I said to the dragon.

"That was the tits," the dragon said.

Milo slowed the dragon, little by little, so the cops were able to get a lead, and finally he came to a stop. When the cops slowed, like they might come back to see what was what, Milo fired the light beam into the sky above their heads until they were well on their way again. When they were out of sight, the metal dragon turned and made its way back to us, Milo always careful to flatten its claws when it went over the road, although the weight alone buckled the tarmac.

The metal dragon stopped on the other side of the little bridge from us. "Maybe you better stay here," I said to the Rain Dragon. "Let me prepare them for the shock."

The dragon laughed again, and I cannot tell you how disturbing that is. "They have seen things that would boggle your little mind," he said.

The hatch on the metal dragon opened and a blonde with surprised hair popped out. "Hey, baby," she said. "Holy fuck, what is that?"

"Rain Dragon, Stilton. Stilton, the Rain Dragon. He kind of made all this happen."

"The Cheese!" said the dragon.

"All right, pal, it's your funeral," I said.

But the Cheese made nothing of it. She just climbed down the steps, jumped off from three up, and ran into my arms. "I missed you," she said.

"Me, too," I said. And I had.

"You're okay with this?" I threw a thumb at the Rain Dragon.

She paused, looked him up and down. "Tiny," she said. "Let me tell you, there's one down there that could wear the Golden Gate Bridge for a belt. It's so big you can't even see it all at once."

"My beloved," said the Rain Dragon.

"Really?" said the Cheese, looking the Rain Dragon up and down. "Okay." She shrugged. "What's all over you guys?"

"Gangsters," I said. "He's small but he packs a mean punch."

"Yikes."

Milo, Myrtle, and Doris had climbed out of the metal dragon and were waiting behind us.

"Nice driving," I said to Milo.

He grinned. "I didn't want to kill anyone, just fuck up some cop cars."

"Well done. What's with the light beam thing?"

"We don't know, moonman stuff, but anything it hits just suddenly isn't there anymore."

"Hey, where *is* the moonman?"

"He ditched us," said Myrtle. "Used us and just tossed us away."

"There's a spaceship down there," said Doris. "And a fucking enormous dragon sitting on it."

"She thinks it's an egg," said the Rain Dragon.

So then I had to do more introductions all around and the Rain

Dragon was right, no one was even surprised that there was a blood-covered talking dragon waiting for them after their ride. They were all out of surprise. No one shook hands, however.

"She thinks it's an egg," repeated the Rain Dragon.

"How did he get it down there?" Milo asked.

"It was there when she arrived. It was there last moon when we made passionate love."

"Forty-one years ago," I corrected. "Time is different for a dragon," I explained to the others.

"So Scooter had us build the dragon so he could get to the ship so he could go home?"

"And he didn't even say good-bye," said Myrtle. "I thought he wanted me and Tilly and Doris to come along so he could motor-boat us good-bye."

"It is the way of his people," said Doris.

"It doesn't even look like an egg," said Myrtle.

"The Earth Dragon is beautiful, but she is not incredibly bright," said the Rain Dragon.

"So you're going back down there, to be with her?"

"I need to rest, recover," said the dragon. "With her."

"Then wake up, do the razzmatazz, and destroy San Francisco again?" I asked.

"Perhaps," said the dragon. "But rest first."

"Come on," Milo said. "I'll show you how to drive her." He started back for the metal dragon.

"She is of my kind," said the Rain Dragon. "We take many forms. You should see the Wood Dragon. She's a fire breather. When she takes form, built by you monkeys, she rages for five minutes, burns to ash, then her spirit lives in a tree for a thousand years. I know my kind."

"So you already know how to drive a dragon built at the direction of a moonman?" I said. "Give him the keys, Milo."

"Perhaps my charm will not suffice. Show me how to drive her, pilot."

Milo hadn't gotten four steps toward the dragon when a beam of light exploded out of the crater the Metal Dragon had made and seconds later a thing, a cylindrical white thing that might have been made of light, shot out of the crater and into the sky, making a steady popping sound, like sparks. In a few seconds it was out of sight, but I could still see the afterimage on my eye, something I'd had before when I accidentally looked at an arc welder without goggles or a helmet.

"Bye, Scooter," Myrtle said, waving. "Ya bum."

Stilton went to her and put her arms around her friend. Myrtle put her head on Stilton's shoulder and stared into the sky.

"He could have explained," said Myrtle. "We built all those machines; he could have built a machine that translated his beeps."

"I know, sweetie," said the Cheese. "Men can be jamokes. Even moonmen."

Sometimes dames need a moment to talk about how awful guys are, so I wandered away.

"Hey, Milo," I said. "You're pretty good with that disintegrator thing. You think when you're showing him how to drive you could maybe clean up that garage building and all those cop cars without, you know, blowing out a crater to the center of the earth?"

"There anybody in there?"

"Nope. Not alive. I mean. Nope. It's clear."

"Sure, no problem," Milo said. "Come on," he said to the Rain Dragon. "Do you like cheese and peanut butter crackers? We got a ton of cheese and peanut butter crackers."

When the Metal Dragon was clearing the entrance, I heard "Ho, ho, ho, merry Christmas," in a big, booming voice right behind me, and I jumped, then turned to see Lone Jones in his Santa suit, sans padding, just behind me. "See," he said. "That why I wear them taps on my shoes. It disturb people being sneaked up on. 'Course, they don't work on grass."

"Why aren't you on the bus?" I asked. "I don't think we can all fit in the Ford."

"I ain't going back to the city, Sammy. Nurse Stacy says they got a job for me here, a place to live. She says I got a way with the patients. And they got a shop here that build wheelchairs and whatnot for the patients. I learned how to weld and do machining out to Hunters Point. I can help them."

"But what about your job? Your stuff?"

"Eddie got a car now. He say he help me bring everything up in a few days."

"Eddie got a car?" I said. The mook could have told me. Fucking Moo Shoes. "But your mama's house?"

"That ain't nothing but a rental. Without Mama in it, it ain't Mama's house. They need me here, Sammy. You got to go where you can help folks."

"I get it," I said. Lone had saved my bacon when I was put on the all-Black welding crew at Hunters Point, and many times since. He taught me how to fight and stepped in when I was too beaten up to fight. Lone told me I would eventually learn to keep my mouth shut and wouldn't get in as many fights, and he had been right.

"You ever coming back to the city?" I asked.

"Oh yeah, I'll come down to Cookie's on my day off, let y'all buy me a meatloaf."

"I'd like that, Lone." I shook the big man's hand and everyone said good-bye all around.

Twenty minutes later Lone stood with us as we watched the Metal Dragon dig back down into the crater from which it had emerged, backfilling as it went. Then he waved and ho-ho-hoed as we drove off, Milo, Doris, and Myrtle in the front of Jimmy Vasco's Ford coupe, me and the Cheese in the rumble under a blanket.

"You promised you wouldn't go with Milo in the Metal Dragon," I said to the Cheese.

"Yeah, I lied," she said. "I didn't want to worry you. Hey, you think Olivia Stoddard blasted anyone with Milo's shotgun?"

"We'll see, I guess. You got any of those cheese crackers? I'm famished."

28

MURDER MOST SOLVED

Stilton DeCheese, Private Eye

I was working undercover at a dive bar in North Beach called Sal's when the call came in about a murder. A tasty little piece of tail called Sammy Two-Toes was bartending and I was watching him work while trying to rid the world of vodka and lime juice for the good of all mankind.

"It's for you," Sammy said, holding out the receiver, looking confused, like he'd only just learned to work a phone. The receiver had a long cord. Sammy handed it over the bar to me.

"DeCheese," I said.

"Oh, Tilly, it's horrible." A dame. "I'm so sorry. I didn't know who else to call. I think he's dead."

"Calm down, kid," I said. It was Olivia Stoddard. "Where are you?"

"I'm at the house in the Mission."

"Hold tight. Don't do anything until I get there." I handed the phone back to Sammy. "Hey, Toots, can I borrow a couple of bucks for cab fare?"

Fifteen minutes later I was knocking on the door of the little Victorian in the Mission. Olivia Stoddard answered, peeked out through the chain.

"Tilly?" she said. She looked me up and down. She'd never

seen me in my pink waitress uniform. I should have been wearing the gray Stetson fedora for professionalism, but Sammy had finally realized I'd swiped it from him and took it back.

"I was working undercover," I said. "You wanna let me in or you going to keep a dead guy all to yourself on account of dress code?"

She let me in. She was wearing the gray pinstriped trousers from one of her custom suits, but no coat, just a white silk chemise, and was barefoot. She obviously hadn't put on her face yet, but there were tear streaks down her cheeks. I could see the dead guy lying on his back on the floor in the parlor entry to the left of the front door. His entire abdomen looked like someone had dumped a bucket of hamburger and shredded guts on him.

I could see that the hallway led through to the kitchen, so I held up a finger to mark my place in the conversation, then ran in and barfed in the sink. Two times. My way of showing vodka and lime juice who's boss.

I returned to the parlor, stepping around the dead guy. Olivia was comforting an older dame, maybe forty, who was crying on the couch.

Olivia looked up. "It's my brother, Four. Marjorie didn't mean to. She thought he was going to hurt me. He hurt me before."

I didn't see the family resemblance. But to be fair, Four was probably not looking his best. Marjorie looked up at me. She was pretty, blond, had short June Allyson hair, wearing a housecoat. She looked like somebody's mom, but there was something there that flashed in her eyes when she looked at me, and it wasn't distress. Anger? Jealousy? I had questions.

"So, Olivia, both barrels?" That seemed like the most important question at the moment. I'd only given her two shotgun shells. Olivia nodded.

"And the shotgun?"

She pointed. It lay on the floor by the edge of the couch. I wasn't much for crime scene analysis, but based on my extensive waitressing experience, and how few pellet marks there were on the wall, I'd say Marjorie couldn't have been more than five or six feet away when she let loose on Alton Stoddard the Fourth. He'd caught it all. But looking at his stiff again, with both his chest and his stomach turned to goo, and a few neat little holes in the hardwood floor on either side of his body, he hadn't taken both barrels at the same time. She'd shot him once, then stood over him and shot him again while he lay there, probably already dead, or certainly dying.

"So, Marjorie," I said. "Marjorie what?"

"Dunne," she said.

"Uh-huh," I said. "Look, I'm going to run out to the car and get my crime kit. I'm going to need an ice pick to help you make this look better. See if you can find one." I headed out the door, down the stairs, and to the phone booth at the corner of Sixteenth and Market, where I dropped a nickel in the phone and dialed zero. I asked the operator to connect me with SFPD homicide. After what felt like a week, a guy picked up.

"There's been a murder," I said. I gave him the address. "The dead guy is a white male, late twenties, early thirties, named Alton Stoddard the Fourth. The killer is still there. Her name is Marjorie Dunne, late thirties, early forties. Blond. Don't hand this case over to Captain Dunne. The killer is his wife, and he'll try to cover it up. And search the joint. I think you'll find evidence in the drag king killings. Look for an ice pick. And oh yeah, she's armed and crazy as a shithouse rat."

The detective wanted to know who I was and how I knew all this, but I hung up and walked onto a streetcar that took me to the cable car at Powell, which I rode into North Beach. I was back in my seat at Sal's less than an hour after I left.

"Hey, Toots," I said to the cutie behind the bar. "You got something that can kill the taste of upchuck?"

"I think I can find something. Listerine on the rocks, maybe? And don't call me Toots."

"Can I get one on the house, for solving a couple of murders?"

"I suppose," he said. "I'm going to need some details."

Sammy

I let the murder case and the debacle with the Christmas party settle a couple of days before getting back to business.

The details of the murder case were still trickling into the papers, which were doing a little tap-dancing on why they hadn't covered the drag king murders before, and as for the Christmas party, well, the police commissioner was plenty sored up at Captain James "the Nun" Dunne when ten SFPD cruisers vanished without a trace seventy miles out of their jurisdiction and twenty cops all experienced a mass hallucination about being attacked by a giant metal monster that disappeared into the sky, leaving only a glass-smooth landing pad where there used to be a garage and office building. By the time any cops got back to Sonoma State Hospital, everyone was tucked snug in their beds, making Dunne's claim that he had been there to break up a debauched Christmas party full of hookers he'd learned about on the word of a hysterical drag queen whose name they'd recorded as Mae Breast seem somewhat less than credible. Dunne had been suspended and was probably going to be fired when the details came out about the murders his wife had committed. He might have gotten away with covering up the drag king killings, but someone had called the office of Alton Stoddard the Third and left a message about the murder of his son before the body was even cold, and Alton was more than somewhat steamed about the scragging of his namesake son, so that wasn't going away. If the rest of the details didn't come out in a week, Fitz, the old homicide cop, was going to slip a file to one of his buddies who was still on the force.

In the meantime, I dropped in on Jimmy Vasco at her place on the wharf one afternoon at about three when I saw the Ford coupe parked out back. It was just me and Jimmy, who had been doing books. We sat in her office, looking over a desk the size of a coal barge, the finish worn off on the corners from people moving around it. She offered me a drink. I took a Coke, straight out of the bottle.

"I'm not giving you the apartment," Jimmy said.

"I figured," I said.

"You didn't find the killer."

"I know. The Cheese did."

"I feel like taking down the Nun is a bonus, though. So I'll cover your expenses. Who would have thought a mousy little dame like that could get the drop on Butch."

"Two grand in expenses," I said. "I need you to donate it to the Sonoma State Hospital. Mark it as funds to build them a new garage at the entrance." I'd gotten the construction estimate from Nurse Stacy.

"What kind of daffy shit is that? And two grand? Are you fucking kidding—"

"Marjorie Dunne didn't kill Butch," I said.

"What?" Jimmy said. "The papers. Wait, what?"

"Two grand. To put your mind at ease. I'll wait while you write the check."

I waited. She wrote the check. Handed it over the desk.

"I could stop payment on that," she said.

"You could," I said. "But you won't. We're pals."

"Okay," she said, not really convinced.

I put the check in my inside jacket pocket. "Alton Stoddard the Fourth killed Butch. I saw Butch beating the stuffing out of him with that big black dildo that night. Later he shaved the mustache, but I still should have recognized him. I told Dunne, by the way, who eventually figured out who it was, but at that point he couldn't tell anyone because there had been a second murder."

"So Dunne was leaving me the threatening notes?"

"No, his wife was. She was thrown out of her house as a kid

when her father caught her with another girl. She had nowhere to go, no way to make a living, so one of the enterprising procurement agents in Los Angeles found her and turned her out on the street. That's where Dunne found her, and eventually rescued her from the life by marrying her, but he didn't rescue her from liking girls. He moved up here right before the war to get her away from anyone who knew her when she was in the life, but when he signed up and shipped out, she started hanging out here and at Mona's. Found companionship among the Sapphic crowd."

"Sapphic? Nice."

"Yeah, my mother was an English teacher. Anyway, she fell in love with Olivia Stoddard, and when she figured out you were moving on her, she started leaving you the notes. She hadn't even killed anyone yet."

"Wait, I wasn't moving on Olivia."

"Yes you were, Jimmy. You know it, I know it, and Marjorie Dunne knew it. The only person who doesn't know it is Myrtle. You were pretending you didn't know who Olivia was for Myrtle's benefit. And since you're going to overcome your natural hound nature, Myrtle never needs to know, right?"

"Right," said Jimmy. "Absolutely."

I said, "When Butch was killed, Marjorie used the opportunity to warn you off. When you showed Dunne the note, he recognized the handwriting as Marjorie's. He'd been seeing it on grocery lists for years. I think he confronted her, and that's when she bolted for the love nest Olivia Stoddard had set up for them—went into hiding from Dunne. Sitting home waiting for her young girlfriend probably sent her over the edge, although I'd guess that going from a puritanical father who throws you out for who you are to a puritanical husband who tries to wipe out sin in the whole city might have done that, too. Anyway, something snapped, and when she saw Olivia flirting with Frankie Fortuna at the show, she followed her and drove an ice pick into Frankie's neck."

"That dame knows how to float a flirt," Jimmy said.

"Yeah, not the point. By this time Dunne had his guys looking for his wife, but only as a witness, according to him. He knew from the notes that she'd been here. That's why he pulled his men off your door and put them on the next pier. Then he visibly covered all the other lesbian clubs, hoping she'd show up here again and his guys could tail her to a place he could find her."

"Did Dunne know about Olivia Stoddard?"

"He did from the night Butch was killed. Remember, during the raid Olivia said something to Dunne and suddenly the cops cleared out. When I first found out who she was, when Stoddard hired me to find her, I thought she'd just told Dunne who her father was and Dunne didn't want any part of that much power, but that wasn't what she said. She told him she was fucking his wife and that unless he cleared out, she would tell every cop in the joint. It wouldn't look good for the Mother of All Virtue."

"What's going to happen to Olivia Stoddard?" asked Jimmy. "That kid's got moxie for miles."

"Yeah, she's a kid, who probably had a similar experience to Marjorie's, except Stoddard couldn't throw her out. He covered up, smoothed over, took away privileges, then gave them back. The brother, Four, was sort of the enforcer. He was supposed to keep an eye on his little sister and he ended up doing a lot more than that. I don't know what he did to the girl, but he definitely developed some twisted tendencies toward cross-dressing dames, which he tried to work out at the whorehouses around the city, until he got thrown out for being too rough with the girls. I'm guessing a lot of that came back on Olivia, and that's one of the reasons she was hiding from him and her father."

"So you don't think that had anything to do with him killing Butch?"

"I don't think he planned that. I think Butch humiliated him, beat him, and as soon as the coast was clear he popped her on the head with a brick and tossed her in the bay. But he was here in the first place looking for his sister, and being a jerk about it, which is what set Butch on him in the first place. She had his number, although she thought he was a jealous husband, not a brother, and she wouldn't let him in."

"But Olivia didn't even show up until after Butch was killed, as far as we know."

"But it was minutes, literally minutes. Maybe Four was following Olivia, lost her, figured where she was going, and got here ahead of her. Funny, him shadowing her and going to her haunts in the same make and color car as hers probably threw the cops off, but they were hands-off because he was a Stoddard. Now Stoddard the Third will send his daughter off to some private butterfly garden to treat her, even though the only thing wrong with her is she falls for damaged people."

"What kind of guy does that to his own daughter?"

"Alton Stoddard the Third is a nasty piece of work. I'm not sure I'd even be alive to tell you this if he wasn't terrified of poor people."

"Well, you got that going for you," Jimmy said.

"Yeah, I do."

"And a terrific girlfriend."

"As do you," I said. I got up. "Myrtle's a stand-up dame."

Jimmy stood and seemed to get sad all of a sudden. "Am I going to see you guys?"

"Oh yeah," I said. "I'll see you at Cookie's. Now that you're done being a hound, right?"

"Right. Absolutely. I'll see you at Cookie's." She got a little twitchy then, like a little kid who has to pee but doesn't want to say anything. "About the apartment—"

"Don't worry about it," I said. "The Cheese and I are renting Lone Jones's mama's place in the Fillmore. They're delivering a new bed tomorrow."

"Okay, I guess I'll see you at Cookie's, then," she said.

I was walking out of the office, but Jimmy called me back.

"What about Marjorie Dunne?"

"No judge is going to send her up for this, with her history. She's nuttier than a squirrel wedding. I figure Camarillo State Nut Hatch."

"How'd you know all that, about Marjorie's past?"

"Once we pegged her for the killer and not just a cop's wife, a friend of mine, ex-cop, was able to get some files pulled down in Los Angeles. She told her whole story to a social worker the first time she got pinched for hooking when she was seventeen. Just a broken kid."

"Yeah, ain't we all?" Jimmy said.

"Some more than others," I said.

I walked out into the bright afternoon sun and hopped to it to get home and shower before my shift.

The Rain Dragon

Oh yeah, I've been talking in your head, being the buzz in your ear, driving you nuts. We dragons are magical, but we are also mysterious and tricky. It is our way. But, before I lie down for a long winter's nap, let me tell you what happened after.

First, motorboating your boobs is not how Scooter's people say hello, and putting probes up people's butts has nothing whatsoever to do with how that little mug puts thoughts in their heads. He's just a little freak. Just so you know.

So, Sammy and the Cheese moved into Lone Jones's mama's house in the Fillmore, but it was only Sammy who could hear Lone's mama's voice, and he did as she told him, and they were happy. They were poor, but Sammy had learned something at the Christmas party talking to Nurse Stacy.

He'd asked, "How long have you been doing this?"

"Twenty-five years," she'd said. "And five years before that, I was a kindergarten teacher."

Sammy'd asked, "And what have you learned in all that time, doing this kind of work?"

She'd said, "That no matter how young or old someone is, or how severe their disability, everyone just wants to help."

He didn't believe it at first, but after looking around at the patients and helpers at the party, he wanted to believe it, he decided to believe it, and he and the Cheese agreed that they were going to believe it together—and that's how they would live their life together, along with heavy drinking and giving each other the razzmatazz.

Sammy made arrangements for Father Tony to look in on the kid, and signed him up for an after-school program with the Salesian Society at Saints Peter and Paul's to keep the kid out of trouble, but nevertheless, he remained a horrible little kid.

Eddie Moo Shoes and Lois Fong started their driving school in Chinatown, got business cards and even a storefront, and Myrtle and Stilton fabricated a second brake pedal on the passenger side of the used Studebaker they had bought, so they could stop if a student got into trouble. Eventually Lois Fong even got her driver's license and there was a lot more driving instructing and less tap-dancing when she was teaching, which annoyed the nut-sack guys to no end.

Milo, after driving the Metal Dragon, lost his fear of driving completely and went back to taking fares and giving rides in addition to selling liquor outside Cookie's Coffee. Unfortunately, he didn't lose his tendency to pass out at the wheel for no particular reason, so Myrtle and the Cheese installed a second brake pedal similar to the one in Moo Shoes and Lois's car, and Doris rode with Milo as his emergency backup when he was driving, which was just fine with both of them. Lars the angry stevedore was never heard from again.

Uncle Ho stayed in Locke with Niu Yun, where he tended the garden and helped prepare their meals and listened to the pigs at a nearby farm talk about mud and slop and other pig things, but he never heard the voice of the Rain Dragon, and as years passed, and with Niu Yun's chiding, he finally forgave himself for the horrible things he had done as a tong hatchet man. Eventually Niu Yun stopped teasing Ho about being the cat fucker, but she never gave up her hatchet, just to keep the old man guessing.

Thelonius Jones became a star employee at Sonoma State Hospital and was beloved by the staff and the patients. He cared for patients, as well as working in the machine shop, where he helped design and build the special machines required to support the patients. The doctors who advised the craftsmen said that Lone possessed a special sensitivity to the needs of the patients, even those who could not speak. Lone and one of the young nurses fell quite hard for each other and they spent many a night together in Lone's quarters, loving each other and thinking that no one knew but them, and Lone was completely happy, until one night, as he was dozing off, he heard a voice in his head, as clearly as if the speaker were right next to him instead of his beloved nurse.

The voice said, "*Secret Service, it is your time to look after the dragon.*"

AFTERWORD AND AUTHOR'S NOTE

I know what you're thinking: "Thanks, Chris. Now you've ruined everything. I was told the alien probings were for science, not recreation! They promised!" Take heart, gentle reader: Scooter was a fictional twisted little moonman; your own alien abductor is probably all about the science. While I made up a lot—well, most—of the stuff in *Razzmatazz,* the context in which much of the story takes place is based on the real world of historical San Francisco and Northern California.

Chinatown

I've lived a few blocks from San Francisco's Chinatown for the last fifteen years, and though I walk through the neighborhood at least once a week, Chinatown remains a mystery, swathed in an enigma, wrapped in a wonton, and fried. I wrote and researched most of *Razzmatazz* during the Covid lockdown of 2020–21, so I wasn't able to do as much on-site research as I would have liked, but historical research opened up a whole world of resilience and racism behind Chinatown's quaint façade that I was only able to touch upon in the novel.

Chinatown was first established in the 1850s, when many Chinese immigrated to San Francisco in search of their fortunes in the "Land of Golden Hills." While they came in search of gold, most of the Chinese immigrants came from Guangdong Province, where agriculture and fishing were the main industries. Many found employment in the gold mining industry in the hills beyond Sacramento, but many more took jobs building the Transcontinental Railroad, which employed thousands from 1863 to 1869. San Francisco acted as the gateway to the West, and a large community of Chinese established itself in an eight-block area of the city (which was the largest population of Chinese people outside of China at the time).

Early on, the population of Chinatown was almost exclusively male, with men outnumbering women by a ratio of twenty to one. Consequently, businesses were established to feed and entertain unaccompanied men, with brothels, gambling houses, opium dens, and restaurants resembling mess halls lining the streets. It was the prevalence of this open "corruption" that led to the justification of the not just systemic but codified racism against the Chinese population that lasted until 1943.

With the end of the Civil War, which threw many soldiers into the labor market, along with the completion of the Transcontinental Railroad in 1869, which released thousands of workers, competition for jobs in the West became fierce. Chinese workers, who would often work for lower wages than their Anglo counterparts, were often blamed for the competitive job market, and anti-Chinese violence frequently broke out in San Francisco, led by groups of outraged laborers.

In 1882 Congress passed the Chinese Exclusion Act, which prohibited Chinese laborers from immigrating, and ten years later the Geary Act extended the Chinese Exclusion Act, while making it illegal to hire a Chinese person at all; required all Chinese people to carry a domestic "passport" to show their identity (papers, please?); prohibited them from owning property or testifying in court; and excluded them from the right of habeas corpus, essentially making it illegal to even be Chinese in the United States. The ratification of the Fourteenth Amendment, in 1868, however, had made it unconstitutional to deprive "natural born citizens" of due process, so the tongs as well as the Six Companies and other Chinese benevolent societies created "paper sons" to allow Chinese people to stay in the United States as well as to bring in new immigrants. With the earthquake of 1906 and the destruction of the records in the San Francisco courthouse, many Chinese people were able to claim U.S. birth in the manner that young Ho does in *Razzmatazz* (by simply showing up).

The Chinese Exclusion Act wasn't repealed until 1943, and only after the Japanese used propaganda about the law to drive a wedge between the United States and her Chinese allies during World War II.

As in *Noir,* many of the businesses referred to in *Razzmatazz* actually existed, including Club Shanghai, where Eddie Shu and Lois Fong worked, and the four-story, eight-foot-wide jook house I renamed Tall House of Happy Snake and Noodle (that was not the name in reality, but Herb Caen, the intrepid street reporter for the *San Francisco Chronicle,* wrote about it in his columns from 1947, without actually giving the name of the place beyond "jook joint"). The fictional ice cream shop, Dong's Dragon, is based on a business that still exists (or did, pre-Covid) called Dragon Papa Dessert at 752 Grant Avenue, where you can still get the Dragon's Beard dessert, purportedly prepared for the Emperor by the Tam family for many generations before they opened their business in Chinatown.

Careful readers will spot the names of Dupont Street, Grant Avenue, and Grant Street being used for the same street in *Razzmatazz*. What we know as Grant Avenue today was once known by interchangeable names in days prior, Dupont Street being the anchor street of Chinatown since the days of the Gold Rush.

Rural "Chinatowns"

When Chinese workers returned to California upon the completion of the Transcontinental Railroad, they found work in much of Northern California applying the skills they had learned in their homeland. Through the latter part of the nineteenth century, Chinese workers, unable to buy or own land legally, were conscripted into a sort of collective sharecropping. That is, Chinese labor leaders would broker the skills of a group of Chinese workers to build levees, establish orchards, raise and harvest crops, and basically terraform most of the Sacramento River valley into some of the most productive farmland in the world. Most of the work was done for a rate of a dollar a day, with no share in the harvest for the workers.

Consequently, a number of rural Chinatowns were established in Northern California, some as part of larger communities, like those in Santa Rosa and Sebastopol, whose workers built many of the wineries in Sonoma County, and others as stand-alone towns, like Locke, which I refer to in *Razzmatazz*. Locke still stands today as a living museum to that period, although few of the original businesses remain, all of which catered to an almost exclusively male population, with dormitory-style rooming houses and dining halls as well as numerous brothels. Most of the prostitutes in rural Chinatowns were Anglo, because there were so few Chinese women there. Locke wasn't established until 1919, so I'm not entirely accurate in sending Ho and Niu Yun there in 1906, but I thought I would be able to visit Locke and get some details to flesh out the description. Unfortunately, once again, Covid-19 prevented me from doing this, so most of my impressions of the town came from maps and the images in *Bitter Melon: Inside America's Last Rural Chinese Town,* a lovely book of photos and text by Jeff Gillenkirk and James Motlow. Most of the original photos in the book were taken in the 1970s and '80s, so little of the seedy underground of Locke in *Razzmatazz* can be blamed on their book, although there are a few historical photos from earlier times. The agreement between the tongs and the rural Chinatowns is entirely my invention.

The Sonoma Developmental Center

I first learned of the Sonoma Developmental Center quite by accident, in the summer of 2016, when my wife and I were staying at our place I've referred to in the past as the Squirrel Ranch. (Just calm down, it's not a squeef [squirrel beef] ranch, it's a ranch for free-range dairy squirrels. Where do you think they get almond milk? You think the barista at Starbucks is just going to squeeze a fresh squirrel into your latte? No. The squirrels go about their business and once a day they come to the house to be milked. And they seem to quite enjoy the process, especially the male squirrels. It's all very humane.) Anyway, there was supposed to be a meteor shower visible at midnight, but the Squirrel Ranch is in the middle of a redwood forest, and the only place the sky is visible is by the Russian River, so we made our way down the Squirrel Ranch dock, and there was already a woman sitting there, visible only in silhouette, waiting for the meteors. We got to chatting, like you do, because a meteor shower isn't really like a fireworks display, and you can wait a pretty long time between meteors, when you are required to stop and say, "There goes one." So we were chatting and we asked one another what we did for a living and the woman said she had just retired after thirty years working at the Sonoma Developmental Center. She went on to describe what was essentially a small city, with its own fire department, post office, and even zip code, that at one time cared for up to 3,000 disabled people, in group homes on the complex, under as many as 1,300 employees. The level of disabilities she described was shocking, and the cooperation of the patients in caring for one another profound. We listened to her for perhaps an hour, at which point I asked her what she had done before working at the Developmental Center, and she said, "I was a kindergarten teacher for five years before that."

I realized that we had been talking with someone whose thirty-five-year career had been spent being actively kind to people. I asked her what she had learned. She said, "Everyone, no matter their age, or their level of disability, just wants to help." (Which is where I got the lines for Nurse Stacy in those chapters.) I was incredibly moved, and went home to do research on the Sonoma Developmental Center and eventually included it in the book.

The center was established in 1886 as the California Home for the Care and Training of Feeble Minded Children with a private endowment from a family with a profoundly disabled daughter. It was supported for years by private donations and was eventually funded by the state of California. While the first home was in Vallejo, California, in the East Bay area of San Francisco Bay, it was moved to Sonoma in the 1880s, near Glen Ellen, adjacent to Jack London's Beauty Ranch. London wrote a short story titled "Told from the Drooling Ward" (published 1914), narrated from the point of view of one of the patients who describes himself and others in the center as "feebs," which is where I found the term. In the story, the narrator leads an escape from the center with a group of patients and encounters London and his wife, who are out riding their ranch on horseback. It reads somewhat like an outline for *One Flew Over the Cuckoo's Nest,* with a patient narrating the escape, but I don't know of any actual connection to Ken Kesey's story. London's story is in the public domain and a quick search will reveal several sites where you can read it.

The Sonoma Developmental Center closed in 2018 and is now used as a center for scientific study (natural sciences—there are no longer patients there). Thank you to Richard Dale, who supervises the researchers and took the time to show me around the grounds of the center as it stands today.

The Tong Wars

The origin of the Triads and the tongs—the story of the five ancestors—that opens the book is taken from Chinese legend. The tongs thrived in San Francisco from the mid-1850s until they went into precipitous decline with the earthquake of 1906 and the destruction of Chinatown. Their connection to the Five Dragons is entirely my invention, although the dragons of earth, fire, metal, and wood are from Chinese myth.

The war among the fighting tongs reached its height in the 1880s, with as many as forty different tongs vying for control of gambling, prostitution, and protection, and even brokering the labor of Chinese workers in San Francisco. They would sign women as indentured servants, who promised to work in the United States for two to three years for their passage but were then forced into sex slavery upon gaining entrance to the city as "paper daughters," much the way Ho is brought to the States as a paper son in the story. While it is an uncomfortable truth that sex slavery thrived in Chinatown in the late 1800s, I felt as if I would have been remiss to exclude it, even in the context of a dark comedy.

The tongs' death knell sounded in the U.S. with the fall of the Qing (or Manchu) dynasty in 1912, but these societies, which were originally formed as the Triads in the 1600s to restore the Ming dynasty, persisted in Asia well into World War II.

The crib brothels were real, and a famous map of Chinatown made in the 1880s shows that nearly every third storefront in Chinatown was a brothel, and sometimes entire blocks of the alleys. Donaldina "Dolly" Cameron, who is only referenced in *Razzmatazz,* was a real woman, the daughter of a Scottish missionary, who liberated Chinese women from sex slavery for nearly fifty years, and whose Cameron House still stands at 920 Sacramento Street (it functions as a youth center today). Cameron did not, however, maintain a farm for rescued women in Sonoma County. That was an invention of my own in order to put Ho and Yun in proximity to the Sonoma Developmental Center.

The Clubs

The drag king clubs of North Beach were real, and Mona's 440 was the most famous of them. The police enforced masquerade laws against the clubs, leaning heavily on the three-articles rule during the late forties and even more in the early fifties, when the clubs were basically run out of business by aggressive public officials. Meanwhile, Finocchio's, a male drag club only a few doors down, remained open and thrived from 1932 until 1999. Jimmy's Joynt was not a real place, but is based on the club Tommy's Joint, which existed but had no connection with the hofbrau of similar name that still exists today.

As with *Noir*, I wanted to portray postwar San Francisco as a dynamic city facing mixes and clashes of cultures, which it was in 1947 and remains today. My thanks to everyone who answered my questions and to the people of Chinatown, who are enduring another ridiculous wave of anti-Asian sentiment as I write this in the fall of 2021.

With the hope that we will someday recognize how the mix of cultures enriches all our lives, I dedicate this silly and absurd novel to the people of San Francisco.

CHRISTOPHER MOORE
SAN FRANCISCO
SEPTEMBER 2021